Praise for *A Perfect Blood*

"The pace and tone of *A Perfect Blood* reflects its protagonist: a
little more cautious, reflective, and purposeful, and the book is
more powerful as a result. . . . Harrison provides the strongest and
most self-assured Rachel we've seen yet."
Miami Herald

"Harrison's colorful cast of supporting characters keeps the story
moving among the fast-paced action scenes. Longtime fans will
obviously be standing in line for this one. However, readers with
any interest in urban fantasy can easily jump into the story."
Library Journal

"With the end of this popular series coming soon, fans will be
savoring the remaining episodes all the more, and those who have
delayed entry will begin jumping on board."
Booklist

By Kim Harrison

Books of the Hollows

THE UNDEAD POOL
EVER AFTER
A PERFECT BLOOD
PALE DEMON
BLACK MAGIC SANCTION
WHITE WITCH, BLACK CURSE
THE OUTLAW DEMON WAILS
FOR A FEW DEMONS MORE
A FISTFUL OF CHARMS
EVERY WHICH WAY BUT DEAD
THE GOOD, THE BAD, AND THE UNDEAD
DEAD WITCH WALKING

And Don't Miss

INTO THE WOODS
THE HOLLOWS INSIDER
UNBOUND
SOMETHING DEADLY THIS WAY COMES
EARLY TO DEATH, EARLY TO RISE
ONCE DEAD, TWICE SHY
HOLIDAYS ARE HELL
DATES FROM HELL
HOTTER THAN HELL

THE UNDEAD POOL

KIM HARRISON

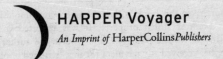

HARPER Voyager

An Imprint of HarperCollinsPublishers

HARPER Voyager

An Imprint of HarperCollins*Publishers*
195 Broadway
New York, New York 10007

Copyright © 2014 by Kim Harrison
Cover art by Larry Rostant
Author photograph by Kate Thornton
ISBN 978-0-06-195794-9
www.harpervoyagerbooks.com

First Harper Voyager mass market printing: August 2014
First Harper Voyager hardcover printing: March 2014

Harper Voyager and) is a trademark of HCP LLC.

Printed in the U.S.A.

10 9 8 7 6 5 4 3 2 1

To the man who knows what makes
the perfect date night

Acknowledgments

I'd like to thank my editor, Diana Gill, for her fabulous insights that make the Hollows the most it can be, and my agent, Richard Curtis, for seeing it before I did.

One

How does the man make checkered shirts and pastels look good? I thought as Trent lined up his drive, head down and feet shifting, looking oddly appealing outside of the suit and tie I usually saw him in. The rest of his team and their caddies were watching him as well, but I doubted they were rating the way his shoulders pulled the soft fabric, or how the sun shone through his almost translucent blond hair drifting about his ears, or how the shadows made his slim waist look even trimmer, unhidden beneath a suit coat for a change. I found myself holding my breath as he coiled up, exhaling as he untwisted and the flat of the club hit the ball with a ping.

"Yeah, the elf looks good in the sun," Jenks smart-mouthed, the pixy currently sitting on the bottom of my hooped earrings and out of the moderate wind. "When you going to put us all out of your misery and boink him?"

"Don't start with me." With a hand held up to shade my eyes, I watched the ball begin to descend.

"All I'm saying is you've been dating him for three months. Most guys you date are either dead or running scared by now."

The ball hit with an audible thump, rolling onto the par-three green. Something in me fluttered at Trent's pleased smile as he squinted in the sun. *Damn it, I'm not doing this.* "I'm not dating him, I'm working his security," I muttered.

"This is work?" Wings humming, the pixy darted off my earring, flying ahead to do a redundant check of the area before we walked into it.

Jenks's silver dust quickly vanished in the July heat, and I felt a moment of angst as Trent accepted the congratulations of his team. He looked relaxed and easy out here, the calm he usually affected true instead of fabricated. I liked seeing him this way, and feeling guilty, I dropped my gaze. I had no business even caring.

As one, the rest started to the green with a clinking of clubs and masculine chatter, undoubtedly feeling pushed by the next team waiting just off the tee. The big guy in the lime-green pants had been talking loudly the entire time, trying to throw Trent's game off, no doubt, but Trent had outplotted corporate takeovers, evaded genetic trafficking charges, slipped murder accusations, and survived demon attacks. One overweight man huffing and puffing for him to move faster would not break his cool.

Sure enough, Trent needlessly fussed over the divot as the rest went on ahead, refusing to relinquish the tee area until he was ready. Smirking, I hoisted his bag, the three other clubs he used clinking lightly as I came to take his driver. I wasn't a caddie, but it was the only way they'd let me on the course and there was no way that Trent would ever be in public without some kind of security.

Even if he could take care of himself, I thought, smiling as I took his club and our separate paces became one. *My God, it's nice out here.*

"Subtle," I said as we found the manicured grass, and he snorted to make me flush, not because I'd seen through him, but because I was one of the few people Trent would drop his mask around. It shouldn't have been that important. But it was. *What am I doing?*

"Watch the guy in the green pants," he said, looking over his shoulder. "He has a tendency to drop his ball into the players ahead of him."

"Sure." Head down, I paced beside Trent, his clubs banging into my back, feeling as if I belonged there almost. I'd been working with him the last three months while Quen, Trent's usual security adviser, was on the West Coast with the girls. This new feeling of . . . responsibility, I guess, bothered me. Jenks's words, though crass, had been echoing in my thoughts in quiet moments, and I looked at Trent's hand, wishing I had the right to take it.

"Are you okay?"

I looked up, almost panicking. "Sure. Why?"

Trent's eyes ran over me as if searching for the truth. "You're quiet today."

I was quiet today? Meaning we'd been spending enough time together that he knew the difference. Forcing a smile, I handed him his putter. "Just trying to stay in the background."

He took it, eyebrows high, and I'd swear I heard him sigh as he turned away. Head coming up, he stepped onto the green and joined in the light banter between the other CEOs. My heart was pounding, and I dragged my melancholy ass out of the way to rest under the shade of the storm shelter.

"Just trying to stay in the background," Jenks said in a high falsetto. "My God, woman. Your aura is glowing. Just admit you like him, bump uglies, and get on with your life!"

"Jenks!" I exclaimed, then wiggled my fingers apologetically at the man lining up his putt.

Smirking, Jenks landed on the storm shelter's rafters, his hand carefully going over a small wing tear to even out a raw edge. "That's how pixies know we're in love," he said as he folded his dragonfly-like wings and wiggled out of his red jacket, wincing as something pulled. "If the girl has glow, she won't say no."

"Nice." Arms over my middle, I set the bag down and

watched Trent, glad the girls were coming back tomorrow. With Quen taking up security, I'd be able to wrap my head around reality. I was confusing my work with everything else—and I was done with being confused.

"How's Cookie Bits's game?" Jenks asked. "He looks as distracted as you."

Frowning, I raised my hand as if to bop him, but it would never land. Cookie Bits. That's what Jenks had been calling Trent ever since he caught us sitting in his car outside the church after a job. I'd only wanted to hear the end of the news, but try telling Jenks that.

"Tink's little pink rosebuds, the local pixies are more stuck up than a fairy nailed to my church's steeple," Jenks said, giving up on getting a rise out of me since it wasn't working. "I'm wearing red for a reason, not because I look good in it. Look! Look what they did to my coat!"

Disgusted, Jenks held up the bright red jacket Belle had made for him, poking his finger through a hole just under the armpit. I stiffened, suddenly seeing his small wing tear in a new way. A pixy wearing red should've been given free passage. I'd been seemingly everywhere in Cincinnati with Trent the last couple of months, but the country club was the worst. I hadn't known Jenks was having issues. He'd probably been too proud to tell me. "You okay?"

Jenks froze, his pale face becoming red and making his shock of curly blond hair look even more tousleable. His wings hummed, sifting a pale yellow dust that colored him from head to toe in working black. He looked like a theater guy, but the sword hanging from his belt was real enough, having had deterred everything from bees bothering his children to assassins bothering me.

"Yeah, sure," he said, embarrassed. "I just don't like dodging arrows when I shouldn't have to. We're cool as a breath strip." He squinted at me, head tilting. "You sure *you're* all right? I'm serious about your aura glowing. You got a temp or something?"

"Jenks, I'm not in love," I replied grumpily, ignoring the

odd tingle rising through me as Trent crouched to line up his putt. Cincinnati's ley lines were faint but discernible, the upwellings of power usable even at this distance if not for the course's ward of no-magic, in place to prevent tampering with the game. I'd found a way around it weeks ago. But it almost felt as if there were a line the next hole over, and I looked back the way we'd come.

That big man in the lime-green pants was standing between the markers with his club. We were too close for them to be teeing off, but even the practice swings were making me nervous. It was only a par three—as in "on the green in one drive."

"Ah, Rache?" Jenks rose up, hovering by my ear as Mr. Lime-Green Pants swung. There was the crack of a ball, and my heart jumped. "Oh no he didn't!" Jenks said, and I stiffened, tracking the ball's path.

"What do you think?" I whispered, skin tingling as if I'd tapped a line already.

"I think it's going to be a problem."

"Fore!" I shouted, lurching out into the sun. Heads turned and Trent remained crouched where he was. Instinctively I sent out a ribbon of awareness, easily bypassing the no-magic ward and tapping the nearest ley line. Energy flowed in with an unusual sharpness, burning the inside of my nose as it seemed to come from everywhere, not just the line, as I filled my chi and forced the energy back out through the pathway of nerves and synapses to my hands.

My eyes widened as I tracked the ball's path, energy burning as it flowed in smaller and smaller channels until it reached my fingertips. Shit, it was headed right for him.

"Derivare!" I shouted, hand moving in the simple gesture that harnessed the ley line charm and gave it direction. It was a small spell, one I'd been using for weeks to tweak Trent's ball to make him slice as I practiced getting around the course's no-magic ward. It wasn't much, but it would divert the ball's path from the green. I didn't even need a focusing object anymore.

My intent sped from me with the surety of an electron spinning. I watched, breath held, as it headed for the ball arching down. Men were scattering, but Trent stood firm, confident that I had this.

And then the charm hit the ball, pain flaring simultaneously from my gesture hand.

I yelped, clutching my wrist as a thunderous boom shook the air, flinging me back to land on my butt. Shocked, I stared as chunks of sod and dirt rained down. Men were shouting, and Jenks was swearing, tangled up in my hair. My lips parted, and I blinked at the car-size crater ten feet off the green and in the fairway. "That wasn't there before, was it?" I said, dazed.

"No fairy farting way!" Jenks said, my tangled red curls pulling as he worked his way out. "Did you have to explode it? My God, woman!"

My hand burned, and I didn't dare rub at the stinging red flesh. Dirt and grass were still coming down, and people were running in from all points. From the nearby clubhouse came an irritating hooting. "I think I broke the course's ward," I said, awkward as I got up and brushed myself off with my good hand.

"You think?" Jenks sifted a glittering silver dust as he darted in excitement. "A little protective, are we?"

Peeved, I frowned. My control was better than this, much better. I shouldn't have tweaked the no-magic ward, much less exploded the ball, even if I had shouted the word of invocation. The men in their pastels and plaids were clustered together talking loudly. The other caddies were in their own group, staring at me. Arms swinging aggressively, Mr. Lime-Green Pants strode forward, distant but closing the gap. The rest of his team stayed on the tee.

Calm and relaxed as always, Trent meandered over, squinting at me from under his cap. "Are you okay?"

Embarrassed, I brushed a chunk of dirt off him. "Yeah," I said, hand hurting. "I mean, yes. Does my aura look funny to you?"

"No." My head jerked up as he took my hand, turning it over to look at my red fingertips. "You're burned!" he said softly, shocked, and I pulled away.

"I am so sorry," I said, hiding it behind my back, but I could feel the sensation of pinpricks as Jenks, sifting dust down on it, checked it out himself. "I only tapped it. It shouldn't have exploded. I didn't use any more line strength than any other time."

Jenks snickered and I froze, mortified as I watched understanding cross Trent's face.

"You . . ." he started, and I flushed. "All last month?"

"Now it's out, Rache," Jenks said, then darted away to check out the crater.

Wincing, I nodded, but Trent's expression was one of amusement, almost laughing as he touched my arm to tell me he thought my messing with his game was funny. That is, until his gaze went past my shoulder to the man in the lime-green pants stomping down the fairway. Trent's hand fell from me with a reluctant slowness, and his attention shifted to his team, waiting to find out what had happened. "This isn't going to be pretty."

The guilt swam up anew. "I'm really sorry. It shouldn't have happened. Trent, you know I'm better than this!" I said. But it was hard to argue with a ten-foot hole in the ground.

Jenks hummed close to drop the twisted mass of rubber and plastic into Trent's hand. "Dude, it looks like a giant spider scrotum. Damn, Rache! What did you do to it?"

Trent held the thing with two fingers. "I'll take care of it," he said, making me feel small. "Don't worry about it. No one got hurt. They can use a sand trap on this hole anyway."

"Yeah." Jenks landed on Trent's shoulder, looking right there somehow. "It could have been an assassination attempt, and your charm prematurely triggered it."

I jerked upright, embarrassment gone. "Excuse me," I said as I snatched the ball away, wanting to do some post-invocation tests on it later. Eyes narrowed, I turned to Mr.

Lime-Green Pants, his pace slowing as he huffed red-faced up the slight rise.

"Rachel . . ." Trent said in warning, and I got in front of him, the ley line humming through me, prickly through the course's no-magic ward. The alarm had stopped, and the ward was back in place. Not that it mattered.

"He doesn't look like an assassin," Jenks said.

"And I don't look like a demon," I said, pulse fast. "Do another sweep, will you?"

"You got it."

"Rachel, it was an accident," Trent said as Jenks darted away, but there was a new slant to his eyes that hadn't been there a second ago.

"It blew up," I said tightly. "Don't let him touch you."

Worry crossed his face, satisfying me that he was taking it seriously, and together we turned to the man, puffing and sweating as he stormed closer. "Where the hell is my ball?" the big man shouted, clearly enjoying that everyone was watching him.

Calm as ever, Trent smiled soothingly. "I am sorry, Mr. . . ."

"Limbcus," the man in the green pants said, and I pulled Trent back a step.

"We had an accident," Trent said, and one of the caddies laughed nervously. "Please accept my apologies, and perhaps a bottle of wine at the club's restaurant this afternoon."

"Bribe? You're bribing me?" Limbcus shouted, and the first hints of red shaded Trent's cheeks. "You used magic during tournament play. You interfered with the lay of my ball!"

I couldn't let that go. "I wouldn't have blown it up if you hadn't dropped it into his game."

Sputtering, Limbcus pointed, focusing everyone's attention on me. "She admits it!" he said loudly. "She used magic to influence the game! You are *out*, Kalamack."

Trent looked up from his phone, the smallest tick of his lips giving away his irritation. "Mr. Limbcus, I'm sure we can come to some understanding."

Limbcus jerked, shocked when Jenks circled us, silver dust spilling down to tell me that the course was clear. I didn't know if that pleased me or not. A thwarted assassination attempt might be preferable to having overreacted.

"We're good," Jenks said, alighting on Trent's shoulder instead of mine. My hair was frizzy enough on its own, and seeing it snarling under the club's ward was scary. "I think it was an honest mistake, but the guy is a class-A dick."

Limbcus almost had kittens, and the pixy laughed, sounding like wind chimes. Peeved, I made a finger motion for Jenks to knock it off, and he sobered. A black-and-gold cart belonging to the pro shop was careening over the course toward us. I relaxed for almost half a second before tensing up again. I'd broken their no-magic ward. I was going to get banned. The best I could hope for was to not take Trent with me.

"Ah! Aha!" Limbcus said, his bulk quivering as he saw the cart as well. "Now we'll see! Kevin!" he shouted. "Kalamack altered the lay of my ball! I want him scratched!"

I cringed as Kevin, apparently, brought the electric cart to a halt, the youngish man blanching at the crater as he got out. Knowing what was going to happen, I waved at him. "It was me, actually. Sorry!"

Kevin looked professional in his black slacks and matching polo top, a crackling radio on his hip and a worn cap on his head. "Is everyone okay?" he asked, his few wrinkles bunching up to make him look older.

Trent nodded, and Limbcus pushed to the front. "She tampered with my game!" the red-faced, pear-shaped man shouted. "Magic during tournament play is grounds for disqualification. Kalamack is out! Scratch him. Right now."

Ever the gentleman, Trent cleared his throat. "I'm afraid this is my fault."

"Ah, no. Actually it isn't," I said. "He dropped his ball into our game and I deflected it."

"More like demolished it," Jenks said, snickering, and I wished he'd shut up.

"She admits it!" the heavyset man exclaimed, pointing again. "Scratch him!"

Kevin met Trent's eyes, and Trent shrugged. Clearly unhappy, the manager nervously pushed in between them. "Mr. Limbcus, is there any way you can see to overlook the lapse? Seeing as it was your ball that instigated the problem?"

"At least let me replace your equipment," Trent said.

Limbcus's eyes widened as he realized they'd sided against him. "I don't give a rat's ass about the ball! We're under tournament rules, and your caddie used magic! Your entire team's scores are suspect, and *you* should be expelled from the club *entirely*!"

"Ms. Morgan isn't my caddie," Trent said coolly. "She's my security."

"I'll bet." The man leered at me, and my chin lifted. It didn't help that I didn't look the part today, dressed in a pair of shorts, sneakers, and a fashion-deprived polo shirt in an effort to blend in. Oh, I was athletic enough, but when a man like that sees curves, he assumes there's no brain or skills attached. But the way I saw it was the less you looked like security, the more likely you were to catch them off guard.

The uncomfortable silence stretched. Mistaking it for agreement, the man shifted his bulk aggressively. "Golf is a gentleman's game. Having women on the course is bad enough, but she doesn't even know how to play!"

My eyes narrowed. "Easy, Rache," Jenks warned.

"She's a demon!" the man bellowed, and there were gasps from the surrounding men. "She's been fixing the game. Can your ward handle demon magic? You don't know!"

"Mr. Limbcus," the golf pro protested nervously.

"Kalamack could be doing his elf magic and you'd never know about it either!"

"Uh-oh . . ." Jenks rose up on a glittering column of blue-tinted black sparkles.

Sneakers silent on the grass, I drifted closer. Trent had gone white—not in fear, but in anger. "You think he's going to do something?" Jenks said, hovering at my ear.

"Doubt it," I said, but I felt a chill when Trent took his hat off. If he had been wearing his spelling cap under it, he had just removed temptation. His ironclad cool had been cracking a lot lately, and I didn't like it.

"His kind shouldn't be allowed to play with decent folk," the man said with a sneer.

That did it. Trent might be downplaying his abilities in order to soothe interspecies relations, but I didn't have to. It wasn't my job to keep Trent out of the papers for assaulting idiots, but Quen would thank me.

With a thought, I reached past the country club's ward of no-magic and strengthened my hold on the ley line. Pissed, I yanked a huge wad of it to me, shattering the annoying ward yet again to make it shrivel up and fold into itself, broken for good this time. In the distance, that warning hoot started up, and Kevin paled, knowing I'd taken out their ward with the ease of a stallion breaking a string. Mr. Lime-Green Pants turned, his anger faltering as he saw me.

"Ah, Rachel?"

I pushed Trent's hand off my arm. "His kind?" I said, hands on my hips as I came to a stop inches from the man's bulging middle and looked up at him. "*His kind* is what kept your momma and daddy alive through the Turn!"

Trent smelled like broken fern. "We're fine," he said. "Rachel, I've got this."

"We're not fine!" I exclaimed, a sliver of satisfaction plinking through me when Limbcus backed up. "That ball would've put you in the hospital and he's griping about me *blowing it up*?"

"Rachel?"

I leaned in until I could smell Limbcus's toothpaste. "How about it, Limbcus? You want that I should call the FIB and file an attempted assault form? I have a license that tells me I can do magic any time I damn well please to protect the person I'm working for." Ticked, I brandished the mass of rubber and burnt plastic under his nose. "I'd shove this ball somewhere nasty if I didn't need it for *evidence*!"

"Rachel!"

I blinked, rocking back when I realized I'd shoved Limb-cus all the way to Kevin's cart. Jenks was hovering behind him, grinning, and that, more than the man's terrified expression, cooled me off. I wasn't doing myself any favors, and sniffing, I stalked to Trent's bag, yanking it up and dropping the blown-out ball into a pocket so I could check it out for tampering later. "You need to read your history before someone makes you part of it," I muttered, jumping when Trent's hand landed lightly on my shoulder. Jenks was dusting an amused bright gold, and sullen, I hoisted Trent's clubs onto my shoulder. It might have been a mistake to butt in, but it was harder to swallow the insults when they weren't aimed at me.

"Mr. Limbcus," Trent was saying, his voice soothing, but I could hear a thread of satisfaction that had been missing before. "I'm sure we can come to some agreement. This is for charity, after all."

Mr. Limbcus still hadn't moved. "If he's not disqualified, I will withdraw from the event and take my entrance fee with me," he said, his jowls quivering. "You may own Cincinnati, Kalamack, but you do *not* own this course, and I will see you expelled before this day is over!"

Actually, his family *had* owned the property at one point, but I managed not to say it. Kevin stood beside the cart looking unsure, and Trent put his cap back on, taking the moment to think. "I will withdraw from the tournament immediately. Kevin, can we ride back with you?"

Distressed, the manager shifted forward. "Of course, Mr. Kalamack."

"Figures," the fat man huffed. "He knows he'll lose without magic."

"My pledges will of course remain in force," Trent said as he put a hand on the small of my back, both possessive and protective as he turned to his team. "Gentlemen? Please excuse me. Lunch is on me."

Surprised he was letting this go so easily, I glanced at

Jenks. The pixy shrugged, but Trent was almost pushing me to the cart. Perhaps the elven slur had caught him off guard. He hadn't been out of the closet long, and knowing how to react gracefully took practice.

"We're gonna get banned, aren't we," Jenks said, and I nodded.

Satisfied, Limbcus strutted and swaggered, talking loudly with the other players about how to score such a gross breakage of the rules. Trent was on my one side, Kevin the other, back hunched and worried.

Thinking he'd won, the man huffed. "It's not the money. I want you out of this club! You'll be hearing from my lawyer, Kalamack."

Trent stopped dead in his tracks. My worry strengthened at the light in Trent's eye. I'd seen it before. He was close to losing it.

"On what grounds?" Trent said coldly as he turned around. "My associate deflected your *assault* in a manner that hurt no one. If anyone should be crying foul, it should be me."

"Ah, Trent?" I said as Jenks hummed nervously.

"You are loud, overbearing, and quite frankly, a poor dresser," Trent said, his steps silent on the manicured grass as he strode back to him. "Your game is erratic, and no one wants to play ahead of you because of your history of *premature releases*."

There was a titter from the watching men, but I didn't like that Trent had his hat on again. He didn't need it to do his magic, but it did impart a level of finesse.

"A true player won't risk the safety of others in a transparent, passive-aggressive action," Trent said, eye to eye with the man. "A true golfer plays against himself, not others. Both I and my security apologized for the destruction of your property and offered restitution, which witnesses have heard you decline," Trent said, the hem of his pants shaking. "If you want to take this to the courts, the only one who will win is the lawyers. But if you want to go that route, Mr. Limbcus, by all means, let's dance."

The man was fumbling for words as Trent confronted him, his wispy hair floating and his stance unforgiving and holding the assurance of kings. Everyone in Cincinnati had seen the glowing lights in the night sky when the demons had hunted and killed one of their own, and everyone in Cincinnati knew that Trent had ridden with them, meting out a justice older than the Bible and just as savage.

Jenks's wings tickled my neck, and I shivered. "Maybe you should rescue him," the pixy said, meaning Trent. "He's good at making his point, but not so good making an exit."

Nodding, I inched forward to stand behind Trent, too close to be ignored. He held the man's gaze a second longer, and with his lips still compressed in anger, he turned and paced back to the cart. I fell into place beside him, guilt tugging at me. None of this should have happened.

Trent touched the small of my back, and I fluttered inside. A surge of energy passed between us, and I quickly grasped my chi's balance before they tried to equalize. He was still on edge. Silent, I walked to the back of the golf cart so Trent could have the front with the golf pro.

"Hey, Rache. You want me to pix the sucker?"

It had been loud enough for almost everyone to hear, and I glumly shook my head.

"Thank you, Mr. Kalamack," Kevin said nervously as he hustled around the cart to drop into the driver's seat. "If it were up to me, you'd be continuing your game and he would be escorted out, but rules are rules."

Mood still bad, Trent slid into the front seat, his eyes on his phone again before he tucked it away. "Don't concern yourself with it. Thanks for the ride back. And please let my office know what the damages are. Not just the tournament, but for the green."

"That's most appreciated, Mr. Kalamack. Thank you."

Flushing, I set Trent's clubs in the rack at the back of the cart. There was a little jump seat, and I flipped it down, happy to sulk at the back with the clubs on the way to the parking lot. My hand hurt, and I looked at it as we jostled into motion, belatedly reaching for a handhold as we took a dip. The wind pushed through my hair, and I took an easing breath, trying to relax.

Had I really overreacted that badly? I *had* shouted the word of invocation, but even so . . . Concerned, I eyed my fingertips, tentatively pushing at the swollen red tips. I didn't like what that might mean. Sure I cared about Trent, but enough to blow up a ball?

A tiny throat clearing pulled my attention up. Jenks was sitting cross-legged on the top of the bag's rim, an infuriatingly knowing look on him. "Shut up," I said as I curled my fingers into a fist to hide the damage like a guilty secret. He opened his mouth, sparkles turning a bright gold, and I smacked the bag to make him take to the air. "I said shut up!" I said louder, and he laughed as he darted out of the rattling cart, sparkles showing his path as he flew ahead.

"I'm sorry, Mr. Kalamack. Interspecies intolerance is not tolerated here," Kevin said, clearly still upset. "I wish you'd file a formal report. There are enough witnesses that Limbcus will be put on probation."

"Don't worry about it, Kevin. It's okay."

But it wasn't, and I held on against the unexpected dips, silent as we made our way back. I'd been watching Trent deal with the crap I'd grown up with ever since he'd come out of the closet as an elf. It had caused him to be less confident in himself, more inclined to deliberate before acting, and his usual calm not as sure—and I felt for him. One would think his being wealthy would've eased the transition, but it only made people envy, and envy leads to hate.

"Mr. Kalamack?"

Trent looked up, a new pinch of worry at his brow. He was now firmly in the "them" camp, and it wore on you after a while. But as I watched, his professional smile became deeper, almost believable. "Mr. Kalamack, I'm truly sorry about this," Kevin said as with a last lurch, we found the pavement of the parking lot and slowed to a stop. "You have every right to protect yourself, and as you said, he has a history of dropping his ball into the players ahead of him."

"We're fine." Trent's hand unclenched from the support bar as he stepped out into the sun, his feet unusually loud in his spiked shoes. "Retreat is better than standing my ground and possibly having him pull his entrance fee. I'm going to need my usual tee time next week. Just myself and one other. No cart. Can you arrange it for me?"

The man's relief was almost palpable as he sat in the driver's seat. "Of course. Thank you for understanding. Again, I apologize. If it were up to me, you'd be the one finishing your game and Limbcus would be cooling his heels."

Trent laughed, and hearing it, Jonathan, Trent's driver among other things, got out of one of the black cars. I liked the man better when he'd been a dog—Trent's version of a slap on the wrist for having tried to kill me. Seeing me take Trent's clubs from the cart, he opened the back of the SUV and waited, a sour expression on his face. I didn't like the man, his tall personage lean and full of sharp angles.

Uncomfortable, I whispered, "This wouldn't have happened if you'd gone bowling. They let you use magic in bowling." Kevin hesitated, and as Trent shifted from foot to foot in an unmistakable signal of departure, I extended my hand to the golf course employee. "Sorry about breaking your field. I can come back this afternoon and help you fix it."

His smile was uneasy and his palm was damp. "No, our people need to do it," he said as Trent took his clubs. "Ahh, Mr. Kalamack, I'm really sorry, but . . ."

Jenks's wings clattered a warning, and I squinted at the regret in Kevin's tone.

"No, it's fine," Trent was saying again, clasping Kevin across the shoulders and clearly trying to make our escape. "Don't worry. It happens around Rachel. It's part of her charm."

"Yes, sir. Ummmm . . . One more thing."

Kevin wouldn't meet my eyes, and I slumped where I

stood. "I'm banned from the course, aren't I," I said blandly, and Trent paused.

Kevin winced, but Jenks was smirking. "I am so sorry," the hapless man gushed. "I would have done exactly what you did, Ms. Morgan, but the rules say if you do any magic on the course, you're not allowed back."

"Oh, for little green apples," Trent said, but I touched his hand to tell him not to get bent out of shape. I'd been expecting it.

"You're welcome to wait at the clubhouse," Kevin rushed. "But you can't go on the course." His gaze shot to Trent's. "I'm so sorry, Mr. Kalamack. We have several caddies licensed for personal security. Your patronage is important to us."

Trent's clubs clattered as he swung his bag over his shoulder and squinted up at the sun. "Can an exception be made?" he asked. "Rachel wasn't playing. She was doing her job."

Kevin shrugged his shoulders. "It's possible. I'll bring it up with the rules committee. You've been a member since your dad gave you your first clubs. Heck, my dad sold them to him. You're good people, Mr. Kalamack, but rules are rules."

Yes, rules were rules, but I was tired of them never helping me.

Frustrated, Trent ran a hand over his hair. "I see," he said flatly. "Well, if Morgan isn't allowed on the course, I won't be needing that tee time."

My eyes widened, and I touched Trent in protest. "Sir . . ." Kevin pleaded, but Trent put up an easy hand in mild protest.

"I'm not angry," he said, and Jenks snorted his opinion. "I'm simply changing my plans. For all his backward thinking, Limbcus is right about one thing," he said, glancing at me. "If you're going to be on the fairways, you should know how to play. I was going to teach you is all."

My heart seemed to catch before it thudded all the louder. "Me?" I stammered, shooting Jenks a look to shut up when he darted backward in glee. "I don't want to know how to play golf." *He wants to teach me golf?*

Undeterred, Trent looped an arm in mine, the bag over his shoulder thumping into me. "I've got an old driving range in one of the pastures. I'll get it mowed and you can practice your drives until this gets worked out," he said. He turned to Kevin and shook his hand. "Kevin, give Jonathan a call later this afternoon and I'll courier over the funds for the game." He winced, but it was clear he was in a better mood. I had no idea why. "This is going to be expensive."

"Thank you," the young man said, all nervous smiles as he pumped Trent's arm up and down. "And again, I'm sorry about all of this."

Trent touched the tip of his golf cap and turned us around. His cleats clicked on the pavement, and my face felt hot. "I don't want to know how to play golf," I repeated, but Trent's pace remained unaltered as we walked to the SUV he'd bought to cart his kids around in. *Why did he want to teach me golf?*

Jonathan stared at us from the open back, and I yanked myself out of Trent's grip. It only made Trent smile all the wider, hair falling to half hide his eyes. Jenks's laughter as he pantomimed a golf swing as he hovered wasn't helping. God, I wasn't stupid! Trent was going to marry Ellasbeth as soon as he was done punishing her for walking away from the altar the first time. But that kiss we'd shared three months ago hung in my memory. He hadn't been drunk—I'd swear to it—but that didn't mean it hadn't been a mistake. You couldn't be two things. I'd tried, and it didn't work. And I wouldn't be his mistress. I was better than that.

Damn it, I'm babbling.

"You don't have to boycott them on account of me," I said as we neared the SUV. Jenks darted to my car in the shade, and Trent's posture relaxed. He liked the pixy, but Jenks was noisy.

"I'm not," he said softly as he handed his clubs to Jonathan. "I don't want to be out here without someone watching my back, and I've seen their security. That ball shouldn't have exploded. Not with that little tap you gave it. You're going to get it checked out?"

I nodded, and reminded it was still in his bag, I went to get it. A chill took me as I held the prickly, twisted mass of rubber and plastic, and I looked out over the overdone green luxury, glad that distance and vegetation hid us from most of the prying eyes. I'd never liked it out here, but I'd thought it was the snobby attitudes. Maybe it was more. "I'm going to ask Al about it."

Trent jerked at the mention of Algaliarept, a new light in his eye making me wonder if he wanted to come with me. "Sa'han?" Jonathan questioned, and the look died as Trent took the dress shoes he was holding out.

"Just calling it early, Jon," Trent said, his voice holding a new weariness. "I got a text about a misfired charm in one of the off-site labs and want to check it out personally."

"You need me?" I asked, and Jenks's dust sparkled from halfway across the lot. He had very good hearing.

But Trent only smiled. "No, but thanks. Those things are almost foolproof, and I want to talk personally to the man who got burned. Make sure I'm not being scammed."

I nodded, my creep factor rising at the siren coming from the nearby interstate.

"I heard shouting," Jonathan prompted, clearly unconvinced as Trent sat on the tailgate and unlaced his shoes.

"We took care of it." Trent stopped. Hunched over his feet to look both out of reach and totally accessible, he tilted his head and eyed Jonathan, clearly wanting him to leave.

Jonathan's thin lips screwed up as if he'd eaten something sour. Back ramrod straight, he stalked to the passenger side and got in, slamming the door in protest. Trent's lips quirked and he went back to his shoes. Jonathan could still hear us but at least he wasn't staring. The wind was catching in Trent's hair, making me want to smooth it out.

Stop it, Rachel.

My car was three spaces down and across the lot, but I was reluctant to leave. Trent looked weary, the sun full on his face and his green eyes squinting as he took a cleated shoe off and slipped his dress shoe on. I remembered how he'd stuck up for me, and something in me fluttered. It had been happening a lot lately. *Don't get involved, Rachel. You know it's because he's out of reach.*

Trent stood, cleats in his hand. "Let me know what you find out."

"Tomorrow. Unless it's bad news," I said, and Trent shut the back of the SUV.

"Tomorrow," Trent affirmed as he came closer, and my smile froze. I wasn't sure what he was going to do. "Thanks for today," he said softly as he gave my hand a squeeze.

"You're welcome," I said, wanting to acknowledge it but afraid to, and his grip fell away. Professional. I was professional. He'd been nothing but professional back to me ever since that kiss, his mouth tasting of wine and me breathless and wanting to know how long it took to get him undressed. I knew that he was going to marry Ellasbeth, that he had a standard to live up to that didn't include a local girl with a crazy mom and pop-star dad.

But he kept touching me. And I kept wanting him to.

Jenks was picking the bugs out of my car grille with his sword and shoving them off with his foot. Meeting my eyes, he made a get-on-with-it gesture, but Trent wasn't making any motion to leave and I didn't know what he wanted. "I'll talk to you later, then," I said, rocking back a step.

"Right. Later." Head down, Trent started to go, then turned back unexpectedly. "Rachel, are you available tonight?"

I continued to back up, going toe-heel, toe-heel, not watching where I was going. There it was again. Professional, but not. My first response was to turn him down, but I could use the money and I *had* promised Quen I'd look after him. Jenks's dust flashed an irritated red at the delay, and I said, "Sure. Business or casual business?"

"Casual," Trent said, and I put my hands in my pockets. "Ten okay? I'll pick you up."

He was going to want to nap around midnight, so whatever it was, it'd be over by then. Either that, or it was a meeting with someone on a night schedule that couldn't be tweaked.

"Ten," I said, confirming it. "Where are we going?"

Trent's head ducked, and spinning on a heel, he walked to his SUV. "Bowling!" he shouted, not looking back.

"Fine, don't tell me," I muttered. It didn't matter. I'd be wearing something black and professional no matter where we went. The kite show, a horse event, the park with Ellasbeth when she came to pick up or drop off the girls and Trent didn't want her on the grounds. Even an overnight trip out of state for business. I liked doing stuff with Trent, but I always felt like a cog out of place. As I should—I was his security, not his girlfriend.

"Oh, for sweet ever loving Tink!" Jenks complained when I got to my car. "Are you done yet? I've got stuff to do this afternoon."

"We're done," I said softly as I slipped in behind the wheel of my little red MINI Cooper. Trent was backing up, and I waited as he leaned across a stiff-looking Jonathan and shouted out the open window "Let me know what Al says!" before putting it in drive and heading for the interstate. If Quen had been here, he would've insisted on driving, but Jonathan could be swayed and I knew Trent liked his independence—not that he had that much.

"Al, huh?" Jenks said, suddenly interested as I sat behind the wheel and watched Trent leave. "You think that's a good idea?" Jenks asked, now hovering inches before my nose.

I leaned forward to start my car. "He can tell me if there was a charm on it," I said, and Jenks landed on the rearview mirror, distrust and unease falling from him in an orangey dust. I was tired, annoyed, and I didn't like the unsettled, more-than-being-said feeling I was getting from Trent. "It shouldn't have exploded," I added, and Jenks's wings slowly fanned in agreement.

If someone was targeting Trent, I wanted to know. It was worth bothering Al over, though he'd just tell me to let the man die.

That ball shouldn't have exploded.

Two

The sun was a slow flash through Cincinnati's buildings as I fought afternoon traffic headed for the bridge and the Hollows beyond. The interstate was clogged, and it was easier to simply settle in behind a truck in the far right lane and make slow and steady progress than to try to maintain the posted limit by weaving in and out of traffic.

My radio was on, but it was all news and none of it good. The misfired charm at Trent's facility wasn't the only one this morning, and so far down on the drama scale that it hadn't even been noticed, pushed out by the cooking class in intensive care for massive burns and the sudden collapse of a girder slamming through the roof of a coffeehouse and injuring three. The entire east side of the 71 corridor was a mess, making me think my sand-trap crater had been part of something bigger. Misfires weren't that common, usually clustered by the batch and never linked only by space and time.

Jenks was silent, a worried green dust hazing him as he rested on the rearview mirror. But when the story changed to a cleaning crew found dead, the apparent cause being brain damage from a sudden lack of fat in their bodies, I turned it off in horror.

Jenks's heels thumped the glass. "That's nasty."

I nodded, anxious now to get home and turn on the news. But even as I tried not to think about how painful it would be to die from a sudden lack of brain tissue, my mind shifted. Was I really seeing what I thought I was in Trent, or was I simply projecting what I wanted? I mean, the man had everything but the freedom to be what he wanted. Why would he want . . . me? And yet there it was, refusing to go away.

Elbow on the open window as we crept forward, I twisted a curl around a finger. Even the press could tell there was something between us, but it wasn't as if I could tell them it was the sharing of dangerous, well-kept secrets, *not* the familiarity of knowing if he wore boxers or briefs. I knew Trent had issues with what everyone expected him to be. I knew his days stretched long, especially now that Ceri was gone and Quen and the girls were splitting their time between Trent and Ellasbeth. But there were better ways to fill his calendar than to court political calamity by asking me to work security—me being good at it aside. We were going to have to talk about it and do the smart thing. For once, I was going to do the smart thing. *So why does my gut hurt?*

"Rache!" Jenks yelled from the rearview mirror, and my attention jerked from the truck in front of me.

"What!" I shouted back, startled. I wasn't anywhere near to hitting it.

Pixy dust, green and sour, sifted from him to vanish in the breeze. "For the fairy-farting third time, will you shift the air currents in this thing? The wind is tearing my wings to shreds."

Warming, I glanced at the dust leaking from the cut in his wing. "Sorry." Rolling my window halfway up, I cracked the two back windows. Jenks resettled himself, his dust shifting to a more content yellow.

"Thanks. Where were you?" he asked.

"Ah," I hedged. "My closet," I lied. "I don't know what to wear tonight." Tonight. That would be a good time to bring it up. Trent would have three months to think about it.

Jenks eyed me in distrust as a kid in a black convertible wove in and out of traffic, working his way up car length by car length. "Uh-huh," he said. "Trent's girls are coming back tomorrow, right?"

The pixy knew when I lied. Apparently my aura shifted. "Yes," I said, trying for flippant. "I can use the time off. Trent is more social than a fourteen-year-old living-vampire girl." And he could text just as fast, I'd found.

Jenks's wings blurred. "No money for three months . . ."

My grip on the wheel tightened, and I took the on-ramp for the bridge. "I've got your rent, pixy. Relax."

"Tink's little pink rosebuds!" Jenks suddenly exploded, his wings blurring to invisibility. "Why don't you just have sex with the man?"

"Jenks!" I exclaimed, then hit the brakes and swerved when the kid in the convertible cut off the truck ahead of me. My tires popped gravel as I swung on the shoulder and back to the road again, but I was more embarrassed about what he'd said than mad at the jerk in the car. "It's not like that."

"Yeah?" There was a curious silver tint to his dust. "Watching you and Trent is like watching two kids who don't know how their lips work yet. You like him."

"What's not to like?" I grumbled, appreciating the thinner traffic on the bridge.

"Yeah, but you thought you hated him last year. That means you really *like* him."

My hands were clenched, and I forced them to relax on the wheel. "Is there a point to this other than you talking about sex?"

He swung his feet to thump on the rearview mirror. "No. That's about it."

"The man is engaged," I said, frustrated that my life was so transparent.

"No, he isn't."

"Well, he will be," I shot back as the bridge girders made new shadows and Jenks's dust glowed like a sunbeam. *Will be again.*

Jenks snorted. "Yeah, he lives in Cincy, and she lives in Seattle. If he liked her, he'd let her move in with him."

"They've got a kid," I said firmly. "Their marriage will solidify the East and West Coast elven clans. That's what Trent wants. What everyone wants. It's going to happen, and I'm not going to interfere."

"Ha!" he barked. "I knew you liked him. Besides, you don't plan love, it just happens."

"Love!" Three cars ahead, horns blew and brake lights flashed. I slowed, anticipating trouble. "It's not love."

"Lust, then," Jenks said, seeming to think that was better than love anyway. "Why else would you explode that ball? A little overly protective, yes?"

My elbow wedged itself against the window, and I dropped my head into my hand. Traffic had stopped, and I inched forward into a spot of sun. I was not in love. Or lust. And neither was Trent, despite that I'm-not-drunk kiss. He'd been alone and vulnerable, and so had I. But I couldn't help but wonder if all the engagements this last month were normal or if he was trying to get out of the house. With me. *Stop it, Rachel.*

A horn blew behind me, and I moved forward a car length. Trent had his entire life before him, planned out better than one of Ivy's runs. Ellasbeth and their daughter, Lucy, fit in there. Ray, too, though the little girl didn't share a drop of blood with him. Trent wanted more, but he couldn't be two things at once. I had tried, and it had almost killed me.

My gaze slid to my shoulder bag and the golf ball tucked inside. "The explosion was probably the same thing affecting the 71 corridor," I said. "Not because I overreacted."

Jenks sniffed. "I like my idea better."

Traffic was almost back up to speed, and I shifted lanes to get off at the exit just over the bridge. We passed under a girder, and a sheet of tingles passed over me. Surprised, I looked up at the sound of wings, not seeing anything. *Why are my fingertips tingling?*

"Dude!" Jenks exclaimed. "Did you feel that? Crap on toast, Rache! Your aura just went white again!"

"What?" I took a breath, then my attention jerked forward at the screech of tires. I slammed on the brakes. Both I and the car ahead of me jerked to the left. Before us, a car dove to the right. Tires squealed behind me, but somehow we all stopped, shaken but not a scratch.

"I bet it was that kid," I said, my adrenaline shifting to anger. But then I paled, eyes widening at the huge bubble of ever-after rising up over the cars.

"Jenks!" I shouted, and he turned, darting into the air in alarm. The bubble was huge, coated in silver-edged black sparkles with red smears of energy darting over it. I'd never seen a bubble grow that slowly, and it was headed right for us.

"Go!" I shouted, reaching for my seat belt and scrambling to get out of the car. No one else was moving, and as Jenks darted out, I reached for a line to make a protection circle. But I was over water. There was no way.

Turning, I plowed right into someone's door as it opened. I scrambled up, frantically looking over my shoulder as the bubble hit my foot. "No!" I screamed as my foot went dead. I hit the pavement and fell into the shadow of the car. Suddenly I couldn't breathe. Brownish-red sparkles flowed into me instead of air, and my ears were full of the sound of feathers. I couldn't see. There was no sensation from my fingers as I pushed into the pavement. There was simply nothing to feel.

My heart isn't beating! I thought frantically as the sound of feathers softened into a solid numbness. I couldn't move. I couldn't breathe. It was as if I was being smothered in brown smog. Panicked, I looked again for a line, but there was nothing. What in hell was it? If I could figure that out, I could break it.

A slow roaring grew painfully loud until it cut off with a soft lub. A sparkle drifted before me, then another. I wasn't breathing, but I wasn't suffocating, either. Slowly the roaring started again, rising to a crescendo to end in a soft hush.

It's my heart, I realized suddenly, seeing more sparkles as I exhaled as if in slow motion, and with that, I knew. I was trapped in an inertia dampening field. There'd been an accident, and a safety charm had malfunctioned. *But why had it risen to encompass all of us?* I thought, reaching deep into my chi and pulling together the ever-after energy I'd stored there. I couldn't make a protection circle without linking to a ley line, but I sure as hell could do a spell.

Separare! I thought, and with a painful suddenness, the world exploded.

"Oh God," I moaned, eyes shut as the light burned my eyes. Fire seemed to flash over me and mute to a gentle warmth. Panting, I cracked my eyes to see it had only been the sunbeam I was lying in. *Sunbeam? I'd fallen into the shade. And where are the cars?*

"Rachel!" a familiar gray voice whispered intently, and I pulled my squinting gaze from the overhead girders to my hand. Ivy was holding it, her long pale fingers trembling.

"How did you get here?" I said, and she pulled me into a hug, right there in the middle of the road.

"Thank God you're all right," she said, the scent of vampiric incense pouring over me. Everything felt painfully sharp, the wind cooler, the sunlight brighter, the noise of FIB and I.S. sirens louder, the scent of Ivy prickling in my nose.

The noise of the FIB and I.S. sirens louder? Confused, I patted Ivy's back as she squeezed me almost too hard to breathe. I must have passed out, because most of the cars were gone. I.S. and FIB vehicles, fire trucks, and ambulances had taken their place, all their lights going. It looked like a street party gone bad with the cops from two divisions and at least three pay grades mucking about. Behind me was more noise, and I pushed from Ivy to see.

Her eyes were red rimmed; she'd been crying. Smiling, she let me go, her long black hair swinging free. "You've been out for three hours."

"Three hours?" I echoed breathily, seeing much the same

behind me at the Cincy end of things. More cars, more police vehicles, more ambulances . . . and a row of eight people, their faces uncovered, telling me they were alive, probably still stuck in whatever I'd been in.

"You weren't in a car, so I made them leave you," she said, and I turned back to her, feeling stiff and ill.

My bag was beside her, and I pulled it closer, the fabric scraping unusually rough on my fingertips. "What happened? Where's Jenks?"

"Looking for something to eat. He's fine." Her boots ground against the pavement as she stood to help me rise. Shaking, I got to my feet. "He called me as soon as it happened. I got here before the I.S. even. They're telling the media an inertia dampening charm triggered the safety spells of every car on the bridge."

"Good story. I'd stick with that." I leaned heavily on her as we limped to the side of the bridge and into the shade of a pylon. "But those kinds of charms can't do that."

"Rache!" a shrill pixy voice called, and I looked up, blinding myself as Jenks dropped down from the sun. "You're up! See, Ivy. I told you she'd be okay. Look, even her aura is back to normal."

Well, that was one good thing, but I was starting to see a pattern here, and I didn't like it. "You got out okay?" I asked, and he landed on Ivy's shoulder.

"Hell, yes. That wasn't multiple spells. I watched the whole thing. It was one bubble, and it came from that black car with the jerk-ass driver."

Hands shaking, I leaned on the cool railing. Two medical people were headed our way, and I winced. "Oh crap," I whispered, grabbing Ivy's arm as they descended on us, medical instruments flopping from pockets and their tight grips.

"I'm okay. I'm okay!" I shouted as the first tried to get me to sit back down, and the second started flashing a light in my eyes. "It was just an inertia dampening charm. I think it was so big ordinary metabolic functions couldn't break it. I got out using a standard breakage charm. And get that light out of my eyes, will you?"

"A breakage charm?" the one trying to fit a blood pressure cuff on me said, and I nodded, glad that ambulance teams were required by law to have at least one witch on staff and he knew what I was talking about.

"I'm willing to try anything," the first said, turning to look at the line of people.

"They're going to wake up thirsty," I said, but they were already striding back to the people under the sheets with a new purpose. Thankful that Ivy hadn't let them put me in that horrible line, I gave her arm a squeeze. "Thanks," I whispered, and her fingers slipped from me.

"It works!" came an exuberant cry, and a cheer rose as a man sat up, groggy and holding a hand over his eyes.

I was *so* glad that I wasn't going to be the only one to wake up from this. "Where's my car?" I asked as I scanned for it, and Ivy winced.

"I.S. impound, I think."

"Swell." My keys were still in it, and tired, I looked in my bag to make sure I still had that golf ball. "Okay, who out here owes me a favor?"

Jenks rose up from Ivy's shoulder, turning in midair to look toward Cincinnati. "Edden."

Nodding, I gathered myself, and as Ivy hovered to catch me if I stumbled, we shuffled that direction. I was surprised. As a captain of the street force of the FIB, or Federal Inderland Bureau, Edden didn't get out much, but this had happened six blocks from their downtown tower, and with both human and Inderland Security fighting for jurisdiction, he'd want to make sure the I.S. didn't sweep anything under the carpet.

The chaos was worse on the Cincy side of things and they were still moving cars out. Unfortunately none of them was mine. Behind the blockade were even more official vehicles, and behind them, the expected news vans. I sighed, trying to hide my face as a helicopter thumped overhead. *Three hours?*

But the shadows on the road agreed with the lapse of time, and as we looked for Edden, I thought back to that inertia bubble. Safety charms didn't grow that big, and it wasn't a cascading reaction of one triggering another, either. It had been a misfired charm in a morning of them. What the Turn was going on?

"Found him," Jenks said, darting away, and Ivy angled to follow his shifting path through the people. It was tight, and I leaned closer to her, not wanting to be bumped. Everything felt uncomfortably intense, even the sun.

"I'm sorry I scared you," I said as I pressed into her to avoid a harried medic looking for a sedation charm for some poor woman. Her husband was fine; she was having hysterics.

"It wasn't your fault."

No, it was never my fault, but somehow I always got blamed, and upon reaching the blockade, I dug in my bag for my ID. Ivy had already flashed hers, and after comparing the picture to my face, the two officers let me past. Jenks was hovering over Edden like a tiny spotlight, and I limped a little faster. There were definite advantages to being a non-citizen, but only if you were four inches tall.

Captain Edden had put on a few pounds since taking over the Inderland Relations division after his son had quit. His ex-military build made the stress weight look solid, not fat, and I smiled as he took off his sunglasses, his eyes showing a heavy relief that I was no longer out cold on the pavement. Standing beside an open car door, he finished giving two officers direction before turning to us.

"Rachel!" he exclaimed, thick hand finding my shoulder briefly in a heartfelt squeeze. "Thank God you're okay. That wasn't you, was it? Trying to stop something worse, maybe? You would not believe my day. The I.S. is so busy with misfired charms that they don't even care we're out here."

"Wasn't me this time," I said as we came to a halt in an open patch of concrete. "And why is everything automatically my fault?"

The bear of a man gave me a sideways hug, filling me with the scent of coffee and aftershave. "Because you're usually mixed up in it somewhere." His tone was pleased, but I could see the worry. "I wish it *had* been you," he said, his eyes flicking to include Ivy and Jenks as he put an arm over my shoulder and moved us away from the news vans. "The I.S. is giving me some bull about it having been a cascading inertia dampening charm."

Jenks rose up, but I interrupted him, saying, "It was an inertia charm, but it was one charm, not a bunch of them acting in concert. It came from about three cars ahead of mine. Probably the black convertible the kid was driving." I hesitated. "Is he okay?" Edden nodded, and I added, *"Nothing* came from my car. If it had, I wouldn't have been able to get out of it."

Edden chewed on his lower lip, clearly not having thought it through that far. The I.S. would have, though. Ivy looked tense, and I was glad I had friends who'd sit with me on the hard road and protect me from helpful mistakes. A guy with an armful of bottled water went past, and I eyed it thirstily.

"If anyone would bother to look," I said, voice edging into accusation, "they could see my safety charm hasn't been triggered. It's probably another misfired charm. Have you listened to the news today? No one's brain dissolved. We got off easy."

Edden shook himself out of his funk and looked over the surrounding heads. "Yes, we did. Medic!" he called, and I waved the woman off as she looked up from putting an ice pack on an officer's swollen hand, probably crushed when they were getting the people out of their cars.

"I'm fine," I said, and Edden frowned. "I could use some water, though. You don't know where my car is, do you?"

Edden's frown vanished. "Ahh . . ." he said, looking everywhere but at me. "The I.S. took everything south of the midpoint."

Jenks's wings clattered from Ivy's shoulder. "Hey, hey, hey. Good-bye."

Tired, I sighed. I was *not* going to take the bus for the

next twelve months while they figured out whose insurance was going to pay for this.

"I can get you home . . ." Edden started.

Ivy put a hand on my arm, pulling me from my souring mood. "It's okay, Rachel. My car is just off the bridge in the Hollows."

That wasn't the point, and I shivered as Ivy's touch fell away with the feeling of ice. The light was seriously hurting my eyes, and even the wind seemed painful. It was almost as if my aura had been damaged, but Jenks said it was okay. *Why had it gone white, and right before the misfire?* "Edden, I had nothing to do with it," I complained, not entirely sure anymore. "I can't tap a line over the water, and the I.S. knows it. If I could, I wouldn't have gotten stuck in that . . . whatever it was. It was all I could do to get out. This is the second misfire I've been in today, and I want my car!"

Edden jerked, his eyes coming to mine from the man with the water. "Second?" He whistled, and the guy turned. "Where was the other one and why haven't I heard about it?"

Jenks's wings hummed—swaggering, if someone flying could swagger—as he landed on Ivy's shoulder. "Out at the golf course," he said, and Ivy's eyes remained steady, telling me he'd already told her. "Someone almost nailed Trent with a ball, and she blew it up instead of deflecting it. Made a new sand trap out on four."

Edden's reach for the bottle didn't hesitate, but he eyed me speculatively as he cracked the cap and then handed it to me. "You're still working Kalamack's security?" he said, clearly disapproving.

"If you call that working," Ivy said, and I felt a chill as the cool water went down. "Edden, I've been listening to the radio the past three hours—"

"As she held poor Rachel's little hand," Jenks smart-mouthed, darting off her shoulder when she flicked him.

Edden's brow furrowed, and he looked back to where I'd woken up. "You could hear the radio from there?"

Ivy smiled, flashing her small and pointy living-vampire

canines. Her hearing was that good. Almost as good as Jenks's. "I've heard nothing new since the bridge. If I had access to the FIB's database, I could confirm it, but I'm guessing the misfires are contained in a narrow band that's moving about forty-five miles an hour, roughly paralleling 71."

I lowered the bottle, cold from more than the water. Across from me, Edden took a breath in thought, held it, then exhaled. "You know what? I think you're right."

Suddenly everyone was looking at me, and my stomach clenched. "This isn't my fault."

Edden went to speak, and Ivy cut him off. "No, she's right. The first incident was just outside of Loveland. Rachel was nowhere near there."

Head down, I recapped my water, a bad feeling trickling through me. I hadn't been out to Loveland this morning, but my ley line was out there. Crap on toast, maybe it was my fault.

"So you're off the hook!" Jenks said brightly, and I lifted my eyes, finding Ivy as worried as me.

Clueless, Edden looked over the heads of everyone as if having already dismissed it. "I don't like you working for Kalamack," he muttered.

"He's the only one who comes knocking on my door looking for something other than a black curse," I said, worried. Damn it all to hell, I had to talk to Al. He'd know if my line was malfunctioning. Again.

Making a small grunt of understanding, Edden touched my shoulder. It meant more than it should, and I managed a small smile. "Sit tight, and I'll see if I can get your car before it goes to the I.S. impound. Okay?"

"Thanks," I whispered as I took a swig of water. It was too cold, and my teeth hurt. Jenks noticed my grimace and the hum of his wings dropped in pitch. Sitting tight sounded fine to me. I wasn't up to dealing with vampires yet, especially if everything was hitting me twice as hard.

Ivy seemed to gain two inches as she scanned for someone wearing an I.S. badge and a tie. Across the cleared pavement, the last of the charmed people were finding their feet. The only one still on a stretcher was the kid. "Mind if I go with you?" she asked Edden. "I don't recognize anyone, but someone out here probably owes me a favor." She looked at me as if for approval, and I nodded. I was fine, and if anyone could get my car back, it would be Ivy.

"Great," Edden said. "Jenks, stay with Rachel. I don't want anyone from the press bothering her." He hitched his pants up and tightened his tie. "We'll be right back. Someone needs a refresher on this sharing information thing we're supposed to be doing."

I rolled my eyes, wishing him luck as Ivy looped her arm in his and they started across the bridge to the Hollows end of everything. "They're just afraid, Edden," I heard Ivy say as they left, a sultry sway to her hips. "FIB forensics can put them in the ground, and they're tired of looking bad."

I couldn't help my smile as I watched them, her svelte sleekness next to his round solid form, both very different but alike where it counted.

"Ah, 'scuse me, Rache," Jenks said, a pained look on his face. "I gotta pee. Don't move."

I looked around, finding a car I could lean up against. "Okay."

His wing hum increased as he hovered right before my nose. "I mean it. Don't move."

"Okay!" I said, resting my rump against the car, and he darted over the edge of the bridge.

Sighing, I turned to the insistent beeping of the last car being towed off. Most of the news crews had left with the recovering spell victims, and it was beginning to thin out. A man in a trendy black suit drew my attention, up to now hidden behind the Toyota being carted out, and I frowned as he looked at his phone, fingers tapping. It wasn't his dress, and it wasn't his haircut—both trendy and unique—it was his grace. *Living vampire?*

A distant pop across the bridge sounded, and the man started, his eyes scanning until they fastened on mine.

A chill dropped through me as I took in his blond hair shifting in the wind, the grace with which he tucked it behind an ear, the knowing, sly smile he wore as he looked me up and down. Suddenly I felt alone. "Jenks!" I hissed, knowing he was probably within earshot. This guy wasn't FIB, and he definitely wasn't I.S., even if he was a living vampire. The suit said he had clout, and confidence almost oozed from him. "Jenks!"

Putting his attention back on his phone, the man hit a few more keys, slipped the phone in a pocket, turned, and walked away. In three seconds, he was gone.

"Jenks!" I shouted, and the pixy darted up, his dust an irate green.

"Good God, Rache, give me a chance to shake it, huh?"

My hands on the warm car burned, and I curled my fingers as I scanned the crowd. Slowly my pulse eased. "Are you sure my aura is okay?" I asked out of the blue.

Hands on his hips in his best Peter Pan pose, he said, "You called me back about that?"

"I think it might be linked to the misfires," I said truthfully, and he looked askance at me.

"Yeah, but you were nowhere near any of the other ones. It wasn't you, Rache."

"I suppose." Heart pounding, I leaned back against the car, arms wrapped around my middle. I couldn't tell Jenks I had been spooked by a vampire, not under the noon sun, and not by a living one. He'd laugh his ass off.

But as we waited for Ivy to return with good news about my car, I shivered in the heat, unable to look away from the crowd and a possible glimpse of that figure in black.

He'd looked like Kisten.

Three

It wasn't Kisten, I thought again for the umpteenth time as I shook two tiny pellets of fish food into my hand, wiggling a finger at Mr. Fish in his bowl on the mantel. But it had looked too much like him for my comfort, from his lanky, sexy build to his funky sophistication and even his thick mass of blond hair. I'd been so embarrassed I hadn't even told Ivy. I knew she'd loved him too—loved him long before I'd met him, loved him, and watched him die twice defending me. But those feelings belonged to someone else, and I now knew what vampires were born knowing: those who tried to live forever truly held no future.

The heat from Al's smaller hearth fire was warm on my shins, and I soaked it in, worried about the beta resting on the bottom of the oversize brandy snifter, gills sedately moving. The wood fire crackled, and I breathed the fragrant smoke, much better than the peat moss fire that stank of burnt amber that he'd had last time.

I dropped the fish food into the bowl and turned, glad to see other hints that Al was pulling himself, and therefore me, out of ever-after poverty. I'd seen other demons' spelling rooms over the last year or so, and they varied greatly as to the theme. Newt's looked like my kitchen, which made me all warm and cozy. But Al was a traditionalist, and it showed in the stone floors, the glass-fronted ceiling-tall cabinets holding ley line paraphernalia and books, and the smoky rafters coming to a point over the central, seldom-lit raised hearth fire in the middle of the circular room. We didn't need the big fire for the spell we were working, and Al sat on the uncomfortable stool at his slate-topped table five feet from the smaller hearth. He liked the heat as much as I did.

The shelves were again full, and the ugly tapestry I'd once heard scream in pain was back on the wall. The hole that he'd hammered between my room and the spelling kitchen had been tidied, and the new solid stone door between the two met with an almost seamless invisibility.

"Mr. Fish is acting funny," I said as I watched the fish ignore the pellets.

Al glanced from the book he was holding at arm's length. "Nothing is wrong with your fish," the demon said, squinting at the print as if he needed the blue-tinted round glasses. "You're going to kill him if you give him too much food."

But he wasn't eating, simply sitting on the bottom and moving his gills. His color looked okay, but his eyes were kind of buggy. Distrusting this, I slowly turned to Al.

Feeling my attention on him, he frowned as he ran an ungloved finger under the print to make it glow. His usual crushed green velvet coat lay carefully draped over the bench surrounding the central hearth, and his lace shirt was undone an unusual button to allow for the warmth of the place. His trousers were tucked into his boots, and to be honest, he looked a little steampunky. Feeling my attention on him, he grimaced. It was one of his tells, and my eyes narrowed. Either it was the fish or the charm I wanted to know how to do.

"He's just sitting on the bottom," I said, digging for the source of his mood. "Maybe I should take him home. I think it's wearing on him."

Al peered sourly over his book at me. "He's a fish. What would wear upon a fish?"

"No sun."

"I know the feeling," he murmured, apparently not caring as he went back to the book.

"His mouth is funny," I prompted. "And his gimpy fin is the wrong color."

Al's breath came out in a growl. "There's nothing wrong with *that fish*. Teaching you how to identify the maker of a spell by his or her aura is a bloody hell waste of time. As you have an interest, I will indulge you, but I'm *not* going to do it myself. If you're done playing zookeeper, we can begin." He looked pointedly at me. "Are you done, Rachel?"

Silent, I took the mangled ball out of the brown lunch bag I'd brought it in and nervously set it on the table beside the magnetic chalk, a vial of yellow oil, and a copper crucible.

Al's eyebrows rose. "Since when do you golf?"

I knew Al didn't like Trent. I knew that the source of his hatred was more than five thousand years old and hadn't lessened in all that time. "I was on a job," I said. "It exploded under a deflection charm. I think it might have triggered an assassination spell."

Shoulders stiff, his eyes narrowed. "You were Kalamack's *caddie*?"

"I'm his security," I said, voice rising. "It's a paying job."

Standing, Al's lips curled in disgust. "I said avoid him, and you take a subservient role?" My breath to protest huffed out when he slammed the book in his hand onto the table. "There's only one possible relationship, that of a slave and master, and you are failing!"

"God, Al! It was five thousand years ago!" I exclaimed, startled.

"It was yesterday," he said, hand shaking as it pinned the book to the table. "Do you think the fact that there can be no viable children between elf and demon is an accident? It's a reminder, Rachel. Lose him or abuse him. There is no middle ground."

"Yeah?" I exclaimed. "You're the one who offered him a circumcision curse. I thought you two were BFFs."

Brow furrowed, Al came around the table, and I forced

myself to not move. "You're making a mistake. There're already concerns that we moved too fast in killing Ku'Sox."

I drew back. "Excuse me!"

"That we were taken in by elven trickery and lured into killing one of our own."

"That is so full of bull!" I could not believe this. "Ku'Sox was trying to kill all of you and destroy the ever-after!"

"Even so," he said as he put a threatening arm over my shoulder. "It would be better if you simply . . ." His words drifted off into nothing, his fingers rubbing together, then opening as if freeing something.

"You spent a thousand years with Ceri. What's the difference?"

His arm fell away, and I felt cold. "Ceri was my slave. You're treating Trent as an equal."

"He is an equal."

Motions brusque, Al reached for his book. "No, he isn't," he growled.

"Yeah? Well, you loved Ceri," I accused. "You loved her for a thousand years."

"I. Did. Not!" he thundered, and I cringed when dust sifted from the rafters.

"Fine," I muttered. "You didn't." This had been a bad idea, and I grabbed my golf ball to go home. He was my easy ticket out of here, though, until the sun set and Bis woke up.

Seeing me standing there, chin high and pissed, clearly wanting to leave, Al relented, stiffly pointing for me to take his chair. Relieved and uncomfortable, I did, setting the golf ball back down with undue force before I sat on the hard stool. The spell book was splayed out in his thick, ruddy hand as he came to stand behind me, and I could smell the centuries of ever-after on him, soaked in until it couldn't be washed off. He'd teach me this, but I was sure our conversation was far from over.

"It doesn't look like much," I said as I looked at the spell laid out before us.

His hand hit the table beside me, and he leaned uncomfortably close over my shoulder. "Good curses don't."

The slate table shifted as he pushed back up, and still lurking more behind than beside me, he peered at the book over his glasses. "Step one," he said loudly. "Sketching the pentagram. You can do that, yes?"

I blew across the table and picked up the magnetic chalk. "You need a book for this?"

"No." He pointedly dropped a colorful square of silk, and I wiped the slate free of stray ions. "I've not done it the long way for ages. Any more questions? Then a standard pentagram of comfortable size. The point goes up if the ley lines are flowing into your reality, but down if they are flowing out." He hesitated, then said sarcastically, "Which way are they flowing, Rachel?"

Hesitating, I tried to guess. We were about four stories deep. "Has the sun set yet?"

He cleared his throat in disapproval, and when I turned, he said, "No."

"Then it's point up," I said, mostly to myself as I began to sketch. I'd only recently found out that the ley lines, the source for most if not all magic, flowed like tides between reality and the ever-after. Energy streamed into reality at night, and flowed out when the sun was up, but since there were lines scattered over the entire globe, it evened out unless a line was unbalanced. And if it was, it wreaked havoc.

I don't know which is worse, I thought, the soft sounds of the sliding chalk mixing with the snapping fire making a singularly comforting sound. *An attack on Trent, or that my line might be wonky.* The misfires were coming from Loveland. Damn it, it was my line. I knew it.

"Better" was Al's grudging opinion as I finished, but I could tell he was pleased. I'd been practicing. "Crucible in the center, ball in the crucible. As you say, simple stuff." The snap of the book make me jump, and he added, "Step two. Burn the object to ash. Use a spell to avoid contamination."

The crucible was cold against my fingers as I placed it in the cave of the pentagram, and I tried to fold the ball so it would all fit in the copper bowl. We needed the ash, apparently. "Do I need a protection circle?" I asked, and then remembering having burned my fingers this morning, I wedged a tiny portion of the ball off to use as a connecting bridge.

Al leaned over my shoulder, his lips so close to my ear that I could feel their warmth. "Do you make a pentagram for any other reason?"

I turned to face him, not backing down. "I do, yes." Maybe bringing Ceri up had been a bad idea, and I looked across the table to the cushy chair that had been hers, still there although the woman was not.

Grumbling, he waved his hand in acquiescence, and using the outer circle linking the points of the pentagram as the circle base, I touched the nearest ley line and set a protection circle. Energy seeped in, connecting me to all things, and I let it flow unimpeded as a reflection of my aura stained the usual red smear of ever-after now making a sphere half on top, half underneath the table. I scooted the stool back a smidge so my knees wouldn't hit it under the table and accidentally break the spell. As I watched my thin layer of smut skate and shiver over the skin of the molecule-thin barrier, I tasted the energy for any sign of bitterness or harsh discord. It was fine. The lines were fine.

But the fear of being trapped in that inertia dampening charm gave me pause. My nudge to Limbcus's golf ball had blown it up, and I was gun-shy.

"We're waiting . . ." Al drawled.

Well, it was in a protection circle, I thought, and maintaining my grip on the line, I held the small bit of the ball I'd peeled off in my hand as I carefully enounced, *"Celero inanio."*

A puff of black smoke enveloped the ball, and for a moment, the reek of burning rubber outdid the stink of burnt amber. The heavy smoke rolled upward, curling back as it hit the inside of my small circle until it finally cleared.

In the center of the pentagram and the crucible was a pile of ash. For an instant, relief filled me. My control was fine. And then my mood crashed. Something from Loveland had caused the misfires. If it wasn't me, what was it?

"Very good." Book in hand, Al sat down before me in my usual chair, and I wondered if he'd been hiding behind me this entire time to avoid a possible burn if I did it wrong.

Peeved, I eyed him, the length of the table between us. "You're such a chicken squirt."

One eyebrow went up, and he pushed the oil across the table at me. "Anoint the ash with oil of marigold," he said dryly. "Don't ask me why, but it has to be marigold. Something to do with the linkages in the DNA allowing a hotter burn."

Unsure, I picked the oil up. "How much?"

Al opened the book back up and peered at it over his blue-tinted glasses. "Doesn't say, love. I'd use an amount equal to the mass of the ash."

My palm itched as I broke the protection circle, carefully spilling what I thought was the right amount of oil onto the ash. This was kind of loosey-goosey for me, but demon magic had more latitude than the earth witch magic I was classically trained for, being a mix of earth and ley line and whatever else they cobbled together.

"Burn it using the same charm you use for making a light," he said, and I touched the oil/ash mixture to make a connection to the slurry so the next curse would act on it and not, say, my hair. But when I reset my circle, he reached out and broke it, shocking me with the reminder that he was still stronger than me—unless I worked really hard at it.

"No protection circle," he said, and I slumped.

"Why not? Something is causing misfires, and I don't want to blow you up. I mean, you just got your kitchen looking halfway decent again."

Al's grimace as he looked over the space was telling. "Your magic is fine," he said, but he was edging backward. "You can't put it in a circle. If you do, then the color of the flame will be distorted from your aura."

My fingers twitched. That was how it worked, eh?

"But I don't think it matters," Al said with a false lightness. "That ball was not charmed by anyone but you."

Which would mean the misfires were responsible for it. Taking a steadying breath, I renewed my hold on the ley line. *"In fidem recipere,"* I said, smearing the ash and oil between my fingers for a good connection. One eye squinched shut, I finished the curse and made the proper hand gesture. *"Leno cinis."*

The ley line surged through me as the oil and ash burst into flame, and I wiggled at the uncomfortable sensation. Almost two feet tall, the flame burned with an almost normal gold color, hinting at red at the edges, and black at the core. I cut back on the energy flow, and when the flame subsided to three inches, both Al and I leaned over the table to get a closer look.

There was the bare hint of a mossy scent coming from Al, so faint I thought I might have imagined it. I must have done something, because his gaze slid to mine, making me shiver at his eyes, again back to their normal goat-slitted redness thanks to a costly spell. "That's your aura," he said flatly, and I began breathing again. "Your aura alone, and very little of it," he added. "You hardly tapped it, indeed. You say it made a crater?"

"And knocked me on my ass," I whispered, wishing the black smut wasn't there at all, but I'd become so used to doing curses that I didn't even consciously accept the smut anymore. It just kind of happened. "This is dumb," I said, depressed, and Al snuffed the flame with his hand. "What could you do just knowing the aura of a practitioner, anyway? Even if it did show something, I can't comb the city with my second sight trying to find a match."

Al took the still-hot crucible up in his bare hand. "You're missing the point, itchy witch," he said, tossing the entire thing into the fire. "Once you know a person's aura, you simply tune yours to it as if it was a ley line and pop in."

He was smiling with a wicked gleam in his eye, and I sat

up, seeing the beauty in it. "That's how you always find me," I said, and his devious expression blanked.

"Stop!" he said, hand up. "Don't even think to try it. You or your gargoyle don't have the sophistication to differentiate between auratic shades to that degree. Line jumping is one thing, jumping to an aura is something else. It's like saying the sunset is red when it's thousands of shades."

I could see his point, but hell, I knew Ivy's aura pretty well. And Jenks's.

"Student!" I started as his hand hit the table inches from me, and irate, I looked up. "What did I say?" he asked, leaning over me, his smile nasty.

"Not to think about it," I said calmly, but I was, and he knew it.

Back hunched, he spun away. "Fine," he grumbled. "Go ahead and burn another line into existence. Let me draw up the papers to annul our relationship first. I'm not paying for another one of your *life lessons*. Have you seen my insurance premiums? My God, you're more expensive than a seventeen-year-old working on his third car."

I had precious little ever-after income from my tulpa at Dalliance—which went to Al, incidentally—but he'd never mentioned insurance before now, meaning it had to be embarrassingly costly. "I'm not thinking about it," I said softly, and he looked at me over his shoulder, slowly spinning to gather the rest of the spelling equipment and lovingly set each precious piece back in its proper spot.

"So if the ball wasn't an assassination attempt and I did the diversion charm correctly, then why did it misfire?" I asked as he slid the curse book away and locked the cabinet.

"It didn't." He slid the key into a pocket, and I felt a tweak on my awareness as the little bump of fabric vanished. "It was overstimulated, not misfired."

My lips pursed as I saw the news reports in a new way. Not misfired, but overpowered? "But I'm better than that!" I protested.

His back was to me, and he lined his chalk up with the rest. "Yes, you are."

It was a soft murmur, and I crouched before the fire to pull the crucible out before it tarnished too badly—since I was the one who'd probably have to clean it. "Then why? Al, we had thirty misfires over a twenty-mile stretch in the span of an hour. Ivy worked it out. Whatever it is, it's moving almost forty-five miles an hour."

"Ivy, eh?" he said. "I'll take that as a fact, then. Perhaps whatever disturbed the energy flow is gone."

My gut hurt, and I set the fire iron aside. "Al, the misfires are coming from Loveland."

There was a telling instant of silence, and then Al turned away, his shoes scraping softly. "Your ley line is fine."

"What if it isn't?" I stood, afraid to tell him that my aura had gone white. If it was overstimulation, then probably everyone's had.

"You fixed it." Eyes averted, he sat in his chair, fingers steepled. "Your line is fine!"

I pulled his coat from the bench, the crushed velvet smooth against my fingers. On the mantel, Mr. Fish swam up and down, his nose against the glass, ignoring the pellets. I didn't say a word. Just stood there with his coat over my arm.

"You want to go look at it?" he finally asked, and I held his coat out. "Okay, we'll go look at it," he conceded, and I quelled a surge of anxiety. This close to sunset, there'd be surface demons, but I was more afraid of what my ley line looked like.

"Thank you," I said, and he grumbled something under his breath, shoving his arms in the sleeves and leaning to throw another log on the fire to keep it going until he got back.

"There are no monsters under your bed, Rachel, or in your closet."

Mood improved, I waited as he checked the buttons on his sleeves and fluffed the lace at his throat. "I found Newt in my closet once."

He gave me a sideways look and grabbed a mundane oil lamp from a shelf. Nose wrinkling, he did an ignition curse and the lamp glowed. "Damn surface demons. If it's not the sun burning your aura off, it's the surface demons harrying you at night." He stood poised, arms wide. "Well, let's go! I've got things to do tonight that don't involve you and your pathetically slowly evolving skills."

I felt better as I came forward to stand with him on the elaborately detailed circle of stone he used as a door. I must have done something right. Sure enough, I felt his satisfaction as the line took us, his kitchen dissolving into nothing as he flung us back to the surface and some place distant from his underground home.

Reality misted back into existence with a gentle ease that made it hard to believe that we had moved. A red-tinted haze struck me, and the gritty wind. Squinting, I turned to the sun still hanging over the horizon. The heat of the day continued to rise from the dry, caked earth, but I could feel a chill in the fading light. Red soil looked as black as old blood in the shadows.

We were at Loveland Castle, and the slump of rock that was all that was left of it here in the ever-after loomed behind us. My ley line hummed at chest height, looking, as Al sourly informed me, as right as rain in the desert, and could we go home now?

Arms about my middle, I spun. Almost unseen in the distance were the crumbling towers of Cincinnati. Nothing but dry grasses and the occasional scrubby tree filled the space between here and there. And rocks. There were rocks. It was the savanna in a decade-long drought.

Except for that odd green circle . . .

"What is that?" I whispered as I realized there was a figure upon the grass, withering on the ground, and Al grunted as he followed my gaze.

"Mother pus bucket," he muttered, head down as he began stomping toward it. "She's at it again."

"She?" But Al hadn't stopped, and I hastened to catch up. *Oh God, it's Newt,* I thought as I saw her unmistakable silhouette standing just outside the circle of green, her arms raised, bare where her androgynous robe had slipped to her elbows. She had short, spiky red hair today, a squat, cylindrical cap done in shades of black and gold atop her head, the colors repeated on her sash and slippers and stained red with the setting sun. A black staff was in her hand as she gestured and chanted at the figure on the living green, crazy as a loon in spring.

"What is she doing?" I said, shocked more from the green grass than anything else.

"Calibration curse," he said softly. "Maybe she heard about the misfires." And then he raised his voice. "Newt, love! What *has* the poor devil ever *done* to you?"

Clearly knowing we were here, the demon shifted her staff to both hands and held it level before her to pause in her magic. Within the fifteen-foot circle, the surface demon looked up, his thin chest heaving as he panted. His aura looked almost solid, the hatred from his eyes clear. There was a sword at his feet, the red light of the sun gleaming cleanly on it, and as I watched, a sun-brown hand crept out and gripped it.

"It exists," Newt said, her voice feminine even if the rest of her looked ambiguous. "It's an affront. What will happen to them when the ever-after collapses? That's what I want to know. Poor fools."

Fear rippled through me, and I looked behind me to the ley line. *It was collapsing. It was falling apart! I knew it!*

"We fixed the line," Al said, as much for her as for me. "Remember? We had a fine hunt. Rachel's line is within tolerance."

Surprise showed on Newt's face, and a small rock clinked as she turned to the line behind us. The surface demon hammered at the circle to get out, the heavy blade doing no damage, even if it was as tall as he was. "That's right," she said, peering at me with her all-black eyes that gave me the creeps. "I forgot, and yet we're both up here in this putrid filth we wallow in."

The sun turned me red even as I shivered in the chill of the coming night. "What is that?" I asked, looking at the demon, but what I really wanted to know was how there was living grass.

As distractible as a child, Newt turned, beaming. "It's a calibration curse," she said in delight, oblivious to the anger of the surface demon beating upon it. I could almost see clothes, so distinct was he in the low sun.

"It doesn't look like the curse I know," I said.

"That's because it's calibrating space and time, not balance and skills."

"Space and time?" I breathed as she began chanting. Immediately the demon dropped his sword and fell to the ground, writhing in pain. Neither Al nor Newt seemed to care. "Al," I almost hissed. "What is she doing?"

Frowning, Al put a fist to his hip. "She's moving a bubble of time into the past. The surface demon is caught up in it intentionally, as a marker."

That explained the green grass, but how far back had she needed to go to find it? "You can do that?"

"She can." Al pointed with the lantern, the flame pale in the remaining sun. "By comparing the rate of adjusted time to a known span, we can see if anything is out of balance."

I shuddered when the sun touched the rim of the earth and bled all over it. Newt thought something was wrong, too. "You do this a lot, right? Like a monthly siren test?"

"No," she said, and the surface demon behind the barrier scrabbled at the edge, his motions becoming erratic. "It hurts."

"I'll say," I whispered.

Newt gave me a sharp look. "Not the demon," she said sourly. "Me. Pay attention. You might have to do this someday. Each surface demon comes into existence at a specific, known time. This one has a particularly long life: watch now. We're close."

With no warning, the surface demon vanished, the grass under him springing up as if he'd never been there. Newt set the butt of her staff on the ground, clearly pleased. Beside me, Al fussed with his pocket watch, making a show of opening it. Not knowing why, I looked at it, glancing up to see Newt had a watch locket on a black chain around her neck.

"Ready?" she said, and Al nodded.

I had no idea what to expect, but as Newt pointed at the bubble and indicated "go," the demon reappeared. I watched in a horrified awe as he flung himself against the barrier, clearly in pain as the green grass grew sparse about him and the sword that had glittered so beautifully tarnished and became dented. With a sudden shock, I recognized it as the one the gargoyle had dropped when he'd come to find out who'd damaged my ley line.

His aura failing, the surface demon fell and a layer of black ash covered him. A bright light crisped the remaining vegetation to ash. Dead-looking sprigs appeared, and then the twisted figure with the tattered aura vanished.

"Mark!" Newt said, and Al nodded sharply, holding his watch out to Newt as the demon hiked her loose-fitting clothes up and came closer. "Perfect," she said, and Al closed his watch with a snap. "Time and space are moving concurrently, i.e., not shrinking," she said, seemingly perfectly sane. "Your line isn't impacting the ever-after, but it feels odd at times."

Scared, I spun to Al. "I told you. I told you something was wrong!"

Newt sniffed as Al frowned at me to shut up. "He didn't believe you?" she said, staff planted firmly before her as the setting sun cast her shadow over both of us. "You should listen to her, Gally. If you had listened to me, we might have survived."

Al shifted to get out of her shadow, screwing his eyes up at the last of the light. "We're not dead yet, Newt, love."

Newt's expression became sour. "Oh, so we are," she said, her gaze dropping to her foot nudging a rock deeper into the grit. "I suppose . . ."

Frustrated, I slumped. "Newt, what's wrong with my line?"

"Nothing is wrong with your line!" Al bellowed.

"He's right," she said, and his bluster died in a huff. "There's nothing wrong with it, but everyone else's is fine."

Okay. I rubbed my forehead. Newt wasn't known for her clarity of decisions, but she was a font of knowledge if you could understand. The concern was in how she might react to whatever she might suddenly remember.

I jumped when Al grabbed my arm and rocked us back a step. "Yes, yes. Everything fine," he said jovially. "Rachel, ready to go?"

My gaze was fixed on that ring where the grass had been. "That's what the ever-after used to look like," I said, stumbling when Al gave me a yank.

Newt turned to look at it. "As I said, it hurts." Her gaze was empty when she turned back. "Why are you here?"

I gave in to Al's tugging when Newt suddenly seemed to have forgotten the last ten minutes. "Ah, Rachel wanted me to check under her bed for monsters," he said, but I'd found the crazier Newt was, the more information you got, even if it was like teasing a tiger.

"I was checking that my line was okay," I said, stumbling when Al smacked my shoulder.

Newt smiled and linked her arm in my free one, making me feel as if we were on the yellow brick road. "You've noticed it too?" she said, having forgotten we'd had this conversation.

"Noticed what?" I asked as Al became visibly nervous.

"Thunder on the horizon," she said, and Al's pace bobbled.

"So sorry, Newt!" he said cheerfully as he pulled me away from her. "We have to go."

I tapped my line and gave Al a jolt. It wasn't anything he couldn't handle, but his grip loosened enough for me to pull away. "A simple charm blew up in my face today," I said hurriedly. "And another one that I had nothing to do with trapped me for three hours. Al says they were overstimulated, but there's a pattern to them, and they're coming from my line."

Newt was staring at the setting sun, just a sliver left. "Thunder like elephants," she whispered. "Have you seen an elephant, Rachel?"

Al's fingers gripped my shoulder, but he didn't yank me back. "We need to go. Now," he whispered. "Before she decides you're one of her sisters and kills you."

I stiffened. "Only in the zoo."

Newt turned back to me, her eyes black as the sun slipped away. From the slump of broken castle, a rock fell. "We exist in a zoo," she said, chilling me. "You know that, yes? I hope our funding doesn't run out. I'd give anything for a better enclosure, one that at least hides the bars." Her focus blurred, then sharpened on me. "Rachel, would you like me to do a calibration on you? See how long your soul has been aware?"

Blanching, I remembered the demon behind the barrier, twisting in pain as he lived his entire existence backward and forward in ten seconds flat.

"No!" Al said, and this time, I did nothing as he jerked me away. "Newt, we must go. Spells to weave, curses to twist. A student's work is never done!"

There was alarm under his cheerful words, but Newt gestured as if she didn't care, turning to look at the red smear where the sun had once been. "Study hard, Rachel," she said, her staff hitting the earth to pinch the rocks and make them skip. "Come again soon. I'm having a party next week when the purple grass flowers. It's beautiful then, when the wave hits them and sends them all crashing into one another."

Al pulled me back another step, and I walked backward, watching Newt sketch out another circle. "How much power does it take to do that?" I asked, pitying her.

"Enough to make you crazy," Al said. "Go home and *leave Kalamack alone*."

My feet were edging my ley line, and I felt its warmth spill into me. "Yeah, whatever," I muttered, deciding it probably wouldn't be a good idea to tell him I needed to get home so I could pick out what I was going to wear tonight with Trent.

"Rachel."

"Ow?" He was pinching my arm, and at my dark look, he let go. Anger had tightened the corners of his eyes peering at me over his blue-smoked glasses. His lips pulled back in a grimace, and I fidgeted, halfway home but realities away. "Give me a break, Al. If I alienate him, I'll never get the countercurse so you all can escape the ever-after. You can understand he's a little reluctant after you collectively suggested to off him for the hell of it."

Behind him, Newt gestured, and another demon contorted on the ground. Al squinted at me, clearly not happy. "You don't have enough money to survive the fallout if you fail. And neither do I."

My heart thudded. "Tell me about it." I stood, waiting for him to jump me home. I could shift realities by myself, but I'd be marooned at Loveland Castle and have to beg a jump home from Bis.

Al shoved me into the line. My anger vanished, turning to worry as I felt the line take me. At least I knew no one was gunning for Trent or me. Almost I wished there was.

Death threats I could handle. Saving the world had always been a little trickier.

Four

"Ivy?" I shouted as I pushed my socks around in my top dresser drawer. "Have you seen my white chemise with the lacy fringe?" The black slacks and short, snappy matching jacket I'd picked out for tonight's job needed something to alleviate the stark security look. Finding something that said work without tacking on fashion dork was harder than it sounded.

Jenks flew into my room, his wings clattering loudly. "The last time I wore it, I put it back where I found it," he said as he came to a pixy-dust-laced halt on my dresser.

Eyeing him sourly, I held up a pair of big hooped earrings, and together we evaluated the effect. They got rid of a large chunk of security, and at Jenks's thumbs-up, I slipped them on. Not only did they look nice, but with my shower-damp hair back in a hard-to-grab braid, Jenks could use them to do his pixy surveillance . . . thing.

Ivy's voice filtered back from the kitchen. "Your bathroom?"

Scuffing my flat shoes on, I went to check. Even with a quick shower to get the stink of ever-after from me, I was doing good for time, but Trent was usually early.

"And you think you don't like him," Jenks said as he followed me across the hall. "It's just Trent, for Tink's toes.

Who cares what you look like? No one is supposed to notice you."

"I never said I didn't like him," I said as I remembered Al's warning.

Wearing security black hadn't bothered me at first, but after three months of it, being professional had gotten old. If it had been a date, I'd wear my red silk shirt and maybe the jeans that were a shade too snug to eat in. Gold hoops and a white chemise would have to do, and I rifled through the dryer, finally finding it hanging up behind the door.

"Out!" I said firmly to Jenks. "You too, Bis," I added, and Jenks jerked into the air, leaving behind a flash of black sparkles like ink as he spun to the glass-door shower.

"Bis! Damn it, you creepy bat!" Jenks swore, and the teenage gargoyle made a coarse guttural laugh like rocks in a garbage disposal. "What the hell are you doing?"

"Practicing," the gargoyle said, his color shifting back to his neutral pebbly gray. Bis hung from the ceiling with his clawlike fingers, his dexterous, lionlike tail with the white tuft wrapped around the showerhead for balance. He was the size of a cat, and I'd be worried about him pulling out the plumbing if he weren't exceptionally lightweight. He had to be for his leathery wings to be able to keep him in the air. I'd felt his presence the instant I entered the bathroom, easily spotting him in the shower practicing changing his skin tone to the pattern of the tile. The mischievous kid had taken a liking to startling Jenks, knowing it made the pixy mad.

"I mean it," I said, chemise in hand as I pointed to the door. "Both of you, out."

Still laughing, Bis swooped out, intentionally making the back draft from his wings spin Jenks's flight into a dangerous loop before he darted out after him. I couldn't help my smile as I listened to Jenks complain to Ivy as I put the chemise on instead of the flat cotton tee.

"Much better," I whispered as I evaluated the results, and grabbing my jacket, I headed for the hall, ambling to the kitchen at the back of the church. Ivy looked up from her slick new laptop as I entered, her eyes skating over my outfit in approval. Her old tower and monitor were gone, and an overindulgent, high-def screen she could plug her laptop into now took up a good portion of the thick country-kitchen farm table pressed up against the interior wall. Her high-tech efficiency went surprisingly well with my herbs and spell-crafting paraphernalia hanging over the center counter. The single window that overlooked the kitchen garden was a black square of night. Al's chrysalis and Trent's old pinkie ring sitting under a water glass were the only things on the sill now that most of the dandelions were done. The radio was on to the news, but thankfully there'd been no new reports of misfires. Maybe it was over. I sighed, and as if feeling it, Ivy took the pencil from between her teeth. "Nice balance."

Pleased, I dropped my jacket onto my bag on the table as I made my way to my charm cupboard. "Thanks. I don't know why I even bother. I'll probably be spending the night sitting outside a boardroom door." Standing before the open cupboard, I fingered my uninvoked charms to find two pain amulets. Both Bis and Ivy were looking at her maps, the gargoyle's gnarly claws spread wide to maintain his balance on the awkwardly flat surface. He really was a smart kid, and I'd been toying with the idea of giving him my laptop so he'd stop using Ivy's—but then I'd have to use Ivy's, and that was no good either.

"What's up?" I asked, and she stuck the pencil back between her teeth, spinning the topmost map for me to see.

Bis looked worried, and with one hand at my hip, the other on the table, I leaned over the map showing Cincinnati and the Hollows across the river, color coded like a zip-code map to show the traditional vampire territories. Everyone looked to Rynn Cormel as the last word in vampire law, but lesser masters handled their own problems unless things got out of hand. Squabbles were common, but the number of red dots on Ivy's map wasn't good. Every section had at least one violent crime within the last twenty-four hours, probably ignored in the current chaos.

"You think it's connected to the misfired charms?" I asked.

"Could be," she said as she turned the map back around when I dropped my charms into my bag and went to the silverware drawer for a finger stick. "David called when you were in the shower. He wants to talk to you about some odd activity he's been witnessing."

Tension flashing, I took the sticky note she pushed at me with one long, accusing finger, recognizing her precise script and the cell number on it. "Thanks, I'll call him," I mumbled as I stuffed it in my pocket. I hadn't talked to him or anyone from the Were pack since an uncomfortable dinner almost a month ago. It had been to celebrate the addition of a few new members, but everyone except David had treated me as if I was some sort of revered personage. I'd left feeling as if they were glad I'd gone so they could cut loose. Who could blame them? It wasn't as if I was around that much. My female alpha status was originally supposed to be honorary—and it had been until David began adding members. I hadn't said anything because David deserved it. That, and he was really good at being an alpha.

"Will you be around for dinner?" she asked, ignoring that I was staring at my open silverware drawer, slumped in guilt.

"Ahhh, I wouldn't count on it," I hedged, wincing when Jenks's kids flowed through the kitchen, jabbering in their high-pitched voices. Circling Bis, they begged him to wax the steeple so they could slide down it, and blushing a dull black, the gargoyle took off after them. "You batching it tonight?"

Ivy set a hand on her papers so they wouldn't fly up. "Yes. Nina is with her folks tonight."

Her mood was off, and I put the finger stick in with my charms to invoke them later. Ivy's control was good, but why put warm cookies in front of someone on a diet? "She doing okay?" I asked, crouching to get my splat gun out of the nested bowls.

Ivy's smile was wistful when I came back up. "Yes," she said, and a small knot of worry loosened. Whatever was bothering her wasn't Nina. "She's doing well. She still has control issues when heated, but if she can realize it in time, she can funnel the energy into other . . . directions." Her pale cheeks flushed, and her fingers clicked over the keys in a restless staccato.

Knowing Ivy, I could guess where that energy was being diverted, and I dropped the splat gun into my bag, peering in to see what I'd collected. Pain charms, finger stick, wallet, phone, keys, lethal magic detection charm . . . the usual. "Hey, I appreciate you trying to get my car back. Edden still working on it?" I said, still fishing for what was bothering her.

The irritating tapping of her pencil ceased. "No one out there knew me, Rachel," she complained, and my eyebrows rose. *She is worried about my car?* "I worked in the I.S. for almost a decade, all the way from runner to the arcane, and no one out there knew me!"

Ah, not my car, her reputation. Smiling, I dropped my bag on the table, glad no one there recognized her. Maybe now she'd be free to live her life. "Jeez, Ivy, you were the best they had. If they ignored you, it was because they're still ticked. There's a difference."

"Maybe, but I didn't see anyone I recognized." Lips pressing, she tapped her maps. "You saw how busy it was. Half of Piscary's children worked in the I.S., and no one was out there."

"Maybe they were out at other calls," I suggested.

"All of them?" Again the pencil tapped, the cadence faster. "Where is everyone?" she said, eyes on the map. "I can see some of them being let go when Piscary died, but Rynn Cormel would still need a foothold in the I.S. Maybe more so since he's not originally from here. You don't think he abandoned them, do you? Now that he's had time to make his own children?"

"No. He wouldn't do that," I said, trying to reassure her, but the truth of it was I didn't know. That Rynn Cormel had taken Piscary's children in when he became Cincy's new top master vampire had been unusual, even if the vampire hadn't had any of his own at the time. It had prevented a lot of heartache, because vampires without masters usually didn't last long, succumbing to blood loss and neglect as they worked their way backward through the citywide hierarchy.

"I'm sure they were just on other calls," I said when the huge farm bell we used as a front doorbell clanged. My heart gave a pound, and my motion to get the door faltered when Jenks shouted that he'd get it. A sprinkling of pixy dust drifted down in the hallway, and I wondered how long he'd been eavesdropping. He worried about Ivy, too.

"That's probably Trent," I said, breath catching at the easy sound of his voice.

Ivy froze, her eyes flashing a pupil black as she looked up from under a lowered brow.

"What?" I asked, liking Trent's voice, especially when it was soft in quiet conversation.

Exhaling, Ivy dropped her eyes. "Nothing. I've not felt that in a long while, is all."

"Felt what?" I said defensively when she arched her eyebrows cattily. "Oh, hell no," I said as I slung my shoulder bag. "I'm not falling for him. It's the excitement of a job. That's it."

"Uh-huh," she said, and realizing I'd forgotten to put my jacket on first, I took my shoulder bag back off. "And that's why you put your best perfume on?"

Motions jerky, I jammed first one arm, then another into the jacket. "Give me a break, Ivy," I muttered, hearing Trent's voice become louder. "You know how hard it is to get rid of the stink of burnt amber? I might be having dinner with the mayor."

Trent walked in with Jenks on his shoulder, and my next words caught in my throat. He was in jeans and a casual top. My eyes traveled all the way down. *Tennis shoes?* "Or maybe something a little more casual," I said, feeling over-dressed.

His smile was as informal as his clothes, and he nodded to Ivy as she pushed back from her laptop, that pencil of hers twirling around her fingers instead of tapping on the table. "Ivy. Rachel," he said in turn, then glancing at his watch. "You look nice. Are you ready?"

"Sure," I said, cursing myself as that same quiver went through me. I saw it hit Ivy, her eyes going even darker. Damn it, I wasn't going to do this. "Ah, give me five minutes to change into some jeans."

His impatience was barely suppressed and I smiled, taking the show of emotion from the usually stiff man as a compliment. "You look fine. Let's go. I have to be back by two."

"But . . ." I said, words faltering as he nodded at Ivy and turned, his steps fast as he vanished back the way he'd come.

"Better get moving," Jenks said, hanging in the air right where he'd been sitting on Trent's shoulder.

"You're not coming?" I asked, and he shook his head.

"Nah-h. Trent told me his plans. You don't need me."

Brow wrinkled in confusion, I turned to Ivy. "See you later, I guess."

She was already bent back over her work, hiding her eyes. "Take it easy out there. There haven't been any more misfires, but it doesn't feel over."

It didn't feel over for me, either, and bag in hand, I followed Trent out. He was waiting for me at the top of the hall, his expression sheepish as he fell into step with me.

"Did I set Ivy off?" he whispered, and my eyes widened. That's why the abrupt departure. But then I flushed. He thought he had set her off. Crap on toast, he thought *he* had set her off—meaning . . .

Stop it, Rachel. "Um, she's fine," I said, not wanting to say no and have him guess that I had set her off, not him. "You don't mind driving, do you? My car is in impound." His eyes went wide in question, and I added, "Long story.

Not my fault. I'll tell you in the car." He almost laughed, and I could have smacked him. "So where are we going, anyway?"

"I told you. Bowling."

"Fine. Don't tell me." He was still smiling and I lagged behind as we passed through the sanctuary, the light from the TV a dim glow as Jenks's youngest watched a wildlife documentary. Bowling. Was he serious? What kind of contacts could he make *bowling*?

Trent's pace was graceful and smooth, his fingers trailing along the smooth finish of the pool table. It was all I had left to remind me of Kisten, and I watched Trent's fingers until they slipped off the end. "So what did Al say?" he asked.

To leave you alone, I thought, and seeing my frown, Trent added, "It was tampered with, wasn't it?"

"Oh!" I forced a smile. "No," I said as we entered the unlit foyer, pulse quickening when the scent of wine and cinnamon seemed to grow stronger in the dark. "It was fine," I murmured. "Al says the charm was overstimulated, not misfired. I'm guessing it is the same thing that caused the rest of the misfires today. How's your employee?"

"He'll be okay with minimal hospitalization. The safety measures in place saved his sight, but if it had happened anywhere else it might have . . . taken out a room." His words trailed off in thought as he reached before me to open the door. "Overstimulated? That makes more sense than misfires. I had a couple more incidents come in this afternoon. Little things, but I sent Quen all the data I could find. He says the misfires are localized into a narrow band that seems to be stemming from, ah . . . Loveland?"

His voice was hesitant, expression doubly so in the faint light from the sign over the door, and I nodded, glad he'd figured it out and I wouldn't have to bring it up. Not many people knew that the ley line just outside the old castle was less than a year old and made by me—by accident. "I asked Al while I was there. We went out to look, and there's nothing wrong with my line."

"Oh!" His smile was oddly relieved as he pointed his fob at the car at the curb, and it started up. It was one of his sportier two-doors, and he liked his gadgets almost as much as he liked driving fast. "You're already ahead of me on this. Good. That frees up our conversation tonight. I'd like to wedge something to eat into the schedule too." He hesitated, one step down. "That is, if you don't have other plans."

I eyed him, not sure why the hint of pleasure in his voice. "I could eat, sure." He still hadn't told me where we were really going, and I closed the door behind me. We could lock it only from the inside, but who would steal from a Tamwood vampire and Cincinnati's only day-walking demon? Scuffing down the shallow steps, I headed for Trent's car, only to jerk to a halt when he unexpectedly reached before me to open the door with a grand flourish.

We're going bowling, I thought sarcastically as I got in. *Right.* Trent shut the door, and the solid thump of German engineering echoed down our quiet street. I watched Trent through the side mirror as he came around the back of the car, his pace fast and eager. I fidgeted as he got in, the small car putting us closer than usual. I leaned to put my bag in the tiny space behind the seat, and Trent was holding himself with a closed stiffness when I leaned back. He liked his space, and I'd probably gotten too close.

My damp hair was filling the car with the scent of my shampoo, and I cracked the window. "Seriously, where are we going?" I asked, but his smile faltered when my phone rang from my shoulder bag. "You mind?" I asked as I leaned to get it, and his foot slipped off the clutch. The car jerked, and I scrambled not to drop the phone. His ears were red when I looked up, and I couldn't help but smile as I found my phone. "It's Edden," I said as I looked at the screen. "He might have something about my car."

Gesturing for me to go ahead, I flipped the phone open.

"Edden!" I said cheerfully. "What's the good news about my car?"

"Still working on it," he said, then at my peeved silence, added, "Can you come out tomorrow, say at ten?"

"What about my car?" I said flatly, and he chuckled.

"I'm working on it. I'd like you to talk to our shift change meeting. Tell everyone what happened at the bridge and give us your Inderland opinion."

Oh. That was different. "That's ten P.M., right?" I asked, fiddling with the vents as Trent drove us down the service roads paralleling the interstate. His usual fast and furious driving had slowed, and I wondered if he was trying to listen in.

"Ah, A.M."

"In the morning?" I exclaimed, and Trent stifled a chortle. Yep, he was listening. "Edden, I've barely got my eyes unglued at ten. I'd have to get up by nine to make it."

"So stay up," the man said. "Call it a bedtime story. I promise I'll have your car."

I sighed. The chance to be included in something professional where my opinion was wanted was a unique and cherished thing. And I did want my car. But ten A.M.?

"Rachel, I could really use your help," he said. "Even if these misfires are over, I'm having a hard time getting a handle on the issues they've caused. That misfired charm on the bridge was one of about two dozen that got reported," Edden admitted. "We're guessing five times that actually happened. I'm down two officers, and with the I.S. scrambling to apprehend the inmates who survived the mass exodus of the containment facility downtown, the vampires at large are taking it as a sign there is no law at all."

We stopped at a light, and I glanced at Trent. His brow was creased, and I frowned. "What happened at the Cincy lockup?"

Edden's sigh was loud enough to hear. "Apparently the high-security wing was in the path of whatever that was, and it unlocked. Most of the inmates are either dead or gone—"

"They killed them?" I said, aghast.

"No. Anyone using magic to escape died, probably from

a misfire. They got it locked down, but I hate to think what would have happened if the sun hadn't been up. At least the undead stayed put." The background noise became suddenly louder as Trent turned us down a quiet street.

"The I.S. isn't handling *anything* right now," Edden said, and a ribbon of worry tightened about me. "Rachel, I don't know the first thing about why a spell shop would explode or what would make a witch's apartment fill with poisonous gas and snuff the entire building. I've got a sorting charm at the post office that took out the back wall of the Highland Hill branch and killed three people. Two construction workers in intensive care from an unexpected glue discharge, and a van of kids treated and released for something involving cotton candy and a hay baler. Even if nothing more goes wrong, I'm swamped. Is there an Inderlander holiday I don't know about?"

"No." My thoughts went to Newt's space and time calibration curse. She didn't think it was over. "Okay, I'll be there, but I want coffee."

His sigh of relief was obvious. "Thanks, Rachel. I really appreciate it."

"And my car!" I added, but he'd already hung up. I closed the phone and looked at it sitting innocently in my hands. "Thanks," I said as I glanced at Trent, the streetlights flashing on him mesmerizingly. "You heard all that, right?"

He nodded. "Most of it. It's a mess."

"I'll say. I doubt I'll come away with anything we don't already know, but I'll let you know if I do."

Again he smiled, a faint worry line showing on his forehead. "I'd appreciate that. We're here."

I looked up from putting my phone away. Surprised, I blinked. It was a bowling alley, the neon pins and balls on the sign flickering on and off. Lips parted, I said nothing as Trent pulled his shining car into one of the parking spots beside a dented Toyota. Jenks staying home resounded in me, and the tension from Edden's call vanished as Trent turned the car off.

"Trent, is this a date?"

He didn't reach for the key still in the ignition. "You never told me how your car got impounded."

"Is this a date?" I asked again, more stridently.

Silent, he sat there, his hands on the wheel as he stared at the front door and the flashing neon bowling pins. "I want it to be."

My face felt warm. A couple was getting out of a truck a few spots down, and they held hands as they went in. *A date?* I couldn't imagine holding Trent's hand in public. Kisten's, yes. Marshal's, yes. Not Trent's. "This isn't a good idea."

"Normally I'd agree with you, but I've got a valid reason."

Valid reason. His voice had been calm, but my skin was tingling, and I fidgeted with my shoulder bag until I realized what I was doing and stopped. "Nothing has changed in the last three months."

"No. It hasn't."

I took a breath, then thought about that. He'd kissed me three months ago, and I'd kissed him back. *Nothing has changed.*

I heard the soft sound of sliding cotton as he turned, and I felt his attention land on me. Looking up, I read in his eyes the question. "Nothing?" I said, my hands knotting in my lap. Things felt different to me. We'd been all over Cincinnati together the last three months, me doing everything from getting him coffee at the conservatory's open house to discouraging three aggressive businessmen who wouldn't take no for an answer. We'd developed an unwritten language, and he'd gained the knack of reading my moods as easily as I knew what he was thinking. I'd seen him laugh in unguarded moments, and I'd learned to be gracious when he paid my way into events that I'd never be able to afford. I'd been ready to defend him to the pain of unconsciousness, and I wasn't sure anymore if it was a job or something I'd do anyway.

But he had another life, one coming in tomorrow on a 747 that didn't include me.

"I can't be like Ceri, showing the world one face and my heart something else," I said, gut clenching.

"I'm not asking you to."

I looked up from my hands, my breath catching at his earnest expression. "Then what are you asking?"

His lips twisted, and he turned away. "I don't know. But Ellasbeth is coming back with the girls tomorrow—"

I pounced on that. "Yes, Ellasbeth." He winced. A second couple was going in, and I looked at the glowing sign. Couples night. Swell. "Trent, I will not be a mistress."

"I know." His voice was becoming softer, more frustrated.

"Yes, but we're still *sitting* here," I said, my anger building. "Why are we here if we both know it's not going to work?"

"I want to take you bowling," he said as if that was all there was to it, and I flung my head back, staring at the roof of the car.

"Rachel," he said tightly, and I brought my head down. "Tonight is my last night before the girls come home and my world shifts back to them. I've never had time for myself like this. *Ever.* Quen will be there evaluating me though I know he doesn't mean to, and until she leaves, Ellasbeth will be doing the same. The girls will be front and center as they're supposed to be, and that's okay. But I've spent the last three months with you and this incredible freedom that I've never had before, and I need to know if . . ."

His words trailed off, and my heart hammered at his expression, both pained and wistful.

"I need to know," he said softly. "I *want* to know what a date with you is like so I can look at it and say *that* was a date. *This* was business. One date. One real date, with a good-night kiss and everything. One date so I can honestly say to myself that the others were not . . . dates."

I couldn't seem to catch my breath, and I looked back down at my hands, all twisted up again. Slowly, deliberately, I opened my fingers and splayed them out on my knees. I knew what he was talking about, and it might not be a bad idea—having a reference and all. But it sounded dangerous. "Bowling?" I questioned, and the worry wrinkle in his brow eased.

"Sure," he said, his hands falling from the wheel. "You can't get banned, so there's no reason for them to kick us out." He hesitated, then added, "Or I can take you back home."

I didn't want to go home. Knees wobbly, I yanked the door handle, grabbing my shoulder bag as I got out of the car. "No kiss," I said over the car. "Not all dates end with a kiss."

His smile hesitant, Trent got out and came around the front of the car. "If that's what you want," he said, and flustered, I put my hands in my pockets so he wouldn't be tempted to take them, flashing him a stilted smile when he reached to get the heavy oak door for me.

Though clearly disappointed about the kiss stipulation, Trent seemed happy that I hadn't said no outright, and he stood behind me as I shifted to the right of the door, breathing in the stale smell of beer and really good burgers. The crack of the pins followed by an exuberant call of success was relaxing, and the sappy couples music made me smile. "I've not been bowling in ages," I said, and Trent fidgeted his way out from behind me.

"This is okay?" he said hesitantly, and I nodded. The soft touch of his hand on the small of my back jolted through me, and I scrambled to catch my energy balance before it tried to equalize between us. I felt overdressed as we approached the counter, and I set my bag down on the scratched plastic to take my jacket off to turn me from security to professional woman coming right from work. Under the plastic top were perfect bowling scores, and I glanced at the bar in the corner, my stomach rumbling at the smell of greasy, salty, wonderful bar food. *Yes, this is okay.* God help me if Al ever found out.

"Two games, please," Trent said as he reached for his wallet. "You have a fast lane?"

The guy behind the counter turned from changing the

disc on the music they were piping through the place. He looked old, but it was mostly life wearing him down. "Three is fast," he said, then blinked as he saw me. *Crap, had I been recognized?* "You, ah, need shoes?"

Trent nodded. "Size 8 women's, and a men's 10."

The bowling guy's chair was on casters, and with a practiced move, he shoved backward to the honeycomb wall behind the counter, grabbing two pairs and shoving himself back. "Ah, with the shoes, that will be forty-three, unless you want to include two burger baskets. They come with two complimentary beers each."

It was couples night after all, and Trent turned to me. "Okay with you?"

"Sure." Oh God, what was I doing? This felt more risky than anything I'd ever done with Trent before, including the time we'd stolen elf DNA from the demons. Nervous, I turned to the bar again. The TV was spouting today's recycled bad news to counteract the love songs, but the love songs were winning.

"I got this," Trent said as I made a motion to get my wallet from my shoulder bag. He was grinning as he counted out the cash. "We're on a date," he told the man proudly as he handed the bills over, and I flushed.

The guy behind the counter glanced at me, then Trent as if he was dense. "I can see that," he said. "Let me sanitize your shoes."

Setting both pairs on a scratched pentagram behind the counter, he muttered a phrase of Latin. My internal energy flow jumped as a flash of light enveloped the shoes. I knew the light was just for show, but it was reassuring, and I took my shoes as the man dropped them before us. The leather was still warm, stiff from having been spelled so often.

"Enjoy your game," he said as he handed us a scorecard and a tiny pencil. "All food stays at the bar." Slumping, he fumbled in a plastic bin. "Here's your food and beer coupons."

Trent was smiling, looking totally out of place despite

his jeans and casual shirt as he took his shoes. "Thank you. Lane three?"

Nodding, the man hit a button on a panel, and it lit up, the pinsetter running a cycle to clear itself.

"This is so weird," I said as I fell into place behind Trent.

"Why?" He looked over his shoulder at me. "I do normal things."

Pulling my gaze from him, I scanned the ball racks for a likely candidate. "Have you ever been here? Doing normal things?"

Trent stepped down from the flat carpet to the tiled floor and our lane. "Honestly? No. Jenks suggested this place when I asked him. But the burgers smell great."

Jenks, eh? Thinking I was going to have a chat with the pixy when I got home, I dropped my shoes on one of the chairs and went to pick out a ball. Trent was tying his shoes when I came back with a green twelve-pounder with Tinker Bell on it. Clearly it had been someone's personal ball at some point, and therefore might have some residual spells built in, charms I could tap into if I guessed the right phrase. Trent eyed it in disbelief when I dropped it on the hopper, but the first feelings of competition stirred in me, and I looked down the long lane and the waiting pins in anticipation. This might be okay. I'd had platonic dates before.

"You're kidding," he said as I sat down and slipped my shoes off to tuck them under the cheap plastic seats.

"They say you can tell a lot about a man by the ball he uses."

His eyes met mine, and feeling spiked through me. *Okay, it didn't have to be completely platonic. Not if we both knew it was the only date we'd ever have.*

"Is that what they say?" he asked, head tilted to eye me from under his bangs, and I nodded, wondering why I'd said that. The shoes were still warm, and I felt breathless as I leaned to put them on. Trent slowly rose, his motions out of sync with the sappy love song, but oh so nice to watch. I fumbled my laces and had to start over when he stopped at a rack and lifted a plain black ball with an off-brand logo. "This one looks good."

Good. Yeah. What *I* liked was the way his butt looked, clenched as he held the extra weight of the ball. Slowly I shook my head, and he replaced it.

"Better?" he asked, hefting a bright blue one, and I shook my head again, pointing at one way down on the bottom of the rack. Trent's expression went irate. "It's pink," he said flatly.

I beamed, tickled. "It's your choice. But it's got a charm or two in it, I bet."

Looking annoyed, he hefted the pink monstrosity, his expression changing as he probably tapped a line and felt the energy circulating through it. Saying nothing, he came back to our lane and set it beside mine. "I am so going to regret this, aren't I?"

I leaned forward, heart pounding. "If you're lucky. You first." Feeling sassy, I stood, almost touching his knees as I edged into the scoring chair. The masculine scent of him hit me, mixing with the smell of bar food and the sound of happy people. My heart pounded, and I focused on the scorecard, carefully writing Bonnie and Clyde in the name box in case anyone was watching the overhead screen.

What am I doing? I asked myself, but Trent had already picked up his pink bowling ball, giving me a sideways smirk before he settled himself before the line, and made a small side step, probably to compensate for a slight curve.

I exhaled as I watched him study the lane, collecting himself. And then he moved in a motion of grace, the ball making hardly a sound as it touched the varnished boards. Trent walked backward as the ball edged closer to the gutter, then arced back, both of us tilting our heads as it raced to the pins to hit the sweet spot perfectly.

"Boohaa!" I cried out, since that's what you are supposed to do when someone pulls a gutter ball back from the edge, and Trent smiled. My heart flip-flopped, and I looked away, scratching a nine in the first box. "Ah, nice one," I said as he waited for his ball to return.

"Thanks." His fingers dangled over the dryer. "But I swear, if you tweak this ball like you do my golf balls, I'll put fries in your beer."

My head snapped up, and his smile widened until he laughed at me. "Leave my game alone," he said, the rims of his ears going red.

"You're going to regret that statement. I promise you that," I said, and he smirked as he took his gaudy pink ball and set himself up to pick up the spare. Damn it, this was so not smart, but I couldn't help but watch him. My fingers were trembling as I wrote down his score and stood for my first roll. I enjoyed flirting, and to be honest, it was almost a relief after biting back so many almost-said comments the last month.

And after all, it was only one date. One night of freedom so we both had something to compare the last three months with and know that they were not dates.

Just one night. I could do one night.

Five

He eats *his fries with mustard?* I thought, watching Trent put the yellow squeeze bottle down and pull his basket closer as we sat at the bar and finished our dinner. The burgers had been heavenly and the conversation enlightening, even as it had been about nothing in particular.

Happy, I made a final notation on the scorecard and let the tiny pencil roll away. "Okay, okay, I'll give you that last one, but only because I'm nice."

"Nice, smice." Trent dipped a fry and pointed it at me. "I took that pin fair and square. I can do magic while bowling." He ate his fry and lifted a shoulder in a shrug. "You not knowing the charm doesn't make it illegal."

"Well, no, but it was kind of cheesy."

"Cheesy?" He chuckled, looking nothing like himself but having everything I liked about him. I'd had a great time, and I'd been watching the clock with the first hints of regret. It had been unexpected, that feeling of forgetfulness, free for a time of who I was, and who he was, and what was expected of us. I didn't want it to end. "Where did you learn to bowl?"

Trent watched his fingers, carefully picking out his next fry. "University. But you can't use magic at the West Coast lanes. It's not illegal, but it's too unpredictable. How about you?"

I chuckled, glad when the music turned off. We were closing them down, and it felt good. "My brother belonged to a young bowlers' league. When my mom worked weekends, he had to watch me. If I promised to leave him and his friends alone, he'd buy me a lane at the outskirts where I could mess around."

Trent's gaze went behind me to the last of the bowlers finishing their games. The cleaning staff was making inroads, but they wouldn't shut the door for almost an hour. "Sounds lonely," he said, dipping a fry.

"Not really." But it had been. He was looking at my mouth again, and I wondered if he wanted to kiss me.

I dropped my head, and he shifted on the bar stool, the motion holding frustration.

"That was the best burger I've ever had to pay for," he said to fill the silence. "I'm going to have to stop in the next time I'm in the area."

"When do you ever get out here?" I could look at him now that he wasn't looking at me.

"Never," he admitted, his attention falling from the TV. "But I'd drive for this. Mmmm. The fries are good, too."

"You should try them with ketchup," I said, and then not knowing why, I pushed my basket toward him. There were a few fries in it, but it was the puddle of ketchup I was offering.

"I have," he blurted, eyes wide to look charming. "I mean, I do, but not in public."

I looked at his pointy ears, and he actually blushed.

"Right," he said, then dragged his fry through my ketchup, not meeting my gaze as he chewed.

He used my ketchup, I thought, and something in me seemed to catch. "The good with the bad, yes?" I said, and when I lifted my pop, we clinked bottles. "Hey, I'm sorry about losing it today at the golf course. I should have handled that better. Bullies get the best of me."

Absorbed with his fries, he shook his head. "Don't worry about it. It surprised me when he brought up my background.

I'll do better next time. I've got a response now and everything."

I took a swig of my drink and set it down. "Good luck remembering it. I always forget." I wasn't hungry, but I liked the idea of sharing a puddle of ketchup with him, and I ate one last fry. "It's worth it, though, don't you think? Not hiding?"

"God yes. I've not had to make any ugly decisions since Lucy came home."

His voice had softened, and it was easy to see the love for his child. I knew he loved Ray just as much even though she didn't have a drop of his blood. Ray was Quen and Ceri's child. Trent had only repaired her damaged DNA, but the girls were being raised as sisters, especially now that Ceri was gone.

"So they come back tomorrow," I prompted, wanting to see more of that soft look.

Trent nodded, the beer he'd nursed the last hour hanging between two fingers an inch above the bar. There was only one couple left at the lanes, the cook scraping the grill, and the guy at the shoe counter cleaning each pair before calling it a night. I liked Trent like this, relaxed and thinking of his kids, and I quashed a fleeting daydream. I couldn't picture him in my church, living with the pixies, waking up in my bed. *Stop it, Rachel.*

A siren wailed in the distance. It felt like a warning, one I needed to heed. I wasn't attracted to Trent because Al told me to leave him alone. I liked Trent because he understood who I was and would still sit at a bar with me and eat french fries. *And it ends tomorrow.*

"I'll be glad when Quen gets back," I said, eyes down.

"Oh? Has watching my back been that onerous?"

"No. It's just that you take up a lot of my time." *And after tonight, I'm not going to have a damn thing to do.*

Trent set my basket atop his and pushed them both to the side, making no move to leave. "You definitely have a different style than Quen. But you did a wonderful job of it. Thank you."

Almost depressed, I watched the cook through the long thin pass-through. "Thank you," I said, meaning it. Again we clinked bottles, and we both took a swallow. I was going to miss it. Miss everything. But the girls would be going back to Ellasbeth in three months. I could wait.

And then what, Rachel?

"I had a good time tonight," he said as if reading my mind. "If things were different—"

"But they aren't," I interrupted. "Besides, you don't pass my underwear test." I needed to leave before I started to cry or break things. This really sucked.

"Your what?" Trent said, his eyes wide.

I couldn't help the mental picture of him in tighty whities, then boxers, wondering which way he went. "My underwear test," I said again, then added, "I can't imagine folding your underwear week after week. That's it."

Seeming annoyed, Trent turned away. "I have people who do that for me."

"That's just it," I said, fiddling with my pop bottle. *This isn't how I wanted to end this evening.* "Even if you didn't have this big thing you're going to do with Ellasbeth, I can't see you living in my church, or anywhere other than your estate, really, doing normal stuff like laundry, or dishes, or washing the car." I thought of his living room, messy with preschool toys. I hadn't ever imagined that, either. "Or trying to find the remote," I said slowly.

"I know how to do all those things," he said, his tone challenging, and I met his eyes.

"I'm not saying you don't. I'm just saying I can't imagine you doing those things unless you wanted to, and why would you?"

He was silent. In the kitchen, the cook began putting the food back into the big walk-in fridge. Trent's jaw was tight, and I wished I'd never brought it up.

"Forget I said anything," I said, touching his knee and pulling my hand back when his eyes darted down. "Laundry is overrated. I really enjoyed tonight. It was nice having a real date."

Trent's annoyance, startled away from that touch on his knee, evolved into a sloppy chagrin. Nodding, he spun his bar stool to take my hands and turn me to face him. It was ending. I could feel it. It was as if our entire three months together had been building to this one date. And now it was over.

"It was, wasn't it?" Trent's grip on my hands pulled me closer. My heart pounded. I knew what he wanted. There wasn't a hint of energy trying to balance between us, but the tips of my hair were floating, and a sparkling energy seemed to jump between us. Trent's eyes were fixed on mine, and I swallowed. He was feeling it too, a slight pressure on his aura, as if passing through a ley line.

Passing through a ley line?

"Do you feel that?" I said, remembering the same sensation on the bridge this afternoon.

"Mmmm," he said, oblivious to my sudden disconcertment as he pulled me closer.

Oh God, he's going to kiss me, I thought, then jumped at the bang at the shoe counter.

Trent jerked, a flash of energy balancing between us as he reached for a line.

My eyes darted to the shoe counter. A dusky haze hung over it. Under the smoke was a hole blown clear through the counter, the plastic melted, and above, an ugly stain on the ceiling. "What the fuck!" came from behind the remains of it, and the two people still on the lanes turned as the counter guy rose up, his beard singed and his eyes wide as he saw what was left of his desk. "Where the fuck are my shoes? Shit, my beard!"

It was smoldering, and he patted the fire out as a big man with suspenders came from a back room, a napkin in one hand. "What happened?" he said, then stopped short, staring at the counter. "What did you do?"

"The fucking shoe charm blew up!" the man said indignantly. "It just blew up!"

My heart pounded. Sparkly feeling, charm reacting with uncontrolled strength: it was starting to add up, and I looked at the couple returning to their game. Not every ball was charmed, but most were. *Shit.* "Stop!" I yelled as I slid from the stool, but it was too late, and the woman had released the ball. I watched it head for the gutter, then make a sharp right angle as if jerked by a string, bouncing over six lanes to bury itself in the wall with a bone-shattering thud.

It was happening again, and the woman turned to her boyfriend, white-faced. "Charles?" she warbled.

"No one do any magic!" I said, voice stark as it rang out. "You in the kitchen! Nothing!"

Everyone stared at me, Trent included, and my pulse rushed in my ears. Silence pooled up, and from outside we could hear pops and bangs followed by screams. The sirens we'd heard earlier took on a different meaning. A cold feeling slithered from the dark spaces between the realities, winding about my heart and squeezing. It was happening again, and it was worse.

"All right then," the manager said, his expression determined as he crossed the bar. Reaching behind the demolished shoe counter, he grabbed a rifle, checking to see if it was loaded before striding to the door. The shoe guy followed, still patting at his beard. The couple from the lanes broke the rules and walked on the carpet with their borrowed shoes, and the cook came out from the back, hands working his stained apron to clean them as he walked.

Trent slid from his stool, but when I didn't move, neither did he. It was happening again. Why? Was it me? Trent took my hand. Our eyes met. He looked worried.

Gun ready, the manager pushed open the door, everyone clustered behind him. Behind him, the sky was a ruddy red. "Good God Almighty," he said, and I realized it was fire reflecting on the low clouds. "Greg, call 911. The Laundromat is on fire!"

People pushed outside around him, and Trent reached across me to take my shoulder bag. "Maybe we should leave," he said, and I numbly nodded as he handed it to me.

Trent left a healthy tip on the table, and we headed for the door. The feeling of security, of a place set aside, was gone, and I tensed at his hand on the small of my back. We had to go sideways between the people to get out, and the smells hit me as I got too close: aftershave, perfume, grease, adrenaline.

My gaze went up as we got free of them, and my pace faltered. One street over, a three-story building was on fire, gouts of flame and black smoke rising through the empty shell, windows showing as bright squares and stark black lines. It reminded me of the ever-after, and I stared, listening to sirens and people shouting. Less than a block away, a car was on fire. The nearby apartment building reflected the light as a dozen people tried to put it out with a garden hose. People were coming from everywhere to help, even the sports bar half a block down.

Across the river, huge swaths of Cincinnati were dark from a power outage, and the gray buildings glowed with the reflected red light against the ruddy night sky. More sirens sounded faintly over the river, and I cringed at the imagined chaos. If it was bad here, it would be worse there.

Cars were starting up, the frightened jerky motions of the people showing their fear. "It's not me," I protested as Trent got me moving. "Trent, Al says my line is fine. It's not me!"

"I believe you."

His voice was grim, and I waited by his car as he pointed his fob and reached for my door. The car fire seemed under control, and Quen wouldn't thank me for hanging around.

"Trent—" I started, gasping when the flaming car exploded. I dropped, pulling Trent down with me. I watched, mouth hanging open as chunks of burning car hit the ground to flicker and go out. A man's high-pitched scream went to the pit of my being, terrifying as he fell to the ground, but the hose was already on him and the flames were out.

More people poured into the streets, the high flames and screams bringing the last of the diehards out of the bar to gawk and shout helpful advice. The man's screaming had shifted to a gasping, pained cry, and the discarded hose spilled forgotten into the gutter. That this was happening all over the city was horrifying. Cincy couldn't handle this. No city could.

"Do you think we can help?" I said, and Trent pulled his phone out.

"I have no signal," he said, dismayed, and then we both turned to the dark street behind us at a terrified scream. It had come from the sports bar, and Trent's grip on me tightened at the masculine shout following it, telling her to shut up and that she'd enjoy it.

My blood ran cold as a woman pleaded that she didn't want to be a vampire.

Shit. My mind went to Ivy's map. Were the misfires and violent crimes connected, or were the vampires simply responding to the overlying chaos? And where in hell were the masters?

"Let me go!" a woman screamed, her frantic cries muting at the slamming of the door. Behind me, people tried to keep the burned man alive. I was starting to get ticked. Living vampires didn't just go bad, but there was a lot of fear in the air. Maybe it was too much for the masters to redirect. Pushing past Trent, I started across the street, swinging my bag around and digging through it. I couldn't do anything to help the burned man, but by God I wasn't going to walk away and leave that woman.

"Rachel, wait."

If the woman was still screaming, we had a little time. Even so, I didn't slow down. She'd said vampire, and they usually played with their food. "I'm not walking away," I said as he fell into step beside me. "We both know what will happen if I do."

"No," he insisted. "Can I borrow your splat gun?"

I jerked to a stop, the woman's frightened pleading a horrific backdrop. Shocked, I looked at Trent, my pulse pounding. *He wanted to help?* "Didn't you bring anything?"

He shifted from foot to foot. "No. I was taking you on a date, not a stakeout."

Yeah, I knew how that felt. I started for the building with a quick pace, an eye out for anyone else lurking in the shadows. "What am I supposed to use? You saw what happened to the ley line magic. Go back to the car. I'll be right back."

"Your magic is fine," he said as he walked fast beside me.

"You call this fine?" I said, and he pulled me to a stop.

"Listen to the noise," he said calmly, and my frantic pulse slowed. "It's moving off. I felt whatever it was right before things went haywire, and it's gone. Whatever it is, it's past us. Try a spell. Something that won't explode."

The woman's cries cut off with a startling smack of flesh on flesh. I had no time. I'd have to trust he was right. Breaking into a jog, I tossed my bag to Trent. "It's in there. Don't let them take her outside. If they get her alone, she's dead or worse."

Our feet scuffed on the sidewalk outside, but I didn't care if they knew we were coming. "Got it," Trent said, and I jerked the door open. I would have rather kicked it, but the hinges went only one way and I would've broken my foot. I'd learned this the hard way.

Trent came in behind me, my eyes going to the ceiling before returning to the three vampires at a back table: one woman, and two men, eyes blacker than the sky outside. The woman pinned to the table was in a bartending uniform. Her eyes met mine, her sobs punctuating the dwindling taunts as the vampires turned to us. My breath came easier. They were living vampires. Trent and I had a chance.

"Is this a bring-your-own-can-of-whoop-ass party?" I said, copping an attitude and pulling enough ever-after through me to make the strands of escaped hair float. The line felt normal, bolstering my confidence. "I got enough to pass if you three didn't bring any."

My gun in hand, Trent gave me a quizzical look. "Seriously?"

Shrugging, I shot him an annoyed look. "I'm kind of winging it here."

The largest vampire let go of the woman, and the female vampire in pink-and-blue tights pulled her to herself, whispering in the terrified woman's ear, her grip so tight it made the flesh between her fingers white.

The leader turned, running his eyes up and down my body, hopefully deciding I was too difficult to add to his evening's entertainment, but the other, a cowering nervous man now that they had witnesses, tugged at his sleeve like a little boy.

"Vinnie. Vinnie!" he said, hunched as he looked at Trent and me. "It's them free vampires. We got to go. Let's go!"

Free vampires? I wondered, watching the leader, Vinnie, apparently, breathe deep, taking in the scents of the room and smiling as he realized we were nothing of the kind.

"Shut up," he said, shoving the smaller man off him. "They aren't vampires. That's a witch and an elf. You ever tasted elf blood before? They say it tastes like wine."

"And you'll never know," I said, finding my balance and pulling heavier on the line. *"In fidem recipere, leno cinis,"* I shouted dramatically, making a glowing ball hang right before me. My pulse raced, but it was perfect, the size I wanted and its construction without fault. It wouldn't hurt them, but if I could cow them into leaving, I wouldn't have to spend the rest of my night filling out forms. "You need to let her go," I said boldly. Beside me, Trent took aim.

The show of force made the smaller vampire jiggle on his feet. "Oh shit. Oh shit. Oh shit. Vinnie, that's Morgan!" he hissed, and the woman vampire finally quit her soft crooning. "Cormel's demon. Come on. Let's go!"

But Vinnie shoved the frightened vampire back, arrogant as he came forward three steps. "Cormel don't scare me. Don't let that woman go. This will only take a second."

I pulled harder on the line, and the light glowed brighter,

making the woman vampire hiss and drag the silent, tear-streaked bartender back. "Let's try this again," I said, and the largest vampire laughed. "You are going to let her go, and sit at a table. Pick one. It's seat-yourself night. Otherwise, I'm within my rights to kick your collective ass until you're unconscious. You know who I am, and that's all the warning you're going to get."

The head vampire flicked his eyes to Trent, vamp pheromones rising like musky desire to make my neck tingle. He dropped back a step, and when I relaxed, he leaped at me, the other vampire screaming as he did the same a heartbeat behind.

"Celero dilatare!" I screamed, and the charm acted on the light curse already going, expanding it in a flash of light to blow them back.

The first vampire hit the floor, his head meeting it with a sodden thud. The smaller one handled it better, and he scrambled up as the woman vampire holding the bartender howled her anger. Even before regaining his feet, he fell, taken out by Trent's first shot. His second hit the larger vampire, still dazed. His head fell back and hit the floor again. Two down, one to go.

"Help me!" the woman screamed as the last vampire dragged her away, and then all hell broke loose when the bartender began to wiggle wildly, thrashing out and clawing until the vampire threw her across the room and spun to run out the back.

"I've got her!" I shouted, hoping Trent didn't down me with my own spell as I launched myself at her.

My breath exploded from me as I hit her and we went down, the vampire shrieking in anger and affront. Grabbing her luscious hair, I slammed her head into the floor. "This is *why* . . . you never *leave* . . . your hair *loose*!" I shouted in time with my motions.

"Rachel! You got her!" Trent cried out, jerking back when he touched me and I almost hit him. "You got her," he said softer. "It's over."

Panting, I stopped. I was shaking, and I scrubbed a hand over my face before I slipped my hand in his and he helped me rise. My elbow felt like it was on fire, and I stood over the downed woman and twisted it to see. I had a floor burn, but if that was all I walked away from here with, then I'd done good.

No, we'd done good, I amended, seeing the gun still in Trent's hand. He didn't seem to know what to do with it, and I understood.

"Where's the bartender?" I said, and we spun when she came out from behind the bar, a big-ass rifle in her hand. Her face was wet from crying, but her expression was of hate and fear. The sound of it cocking shocked through me, and I put my hands in the air.

"Whoa, whoa, whoa! It's okay! We got 'em!" I said, and Trent shoved the gun behind him into his waistband and out of sight.

Hunched, she came closer, the gun pointed at the largest vampire. "They tried to take me!" she screamed, and the adrenaline was a slap, clearing my thoughts. "They were going to turn me into a *doll*! I'm going to *kill them*! This is my place, and I'm going to *kill them*!"

Her eyes were darting between all three, and I let my arms come down. I nudged Trent, and he did the same. "Look, they're all unconscious," I said softly. "It's over. You're safe."

"The *hell* I am! We have laws against this! Where are the master vampires! They're supposed to protect us! I called the I.S. and no one came! If I ever see another vampire in my place, I'm going to *shoot them on sight*!"

I totally understood, but I edged closer, trying get between her and the vampires. "It's over. You're okay," I said, hands out in placation. "You're not marked or bitten, you're okay. Tomorrow will be the same as today. Put the gun down. They aren't getting up."

"Rachel!" Trent shouted, and I turned, seeing the last female vampire I'd knocked unconscious coming at me.

"No!" I shouted, then dropped as the rifle went off.

"Leave me alone!" the bartender screamed, shaking as she stood with the smoking rifle in her hand. "I'll kill you! I'll kill you!"

Yep, she killed her, I thought. The female vampire had a hole in her chest big enough to put your fist in. The hole in her back would be bigger, and I thought the woman would look better with less makeup as she sighed her last breath and her pale hand fell against the scratched floor.

"Give me that," Trent said, jerking the gun from the bartender's slack grip as she stood, a shocked expression on her as she watched the vampire die her first death. Collapsing to the floor, the bartender began to sob, rocking back and forth with her knees drawn to her chin.

Gunpowder pricked in my nose. I got up as Trent took the last shell from the rifle, tucking it in his pocket before gently setting the weapon on the nearest table. There was no blood on me. No blood on Trent. There was a growing puddle of it on the floor under the woman vampire, and I looked at the clock over the jukebox. They'd want to know what time she died to better estimate her rising, though by the look of it, it might be weeks.

Silent, Trent eased to stand beside me. "I'm going to go out on a limb and say that a date with you is nothing like having you work security. Let's not tell Quen about this, okay?"

I slowly looked him up and down. He seemed to be taking this rather well, but then again, I'd seen him kill a man in his office. Flashing me a mirthless smile, he started scanning the place. "You see a tablecloth anywhere?"

To cover the dead vampire, I thought, shaking my head. The woman was still crying. I knew I should comfort her, but I was kind of pissed at her right now. Leaving her to cry, I found my shoulder bag and dug out my phone.

"How come you got a signal?" Trent said, grunting when he checked his phone and found the towers were back up. Unfortunately the 911 circuits were busy, with a recorded message saying to hold for a thirty-minute wait time.

"Nuts to that," I said, thinking I wasn't going to spend my night here with a dead vampire. Hanging up, I called Edden's direct line. "Edden," I said as soon as his deep, low voice came clear over the sound of ringing phones and tense voices.

"Rachel? I don't have time right now."

Impatient, I pressed the phone to my ear. "I'm in a bar on Hostant Drive. I've got two vampires under sleep charms and another dead, possibly twice from a hole in her chest."

Edden went silent, and the woman stopped crying at the sound of Trent locking the front door. "Oh," Edden finally said. "Did you call 911?"

"Duh! There's like a thirty-minute wait time. Edden, is there a vamp war going on? They mentioned something about free vampires." Suddenly itchy, I turned to the door, wanting to leave.

"If there is, it involves all of them." Edden's voice went distant for a moment, then came back stronger. "My God, it's a mess. The I.S. is completely down. Looks like one of your misfire waves came through again. Hold on."

"It's not my wave," I grumbled, one arm across my middle as Trent finally got the woman to get up off the floor and into a chair facing away from the blood and violence. "Edden," I started when I heard the phone picked back up.

"Do you have the situation contained?" he asked, and my eyes met Trent's. He probably didn't want to be seen here with a corpse on the floor.

"Unless their friends show up. Yes."

"Okay. Good. I'm sending someone right now. There's a fire a few blocks from you, so it won't be but five minutes. Just sit tight. Can you do that?"

I looked at the woman sobbing quietly to herself. It was more gentle, broken almost, but I remembered her fear and her outright decisive lethal action. Forty years of carefully built coexistence gone in five terrifying minutes. We were that close to losing it all.

"I'll be here," I said softly. "We could really use an ambulance while you're at it. Someone was burned very badly at the fire. And thanks."

Muttering something, he hung up. Not closing the phone, I called David's number, but there was no answer and I didn't leave a message. Trent was standing behind the bar, pouring vodka into a single glass when I texted Ivy that I ran into some difficulty but was okay and would be home a little later than planned. No need to tell her that vampires were behaving badly. She probably already knew that. I hoped Nina was okay. The safe houses would be busy tonight.

"You ever hear of free vampires?" I said as I went to the bar to sit and wait. Head shaking no, Trent set the vodka beside the woman and returned to stand beside me and lean against the bar, his entire body stiff with tension. "That was fun," I said sarcastically, then noticed a darker anger in him, one deeper than the mess before us would warrant. "You okay?"

"I called to tell Quen that I was all right, and he informed me Ellasbeth is refusing to bring the girls home."

Lips parting, I reached out. "What? She can't do that! Ray isn't even hers!"

My eyes darted to the dead vampire, unsure if that sigh had been caused by a muscle release or voluntary.

"Ellasbeth says that with the misfires impacting Cincinnati she has every right not to bring them into a dangerous situation," he said. "That the estate is outside of the area doesn't seem to matter."

Worried, I gave his arm a squeeze. "I'm sorry. You know you'll get them back. She can't do this."

His expression eased as his attention came back to me, and I suddenly realized we were inches apart. "Yes, I will," he said softly. "How are you? Still shaky?"

Feeling the warmth between us, I looked at my skinned elbow. "Fine. Edden's sending someone. You can go if you want. We'll be okay." Unless the bartender had another gun stashed somewhere.

He glanced over at the bar, gaze settling on the rifle with

his prints on it. "I'll wait. Besides, this is the most excitement I've had in three months." His smile went right through me, warming me from the inside. "I'm glad we did this," he said, tucking a strand of hair behind my ear.

"The date, right?" I said, trying to lighten the mood. "Not the . . . this?"

Eyebrows high, he brushed me as he leaned over the bar for a bottled water. Tingles raced up my arm, and I didn't move. "I can honestly say that a date is nothing like working with you," he said as he cracked the top of it and handed it to me.

I took a swig before handing it back. I was curious to see if he'd drink from it as well. My skin was still tingling, and my heart pounded when he looked at his watch, smiled, and then leaned in to kiss me.

My first flash of annoyance evaporated in a puff. His hands pulled me closer, and the sensation of fire dove through me, plinking every single trigger I had. The scent of cinnamon and vampire pheromones rose, and a soft sigh escaped me. This wasn't enough, and uncaring of tomorrow, I slid from the stool. Our lips parted as he stumbled, and then I pulled him to me, arms going around him and up into his hair.

I had spent the last three months looking at his hair, wondering what it would feel like in my fingers again. Three long months I'd watched him move, seen him in every possible piece of clothing and wondered what he'd look like out of them and how he might move against me when the darkness was velvet and the sheets were cool. Three months of saying no, be good, Rachel, be smart, Rachel.

I wanted one damn kiss, and I was going to have it, by God.

"You are fucking animals!" the woman at the table exclaimed, and when Trent's lips threatened to slip from mine, I sent the barest dart of tongue past his lips to recapture his attention. It worked. His breath caught, and I swear the man growled. His arm crushed me to him, and it was all I could do to not wrap my legs around him. Bar stools could hold that much weight, right?

"There are three dead vampires on my floor, and you are making out?"

Energy darted between us, and breathless, I pulled back, the sound of our lips parting sparking through me. Trent's eyes smoldered. I held their heat, tasting him on my lips. It wasn't the vampire pheromones in here. It was three months of saying no.

"Relax," I said to her, never dropping Trent's gaze. My heart was pounding, and I still didn't care about tomorrow. "Only one of them is dead, and I think she's going to make it. You probably won't even have any jail time."

"Jail time! They tried to blood rape me!"

"Like I said. No jail time."

Trent was still silent, but he was smiling at the sound of boots and the flash of cop lights on the front sidewalk. The woman made a tiny sound and ran to unlock the door. We slowly parted, his hand slipping from me in a sensation of tingles. My smile faded as I looked at his hand and realized I'd never hold it again.

That hadn't been our first kiss, but it had been our last.

Six

"And there are no indications it will be any better to-night," Edden said, his hand smacking the podium with a loud pop.

My head snapped up at the sharp sound, but not before my chin slipped off my palm and I did a classic head bob. Jerked awake, I looked over the FIB's shift change meeting to see if anyone had noticed. The dream of purple, angry eyes and spinning wheels lingered, and I thought I could still hear the sound of wings beating upon me in punishment.

Sheepish, I resettled myself. I wasn't surprised I'd nodded off, having come in early to the FIB to first fill out a report about the bar incident and, second, to get my car out of impound. Sleep had been a few hours on the couch, fitful and not enough of it. Coffee had lost its punch, and a vending machine no-doze charm wasn't going to happen. Those things could kill you, especially now, maybe. It was starting to become really clear what might be going on, and even though there were more questions than answers, it didn't look good.

Edden was up front between a podium and a big map hanging from the dry erase board. The city was cordoned off like one of Ivy's maps, little red stickers showing vampire crimes, blue ones the misfired charms. There was an obvious pattern to the misfired charms, but the vampire crimes were widespread within the confines of Cincy and the Hollows, with no recognizable linkage to the sporadic waves other than they seemed to start at the same time.

Edden was hiding a smirk, clearly having caught my head bob, but his voice never faltered. There were rows of officers between me and him, and you could tell which officers were going off shift by the fatigue.

"I need some coffee," I whispered to Jenks, tickling the roof of my mouth with my tongue to try to wake up.

"Yeah, me too," he said, rising up with an odd blue dust. "You know what they say. You can tell a human by how many meetings he has. I'll be back. I gotta get me some of that honey."

"Honey!" I whispered, but he was gone, flying right down the center aisle and turning heads as he went for the coffee urn set to the side at the front of the room. Oh God, he was going to get drunk, right when I was trying to show them all how professional I was.

"We're all pulling the occasional double shift until we're sure this is over," Edden said as Jenks saluted him and landed by the little packets of honey there for the tea drinkers.

"Captain," one of the more round officers complained as a general air of discontent rose.

"No exceptions, and don't trade with anyone," Edden said, then hesitated as Jenks stabbed a honey packet with his sword, his dust shifting to a brilliant white when he pulled a pair of chopsticks from a back pocket and started eating. "Rose is doing the schedule so no one gets two nights in a row. I say again—no trading."

The officers not griping were watching Jenks, and the pixy looked up, his chopsticks lifted high over his head as the honey dribbled into him. "What?" he said, his dust cutting off in a reddish haze. "You never seen a pixy before? Listen to Edden. I'm eating here."

Edden cleared his throat and stepped from the podium. "As for our last item, I know it was a rough night, but before you go, I'd like those of you who dealt with something . . . ah, of an Inderland nature to share what you did and how it worked for those coming on shift."

"Inderland nature," an older cop with a raspy voice and belligerent attitude complained. "I was almost eaten last night."

Snickering, Jenks dribbled more honey into his mouth, but I didn't see anything funny. Whether he knew it or not, the craggy officer probably wasn't exaggerating.

"I didn't see you complaining at the time," said the cop next to him, and the first officer turned to stare him down.

"Callahan!" Edden said, shouting over the sudden ribbing. "Since you volunteered. Let's hear what happened on your Inderlander encounter and how you dealt with it."

"Well, sir, I believe the woman bewitched me," he said slowly. "My partner and I were responding to a misfired charm up by the zoo when we spotted two suspects outside a window, trying to break in. I politely asked them if they had lost their keys. They ran; we followed. One got away. When I tried to apprehend the other, she got all . . . sexy like."

Hoots and whistles rose, and Jenks, deep into his honey drunk, gyrated wildly.

"Eyes black and coming on to me like one of those legalized prostitutes down in the Hollows," he continued. "It was enough to embarrass a man."

Jenks almost spun right off the table and I hid my eyes, mortified.

"I don't see an arrest," Edden said as he leafed through a clipboard.

"You get yourself some vampire ass, Callahan?" someone shouted, and the man cracked an almost-not-there grin.

"When I turned around, she was gone," Callahan said.

A woman made a long "awwww," and I smiled. They had a good group. I missed that.

"She wasn't going to bang you, she was going to smack you into next week," I said, and Edden hid a cough behind rubbing his mustache. "That is, if you were lucky."

Callahan turned in his chair to give me an irritated look. "And you would know how?"

I shrugged, glad everyone was looking at me and not Jenks making a wobbly flight to the podium. "Because when a vampire gets sexy, they're either hungry or mad. Cornering her was a mistake. You're lucky. You must have left her an out. She was smart and took it."

They were silent. Slowly the tension rose. But I wasn't going to keep my mouth shut if a little information might keep someone out of the hospital.

"Everyone, if you don't recognize her, this is Rachel Morgan," Edden said, and I could breathe again when they turned away. "I asked her to come in and give us some ideas on how to handle the issues falling to us right now as the I.S. takes care of an internal problem."

There was a rising muttered complaint, and Edden held up a hand, then scrambled to catch Jenks as he slipped backward down the slanted podium. "Morgan is a former I.S. runner, and if she says you're lucky, Callahan, you're lucky. Rachel, what should he have done?"

I sat up, glad I'd pulled something professional from my closet today. "Not follow."

They all protested, and my eyes squinted. *You can lead a troll to water . . .*

"She's right!" Jenks shrilled, cutting off most of the grousing. "The woman is right! Righter than . . . a pixy in a garden." He belched, wings moving madly as he tilted to the side.

I wondered if I should stand, then decided to stay where I was. "If you don't have the skills or strength to back up your badge—and I'm sorry, but your weapons won't do it—it's best to just let them go. Unless they're threatening someone, that is. Then you're going to have to work hard to distract them until they remember the law can put them in a cage."

Damn, even the women cops were looking at me like I was a hypocrite. "I don't care if you don't like it," I said. "One vampire is enough to clear this entire room if he or she is angry enough. The master vampires will bring them in line."

"But they aren't," said a woman who had clearly, judging by her bedraggled appearance, come in off the night shift. Around her, others nodded. "No one has been able to contact an undead vampire within the Cincinnati or Hollows area since yesterday afternoon."

Surprised, I looked at Edden, becoming uneasy when he nodded. "How come this is the first I'm hearing about it?" I said, suddenly very awake. If the master vampires were incommunicado, that'd explain the increase in living-vampire crimes. For all the loving abuse the masters heaped upon their children, they did keep the bad ones in line when no one else could.

Edden straightened from his concerned hunch over Jenks. "Because we agree with the I.S. that it would cause a panic. The masters aren't dead, they're sleeping, and so far, it's confined to the Cincy and Hollows area. The I.S. tried bringing in a temporary master vampire from out of state to handle things yesterday, and she fell asleep within five hours."

I bit my lip, processing it. All the undead sleeping? No wonder the I.S. was down.

"Which brings me back to you, Rachel," he said, and my head snapped up. "I originally asked you here to give us options for dealing with aggressive Inderlanders, but I think we've gone beyond that. What's your Inderland take on the situation? Are the misfired charms and the sleeping undead vampires linked?"

Silence descended as everyone looked at me. That they were linked was obvious. The real question should be, was any of this intentional or simply a natural phenomenon, and if deliberate, was the goal to put the masters out of commission, create havoc with misfired charms, or both? If someone was creating the wave, it could be stopped. If it was a natural effect, it was going to be up to me—seeing as the wave was coming from my line.

Nervous, I picked up my shoulder bag and got to my feet.

Jenks saw me coming, trying to sit up as his one wing refused to function, swearwords falling from him as his heels flipped up and he toppled backward down the podium. "Upsy-daisy," Edden said as he caught him slipping off the edge, and Jenks giggled, his high voice clear in the dead air.

"Why would she help us? She's a demon," someone muttered, and Edden frowned.

"Because she's a good demon, Frank," he said, voice iron hard as he held Jenks gently in his cupped hand. Giving Edden a wry smile, I held my bag open and he dropped Jenks inside.

"Hey!" the pixy protested, and then, "Tink's little pink dildo, Rache! Haven't you gotten rid of those condoms yet? They got a shelf life, you know."

I flushed, handing the bag to Edden as I turned. That awful map was behind me, and I shifted until I wasn't behind the podium, not liking the feeling of separation I got behind it. "That the waves, the sleeping undead, and the vampire violence are linked is obvious," I said, half turning to glance at the map. "I don't know how to stop the waves, but until we figure it out, there are a few things that can be done to minimize the damage from the superpowered waves."

"Superpowered?" someone in the back questioned, and I nodded.

"According to, ah, a reliable source, the misfires are actually an overexpression of what the charm is supposed to do, so a charm intended to clean grease removes the fat not just from the counter but from the person who invoked it. Fortunately, the waves appear to impact only charms invoked right when the wave is passing over them. Those already running aren't affected."

Most of them were staring at me in bewilderment. It was frustrating. Another witch would know exactly what I was talking about, and I wondered how charismatic Edden's public relations person was. This was going to go down hard in the Inderland community. "You might want to work with the I.S. and get an early warning detector out to Loveland where the waves are originating. If you tell people not to invoke any magic ahead of a wave, that will probably minimize or eliminate probably ninety percent of the magic misfires."

"What about the vampires?"

Good question. "Which brings me to the vampires. It's a good bet that the increase in crime is simply a combination of the heightened fear brought on by the misfires and the masters being asleep and unable to curtail it. Take out one of the three legs, and the stool will fall. If you wake the undead up, the violence will stop. Curtail or eliminate the misfires, and the violence will probably diminish. Fear is a trigger to bloodlust, and the fewer misfires, the less fear there will be to trigger a twitchy vampire."

Again silence fell, but it was the quiet of thinking. "So who's making the waves?" someone asked.

Good question number two. "I'd guess someone who would benefit from the chaos. Someone trying to hide a crime? Or a firm specializing in disaster recovery?"

Or a demon, I thought, thinking this was just the thing to amuse a bored sadist. Newt, though, had seemed genuinely concerned. Damn it to the Turn and back, I didn't have enough clout to work another deal with the demons. I'd barely survived the last one.

Edden rubbed his face, starting at the feel of his bristles, and I wondered how long he'd been here. The officers, too, were getting fidgety, and it felt as if I should wrap this up.

"In the meantime, it might be a good idea to block off access to some of the smaller parks to minimize large gatherings. Or better yet, Edden, have you given any thought to installing a curfew? Blame it on the magic misfire, not the vampires."

Edden winced. "Ye-e-e-es. Cincinnati has more people on the street at night than the day. We saw a drop last night except for gawkers, but even they became scarce when the vampires took over the streets."

An officer at the edge sat up. "What if we just shut down

the buses? We wouldn't have a repeat of what happened out at the university."

"What happened at the university?" I asked, then put a hand in the air. "Never mind. You could always put a cop on the buses going from the Hollows to Cincinnati. That would probably take care of most of it."

Callahan made a bark of laughter. "And where do you expect to get the manpower, missy? We're double shifting as it is."

Missy? I was losing them. "That's another thing. The I.S. can't be completely down, just disorganized, and if there's something the FIB is good at, it's organization. Has anyone thought to ask the witches or Weres in the I.S.'s runner division to sit in with you in your cars or walk the streets with you? Mixed-species partners are encouraged in the I.S. for a reason. I'd think having someone next to you who can smell vampires a block away is worth looking into. Besides, if the I.S. is down as far as you say it is, the witches and Weres are probably ready to take things into their own hands. You give them a well-structured outlet, they'll jump at it."

Edden shifted from foot to foot behind me. My jaw tightened as they just stared at me. "Fine," I said sarcastically. "Last night I watched a woman blow a hole in a vampire because she lost faith in the I.S.'s ability to protect her. If you don't get a hold of this, and I mean *now,* you're going to have an entire city of vigilantes out gunning for vampires, good or bad. Or you can swallow your pride and not only show the witches and Weres your stuff, but demonstrate to a frightened demographic that you can work with other species instead of killing them."

"O-o-o-okay!" Edden said as he put a hand on my shoulder, and I jumped. "Thank you, Rachel. I appreciate you sharing your thoughts and ideas with us this morning. Gentlemen? Ladies? Smart decisions."

It was clearly his catchphrase to release them, and disgusted, I dropped back as the assembled officers began to collect themselves. Their expressions were a mix of distrust and disgust, ticking me off.

"If you're interested in a joint effort of I.S. and FIB, tell Rose to put your name on a list," Edden said loudly over the noise. "If your name is on the joint-effort list, it won't be on the double-duty list. It's as easy as that, people. Keep it safe!"

"That's not fair, Captain . . ." someone complained, and Edden turned away. His expression was pained as he handed me my bag, Jenks still sleeping his honey drunk off inside.

"Think they'll go for it?" I asked.

"Some will to get out of pulling double duty. A few more will because they're curious."

"Good," I said as the room emptied and he began to take down his map. "I meant it when I said the witches and Weres will try to pull the I.S. together, but most of the top bosses there are the undead. They'll lose a lot of time organizing unless they agree to work with the FIB."

His expression was sour, and he wouldn't meet my eyes as he rolled the map into a tube.

"Edden, you need their help," I pleaded. "It's not just an issue of manpower or officer safety. Right now the living vampires are skittish, but if their masters don't wake up soon, we're going to have more abductions and blood rapes than graffiti and trash parties at the university."

Map in one hand, he gestured with the other for me to head to the hall. "I'm taking names and will make a call. The rest is up to them. Not everyone with a badge is an Inderland bigot."

Edden's eyes were pinched as I fell into step beside him. I knew he missed Glenn, and not just because the Inderlander Relations division that Glenn had been in charge of had tanked when he'd quit the FIB. "I read your report," he said. "Why was Kalamack with you last night?"

Wow, word gets around fast. "His girls come back tomorrow. It was a thank-you dinner."

Edden's eyebrows rose knowingly. "At a bowling bar?"

I smiled as we made our way to the front of the building. "They have great burgers."

"Yeah?" Edden tapped the rolled map on his chin. "And he stood back and let you work."

"Yup," I lied cheerfully. I'd thought Trent had been trying to stop me, but he'd only wanted to borrow my gun. Not that he was a slouch with the elven magic, but he didn't have a license to throw charms around as I did. Magic could be traced back to its maker, even a ley line charm, and if the FIB thought I'd shot the vampires, then Trent's name wouldn't even make the papers. He had surprised me, and I liked being surprised.

And the kiss . . . A tingle raced through me. Slowly my smile faded. Ellasbeth didn't know what she had.

The noise in the reception hall swelled as we entered, and Edden sighed at the angry people at the front desk, none of them listening to the officers trying to get them to take a form and go sit in the chairs to fill it out. I could understand why they were upset, seeing as all the chairs were occupied and the take-a-number dispenser they'd put up was only six numbers different from when I'd come through about an hour ago.

"Thanks for this, Rachel." Edden halted before the glass doors. "You got your car?"

I carefully opened my shoulder bag, easily finding my keys by the light of a snoring pixy. "Thanks, Edden," I said, shaking the pixy dust off them so they wouldn't short out my ignition. "It was worth the early morning. Speaking of which, you need to go home."

Hands in his pockets, he looked out uneasily at the sunny street, the lack of cars obvious. "Maybe next year." He again scrubbed a hand over his face, dead tired, and I remembered that he didn't really have anyone to go home to. "We might find something good in this mess."

Smiling, I put a hand on his shoulder, leaning in to give

him a professional kiss on the cheek and making him redden. I knew he was talking about Inderlanders and humans working together, and I hoped he was right. "Let me know if something changes."

He nodded, pushing the door open for me, and my hair blew back in the draft. "You too."

It was almost eleven, right about the time I usually got up, and feeling a faint sense of rejuvenation, I strode into the sun. "You want some coffee, Jenks?" I said loudly, knowing he wouldn't be up for at least ten more minutes. Junior's was only a couple of blocks away, and a grande, skinny double espresso, with a shot of raspberry, extra hot with no foam, would have a much-appreciated dose of fat and calories in it. "Yeah, me too," I said, taking the stairs with an extra bounce to pull a tiny groan from my bag. My car could stay at impound a few minutes more.

But as I took to the sidewalk, my fast pace quickly faltered. The streets were more empty than usual, and the people who *were* out moved with a fast, furtive pace, very unlike the angry frustration inside the security of the FIB. Pamphlets skated down the gutters, and new graffiti was everywhere. Some of it I couldn't match to a Were pack, making me wonder if it might be vampire, as odd as it would be. The scent of oil-based smoke was a haze between Cincinnati's buildings, visible now that the sun was up, and I tugged my shoulder bag higher, uneasy.

No one was meeting my eyes, and the obnoxious men who usually refused to shift an inch out of their way so we could actually—I don't know—share the sidewalk maybe, were quick to make room as if afraid I might touch them. It wasn't just me, though. Everyone was getting the extra space. Tempers were short, and there were lots of quick accelerations when the lights turned green. Most telling, the usual sign-toting beggars were off the streets.

The wind lifted through my hair, sending the escaping strands of my braid to tickle my neck, and realizing I'd been out of touch for almost an hour, I turned my phone back on. "Oh," I said, pace faltering as I saw all the missed numbers. *David.*

Wincing, I stopped, shifting myself up the steps at Fountain Square to get out of the foot traffic. Guilt swam up from the cracks of my busy life. I was not a good female alpha, too involved in my own life's drama to include much of anyone else's, but damn it, when I agreed to it, David had said it was only going to be him. That had been the entire point. He'd added to the pack since then, not that I could blame him. He was a fabulous alpha male, and I was beginning to feel as if I was holding him back.

Sighing, I hit send and tucked my increasingly dilapidated braid out of the way. He answered almost immediately.

"Rachel!" His pleasant voice sounded worried, and I could picture him, his clean-cut features and tidy suit he wore at his job as an insurance adjuster making his alpha status clear. "Where are you?"

Head down, I rested my rump on one of the huge planters, feeling about three inches tall. "Ah, downtown Cincy," I said hesitantly. "I tried to call yesterday, and then that wave came through and—"

"Ivy said you were at the FIB. I need to talk to you. Do you have some time today?"

Talk to me about me being a lousy alpha, no doubt. "Sure. What's good for you?"

"She also told me what happened at the bridge yesterday. Why don't you tell me these things?" he said, adding to my guilt. "Okay, that's funny. Look up."

I took my fingers from my forehead, head lifting.

"No, across the street. See?"

It was David, standing at the corner beside a newspaper box and waving at me. He was in his long duster, heavy boots, and wide-brimmed hat, which made him look like a thirtysomething Van Helsing. It suited him more than his usual suit and tie, and being an insurance adjuster wasn't the cushy, pencil-pushing job it sounded like. He had teeth, and he used them to get the real dirt on some of the more interesting Inderlander accidents. That's how we had met, actually.

"H-how . . ." I stammered, and he smiled across the street at me.

"I was trying to get to the FIB before you left," he said, his lips out of sync with his voice. "I've got coffee. Grande, skinny double espresso, shot of raspberry, extra hot, and no foam okay?" he said, taking up a coffee carrier currently sitting on the newspaper box.

"God, yes," I said, and he waved me to stay where I was. Smiling, I ended the call. Not only did he know I liked my coffee, but he knew *how* I liked my coffee.

Motion easy, the medium-build man loped across the street against traffic, one hand holding the tray with the coffees, the other raised against the cars. Every single one of them slowed to let him pass with nary a horn or shouted curse, such was his assurance. David was the apex of confidence, and very little of it was from the curse I'd innocently given him, accidentally making him the holder of the focus and able to demand the obedience of any alpha, and hence their pack members in turn. He wore the responsibility very well—unlike me.

"Rachel," he said as he reached the sidewalk and took the shallow steps two at a time. "You look beat!"

"I am," I said, giving him a hug and breathing in the complicated mix of bane, wood smoke, and paper. His black shoulder-length hair pulled back in a tie smelled clean, and I lingered, recognizing the strength in him in both body and mind. When I'd met him, he'd been a loner, and though he had firmly established himself as a pack leader now, he'd retained the individual confidence a loner was known for.

"Thanks for the coffee," I said, carefully wedging it out of the carrier as he extended it. "You can hunt me down any day if you bring me coffee."

Chuckling, he shook his head, his dark eyes flicking down from the huge vid screen over the square, currently tuned to the day's national news. Cincy was in it again, and not in a good way. "I didn't want to talk to you over the phone, and I've got the day off. You got a minute?"

My guilt rushed back, my first sip going bland on my tongue. "I'm sorry, David. I'm a lousy alpha." I slumped, the coffee he'd brought me—the perfect coffee he knew was my favorite—hanging in my grip. It was never supposed to have been anything other than the two of us. The larger pack just sort of happened.

Blinking, he fixed his full attention on me, making me wince. "You are not," he admonished, coffee in hand and leaning against the planter, looking like an ad for *Weres' Wares* magazine. "And that's not what I wanted to talk to you about. Have you heard of a group called the Free Vampires?"

Surprised, I relaxed my hunched shoulders. "One of the vamps last night thought I was one, but no. Not really."

His eyes shifted to the people around us, the motion furtive enough to pull a ribbon of worry through me. It was busy at the square, knots of people clustered around their laptops and tablets, but none nearby. Leaning closer, he dropped his head to prevent anyone from reading his lips. "They're also known as Free Curse Vampires or Vampires Without Masters," he said, sending a chill through me. "They've been around since before the Turn. That's their mark there, up on the vid screen."

My eyes followed his twisting head, only now noticing that the huge monitor overlooking Fountain Square did indeed have a gang symbol spray-painted on it, the huge symbol looking as if a V and a F had been typeset over each other, the leg of the F merging seamlessly with the left side of the V to look elegantly aggressive. It also looked impossible to have gotten it up there.

"Huh," I said, now remembering seeing it on some of the buses this morning. And in the intersection outside of the FIB. Light poles. Corner mailboxes . . . Concerned, I leaned to pick up one of those flyers, finding it read like wartime propaganda. "How can they survive without a master? I'd think they wouldn't last a year."

David watched me shove the flyer in my bag. "Hiding, mostly, maintaining the same patterns that kept all vampires safe before the Turn. It's not hard to file their canines flat or take day jobs to avoid their kin. It's sort of a cult following, one not well represented because, as you guessed, they don't have a master vampire to protect them. We occasionally insure them, seeing as they can't go to a vampire-based company. There's been a jump in their numbers the last couple of days. Some of it could be attributed to the undead being asleep, but—"

I choked on my coffee, sputtering until I got my last swallow down. "You know about that?" I asked, my watering eyes darting. We were right next to the fountain so it was unlikely anyone would hear, but Edden had made it obvious that it was privileged information.

Smiling an easy smile, David put his back to the planter and us shoulder to shoulder. "You can gag the news, but you can't blind an insurance company intent on adjusting a claim. They're coming out of the woodwork, making me think they're more represented than previously thought, perhaps the fringe children who aren't really noticed much and get little protection anyway. They have a statistically improbably high rate of immediate second-death syndrome, which is why I know about them. My boss is tired of paying out on the claims."

David took a sip of his coffee, eyes unfocused as he looked across the street. "One of their core beliefs is that the undead existence is an affront to the soul. Rachel, I'm not liking where this is going."

I thought about it, the July morning suddenly feeling cold. "You think they might be responsible for putting the undead asleep? To show their living kin what freedom is?" I said incredulously, almost laughing, but David's expression remained anxious. "Vampires don't use magic, and that's what this wave is made of."

"Well, they've been using *something* to survive without the protection of a master. Why not witch magic?" he said. "What worries me is that up to now they've been very timid down to the individual, hiding in the shadows and avoiding conflict. Their entire belief system circles around the original vampire sin and that the only way to save their souls is to promote an immediate second death after the first. That they'd put the masters to sleep doesn't bother me as much as that they would *keep* doing it after they realized it promoted vampire violence." David shook his head. "It doesn't sound like them."

But someone was pulling these waves into existence. That the only faction who might want to see an end to the masters didn't have the chutzpah to do it wasn't helping. Frustrated, I slumped back against the planter, squinting up at FV mashed into one letter. Behind it, someone had their "magic wall" showing a replica of Edden's map of vampire violence, the enthusiastic newsman tapping individual dots to bring up the gory details to focus on individual tragedies with the excitement of a close political race.

No undead existence? I thought. Ivy would embrace that, even if she'd never take her second life. Though we'd never talked about it, I knew she was terrified of becoming one of the undead, knowing firsthand what they were capable of in their soulless state and the misery they could heap upon their children, most of them beautiful innocents kept in an intentional childlike state who loved their abusers with the loyalty of an abandoned child suddenly made king.

Kisten had died twice in quick succession, both times in an attempt to keep me alive and unharmed. His final words still haunted me: that God kept their souls for them until they died their second death. To get it back after committing the heinous acts necessary to survive would send them straight to hell—if a hell existed at all. A quick and sudden second death might be the only thing to save a true believer.

Uneasy, I dropped my eyes. Vampires were truly messed up, but I didn't think a quick second death was the answer.

"I need to talk to a Free Vampire," I said softly, and David chuckled, a rough hand rubbing his chin and the faint hint of day-old stubble.

"I thought you might say that. I can't, of course, give you an address, as that would be a breach of Were Insurance policy."

"David . . ." I protested.

"No-o-o-o," he drawled, pushing himself up and away from the planter. "Go home. Get some sleep. Give me some time to be subtle."

Subtle? My lips curled into a grin, and I mock punched him. "Let me know when you're going, and I'll come with you. It'll be a good chance for me to do something with the pack."

His smile brightened, making the guilt rise anew. "I was hoping you'd say that," he said, his words warming me from the inside. "Some of the new members have you on a pedestal. That has got to change."

"You think?" I said, and he gave me a brotherly sideways hug that pulled me off balance.

"I'm *so* sorry about the pack dinner last month. I didn't realize it until you'd left. Did McGraff really scoot your chair in and put your napkin in your lap?"

Feeling good, I nodded, embarrassed even now. "Maybe if they saw me screw up once in a while it might help."

He laughed, the honest sound of it seeming to push the surrounding fear from the nearby people back another inch. "I'll call before we go out."

"I'll wait for it. And thanks for the info. It's a good place to start."

Inclining his head, he gave me a squinting smile. "You going to tell Edden?"

"Hell, no!" I blurted, not a glimmer of guilt. Well, not much of one, anyway. This felt like an Inderland matter; humans, if they knew how fragile the balance was, would start taking Free Vampires out one by one and end the curse that way.

"Thanks," he said, and with a final touch, he turned away. "Give me a day or two!" he said over his shoulder, and I smiled, thinking I didn't deserve friends like this.

He walked away, and as I watched his grace, my smile slowly faded. If the master vampires didn't wake up soon, this could get really ugly, really fast.

Seven

"Jenks, get me that black marker in my room, will you?"
Ivy asked, looking lean and svelte as she stretched over
the big farm table to reach the FIB reports Edden had couriered over. She was trying to make a correlation between the
misfires and the vampire mischief. She rated the mischief, I
rated the misfire severity. Everything went on the map, and
so far we'd not found a link from the precise pattern of misfires to the random acts of violence. But we had to do something as we waited for David to call. The waves were coming
more frequently now, and people were scared.

"Who was your slave last week?" Jenks said from the
sink, and Ivy's head snapped up.

"Excuse me?"

"I said, you are such a pen geek."

I stifled a smile, thinking it was odd of her to ask, but
Nina was napping in Ivy's room, exhausted and scared to
death that Felix was going to make another play for her. Impossible since all the undead—masters and lackeys both—
were sleeping, but she was terrified, and logic meant nothing
when you were scared. Jenks could be in and out without her
ever knowing.

"Thick or thin?" the pixy asked. He was catching drops
from the faucet to wash a cut one of his youngest daughters

had come in with, and after giving her a fond swat on the butt, he rose up, smiling after her cheerful vow to stab her brother in the eye as she flew out.

"Thick," Ivy said, and Jenks darted out of the kitchen.

His dust slowly settled, and I blew it off the pictures arranged before me on the center counter, trying to decide which was more destructive: the first-aid mishap that shifted the spell caster's skin to coat the bare lightbulb, or the dog walker who suddenly didn't have a lower intestine. Shuddering, I put a sticky note with the number eight on the dog walker, seven on the skinned man. The dog walker might survive, but the skinned man hadn't made it to the phone.

We'd had three more waves since the one that caught Trent and me at the bowling alley, and I didn't like that they were regularly making it across the river and into the Hollows now before dying out. I was still hopeful that the waves were a natural effect that simply had to be understood to be stopped. I didn't want to believe that anyone, unhappy vampire faction or not, would do this intentionally. Feeling ill, I put a four on the report of an entire middle-school class gone blind in a routine magic experiment.

"Your pen," Jenks said, a bright gold dust slipping from him as he dropped it into Ivy's waiting hand before landing on one of the more nasty pictures. Hands on his hips, he stared in disgust as the whining squeak of the pen on paper mixed pleasantly with the shouts of his kids in the sunny garden, where they were playing June bug croquet. It was as much fun as it sounded—unless you were the June bug.

Nervous and fidgety, I opened the bag of chips I'd bought for the weekend—seeing as we probably weren't going to have the expected Fourth of July cookout. Crunching through a chip, I rated a few more reports. The over-the-counter glass cleaning charm that had melted the glass and then moved on to the insulation in the surrounding walls got a seven despite no deaths. The charm to inflate a tire taking out the lungs of the man who had invoked it got a two simply because it didn't take much to explode lungs. He hadn't survived. Then there was the carpet cleaner in the Hollows where the charm ate the carpet away, foam and all. The homeowner had been delighted at the hardwood floor underneath. I wished they all had happy endings.

Weary, I pushed at the picture of the university floor, broken open like a ground fault from the small-pressure charm that was supposed to cut a molecule-thin section of fossil from the parent rock. It got a ten. How in hell was I supposed to rate these without taking into account the cost of human life?

"You okay?" Ivy flipped through a report until she found what she wanted.

"Not really." I ate a chip, then went to the fridge for the dip. Everything was better with sour cream and chives.

Jenks's wings hummed at a higher pitch, startled when I dropped the chip dip on the counter. "You really think vampires are doing this?" he asked.

"David seems to think so." I watched Ivy's jaw tighten, already knowing what she thought about that theory. "Me, I'm not buying that vampires would use magic on a scale such as this, even if they think it will save the souls of their kin." Especially after reading that pie-in-the-sky flyer, and I glanced at it on the counter where Ivy had dropped it after I'd showed it to her.

Ivy frowned, still bent over her work. "Did you know they made a saint out of him?"

"Who?" I ate a chip before dumping them into a bowl.

"Kisten," she said, and I froze, remembering the Kisten look-alike on the bridge. *That doesn't mean they're responsible for it.* Then I did a mental jerk-back. *Kisten? A saint?*

"No shit!" Jenks exclaimed, and I just stared at her. *Our Kisten?*

Only now did she look up, the love she once had for him mixing with the sour disbelief for the misled. "Because of what he said to you," she added. "They think he died his second death with his soul intact and unsullied by the curse." Her head went back down, leaving me feeling uneasy. "Cincinnati has the highest concentration of Free Vampires in the United States. If they were going to try to eradicate the masters, they'd try it here first."

"But why? Cincy is in shambles! It's not working!" I said, scrambling to wrap my head around Saint Kisten. Saint Kisten, with his leather jacket, motorcycle, and windblown blond hair. Saint Kisten, who had killed and hidden crimes to protect his master. Saint Kisten, who willingly sacrificed his second life to save mine . . .

"Nina says she's seen some of them," she said, and my attention fixed sharply on her. "I thought she was making it up, but if David comes up empty, I'll ask her."

I rolled the top of the bag of chips down, not hungry anymore. "Sure."

Taking the pen out from between her teeth, Ivy leaned in to the map. "Jenks, what time did you and Rachel leave the golf course yesterday?"

I'd be offended, but Jenks was better than an atomic clock. "We left the parking lot at twenty to eleven," he said, and I moved the bowl of chips before his dust made them stale.

"And then you got on 71 and came home." She frowned, waving Jenks off when his dust blanked out the liquid crystal. "No stops between? Good roads? Not a lot of traffic?"

"No," I said, wondering where this was going. A cold feeling was slipping through me. "Traffic was fine until we got downtown. Then it was the usual stop-and-go." Worried, I dragged my chair around to sit beside her and stare at her huge monitor and the gently sweeping wave of blue markers. It looked just like every other wave map she'd made, except it was the first and there weren't as many violent crimes to go with it.

"Okay." Ivy was clicking, and the city map was covered by a graph. "This is the wave you got caught up in last night at the bowling alley. It's the first one that the FIB took note on the times associated with the misfires. I'm guessing the wave has a top speed of forty-five miles an hour, but that can vary. That first one seemed to be slower, especially."

She had a page of math, and I gave it a cursory look. "And?" I asked, and she moved the mouse, bringing up a new map.

"Last night's wave that ended at the Laundromat was straight. The one that came through this morning before dawn was too, but the tracks were slightly different. It dissipated before it got to the church," Ivy said. "And since most Inderlanders are asleep about then—"

"I'm not," Jenks said, and Ivy sighed, bringing up a new map.

"Most *magic-using* Inderlanders are asleep then, and it wasn't noticed much. But if you look at the one that hit you first at the golf course and then again at the bridge, you can see they *do* shift direction."

My eyes narrowed as she drew her line, making a slight angle shift obvious. If it had continued on its original path, it would have missed the bridge completely.

Ivy was quiet as she eyed me. "Rachel, it shifted to follow you. They all are."

Panic iced through me. "Oh, hell no!" I said, standing up fast when Ivy's eyes flashed black at my fear. "You mean something is getting out of the line and is hunting me?" I said, pointing at the monitor.

But Ivy simply sat there, calm and relaxed, that pen back between her teeth. "It's not very responsive. After you left the golf course, it took almost ten minutes before it realized you were gone and shifted to follow."

Feeling icky, I stared at the map, wishing Ivy wasn't so damn good at her job. Jenks hovered between us. "So it's more like a slime mold after the sun."

Jenks shrugged. "You have the same aura signature as the line. Maybe it's trying to get back to it. Whatever it is."

"You think it's *alive*?"

They said nothing, and I stifled a shudder. I didn't know if I liked this better than Free Vampires trying to change the world. "I have to call Al. Where's my mirror?"

Jenks spun in the air to look at the front of the church.

He darted out, and from the front came a familiar-sounding boom of the heavy oak door crashing into the doorstop, followed by a woman's voice raised in anger. "Where are my children!"

Oh my God. *Ellasbeth*. I flushed, the memory of that last kiss with Trent flashing through me.

"You ever hear of knocking?" Jenks said, his voice hardly audible from the distance, but his voice carried when he was ticked. "Hey! You can't just barge in here!"

I came up from my crouch behind the center counter, my scrying mirror in my hands. "Ellasbeth?" I said to Ivy as the woman stomped down the hall, her high heels clicking. What was she doing in Cincinnati?

Where are my children? I thought.

Ivy put her computer into sleep mode and turned her charts and figures over. "If she wakes up Nina, I'm going to be pissed."

"She threatened to keep the girls," I said as I set the mirror down. "My guess is Quen ran off with them."

"So of course she comes here."

I brushed the hint of chip crumbs from my front. "We're on the way from the airport."

"Trenton?" the woman called, eyes all but sparkling as she came to a breathless halt in the archway to the kitchen. She was dressed in cream slacks and a white top, matching jacket, a wide-brimmed hat askew on her head. My eyes went to my ugly crime scene photos, and I left them there. "Where are my children?" she demanded, an indignant flush on her cheeks.

"I don't know." I fell back against the sink to keep my distance. Jenks had followed her in, a few kids with him all shouting at the top of their lungs. Ellasbeth waved her clutch purse at them, and Jenks pulled his youngest, the one with the cut, out of the woman's way.

"Is Trent here?" she demanded, then blanched at the picture of the woman with no hair.

"I'm sorry, Ellasbeth," I said, rubbing my forehead. "Is

there a reason for you to walk into my house and scream at me, or is this some kind of elven tradition I'm unaware of?"

Immediately she glanced at Ivy, then back at me. "Quen took Lucy and Ray last night. Ran off with no warning. Neither he nor Trent will answer my calls. You're his best friend in this godforsaken dead zone of culture. Where has he hidden them?"

Best friend? "You shouldn't have threatened to keep them," I said as I looked for the phone, not seeing it in the cradle. It was somewhere under the mess, and I began lifting papers. I never should have kissed him back. Never.

"It's not safe here," the woman said with a huff, and Jenks snickered. "Magic is behaving erratically. Even you can see that they're safer with me."

"No, I can't." I moved the chip bag. No phone. "Have you met my roommate Ivy?"

The first hints of embarrassment tensed her shoulders, and she held out a thin, manicured hand. "Ellasbeth Withon," she said by rote as Ivy rose, her motion both sexy and aggressive.

"Ivy Tamwood," Ivy breathed, and Ellasbeth blanched. "If you wake up my girlfriend, I'll let her eat you."

Ellasbeth's lips parted. Then she thought some more, presumptions visibly tumbling through her head as she looked at Ivy, then me, then back at Ivy. I would've said something, but it really wasn't any of her business.

Maybe the phone is under Ivy's mess. "Ellasbeth, I don't know where the girls are. Hold on a sec. Let me call Trent."

"He won't take my calls," she said, still by the door and now holding her purse before her like a little shield. "Those girls are mine!"

"Not for the next three months they aren't," I said, giving up on the landline and getting my cell phone from my bag on the table.

Jenks finally got his kids out—through the hole in the kitchen window screen since they were too afraid to go past Ellasbeth. I hit Trent's number and put the phone to my ear, noting Ellasbeth's annoyance that I had him on speed dial. I could sympathize, and it probably didn't help that she was cranky from having been in the air the last six hours or so, but she shouldn't have threatened to keep the girls.

Ellasbeth glanced at my scrying mirror nervously, and the line clicked open on the third ring.

"Rachel. Get your car back?" Trent asked cheerfully. "How did the FIB meeting go? Did Edden tell you the undead are asleep? No wonder it's a mess out there."

His voice had been loud enough for Jenks to hear, way over by the fridge, and by Ellasbeth's thinly hidden anger, I figured she could hear it too. "Car is in the carport, thanks. Edden told me about the undead. I'm waiting to hear back from David about those Free Vampires, but I need to talk to you about something Ivy pieced together if you have the time."

"Now's good," he said, and I glanced at Ellasbeth as she flipped her strawlike hair from her face. It looked fake next to Trent's and Lucy's transparent blond, and I knew it bothered her.

"I'd rather tell you in person," I said, holding the woman's eyes. "Ah, Ellasbeth is standing in my kitchen."

Ellasbeth lurched into motion, her thin hand reaching. "Give me the phone."

Jenks darted down and away, coming to a sword-swinging halt by my ear. My pulse jumped, and Ivy jerked at the sudden smack of adrenaline. "Excuse me! I am *not* your employee," I said, and she dropped back, shocked when she realized Jenks had scored on her and her knuckle was bleeding from a small scratch.

I backed up to put more space between us, phone at my ear. Lucy's voice was in the background, her words simple but clear, but on the chance Trent didn't want Ellasbeth to know where they were, I simply said, "She wants to know where the girls are."

His sigh was a long exhalation. "I'm sorry. I'll be there in fifteen minutes."

I glanced at the clock on the stove. It took longer than that for me to get out to his estate. "Really?"

"Quen didn't pack anything when she threatened to keep them, and they outgrew everything I have. We went shopping. The Hollows has had fewer misfires."

My smile was unstoppable as I imagined the two of them handling the girls with grace, both of them proficient daddies. "Fifteen. See you then."

Pleased at the chance to see the girls, I clicked off and shoved my phone into my back pocket. My smile faded as I realized everyone was staring at me. My finger was wound around a strand of hair. I didn't remember having done that, and I untangled it, embarrassed. "What?"

Jenks hummed his wings, and I didn't like that knowing look he and Ivy were sharing.

Ellasbeth shifted her shoulders, clearly uncomfortable for having crashed our church, but not willing to sit down until invited. "I wanted to talk to him," she said, temper frayed.

"Well, he didn't want to talk to you." I barely breathed the words, but I knew she heard me. "And lower your voice. Not everyone sleeps in four-hour naps. You want to sit down? He'll be here in fifteen minutes."

Ellasbeth looked at my chair pulled up to Ivy's, then edged around it to sit at the far end of the table by the fridge. No one ever sat there, and she looked stiff. "I'm sorry for bursting in on you. I was understandably distressed."

Distressed? I glanced at the mostly full coffeepot. *And that makes it okay?* I thought, and Ivy shook her head, bringing up her computer's screen now that Ellasbeth couldn't see it. "No doubt," I said, getting a mug from the cupboard.

"Yes, but if you don't start treating me with respect—"

I set the empty cup beside her, leaning in to cut her words off. That big honking engagement ring was still on her finger, catching the light like Jenks's wings. *Who in hell does she think she is?* "I'll start treating you with respect as soon as you give it, missy."

"She called her missy," Jenks said, and Ivy raised a finger to high-five him.

I pushed back, letting her breathe again. "You walked into my house uninvited. Threatened my roommate."

"I did not!" she huffed, indignant as she looked at Ivy.

"I was talking about Jenks. You reneged on your agreement with Trent, and if he wanted to talk to you, he would've answered your calls. He's on his way here, and you're welcome to stay until he gets here because I heard the cabdriver dump your luggage and drive off right after you got out."

Long face becoming longer, she sat stiffly, making me wonder if she was going to cry. I was trying to be calm, not only because it looked good but because an easily unbalanced vampire was sleeping in the next room over and Ellasbeth was kicking out enough anger to wake the dead.

"Now, would you like some coffee while you wait?"

"Yes, thank you." Her voice was softer, not subdued, but it had lost that I-sneeze-sunshine lilt she had. "I've been up for hours."

"Welcome to the club." I took the pot to her and filled her mug. She made sure I saw that ring again, and Ivy quietly went back to work.

"Actually, I'm glad to have this time with you," Ellasbeth said, and I leaned back against the counter. "May I be frank?"

You can be Frank, Paul, or Simon, I don't care, I thought, and Jenks snickered as he sat at the window where he could watch his kids as he sharpened his sword. He knew the joke. "I wish you would."

Ellasbeth eyed Ivy across the table. "Alone?"

Ivy's eyes met mine, and I sighed. "Sure. Garden okay?"

Again she looked at Ivy, as if wondering why the woman wasn't leaving. Grimacing, Ellasbeth stood. "That's fine." Heels clacking and purse held tight to herself, she set her mug down and headed out, already knowing the way. She'd been here once before to pick up Lucy when I'd rescued her from Ku'Sox.

Jenks landed on my shoulder as I went to follow. "You want me to keep an eye on you?"

"No. Yes." I hesitated. I'd likely be more vocal in my opinions if we were out of the church and away from Nina. "Eye, yes. Ears, no."

He flew backward, out of my way. "You're no fun."

Ivy took the pen from between her teeth. "Be nice," she said, and I smiled, then hustled to catch the screen door before it slammed.

Ellasbeth was already outside, her cream heels looking odd in the sun-starved grass that eked out a living under the big tree. Her nose was wrinkled, and I could hear pixies in the branches. I hoped to God that they wouldn't start dropping things on us. "Okay, shoot," I said as I came down the stairs, and she turned to me, that ring of hers sparkling even in the dim light.

"I'd like to ask you to stop confusing Trent."

Tired, I sat down at the picnic table, the wood still slightly damp from the last rain. "No problem." I'd missed a chip, and I flicked it off me.

"Stop being so flippant," she said, frowning. "I'm not blind. You're confusing him. Making this harder than it needs to be."

For who? You or him? "Ellasbeth, Trent and I already had this talk." *And then we went on a date.* "As long as Quen is making the trek out to your place every three months, I'm going to be doing security while he's gone. I know he's going to marry you, and quite frankly, I can't stomach the idea of being a mistress even if I did like him that way." *Liar, liar, pants on fire.* "So as long as Quen keeps leaving, I'm the one for the job. And it is a job."

She was eyeing me, looking for lies, her hat shading her face whereas it shone hot and full on mine. "Then you're not . . ."

Guilt tugged at me. Want was not an action. "I'm not sleeping with him, no." *Damn fine kiss, though.* "Never have." My gut hurt, and I looked out over the graveyard. The grass was long and needed cutting. Everything was going to hell with Jenks's kids leaving.

"Thank you," she said, appearing to take that on faith.

Reclining against the damp wood, I looked at her. "But if I find out you're not treating him right, I'll make your life miserable."

Her expression blanked, and I wondered if she was trying to figure out if it was a joke. Above us, the eavesdropping pixies shot out of the trees, arrowing for the chimney and vanishing down it as if someone had shouted "Honey!"

From inside, Ivy's voice rose. "Nina! No!"

I stood as the torn leaves drifted over us. "You had to wake her up," I said bitterly, then strode to the steps. Ivy might need some help. "Stay out here!" I told Ellasbeth. "You're too angry to be around her right now."

"Rache!" Jenks shouted from inside, and I took the stairs two at a time.

I yanked open the back door, reeling as the vampire pheromones hit me like a wall. My hand clamped to my neck and I staggered through the living room, other hand on the archway, to look into the kitchen. Ivy had Nina pinned front-first to the wall, Nina's head turned to me as Ivy wrenched the woman's arm up behind her. There was a huge knife in Nina's hand, and I felt myself pale. Both women's eyes were black, and Ivy looked scared that she might hurt Nina.

"It's okay, Nina. Breathe," she said as she struggled to keep Nina unmoving. "Look at me. I'm not angry. Breathe."

"Morgan," Nina snarled, a heavy intelligence glittering in her eyes. "Tell Tamwood to let me go."

"It's Felix," Jenks said, and I pushed up from the archway and edged inside. My pulse pounded. The elegant, young Hispanic woman with her face pressed into the wall struggled, and Ivy slipped a foot between hers, ready to pull her down. I could see the sick master vampire in Nina's stance, belligerent and angry that Ivy, a living vampire, had managed to best him, even if he was in the body of a weaker, inexperienced woman. It had been weeks since the master vampire had taken Nina over. But how? All the undead vampires were sleeping!

"Let me go. I can help!" Nina shouted, the domination in her voice coming out in a frustrated howl. She wiggled again, and Ivy yanked her foot out from under her. They both hit the floor, chairs sliding out of the way as they fought for control of the knife.

"I'm sane, I tell you! I need Nina!" Nina screamed as Ivy got the knife. With a backward flip of the wrist, she flung it into the wall where it stuck, quivering. "Let me go! I am cognizant. I'm not ill!"

Tears fell freely from Ivy as she pinned Nina to the floor. "Fight him, Nina. You can do this. You can! You're stronger than him, and it pisses him off that you know it!"

"Get off!" she howled. "I'm no longer ill! I can help, but only if I'm in Nina!"

Hair falling to hide her face, Ivy leaned low over her. "I love you, Nina. Don't believe him. He lies. He can't hurt you if you push him out. I'll keep him away. I promise. I promise. Just get him out!"

The soft scuff behind me gave me warning, and I spun, trying to force Ellasbeth back. Any more fear in the air might give Felix the strength to completely break Nina's mind.

"I told you to stay out," I hissed, pushing her into the hall.

"Oh my God!" Ellasbeth said as Nina bucked to get Ivy off her.

"I'm not sick! With Nina, I can help!"

Ellasbeth's face was white, and she looked into the kitchen as I shoved her into the living room. "This is a madhouse!"

Right now, I couldn't argue with her, but she'd caused the problem to begin with. "We told you not to wake her up," I said as I finally got the woman into the living room. "Sit down and shut up." I pointed to the couch, and she sat.

Shaking, I went back in case Ivy needed me. They'd sat up, Ivy's long legs wrapped around Nina as she held her unmoving before her in her lap. Nina's hair was everywhere, mixing with Ivy's, the ponytail long gone. I could tell just by Nina's snarl that Felix was still in her.

"Together," Ivy breathed, the strain showing in her arms as she held Nina unmoving. Tears made her cheeks shine, and I ached for her. "I will let go of you as you let go of him. I know he fills you with power, but you have to let him go," she demanded. It was an addiction on both ends, and Ivy had survived both its presence and absence.

"Ah, Ivy?" Jenks said, his dust a thick, dark green falling from the overhead rack. "Is that such a good idea?"

I looked at my shoulder bag. My splat ball gun was in it, but before I could move, Ivy whispered, "I trust you." She kissed her, and then let her go.

"Wait!" I cried out, reaching to tap a line as Nina sprang from her, spinning into an ugly crouch.

Ivy reached out a trembling hand. "Nina. I love you. Leave him."

"No!" Nina howled, the sound raging from her with the strength of the undead, and then her tension broke and she collapsed.

Ivy lurched forward. Catching Nina, she pulled the woman to her, rocking Nina, gentling her head to her shoulder and whispering. Nina stiffened, and then she began to cry in great gasping sobs.

"He came!" she cried, words hardly recognizable. "Ivy, he came in my dreams. I didn't even know. I can't do this anymore! I just want it to *stop*!"

I exhaled, shaking as I wiggled the knife out of the wall and set it lightly in the sink.

"You didn't hurt anyone," Ivy was saying, holding her gently now. "It's okay."

"He wanted me to kill you!"

Tears still spilling from her brown eyes, Ivy took Nina's face in her hands and smiled at her. "You didn't hurt me. Look at me. Look at me!" Nina's sobbing hiccups eased, and she blinked tearfully at Ivy. "It's okay," Ivy said firmly, even as moisture shined her cheeks as well. "I'm so proud of you."

It was over, and as Nina continued to cry, I went to get her a glass of water. "That was fun," I said as the tap ran, then looked up as Ellasbeth was suddenly in the doorway, an unusual silence in her stance as she took everything in, the chairs knocked aside, the knife in the sink, the women sobbing on the floor—one in relief, one in love. Maybe now she understood. Maybe now she'd know Ivy was trying to save a strong, intelligent woman from a circular trap. And if she didn't, then the hell with her.

"I told you not to wake her up," I said, fingers trembling as I turned off the water and took the glass to Nina.

Ivy slowly stood, extending a hand down to help Nina from the floor. "It wasn't her fault," Ivy said, and Nina bobbed her head, thanking me as she took the water and gulped at it.

"Jenks, go open the front door," I said as I shoved the window open all the way. "We need to air the place out."

"Got it," he said, then darted off to work the series of pulleys Ivy had come up with for him to open the heavy oak door.

Ellasbeth still hovered in the doorway, a new understanding in her. "I'm sorry."

Ivy's expression was empty. "It wasn't your fault. He attacked her in her sleep."

"Still, I'm sorry. I didn't know."

It was the first honest thing I thought I'd ever heard from Ellasbeth, and I almost liked her as I leaned against the counter and just . . . breathed. "You did good, Nina. It won't be so hard next time. I promise."

Nina managed a smile. "Thank you."

There were tears in Ivy's eyes as she helped Nina to the table, tears and love for both of us. The love for me in the past, and the love for Nina in the future. And somehow, as the four of us women slowly picked up the threads of our lives and began to awkwardly weave them anew, it didn't hurt anymore.

Eight

Ray was a comfortable armful of quiet as she sat on my lap in the kitchen, her eyes on the book that Lucy had brought in from the toy box I had for the rare occasions that Trent brought them to the church. Even the distraction of Jenks's kids couldn't take her attention from the picture book. Still, she didn't reach for it when Lucy ran to me, collapsing on my knees in excitement and a bid for my attention.

"Sasha!" the little girl said brightly as she shoved the book at me and ran out.

"That's the name of her pony at the Withons' estate," Quen said, and I scrambled to catch it before it slid to the floor. Only now did Ray reach for it, and I shifted her so she could hold and turn the pages herself. I didn't think Ray's reluctance to reach for the book earlier was because she was afraid of her sister, but simply knowing that her distractible sibling would keep it if Lucy knew Ray wanted it too.

"I didn't think horses were that important to the Withons," I said, and the man turned his attention from his daughter to the hallway. Ellasbeth and Trent were having a chat in the back living room, one that was probably long overdue, and their voices were a soft murmur.

"The pony was my idea," he said, his motions smooth as

he moved deeper into the kitchen. Quen wasn't small, but a person tended not to notice him unless he wanted to be noticed. Both he and Ray had dark hair, uncommon to elves. It might be a remnant from the elves' recently dropped tradition of hybridizing with humans, but I doubted it. Quen was one of the most elven elves I knew, clever, powerful in his magic, and graceful beyond reason.

"I didn't want their horsemanship to suffer in the time spent away from home," he added as he clasped his hands behind his back, stoic as he waited for Ellasbeth to say what she wanted so he could, hopefully, take her back to the airport.

I smiled as Lucy ran back in, blond hair flying. "Belle!" the excited toddler shouted, dropping a sparkly fairy doll on Ray's book and running out, pixy girls in tow. Ray promptly threw the toy after her and returned to her book. The tension from the back room was ebbing, but I was still glad that Ivy and Nina had excused themselves shortly after Trent's arrival. Belle, too, had retired to the garden. The wingless fairy was a brilliant strategist, but she was pretty much helpless against the grasping toddlers, especially when Rex, Jenks's cat, had dumped her to hide under my bed at the first little-girl "Here kitty, kitty."

"Jenks, stay in here," I said when the pixy rose from the windowsill to follow her out.

"I can't hear crap from here, Rache," he muttered as he landed on my shoulder. Ray looked up when his dust fell on her fingers. Slowly she turned her palm up, mesmerized at the spot of sunshine she could touch.

"That's the idea." I'd watched Ellasbeth turn green when the girls had greeted me with enthusiasm, then white when they'd toddled off to the toy box, clearly knowing where it was.

Quen smiled thinly, finally lowering himself to sit on the edge of a chair beside the fridge. "Any problems while I was gone?" he asked, looking at Ivy's new monitor in envy.

"Apart from the recent magic misfires and no functioning undead vampire in the Cincinnati area?" I helped Ray turn the page, and she sang out, "Thank you," charming me with her little-girl voice. "No," I said softer, the scent of her hair tweaking my maternal instincts. "Mr. Ray and Mrs. Sarong have started campaigning for their picks for the next mayoral battle, and there's been some noise about the parks Trent made in the abandoned warehouse district being better used for commercial, meaning gambling. Couple of death threats with low credibility, but I forwarded that to you."

Quen squinted as he noticed the scratches Bis had made on the ceiling. "Thank you."

His attention fell to Lucy as she ran in and dropped a train book on Ray's lap. "No!" Ray demanded, shoving it off, but Lucy was gone.

I leaned to pick it up and set it on the table, now cleared of any and all FIB-gathered evidence. "It's been my pleasure. I'm glad you're back, though. These misfires and increased vampire violence have problem written all over them."

"You think the two are linked?" he asked, his concern obvious, and I nodded.

From the back room, Ellasbeth's voice rose in hurt. "I'm staying until this matter is settled. If not with you, then downtown. There's one decent hotel in Cincinnati. The service is lacking, but the food is bearable."

"I didn't say you weren't welcome; I asked you to not antagonize my staff," Trent said. "Maggie has been with me since my parents died. She's not an employee, she's family."

"I'm sorry. I wasn't aware," Ellasbeth said softly, and I winced. She was being very contrite—meaning she was up to something.

Lucy came back in, and Ray looked up in annoyance at the glitter ball in her hands. "I'll take it, Lucy," I said, and laughing, the little girl threw it, watching it bounce on the floor before running back into the living room. The ball rolled to a halt and Quen scooped it up.

"How's the weather on the coast?" I asked, wishing they'd hurry up.

"The lines are intolerable. I'd do this for the girls, no one else." He shifted the ball in his hands, watching the glitter move before he set it on the table beside the book of trains. His expression froze when Trent said, "I'll have your room refreshed immediately."

Jenks snickered, and Ray patted the dust suddenly spilling over the book. She looked up at him, beautiful as she smiled and held a small hand up for him to land on.

"My room?" Ellasbeth said. "Trent, I was hoping—"

Her voice cut off at his soft comment, and I cringed. TMI. I was getting too much information. I knew her moving back in with Trent was inevitable, but did she have to bring it up where I could hear it? But remembering how she'd flashed that never-returned engagement ring, she probably did.

I couldn't help my sigh. Ray looked up and patted my cheek, and I flushed when Quen's brow furrowed in suspicion. "So you've been enjoying the work?" he asked, and I was saved answering immediately when Lucy raced in with a Bite Me Betty doll.

I set the doll aside as she ran out. "I don't care to work for most of the people looking to hire a demon," I said, thankful the solicitations for evil curses and bad karma spells had stopped.

Trent's expression was closed when he came in with Ellasbeth. The woman had Lucy on her hip, and the toddler was fussy, clearly not happy with half the toy box still unemptied. There was a book in Ellasbeth's hand. I knew that wasn't going to fly: Ray studied, Lucy explored. They were going to be a potent team if they ever learned to understand each other. Seeing Ellasbeth, Trent, and Lucy together, the resemblance was more than obvious, and my smile faltered. Lucy looked a lot like her mother, too. They were the perfect family.

"Ellasbeth is going to stay and help with the girls until the misfires can be explained and rectified," Trent said as he stood just within the kitchen, not a hint to his mood in his tone.

"Nice," Jenks muttered, then took off from my shoulder. Lucy began to wiggle, clearly wanting to play in the temporary sunbeam. Ignoring her, Ray turned a page.

Ellasbeth pulled out one of the chairs from the table and sat, expertly wrangling the complaining toddler. Her gaze shifted between Trent and me as if looking for evidence we were lovers. It made me nervous, guilty almost, and I hadn't really done anything. "It's not the misfires as much as the out-of-control vampires I'm concerned with," she said as she tried to distract Lucy with the book.

"Me too," I said faintly.

Quen, who had stood when Trent came in, nodded. "Very good, Sa'han. I'll call ahead and have Ellasbeth's room refreshed."

Ellasbeth smiled stiffly, giving up on the book and taking the Bite Me Betty doll when I handed it to her. "Thank you, Quen. I'd appreciate that."

Trent clapped his hands once. "So, Rachel. What have you and Ivy pieced together?"

"Ah, it's rather sensitive," I started, and Ellasbeth frowned. "I don't mind telling you, Ellasbeth," I added quickly. "Especially since you'll be dealing with it, but don't go telling your best friend on the coast."

She made a short bark of laughter. "I'm a scientist," she said, sour enough to curdle milk. "I know how important proprietary information is. I can keep my mouth shut."

She probably did, I mused, having forgotten that aspect of her. "Sorry." I stood and set Ray down, not liking the image of the two of us dueling over the girls' affections. The little girl wobbled for a moment, then carefully toddled into the living room and the toys. Lucy wiggled until Ellasbeth had no choice but to let her down.

"Mine!" Lucy shouted, and Jenks darted after them. Ellasbeth stared at Trent, then Quen, frowning when neither man followed them to supervise.

"Jenks is in there," Trent finally said, and the woman

eased back in her chair, clearly not liking it but wanting to leave the room even less.

"Ah, we still have no clue as to why the wave is making the undead sleep," I said, retreating until the center island counter was between me and Ellasbeth. "But Ivy has been over the raw data from the misfires, and when you figure in my location, there's an indication that it is ah, attracted to some degree to, ah . . . me."

Trent swore softly. Quen started, and I nodded, feeling ill. Ellasbeth brought her attention back from the too-quiet living room. "Jenks thinks it's because my aura has the same signature as the line it's coming from," I said. "Whatever it is, it's not too bright. It went right past me when we were at the golf course, continuing on until I'd moved my location, so maybe it's more like a delayed magnetic response."

"Interesting." Trent took Ivy's chair, sitting down with a thoughtful look.

"Trent," Ellasbeth prompted when the girls began to fight over something.

"They're fine," Trent said distantly. "The room is baby-proof and Jenks is in there."

But Jenks let his kids tease bumblebees, knowing a sting might mean their death. Uncomfortable, I crossed my arms over my chest and leaned against the counter. "David thinks the wave might be caused by a vampire faction that promotes a masterless lifestyle."

"Free Vampires?" Trent said, surprising me.

"That's them." I pushed the flyer to him, and he took it. "There's been a big jump in their numbers since, ah, Kisten died." Which was sort of embarrassing, but at least they hadn't tried to make me a saint's concubine.

"I looked them up this morning." Trent's lips were quirked in an almost smile, knowing firsthand about the playboy living vampire. "They didn't seem that well organized."

Ellasbeth sniffed. "David? Isn't that your insurance friend, Rachel?"

I took an irate breath, words cutting off when Trent interrupted me, saying, "You'd be surprised at the amount of sensitive information insurance companies gather, Ellie. If David says there might be a connection, then it's worth giving more than a little consideration."

Miffed, she fiddled with the strap on her purse.

"Personally?" I said, feeling the weight of her stare on me. "I'd rather believe that it's a natural phenomenon, even if it's coming from my line and tracking me like a slime mold, because if vampires are doing this, they're getting the magic to control it from somewhere."

"Demons," Trent whispered.

"Well, it wouldn't be witches," I said sourly. "I'm scared to even wear a makeup charm." Especially after seeing what one did to the face of that poor woman at the theater. "There're easier ways to get rid of vampires. Ways that don't cause this much fallout."

I wanted it to be a natural artifact so bad, but with that Kisten look-alike on the bridge, Felix being awake, and the Free Vampire graffiti . . . The living didn't prey on the undead. It was the other way around. "I was thinking about talking to Al today," I said hesitantly.

Immediately Trent brightened. "You think he'd tell you if it was demon mischief?"

"No, no, Lucy!" Jenks yelled from the living room. "Don't put that in your mouth. Hey!"

I shrugged. "I want to look at my line again before I tell Edden about the Free Vampire angle, but honestly, he probably already knows. Their graffiti is everywhere," I said as Ellasbeth glared at the men to do something about their children. "I should probably tell Edden the waves are following me, though." Telling Al might be a mistake. Maybe I should take the afternoon and drive out to Loveland and look at my line myself.

The screams from the living room grew more strident. No one moved, and finally Ellasbeth stood, her chair sliding dramatically. Trent touched Ellasbeth's hand in thanks in passing, then turned to me. "Mind if I come with you?"

Ellasbeth's pace jerked to a stop, and I blinked. *To Al's? Was he serious?*

"A-Ah, why?" I stammered as I pushed up from the counter. "I mean, I don't mind . . ." I hesitated, remembering how Trent's freedom seemed to be halved when Quen was around. "Sure. Jenks can't be in the ever-after when the sun is up, and I'd appreciate the company."

Quen's face lost its expression and Ellasbeth stiffened, ignoring the increasing pixy panic from the living room.

"I've not seen Algaliarept for over three months," Trent said, clearly trying to head off their coming protests. "I want to keep the lines of communication open. And I need to thank him for a few things. Or I could just use the vault door and pop over."

"Sa'han," Quen said, warning thick in his tone, and Trent leaned confidently back in his chair, ankle coming up to rest on a knee. When done in his office surrounded by his things, it was effective. Here in my kitchen on a hard-backed chair—not so much.

"I'll be fine," Trent said confidently. "You and Ellasbeth can mind the girls for a few hours. I'm perfectly safe over there."

Ellasbeth turned her back on the rising, shrill "Noooo!" from the living room. "Trenton. They're demons!"

"So is Rachel, and she saved me from a wildly driven golf ball yesterday." He was being flippant, goading her. "I've ridden the Hunt with every demon alive. They all know me. Besides, I'm talking to Algali—" He changed his mind. "I'm talking to Al. Not the entire collective."

"Sa'han. It's an unnecessary risk."

Trent put his foot solidly back on the floor. "Keeping good relations with possible allies is never a risk."

Framed in the doorway, Ellasbeth put a hand on her hip. "Someone else can do it!"

"There is no one else," Trent said calmly, but both Quen and I knew that when his hands laced together, it meant he was pissed, and the older elf sighed and backed off. "Things change, Ellasbeth. Ku'Sox is dead. I'm still officially Rachel's familiar though admittedly emancipated. I'm as safe as you in your lab. Safer."

There was an uncomfortable silence broken by the girls giggling and then Lucy's shout.

"Good. We can go this afternoon," I said to end the discussion, and Trent shot me a grateful glance, even as Ellasbeth let her hand hit her side in disgust. Yawning, I looked at the clock. It was after noon, and Ellasbeth looked dead tired. If she was on West Coast time, it was long past nappies. Trent, too, would be ready for some shut-eye. "You want to wait until after four?" I said. "I want to make some cookies first. Distract him."

"Mine!" shrilled from the living room, followed by Ray screaming and Lucy's wail.

"Excuse me," Ellasbeth said tightly, turning to go into the living room. "No, Lucy, dear. Take him out of your mouth."

Jenks flew in, looking frazzled as he landed on my shoulder leaking dust from a bent wing. "You okay?" I asked.

"I don't want to talk about it."

Trent leaned to look through the hall to the living room, then sat back. "We can go now if you want. My sleep schedule hasn't been predictable lately."

"Mine either," I said, wishing Ellasbeth would leave. "I keep dreaming of purple eyes and wheels with wings."

Quen's head snapped up, and I stared at him. *What did I say?* "Purple eyes?" I prompted, and Quen made a curious, pained expression. "Wings?" I added, and he looked at Trent. A cold feeling slithered out from between my thought and reason, ready to smack me. "What?"

"I don't know," Trent said to Quen, not me, mystifying me. "But now that you mention it, it did feel like wild magic at both the golf course and the bowling alley." Gaze distant,

Trent fished his phone out from a pocket. "I thought Rachel was doing some kind of magic."

"I think she was," Jenks said sourly, leaking dust as he flew to the sink, and I gave him a look to shut up. Catching a drop from the faucet, he dabbed at his shirt. "But if it's wild magic, that would explain why her aura goes white every time a wave hits it."

Quen's eyes widened, and I pulled myself straight. "Whoa, whoa, whoa!" I said, feeling the conversation spiral out of control. "Jenks, are you telling me that wave is wild magic?" *Why is wild magic leaking from my line? And what does that have to do with wheels and wings?*

"Sa'han," Quen protested, but Trent was scrolling rapidly through his numbers when Ellasbeth came to the kitchen archway. Ray was on her hip and Lucy's hand firmly in her grip. There was a book in the little girl's hand, and she'd been crying. Ray just looked mad.

"Jenks, you say Rachel's aura went white?" Trent asked, his intentness scary, almost.

"As white as her ass," Jenks said, and Ellasbeth walked stiffly between us, pointedly sitting down with the girls and the book. *That book is going to last about thirty seconds.*

"The waves can't be wild magic," I protested.

"I did promise the Goddess two goats I've never delivered on."

"Sa'han," Quen protested as Ellasbeth looked up from arranging the book before the two girls. "Cincinnati is not plagued with misfires because you haven't sacrificed two goats."

Trent tucked his phone away. "No, of course not. But that these waves might be natural phenomena is easier to believe than living vampires preying on the undead. We need more information. Quen, I want you to get ahold of Bancroft's assistant as soon as you get back to my office. I don't have his number with me. Invite him out to help me settle a debt with the Goddess and tell him—and only him—what's going on here, including the undead's inability to wake up. Offer him the use of a jet to get him here. Oh, and arrange for two goats."

Suddenly the idea that this might be a natural event didn't thrill me. Wild magic? Al was going to be pissed.

"You cannot be serious!" Ellasbeth protested, prompting Lucy to begin to bounce, mimicking the woman's cadence perfectly.

Trent smiled, undeterred. "It's a good excuse to get him to visit. If we're going to be elves, we're going to be elves, by God. I'd like him to officiate so I get it right."

Ellasbeth simply stared at him. Slowly the book slid to the floor as she struggled with a squirmy Lucy and Ray quietly pushed on her sister to get down. "Bancroft is an old man clinging to traditions we don't even know the beginnings of anymore," the woman said. "And you are *not* going to sacrifice two goats. We aren't savages!"

"Who is to say what we are, Ellasbeth," Trent said coolly. "In the meantime, I'll be partaking of another elven tradition of demon discourse." His tone was far too blasé for my liking. Ceri had followed that tradition, only to end up Al's slave for a thousand years.

An awkward silence grew, and Jenks shrugged when our eyes met. Trent stood, taking Lucy and handing Ellasbeth her purse. "The wave feels like wild magic," he said. "It resonates with Rachel's aura and seeks her out. Bancroft might give us something to investigate, a new direction to think about. Everything circles back, Ellasbeth. Quen can drive you and the girls home."

Silent, the woman rose with Ray, lips pressed into a thin line and her feet unmoving. "So, who is Bancroft?" I asked as I began gathering up the toys.

"Just a man." Trent handed Lucy to Quen and motioned for the unmoving Ellasbeth to head for the front of the church. "He knows more about the Goddess than anyone."

"He's a priest?"

"If you can be a priest in a land with no church. Wild

magic was said to live in the space between spaces in the lines. It sounds as if it's leaking from your line. He might know why, and then we can stop it."

Sure, it sounded easy, but I was willing to bet someone would be dead before it was over.

Ellasbeth still hadn't moved. Trent's arm fell, and he looked expectantly at her. Clearly frustrated, Ellasbeth waved at the pixy kids wreathing her, all of them shrilling good-bye to the girls. "I think Bancroft meeting Rachel is an excellent idea," she said. "Rachel, you *will* come out and give Bancroft your experiences firsthand, won't you?"

Distrusting this, I fumbled for a moment, then managed, "Ah, yes, of course."

Trent eyed her suspiciously as he handed his keys to Quen. "Good. It's a date then. Quen, you and Ellasbeth can take the girls home in the SUV. I'll go to the ever-after with Rachel and talk to Al. If I need a way home, I'll call."

Looking pained, Quen took the keys. "Certainly, Sa'han."

Things were happening fast, and I stood there with my arms full of toys.

"It's good to have you home again," Trent said, giving Quen an honest smile. Lucy wiggled, demanding attention, and he focused on her in Quen's arms, his voice rising as he said, "And you, too, Lucy. It's been too quiet without you and your sister."

I smiled as the little girl gave him a sloppy kiss and shouted, "Good night!"

"It's good to be home," Quen said, his expression fixing to a bland nothing as he turned to Ellasbeth. "Will we be needing to stop somewhere on the way home, Ms. Withon?"

"Actually, I do need a few things," Ellasbeth said as she took a step to the hallway. "But it can wait. The girls need to go down for their naps. Trenton, can I have a word with you?"

Looking resigned, Trent edged past me and into the hall. "What?"

Quen worked hard to hide his smirk as she click-clacked

into the sanctuary, Ray on her hip and dragging Trent behind her.

"Sorry about all this," I said to Quen as I tucked Lucy's flyaway hair behind an ear and gave her a tickle under her chin.

"It's not your fault," he said, his tone making it clear he wasn't entirely sure. "You will keep him safe?"

"Always." But I couldn't help but worry over how Al was going to react with me dropping in with his *most favorite* elf.

Our attentions flicked to the hallway as Trent's voice rose in a hushed anger, and I felt myself warm. "She has saved my life more times than you have rings for your fingers, Ellie. I'm not going to let her go alone to tell a demon that wild magic is leaking from her ley line. She needs someone to watch her back, and pixies can't be in the ever-after until sunset. I'm going. End of discussion."

On second thought, Al probably wasn't going to care about Trent once he found out that wild magic was not only leaking from my line but crossing Cincinnati to find me. Maybe we should just go out to the Loveland line and see it for ourselves.

Nine

The engine's thrum muted as we got off the interstate. I tried not to listen to Trent's phone conversation as the wind noise dropped, but my car wasn't that big. It wasn't as if Trent minded talking to Quen with me listening, but I knew Trent wasn't happy that Quen had called in the first place, prompted by Trent's text that our visit to Al's had been nixed in exchange for a personal visit out to my ley line. If Trent had wanted to turn it into a committee decision, he would have called.

"Good," the man said, wind in his hair. "Keep an eye on the news. Rachel has talked to the FIB and there's going to be a public announcement in the next half hour. Whenever you hear sirens, don't do any magic for an hour."

"No," Trent said as he fiddled with the level of the window. "If it's already running, the charm will be untouched. Don't shut them down." His eyes flicked up and away. "Ah, me too. See you tonight, Ellie," he said, then ended the call.

Not Quen, then. I'd wondered. His tone hadn't been quite right. Eyes fixed firmly on the road, I took a yield, my little car straining at the unusually steep dirt road as the paved road quickly became very country. Sighing, Trent checked his e-mail before tucking the phone away. "Thanks for coming with me," I said, noticing his ears were red on the rims. "I know you wanted to talk to Al."

"I like this just as well. A trip to your line will probably result in more information." Smiling, he reached across the small space, taking my hand and giving it a squeeze.

Eyes firmly on the road, I pulled into the parking lot at Loveland Castle. Smile never dimming, Trent took his hand back, and I exhaled, glad that no one was here. There were posted hours, but the castle itself was seldom locked up, open to the public from dawn to dusk. The antitheft and vandalism hex on the door wasn't legal, but the local cops probably appreciated it, not wanting to police such a lonely, trouble-inviting place.

Gravel popped as I put the car in park and turned the engine off. For a moment, we sat. Slowly the chatter of the unseen river and the haze of insect sound became obvious. Reluctant to get out of the car just yet, I looked past the crumbling icon to one man's idea of perfect nobility to the never-finished garden, tall with weeds and terraced with crumbling stone.

I'd fought Ku'Sox there, surviving with the help of Quen and Etude, Bis's dad. It was becoming increasingly hard to live with the fact that my errors could end up with others getting hurt, and as Trent undid his seat belt and got out, I stifled the urge to tell him to stay in the car.

He could take care of himself, but after three months of watching his back, I found it hard not to be protective.

We're just going to look at my line, I told myself, hastening to follow him. No harm ever came from just looking at the ever-after.

Worried, I brought up my second sight, but as expected, my line was humming with a peaceful reddish haze, the glowing twenty-by-three-by-two horizontal column hovering at chest height. Hands on his hips, reminding me of Jenks, Trent stood with his feet in the knee-high grass and scanned the open area between the fallow garden and the hidden river. He looked good there in the sun in his faded jeans and pullover shirt that he'd gone shopping with the girls in, and a sudden thought of waking up to find him between my sheets flitted through me and was gone—chased away by the memory of Ellasbeth.

"Your line appears fine," he said, then strode into the meadow for a closer look.

Embarrassed, I unfocused my attention even more, almost losing my vision of reality as I concentrated on the ever-after. A gritty red haze overlaid itself across the quiet green, making the trees look black. My tennis shoes brushed through the dry grass, sending up puffs of imaginary ever-after dust as I followed him. Sending a thought out, I connected more firmly to the line, letting the force of it pour through me, shocking me awake. Still it felt okay, and I carefully tasted the energy, hearing the pure sound/color and calling it good.

I'd created this line by accident when sliding through realities. It carried the taint of my aura, differentiating it from everyone else's and making line jumps possible. But the memory of burning my aura off was still too new for me to try line jumping again, especially with Bis sleeping until sundown.

Slowly I came to a weed-shushing halt beside Trent. "It looks fine," he said, squinting at it in the sun. "When was the last wave?"

"Ivy said one went through about five this morning." Not that it made much difference. We had yet to find a pattern to them. Most Inderlanders except pixies and elves would've been asleep right about then. Was it just luck, or was someone trying to minimize the misfires?

The tall grass smelled wonderful, and I tugged at a knee-high tuft of it as I listened to the crickets. I breathed deep, smelling the hot grass and the July heat rising up from the earth, enjoying how it mixed with Trent's scent of shortbread and wine—making me wish we were here for some other reason than checking for telltale signs of wild magic.

"I'm going to check it out from the inside," Trent said, startling me.

"I'm starting to think you like the smell of burnt amber," I said, and he surprised me with his sudden flash of embarrassment.

"It's more to do with not having Quen lurking about," he admitted as he strode right into my line, reminding me that he had one running through his office and probably was used to the idea. "The ever-after is very . . . I don't know. Clean in a way? Uncluttered?"

That's not how I'd describe the ever-after. It was uncomfortable, the sun was too bright, the wind too cutting, and the grit got into everything. And it smelled. The only things able to survive on the surface for any length of time were the indigenous gargoyles, who slept during the day, and surface demons, who weren't really demons at all.

But the nasty things wouldn't be out in the daylight, and I watched Trent look over Loveland's lush setting, knowing he was seeing it as if standing in the ever-after himself.

His thought-provoking harrumph pulled me closer, and I dipped my hand right into the line to feel the energy push against it, sort of like wind except that the flowing sensations came from all directions, not just one. I played with it, cupping the energy and trying to pull it from the line only to have it spill back into its course as if it was magnetized.

Trent turned at my intrusion, a startled look on him. "There's someone on the surface."

"Surface demon?" I blurted, stepping into the line so as to see better. Immediately the sensation of gritty wind strengthened as the clean, moist heat of the summer meadow was entirely replaced by the sucking heat of the desert.

"No, it's a girl!" he said, and my concern focused to a sharp point.

Newt, I thought even before I saw her. "I don't see . . ." I hesitated, finding a dancing figure in white just across the shallow riverbed, jumping to catch something over her head. "Oh. Ah, I think that's Newt."

Trent's attention jerked to me. "Newt?" he said, clearly doubtful. "Mmmm. Maybe we should show our respects."

Jeez Louise, he wanted to go over? I'd just gotten the burnt-amber stink out of my hair. But my immediate refusal to shift realities faltered. If anyone could give me an answer about wild magic, it might be Newt. As the ever-after's only female demon, and not entirely sane all the time, she was a font of information—if you could figure it out.

"Why not," I said, reaching out to find his hand. "I'll do it."

He started, his grip becoming firmer as he gave me an appreciative smile. Shifting realities wasn't hard when you were standing in a ley line. Any trained elf could do it, and witches. No one did because up until recently, it usually resulted in being kidnapped and forced into slavery. It was like stepping through a door where line jumping was like a transporter. This, I could do. But so could Trent.

Eyes closed, I felt the line's resonance, making minute changes to my aura to match it exactly. A weird titillating feeling raced through me as I tried to hold on to everything and shift Trent's aura at the same time. With an odd inward sensation, I felt my insides shrink to nothing, taking us with it. The line became my world, and I snapped a protection bubble into place, the shimmer on it the same as the line's.

All that was left was to artificially shift my aura to push us back out, and with a jerk, reality re-formed. My balance was off, and I lurched until Trent caught my arm. The red glare of the ever-after sun slammed into me, and the gritty wind lifted through my hair. "I love it here," I whispered sarcastically.

Trent was smiling, making me wonder why until he tucked a strand of hair behind my ear. "Most shifts like that would cost someone their soul," he said softly.

Uneasy, I scanned the horizon, watching the heat shimmer up from the rocks. "It still might," I said, then began to walk toward the lithesome shape Newt made dancing in the heat. As I watched, a lump of dusty rock seemed to shake itself, evolving into a tall figure in a top hat, crushed green velvet tails furling as he spun to see us. Al. Great.

"Is that . . ." Trent said as he slid down the shallow incline that was the river in reality.

"Yep." This was so not what I wanted, but we'd been spotted, and leaving would only bring him barging into my church. "Don't tell him about the wild magic following me, okay?" I whispered as Trent scrambled up the other side and extended a hand to help me up.

"Not a problem."

My pulse hammered as we closed the gap. I didn't like Trent's eagerness, nor that Newt had seen us and was energetically waving. She looked like a fourteen-year-old girl, verging on womanhood in a long nightgown that did little to hide what was underneath, her figure slight with early adolescence. Clearly not one of her better days. I'd seen Newt as a child before, and she gave me the willies. "You do know she's nuts, right?" I said as Trent hustled us forward. Al had his hands on his hips, looking nothing like Jenks, and was frowning at me.

"Yoo-hoo! Did you come to catch fireflies?" Newt called, and Trent's pace bobbled when a black film of ever-after slithered over her and her thin, childlike shape grew to the more usual, androgynous, hairless, barefoot, martial-arts-uniform-clothed Newt that I'd once found hammering holes in my back living room. "They make fine night-lights for when the world ends," she added, and then, as her eyes traveled over me, she gave herself hair, a sundress, and a big, wide-brimmed hat. "Hi, Rachel."

Crap on toast, she looked like my mother, and I dropped my eyes before she could see my shock. Trent valiantly struggled for words, pulling himself together to extend his hand to Al. "Algaliarept. Well met," he said, and Al all but bared his teeth.

"Call me Al," he said, clearly not liking that we'd found him up here with Newt. "I insist."

"Al," Trent said simply, his hand falling as he turned to Newt. "Newt. Good to see you."

Newt beamed, seemingly coy as she focused on him.

"Hello, Trenton Aloysius Kalamack," she said, and he stiffened at her seductive tone. Beside me, Al sighed. "You're very dapper out in the ever-after sun. I'd forgotten how the light hits elven hair."

She sidled up to him and I backed out of her way. "I'd advise not moving," Al said, and Trent froze.

"Ooooh, so soft, even when it's full of grit. Come home with me and I'll wash it for you."

"Ah . . ." he stammered, and Newt spun to me, her hair now looking exactly like mine, frizz and all.

"Rachel. Love. You want to trade? I have Nicholas Gregory Sparagmos about somewhere. I put him somewhere safe. I can't remember exactly, but if I put my mind to it, I'm sure I can find him."

Nick? Shaking my head emphatically, I grabbed Trent's arm and pulled him to me. "No. Thanks anyway."

"No?" she echoed, her expression falling. "Pity. I'm catching fireflies," she said, black eyes a startling contrast to her innocent oblivion as she worked the lid off the large jar now in her hand. "Firefly, firefly, glowing there in the sky," she sang, dancing away with the jar swinging in the air as a film of ever-after coated her and she was fourteen and sickly again. "Play with me and don't be shy. Bring your light that will not die. Pretty little firefly."

Trent's face was pale as he watched her dance in the red light hammering down on us. "She wasn't like that before."

Ruddy face sour, Al swung his cane in a wide circle and watched her. "It comes and goes. We tried chaperoning her, dosing her into forgetfulness, spelling her into memory . . ." He shuddered. "Nothing seems to work but Rachel."

"Me?"

Al gave me an unreadable look. "It's especially bad when she's remembered something. That's why I came up here. I don't like her mucking about with your line. Which is fine, by the way. Why are you here? With that elf?" he finished darkly.

Uneasy, I licked my lips, immediately wishing I hadn't

when acidic dust coated my tongue. "I might ask the same of you," I said, avoiding him.

"I'd forgotten how barren it is up here," Trent said, pointedly changing the subject, and Al pulled his eyes from Newt, hopping about as she tried to catch something in her Mason jar.

"Yes . . ." he drawled. "You made a fucking mess before you left us to die in it."

Trent didn't even flinch. "My ancestors, maybe. But not me." He tilted his head. "What *is* she doing?"

Huffing, Al pulled his velvet coat straight. "And yet you're still not going to do anything about it. Don't tell *me* you're innocent of the blame."

"Newt!" I called, and Trent gasped when Al moved to cuff me to be silent. Dodging it, I shifted away from him. "Newt? What did you remember?"

The image of innocence, Newt ran back to us, a cover on the top of the jar. "I caught four this morning," she said, little-girl voice excited. "They'll be calling them out again soon, and I'll be ready with jars and jars. If I catch enough, my room will be bright when the sun goes dark." Head tilting, she looked straight at the sun, unblinking and with no ill effect. "I don't like the dark," she said, her enthusiasm dimming. "If you give them a good shake, they glow even brighter. See?"

Al cleared his throat as Newt energetically shook the jar and held it up, proud of something none of us could see.

"Delightful, delightful," Al drawled. "Newt, love, can I have them? Pretty please?"

Her expression darkened suspiciously until he smiled his best and she coyly conceded. "You may," she said as he took it, and another, identical jar appeared in her hands. "I can get more." And off she skipped, making me shiver at the aspect of a sickly girl in hospital pajamas dancing in the desert.

Frowning, Al's eyes narrowed. "Why are you here?" he asked Trent point-blank.

Oh God. I wanted to know that, too. "He's here so I'm

not alone," I said before Trent could open his mouth. Behind him, Newt had caught something, setting her jar beside a rock before another appeared in her hand and she started jumping again.

"You don't trust me," Al said, and my eyes jerked to his.

"I trust you, but he doesn't."

Trent's hands were behind his back, the windblown grit turning his hair red. "There've been some new developments with that overactive wave. We came out to look at Rachel's line, knowing if she went to you, your answer would be that it was fine."

"That's because it is," Al growled, his mood worsening.

"And that's why both you and Newt are up here?" Trent asked, squinting at Al as the demon glared at him over his round blue glasses. Good grief. They were like little boys.

"Al," I said before it got any worse. "My line is leaking wild magic."

"It is not—" Al's words cut off, and he turned to Newt cavorting in the dust. "No," he breathed, but it sounded more like wishful thinking at this point.

Trent eased closer to me, and Al stiffened. "I think it's intentional," Trent said. "Someone is pulling wild magic from her line, either because it's the newest or perhaps because she lives in reality and it's easier to pull it from her line than another."

"Is that so," Al said snidely.

Undeterred, Trent nodded. "The overstimulation of witch magic is about what I'd expect, tracking through Cincinnati and the Hollows until the energy is spent. I'm guessing they average a life span of an hour or so before dying out."

He and Trent were inches apart, and Al took a deep breath, hesitating when he noticed Trent's scent and pulled back. "Then you'd be wrong," Al said, and Trent frowned. "Wild magic has a half-life of a decade. If it was wild magic, it would circle the globe before dying out, wreaking havoc the entire time. Therefore, it's not wild magic." Seemingly not caring, Al took a tin of Brimstone from a tiny pocket, delicately sniffing a pinch. "Not everything is about you, itchy witch."

"But they hardly get past the river!" I protested, sure it was.

"Which fits with my idea that this is intentional." Trent took my hands persuasively, and Al's brow wrinkled. "Someone is creating the waves and then catching them, either to contain the disastrous effects in Cincinnati, or they are simply collecting the energy for another reason. We just have to find out who's doing it, and why."

Not liking Al's expression, I ran a hand over my hair to find it was a snarly mess. The light of discovery was in Trent's eyes, and something in me quivered. "If it's intentional, then who's helping them with the magic?" I asked pointedly, and we turned to Al.

"You think it's one of us?" he said, affronted, then grinned to show his flat, blocky teeth. "What a marvelous idea. Alas, no, it's not. No demon alive would stoop to using wild magic, even to kill vampires. Why would we kill them? We made them."

"Kill them?" I questioned. "No, they're just sleeping."

Still smiling, Al leaned in until I could smell the Brimstone on his breath. "If they don't wake up soon to feed, they will die from a lack of aura. The undead are starving, Rachel."

My God, he was right, and my focus blurred as I thought of Ivy.

"Imagine!" Al said fervently, cane swinging jauntily. "An entire city without master vampires. How intoxicatingly chaotic. It's almost enough to make me wish I *had* thought of it."

"We'll never survive it," Trent said softly.

"HAPA?" I guessed, knowing the Humans Against Paranormals Association dabbled in demon magic, so why not wild. "The men-who-don't-belong?"

"It is not wild magic," Al said, but his tone lacked conviction.

"Then what is it?" I said, tired of his attitude; just then

Newt called to me as she skipped her way to us, her slippered feet sending up little puffs of dust in the hot sun.

"Rachel!" Mason jar tucked under her arm, Newt hopped a hopscotch pattern. "Do you want to put your pajamas on and have a sleepover with me?" She came to a breathless halt, the hem of her nightgown coated with ever-after dust. "Al." She gave Al a shove, and the demon jerked, startled. "Tell the girl she can have a sleepover. You work her too hard. Look at the dark circles under her eyes."

"It's not because I work her," he grumbled. "The witch can't seem to find her way to my kitchen except when she's in trouble. And she can't have a sleepover!" he added when Newt began tugging on my sleeve, her black eyes glinting. "Leave off, you bitch!" he shouted, and Newt dropped back, looking hurt.

"At least this time, it's only one world," Newt said, and I wondered if her sudden burst of clarity would last. "I don't know if she can do it. She looks tired already, and it's only going to get worse." Newt's eyes widened. "Oh, look!" she exclaimed, looking across the dry river to the remains of Loveland Castle. "They're starting to come out again!"

Trent jerked as Newt ran off, startled by her cry of delight.

"What the mother pus bucket is wrong with her!" Al said, peeved as she ran across the broken earth. She was headed for the dry riverbed, and she jumped right over it, red-stained white nightgown streaming out behind her. Sighing, Al looked at the jar he'd gotten from her. Handing it to Trent, he began trudging after her. Not even glancing at it, Trent passed it to me, and after a moment, I jogged to catch up, jar pressed to my side.

"Newt, love!" Al was calling. "Tell me about your fireflies!"

"That demon is certifiable," Trent said, voice low as we lagged behind. "How can they let her wander around like this?"

Al was waiting for us at the shallow ditch, and he took

the jar as I slid down, then I caught it as he tossed it to me. "Because she might just be the most sane demon here," he said when Trent slid down after me. "I haven't been able to decide if stress pushes her over the edge, or if when she starts digging into her past, she simply loses her way, but usually it's because she's remembered something important."

I started up the other side, startled when Newt's face, somehow both sickly and lively, peered over the edge at me. "Rachel!" she crowed, a thin white hand extended to help me up. "I think they like you!" She pulled back before I could take her hand, and I scrambled up, jar tucked under an arm.

"Oh, so pretty!" Newt was saying as she danced, her bare feet among the stones and her hands in the air as she caught nothing. "Look at them light up!"

"Newt . . ." I started, then my head snapped up as the prickling of wild magic flowed over me. Goose bumps rose, and I set the jar down to help Trent. "Get up here!" I hissed, then gasped at the feeling of sexual titillation that poured through me as his hand smacked into mine. "Holy crap," I breathed.

"Rachel?"

I yanked him up, sitting down where I was as his hand left mine and he stood at the edge of the gully. "Can you feel that?" I squeaked, waves of sparkles cascading through me. It was wild magic, stronger and more unfocused than I'd ever felt before. It was easier to bear if Trent wasn't touching me, but disconcerted, I held that glass jar to me and just sat there, wishing it would both stop and never end.

"That's . . . what is that?" Trent said as he watched Newt dance in delight, shivering.

"Feel what?" Al snarled as he stood beside Trent. "I don't feel anything."

"Wild magic," I said, still sitting as the sensation began to ease. "It's the wave. It's happening." Alarmed, I looked at Newt. "Newt!" I called. "Don't do any magic!"

Spinning and dancing, Newt laughed, the sound pulling all expression from Al's face. "Look at them!" she sang, catching nothing. "They're swarming! Hurry! We need them for when the sky falls!"

"Wild magic?" Al whispered in a sudden horror, and I yelped when he yanked me to my feet. "You little bitch!" he shouted, shaking me so hard I lost my hold on the jar and it fell, breaking. "I told you to leave the wild magic alone!"

"You're hurting me!" I shouted, and Newt turned, her dancing stilling to a cold silence.

"He is an elf!" Al raged, his grip becoming even tighter.

"I haven't done anything!" I protested. "Al. Let me go!" I couldn't do magic. Not with the wave still over us.

"Let her go! You're hurting her," Trent said, and the demon's grip tightened, his eyes almost black in the sun.

"And you're going to make me?" Al said, each word drifting into existence with the sound of falling dust.

Grim faced, Trent stood before us, the hair falling into his eyes as sparkles seemed to dance between his fingers. Al shoved me from him, and I lurched to keep my feet. The demon was hunched like a bear, his feet easing deeper into the ruined earth. *Don't do this,* I begged them silently as I backed up. *Please don't do this.*

"Right now, I probably could," Trent said.

"I'd like to see you try," Al taunted.

"Stop it!" I shouted as Trent made a fist. I could feel the wild magic streaming into him. Al took an eager breath, and I dove for Trent, plowing into him and knocking him down. The red earth slammed into us. My shoulder twinged, and I flung a hand out. "Rhombus!" I screamed, cowering as Al's magic slammed into the barrier.

My heart thudded. Beside me, Trent rolled to a crouch. He was pissed.

"I will not be bullied," Trent snapped as he pushed me into my circle and the barrier fell, tingles of magic exploding into cramps until the force ran back to the line. And then he was gone as Al physically grabbed him, yanking him up and away.

"Stop it! Both of you!" I shouted as I rose. They were

grappling, waves of energy sparkling in the ever-after sun. He wouldn't be bullied. Damn it, I was the one who taught him to stand up to bullies, ages ago at camp. And now it was going to kill him.

Trent screamed in pain, and then Al flung him away, his own cry of agony lost in the gritty wind. Magic exploded in a white-hot flash of silence between them, and I cowered, hands over my head.

An eerie stillness fell. *Ten fingers, ten toes,* I thought, lifting my head at the moan of pain.

"That is quite enough," Newt said, and I looked up to see her back to what passed for normal for her. Lips pressed, she walked through a field of open jars, hesitating to frown at the one I'd broken. "Are you okay?" she asked as she extended a hand to help me up.

I looked at it for a second, and after tightening my grip on my energy balance, I put my hand in hers, wondering if it was the first time I'd ever voluntarily touched her. I didn't think so, but she looked at her hand before hiding it in a wide sleeve when I let go.

Al was on his back, choking. Trent looked about the same. They were both breathing though, and I stifled a shiver. That last blast had come from Newt.

"Rachel, love," Newt said softly, pulling me so I couldn't see them. "Remind me why Gally is trying to kill your familiar?"

My arm hurt, and I rubbed it. "I'm not sure."

Newt looked over the jars, sad when her gaze came back to me. "Sometimes it's better to not remember."

From the dirt, Al choked out, "He's teaching her wild magic! She's already sensitized to it. Waves of it are coming out of her line. He's going to enslave us again. He needs to die. Now!" He was enraged, staring at the sun as if it was all he could do to speak. Slowly he turned himself over, grunting from the effort. "Oh God," he moaned, his words making puffs in the dust. "I'm going to die."

Newt blinked her black eyes at him. "Not today" was

all she said as she looked at Trent, silent but unmoving. I jumped when she put an arm over my shoulder and turned our backs on them. "Rachel, dear, we need to talk."

I looked over my shoulder at Trent. "But . . ."

Newt waved a hand, and I froze, terrified, when both Al and Trent vanished. "Just us girls."

"Newt! Where are they!" I cried, and the crazy demon sniffed.

"Somewhere safe."

Eyes wide, I stared at her. "Tell me before you forget?"

Again, the demon seemed annoyed at herself, and she tapped the butt of her staff into the dirt as she thought that over. "Perhaps you're right," she muttered, and I breathed a sigh of relief when they popped back into existence. Al was white as he sat on the dry earth, and Trent's eyes were wide, but at least they could move now.

"Behave yourselves!" Newt said, clearly ticked. Nose wrinkling, she looked over the rain-starved ground. "I feel wild magic. Who pulled this? You?"

She was talking to Trent, who was currently wedging a rock out from under himself. "No," he croaked, hand to his throat. "But I intend to find out who did."

"He lies!" Al raged, then slumped back when Newt glared. "He's going to seduce her and enslave her, and us with her!" he added.

"Nonsense." Newt gazed at Trent, the elf still preoccupied with trying to breathe. "You're not going to have sex with Rachel, are you?"

Trent's head came up, and I could do nothing when his eyes met mine. "Ah, what does that have to do with it?" he said.

Newt spun fast enough to make me jump. "There, see?" she said triumphantly to Al, her psyche beginning to slide back toward instability. "He doesn't know the only way to enslave her is with sex. Now sit there and have your demon-to-elf chat. We'll be right back. Behave, or I'll put you back somewhere safe until we're done."

Numb, I stayed pliant when she linked her arm in mine and began picking her way through the rubble to one of the larger slumps of rocks.

"Rachel, love," she murmured as she caught sight of the glass jars. "What on earth are you and Al doing up here with all these jars?"

I gave her a sidelong glance. "Collecting fireflies for when the sun turns black. Your words, not mine."

Her pace bobbled, and then she renewed it with a firm determination. "Would you care for some tea?"

The idea of eating anything out here in the baking sun and gritty wind was repellent, but I nodded.

"I'd suggest something with a lot of rosehips," she said, grimacing as she elegantly sat on the wire-rim chair that suddenly appeared. "It masks the taste of grit." A matching chair misted into existence, and then a white cloth-covered table and sunshade. The billowing shade was a relief, and I sat, shifting my chair so I could see Al and Trent, both of them staring at me in anger as they got to their feet and brushed the ever-after dirt from them. If the only common ground they could find was anger at me, then so be it.

"Now," Newt said primly, reminding me of Ceri as she poured out the tea into red-dusted cups. *Tea in the Sahara.* "It's high time we talk about the birds and bees. Lovey, have you had sex with Trenton Aloysius Kalamack?"

Startled, I reached for the cup. "No."

Newt eyed me, making no move to her cup. "You have had that elf as your familiar for over a year, and he's not put the sparkle in your scrying mirror even once?"

Embarrassed, I took a sip, then spit it back in the cup. "I didn't even like him until recently."

"Like?" Newt waved a hand in the air, and hair spun down from her head in a wave. "When does like ever enter into good sex?"

"Why does everyone assume I'm having sex with him?" I said, exasperated.

"Because he's an elf, love, and elves are very good at

it." Newt eyed Al and Trent across the distance, her brow creasing when Al shoved Trent, pinning him to a rock as he whispered threats into his ear. "Why do you think Al spent all that time with that elf? Ceri, wasn't it? It wasn't because he loved her. Oh, wait a moment, it was . . ." Her eyes unfocused, then cleared. "The tea is rancid. Have a cookie."

I looked at the plate of cookies that shimmered into existence, lips parting when I realized they were still soft—almost warm—and that I could smell a faint hint of chocolate under the heavy burnt-amber stench.

Newt took a cookie, waving it about as she talked. "It's not the sex, it's the magic. You've tasted it. I can see it in you. I pray that you've not drunk so deep you're caught."

Alarmed, I looked across the broken earth to Trent, standing defiantly under Al's harangue.

"Elven magic is a sweet, sweet addiction." Newt said the words softly, hardly breathing, watching Trent with a scary longing. "You think it has no cost because there's no smut, but *she* always wants payment." Her black eyes came to me. "Their Goddess is a trickster. You align yourself with her, you may as well end your life now. It will be nothing but misery and betrayal upon betrayal until the bitter end, where she laughs and collects your soul to make new eyes for herself."

I thought of my dream of a thousand purple eyes with wings. Slowly I took a bite of the cookie, wondering where she'd gotten them. "You, ah, know about the Goddess?"

"Of course I do. I was there when we killed her."

Leaning forward, I brushed crumbs from myself. "Then she's real?"

"Oh, she's real. The only reason we beat the elves off was because we convinced them she wasn't." She pointed her cookie at me. "An elf who doesn't believe in his magic can be bested. One who believes will always survive. That's why Al is upset that wild magic is being pulled from your ley line. Coupled with belief, it's stronger than demon magic, though none would admit it."

I thought about that as she put the cookie in her mouth and bit down. She cringed, as if having not wanted to do that, and then she froze, actually tasting it. Fingers trembling, she ate another bite. "This is a good cookie," she whispered.

"Then my line is leaking wild magic," I said, looking at it.

"No." Blinking fast, she reverently took another bite. "Someone is pulling wild magic from between the spaces, and your line is small and remote. Easy to manipulate. What are you going to do about it?"

I thought about the world she lived in where a chocolate chip cookie was grounds for reverent tears. This had to end. "Find out who and why and tell them to stop."

"Good." She pushed the plate at me. "Have another cookie."

"You have them," I said, and she smiled at me.

Her black eyes lost their focus as she gazed out over the broken ever-after, the wind kicking up dirt devils from under the rocks. "You know why Al kept Ceri for so long? Taught her everything he knew?" she said as she watched Trent and Al.

"She was a showcase for his talents as a maker of fine familiars," I said, knowing it was false even if it was what he'd once told me.

"He was trying to find a way to give her children," she said, lost in a memory. "He'd never admit it now. Kill you for even mentioning it. He was delirious when he told me, dying from that aura burn he got from Ku'Sox. The fool looked for the better part of a thousand years through magic and science, knowing it might be the only way that he could have her as more than a slave. I suspect if he had succeeded, he would have fought us all to the grave rather than let her go, but when he failed, he simply . . . walked away." Newt fixed her black, unblinking focus to me, and my breath caught at the sudden glint of lucidity. "It took that long for his hope to die. We are a stubborn people."

Uneasy, I looked away. I'd loved Kisten knowing that

there'd never be children between us. It hadn't seemed to matter, but I suppose when your species was barren, children would carry a lot of weight. Enough to end a war, perhaps.

"Elves are dangerous, Rachel," Newt said, and I pulled my thoughts from Kisten's smile. "Wickedly clever. Powerful. Alluring. And in a moment of weakness, trust comes ill to the unwary. When they practice, their magic seeps into every corner of their soul, able to lift you up beyond what you ever imagined. Are you sure you've not had sex with your elf and just forgotten?"

Unhappy, I shook my head. "He's going to be married by the year's end." *And then, it wouldn't matter.*

"To you?" she said, shocking me.

"No, another elf."

Newt settled back, dragging the plate of cookies closer to her. "More elves. I don't understand this. You free us from Ku'Sox only to enslave us again."

I shook my head, wondering what it might have been like to have Trent between my sheets, his hands on my skin, the feel of his muscles under my fingers. Sighing, I shook the image from me, hoping Newt couldn't see the goose bumps. "He knows how to free you from the curse."

"And yet he won't," she said, voice soft. "It doesn't matter. I don't think we could leave our prison now even if we tore the walls from space itself. We're like fireflies in a jar." Head tilted, she picked up a nearby jar, eyeing it. "What are you doing with all these jars, anyway?"

Concerned, I looked at Trent and Al, and she tapped the table. "I'm watching them," she said sharply. "What are you doing with the jars?"

Feeling pity, I said, "You were the one with the jars. Trying to catch fireflies."

She slumped in her chair, mood distant. "I don't remember," she breathed, handing it to me. The glass seemed to tingle in my fingers, and she pulled herself together when it left her. "I'm so glad we had this chat."

I breathed a sigh of relief tinged with worry. I'd learned everything, and nothing. "Me too," I said as I stood, jar still in hand. Somewhere between sitting down and now, she had put on a long flowing white gown that might look good next to Al in his British lord finery.

"Go collect your elf from Gally before the silly demon kills him. You're going to want the pleasure of that yourself," she said. "And, lovely, be sure to have sex with him before you do. Elves know what magic is good for."

"B-but you said . . ." I stammered, shocked when I felt the line pull through me and she vanished, leaving the sunshade and the spoiled tea to go bad. The cookies, though, she'd taken.

"This is so messed up," I whispered as I picked my way to Trent and Al, my jar of nothing tucked under an arm.

Trent took my elbow. "You don't need to worry about Nick anymore."

I thought of Newt's somewhere safe, and I jerked away. "If you ever attack Al again, I'll never speak to you," I said.

Huffing in satisfaction, Al sidled closer, his burnt-amber-scented bulk domineering.

"That goes for you too," I added, shoving him back with a finger on his chest. "Honestly, you're both an embarrassment, rolling around in the dust, trying to see who has the biggest magic wand."

Al frowned. "What did the crazy mother pus bucket say?"

I looked out over the baking dirt, trying to see it green and moist. *That you loved Ceri so much you made a slave of her for a thousand years because that was the only way you could have her. That the Goddess was real and you all killed her. Not to have sex with Trent.* "That someone is pulling wild magic out of the lines and to find out who and stop them," I said, and Al growled something almost unheard.

"I'll find out who," Trent said grimly. "And we will stop them, Rachel."

I turned my back on the ruined earth and the ugly nothing

that the elves and demons had made of the ever-after. That we would find them and stop them was a foregone conclusion. What had me concerned was that Newt, dancing about catching fireflies, could feel the wild magic as well as I.

I wasn't the only demon sensitized to wild magic. Newt was too.

Ten

Jenks's kids laughing in the garden was like audible sunshine, keeping me awake as I lay on my bed and stared at my shadowed ceiling. The heavy covers had been kicked off hours ago to leave me chilly under just the sheet, my arms crossed behind my head and my foot moving slowly back and forth to make a moving bump that Rex occasionally patted. It was around four in the morning, but slumber had been elusive and I was beginning to think I might see the sunrise before I dropped off.

"Just go to sleep," I moaned, and the cat purred.

My mind wouldn't shut off, circling around and around what had happened in the ever-after. I was sure everything would make sense if I looked at it from the right perspective, but it never moved toward understanding: Newt with her jars of nothing, Nick dead in Newt's hidey-hole, the feel of wild magic prickling over my skin intensifying as I took Trent's hand, Al hurting me in his outrage that Trent was going to enslave them through my ignorance, Al spending a thousand years trying to find a way for elves and demons to have kids, Newt being sensitized to wild magic—the same wild magic that had set Al off.

Demons didn't practice wild magic, but clearly it was a cultural bias, not a physical inability. I thought it telling that

Newt believed in the Goddess when much of the elven population didn't. Was she insane, or just aware of more than the rest of us?

Did Trent believe? I wondered. He was going to sacrifice two goats to her. Was it rote or belief? Did it matter to the Goddess if he believed as long as the goats were dead? Did I believe?

I recalled the scintillating feel of wild magic prickling over my skin like the chime of a bell—and then last spring when a presence had acknowledged me and helped me invoke those elven slave rings. Cold, I pulled the covers up to my chin. *And how did sex figure into it?* My focus blurred as I pulled the grit-coated memory of Trent to me, imagining how he had looked with the ever-after dust running off him in the shower, the sigh of relief he must have made, the slowly dissipating red puddle under him and the soap bubbles among his toes, the glisten of water on his clean skin, both slippery and firm as he shook his head and the drops went flying. His hair would still look light under the water. I'd seen it once. But his eyes would be a brighter green.

"Oh God, stop it, Rachel," I moaned, rolling over and burying my head under the pillow. Just how long had it been since I'd been with anyone? Much less someone I loved?

But I don't love Trent.

My breath grew stale, and in a sudden flurry of motion, I flung the covers off and sat up. Rex dropped down, going to the door with a hopeful chirp of an early breakfast. The oak floor was cold on my toes, and I felt ill from lack of sleep. Pushing my hair back, I looked at my clock blinking a slow four A.M. The sun rose at about ten after five this time of year, and giving up, I reached for my robe, angry almost as I stuffed my arms in the blue terry cloth sleeves and tied it closed around me. Maybe warm milk would help.

The church was silent apart from the pixies outside, and the air was cold on my bare legs as I padded to the kitchen. Ivy and Nina were sleeping, and the mental image of them spooned together, their hair mingling as they shared the same pillow, drifted through me. I smiled and left the kitchen light off. Happiness was happiness wherever you found it.

Warm milk alone wasn't going to do it, and I quietly got out the hot chocolate mix. The coming dawn let in enough light to see by, and I found things by memory, fingers moving sure in the dim light as Rex twined about my feet and got in my way. Newt's empty jar sat on the sill next to Al's chrysalis and Trent's pinkie ring. I knew it was empty, but it gave me the creeps—the early light catching the edges of the glass and making them glow.

My phone was in my bag, and I eyed it as I got out the sugar. If the pixies were up, Trent would be too. Squinting in the light from the fridge, I smiled as Jenks came in, probably drawn by the activity. "Morning, Jenks," I whispered as I filled a mug with milk and added the cocoa.

"Can't sleep?" he said as he perched on the roll of paper towels.

A bright silver dust spilled from him. Morning and evening were truly his time. Feeling fuzzy, I shook my head and looked out the small kitchen window. Most of the red glow in the clouds was from the fires in Cincinnati. Sirens, too, had been a faint, almost nonstop background. Edden hadn't asked me to come in, and for that I was thankful. Today he'd probably be screaming for help as he tried to cope with rising vampire violence.

"Too much going on," I said as I put the mug in the nuker and hit go. I leaned back against the counter while the microwave spun, the square of light diffusing into nothing. Trent had once made me hot chocolate. *Stop it, Rachel.*

The seconds on the microwave counted down, and not wanting to wake up Ivy and Nina, I cut it short. Jenks was a quiet hum of accompaniment as I took the hot chocolate out onto the back porch. The door would thump if I closed it, so I left it open, carefully easing the screen door shut before padding over the slightly damp wood and sitting on the top step, my knees almost to my chin. God, I was tired, but sleep wouldn't come.

Mug held to warm my fingers, I looked over the garden to the glow of Cincinnati. The news last night had been awful, even if there were fewer misfires to focus on. Magic was being voluntarily curtailed above and beyond reason, creating almost more problems than the misfires. A bright spot was that the I.S. was beginning to function on a reduced level to try to contain the more aggressive living vampires. Nonvampire agents were teaming up with the FIB street force out of frustration as their living vampire managers became more and more circular in their thinking, unable to make a decision. It was scary how dependent they were on the undead.

The forensic and investigative teams of both factions were working together the best, giving weight to my theory that magic and technology were the languages of common sense. Still, there were more than a handful of ignorant good old boys and girls on both sides of the fence resisting. Edden was in his personal heaven and hell as he got what he'd been working toward the last three years. There was almost as much friction between the new interspecies partnerships as there was between unruly citizens and the authorities. There was talk of putting Cincinnati and the Hollows under quarantine in the fear that whatever was keeping the undead asleep might spread. We were truly on our own while the world watched.

My toes were cold, and I hid my left foot under my right. The chocolate was beginning to scum up, and I blew it to the far side of the mug before I took a sip. It was quiet, and neither Jenks nor I said anything as we listened to Cincinnati slowly shift from fear and sirens to an exhausted quiet as the day approached.

Jenks hummed a warning, but I felt Bis long before he dropped from the steeple, landing with an almost unheard thump. I turned, smiling at the serious adolescent as he shifted his batlike wings and blinked sleepily. "Kind of pushing it, aren't you?" I asked him, seeing as he had a hard time staying awake when the sun was up.

He glanced at the steeple. "I got about an hour yet. Put me in the belfry if I zonk out, will you?" he said, the vowels grinding together like rocks. "We had six patrols drive by, but most everyone is minding their own turf."

Especially when the world's only day-walking demon lives on your street, I thought sourly. "We'll get it figured out," I said, wondering how I was going to get through today on the scant sleep I'd managed. Trent wanted me to come out tonight around six to talk to Bancroft. That might be difficult with the curfew Edden had going, but perhaps if I got a note or something from him I could get through the roadblocks.

Or I could call Trent and tell him I can't come. I didn't like that he'd adroitly sidestepped telling me what he and Al had discussed. But then again, I hadn't offered to tell him about Newt's and my conversation, either.

"You gonna call him?" Jenks said, somehow knowing where my thoughts were. "He's probably awake."

Bis looked behind me into the church, and the soft sound of footsteps intruded. "Everyone is awake," I said as I turned to Ivy looking rumpled and sexy in her black silk top and pajama bottoms. Expression listless, she pushed the screen door open and shuffled out, squinting disparagingly at the horizon. She looked half dead, and I slid over a few feet to make room for her. Still not having said a word, she sank down, her feet on the step below mine. *She's wearing nail polish?* Bis shifted his wings, and we all settled in again. Seeing she needed it more than me, I handed her my hot chocolate.

"Thanks," she rasped, her voice uncharacteristically rough.

"Tink's little pink rosebuds, Ivy. You look like hell," Jenks said, and she gave him a black-eyed stare over the mug. The spicy, nose-prickling scent of vampire incense became stronger, and Bis wrinkled his face. I was starting to be able to pick out Nina's characteristic scent off her. It was lighter, almost flowery compared to Ivy's darker shadow scent, but lacing it was a thread of blackness—Felix.

"Nina okay?" I asked, thinking it was odd we were all out here on the steps while Cincinnati shook off the night.

A smile made Ivy look almost alive. "She's sleeping like—ah, a rock," she said. "Thank you. For caring, I mean," she added, unable to look at me.

"Nina is a good person," I said. Jenks darted off, unable to handle the emotional, flowery crap, as he put it, and I gave her a sideways hug. "She's good for you, and you're good for her. If they cancel the fireworks, you want to have a cookout when it's all over?" *When was it ever over?*

Ivy took another sip. "Or sleep," she said, focus distant. "I could use some sleep."

"Me too," Bis said. "I woke up yesterday when a fire truck went by. That never bothers me."

"Maybe you're just getting older," I said, and he smiled, his black teeth catching the light. Giving me a nod, he took to the air, and my hair flew as he went back to the steeple to talk to Jenks. A lonely hoot of a train pulled my attention back to Cincinnati, and I wondered if they would continue to stop if we were put under quarantine. Though the waves were still occurring with no discernible pattern, the misfires were under control. I'd noticed an odd, unexpected sense of superiority from humans that their science was holding up in the face of no-magic.

The brum of a motorcycle roaring to life echoed in the quiet street behind us, and I sighed again. So much for my idea of catching a few more winks.

Ivy straightened, her expression shifting from alarm to fear when Jenks made a wide arcing path around the garden, arrowing to us. "That was Nina's bike," Ivy said, pale.

"Someone is stealing it?" I said in disbelief, and Ivy stood, the mug of hot chocolate spilling down the steps.

"Nina!" she cried, racing inside.

"Nina is gone!" Jenks shouted, and I froze at Ivy's cry of heartache. It iced through me as I stood on my back porch, falling to the pit of my soul and tightening into a black knot.

I bolted inside. "Ivy!" I called, running through the back

living room and into the hallway. Their bedroom door was open, and I came to a sudden, breathless halt when Ivy almost ran into me. Her eyes were black, and fear had made her beautiful. A pixy girl hovered over her, tears slipping like sun from her eyes as she wrung her dress and apologized in high-pitched, fast words. "Where's Nina?"

Ivy shoved past me on the way to the kitchen. Her katana was in her hand. Jenks and I followed her as the pixy who'd been on watch wailed, a black dust slipping from her. "Gone," Ivy said as she pulled out a drawer for her set of throwing knives. "He took her. He waited until I left, and then he walked her right out of the church."

Felix? Her voice had no inflection and her movement was vampiric fast as she jerked to a stop, stymied from tucking her knives away when she realized she was in silk pajamas, not leather pants.

Ivy turned, expression riven with grief. "He must have been there all the time, waiting for me to leave."

"I'm so sorry!" the pixy girl wailed. "She looked okay. She talked to me and looked okay. She said she was going to get some ice cream to surprise you."

Ivy stood shaking, one hand full of knives, the other holding her katana, her hair falling to hide her eyes. "I can't let him destroy her. Not now."

"She said it was a surprise!" the pixy cried, and Jenks hovered helplessly.

"It's okay," I said to the little pixy. "Go back to the lines." But she didn't, clearly upset. I gave Jenks a pleading look, and he darted down to take the crying girl outside.

"He's going to kill her," Ivy said in the new quiet. "I can't lose her, Rachel. Not to that madness!"

Her head came up, and my resolve strengthened. "Give me five minutes to get dressed."

"She could be dead in five minutes!" Eyes black, she ran for the hallway.

I stumbled out of her way. Fear hit me hard, and my heart gave a pound as I heard her throwing on clothes, her breath coming in quick, almost sobbing pants. *Felix was awake?* Ivy didn't have a chance.

"Ivy."

I found her in the hallway, katana in one hand, stakes in the other, the knives now tucked away.

"This is a vampire issue," she said, then turned her back on me and walked steadily to her death.

"Do something!" Jenks shouted from the ceiling, and I ran at her.

Ivy gasped as I tackled her, and we slid into the sanctuary. "You are *not* going without *me*!" I shouted, and then the world spun as she shoved me off her.

"I can't leave her to that!" she screamed, pinning me to the oak floor, straddling me with her sheathed blade under my chin and her hair mingling with mine. "Rachel, I love her!"

The hard leather was cold against me, and her hand on my shoulder warm. "Ivy," I said softly, tears blurring my vision. "Look at me. He didn't call her to him to kill her. He wants her alive. He needs Nina alive in order to see the sun."

Ivy's face twisted in fear, and the scent of vampire incense poured over me, making my neck tingle. I was losing her.

"Ivy!" I called, and her gaze came back to mine. "He won't kill her unless by mistake. We have some time. We can get her back. Give me a chance to get dressed and grab my charms so I can come with you. You're not alone. We'll do this together."

Fear showed in her eyes, and she took a heaving breath, the blade beginning to shake against me. Jenks's dust glowed in her hair, and for some dumb reason, I felt more love— more loved, maybe—than I ever had before.

"He probably took her to Cormel's," I said to give her something to focus on so she could find herself. "That's where Felix has been staying. You have to figure out how we are going to get in. That's what you do."

Her hand shook, and with a thump, the sword hit the floor and slid four feet. My breath came in a gasp as she spun away off me. Shaking, I sat up. She was huddled on the floor, her knees to her chin as she held herself together and cried great gasping sobs of heartache and frustration. "How can I save her?" she moaned. "How? It's like heaven in his arms. Hell in his mind . . ."

I glanced up at Jenks, then pretty much crawled over to her, pulling her to me so she didn't have to cry alone. She was real and solid, her fear and grief shaking in her. The world had shifted. I didn't need her anymore. She needed me, and I wouldn't fail her.

"We will get her back," I said, my arms holding her against the tremors, my words a breath in her hair as she shook. "I promise."

Eleven

Phone to my ear, I sat in the passenger seat of Ivy's mom's big blue Buick and listened to the background FIB office chatter as Rose, Edden's secretary, looked for Edden. I hadn't had any luck getting ahold of David, his voice mail full and his cell going unanswered. It wasn't unusual for him to let it ring, especially when working, but I didn't like that the last time I'd talked to him, he'd been investigating the Free Vampires.

We were parked outside of Cormel's, Ivy fiddling with her scarf as she stared at the unassuming two-story tavern turned residence, filling the car with the intoxicating scent of frustrated vampire. As we waited for Jenks to return from his recon, the memory of our trip out west bubbled up from the recesses, pulled into existence by the faint scent of elf from the back. The two aromas were combining to make my libido run a tingling path from my neck to my groin and back again.

Vampire pheromones and curiosity once drew me into a possible lifelong path with Ivy, but we were truly better apart. She needed to be needed, and I couldn't be that person anymore. I was too much a demon, and not enough witch.

A huge Free Vampire glyph had been spray-painted on the twin oak doors, making me wonder if it was coincidence or if the cult had fixed on Felix as something special, seeing as he was awake and no other undead vampire was. The sun would be up soon, and a bright glint hazed the pristinely clean windows on the upper floor. If he was still here, Felix would be trapped in the more elaborate underground apartments, making him more aggressive in his madness. I wasn't about to ask Ivy to wait for reinforcements, though. I agreed that the longer Nina was there, the harder it would be to not only pull her out but separate their minds.

I stiffened when the chatter on the line turned into a woman's tired voice. "I'm sorry," Rose said, clearly distracted. "Captain Edden is in a meeting. Can I take a message?"

A message? I thought, then I exhaled, trying to not get mad. Ivy was tense enough. "Sure. Tell him that Rachel, Ivy, and Jenks are at Cormel's rescuing Nina from Felix. Free Vampires might be involved, and any help the FIB could provide would be appreciated," I said sarcastically. "But I realize you're a little busy this morning. What with your meetings and all. I'm turning my phone off, but I'll check my *messages* when we're done. Bye-bye now." Not waiting for a confirmation, I hung up.

Ticked, I hit the dash, then winced when I noticed Ivy's eyes had dilated at my anger. "Sorry." I needed David and the muscle he commanded. Why didn't he answer his damn phone!

Ivy's jaw tightened. "They must have caught Jenks. Let's go."

She reached for the door handle, and I took her arm, stopping her. Her eyes fixed on mine, and I let go, stifling a shiver at the depth of fear in them. "No one caught Jenks," I said, looking over the quiet parking lot with its handful of cars and a sad attempt at landscaping between us and the twin-door front. No one had bothered to take down the Pizza Piscary's sign, and it looked old and tired. "But we can get out of the car. The cameras are down."

Get out. It was a good idea. Between her frustration, my fear, and a car smelling like an aphrodisiac mix of both of us, it was a wonder she hadn't tried to jump my jugular. And the cameras *were* down. Jenks had made us wait a block over while he spent five minutes clearing our way. Anyone watching the video feeds might notice that the sun never got any closer to rising, but I doubted it.

We reached for our doors simultaneously, not worried about anyone actually looking out a window. The fresh air shocked through me, clearing my head. Ivy, too, seemed to breathe easier. A siren lifted from across the Ohio River, then faded, pulling my attention to Cincinnati and the brightening sky. Ivy got her katana out from the backseat, leaving the sheath on as she made a few practice moves to loosen up and get rid of some adrenaline. Me, I leaned against the car and tried calling David again to no avail, deciding to mute it instead of turning it off. If worse came to worst, I could be found with the built-in GPS—providing we weren't too deep.

"There he is," Ivy said in relief, and I dropped the phone into my pocket and leaned into the car to get my shoulder bag. Jenks was a silver trace of dust when I levered myself back out, and I tugged my red jacket down and made sure the cuffs of my jeans weren't rolled up.

"I think I know why David isn't answering your calls," the pixy said as he came to a hovering, white-faced halt before us, and my heart dropped. "I didn't see Nina," he added quickly when Ivy paled. "Or David. But the ground floor where the restaurant used to be looks like a blood orgy just finished and your pack was the main entertainment, Rache."

Shit.

Weres couldn't be turned, but they could be bound. Anger mixed with fear, the icy slurry setting my heart pounding as I strode for the front door. Anger won, and I pulled my splat gun with a cold certainty I'd use deadly force if needed. David was my rock, the one person in my life who could walk into any situation and find justice with a no-holds-barred force that held no apology, no thought to the future. Heaven help the person who hurt him.

"And you think you're a bad alpha," Jenks said, easily pacing me.

"Rachel, wait up!" Ivy all but hissed, jogging until she caught up. With a shake, she shook the sheath from the katana.

"Go right in," Jenks said as we got closer, the old oak door silent and unmanned. "No one is conscious."

Asking Ivy to wait, I pulled my phone back out and hit 911. I already knew which button to hit to go to their answering machine, and as soon as I got the beep, I rushed to say, "This is Rachel Morgan. Runner number 2000106WR48. I'm at Pizza Piscary's. It's sunrise. There are multiple unconscious vampires and Weres needing medical assistance. Use caution as a master vampire may be awake and violent. And try not to shoot us, okay? It's me, Ivy Tamwood, and Jenks Pixy."

I ended the call, and Ivy moved. Grimacing, she yanked one side of the big oak doors open and lurched in. I almost ran into her when she stopped dead in her tracks.

The predawn light didn't go very far, and I stared, hand over my nose as I tried to figure out what my still-adjusting eyes were seeing. "Holy crap," I whispered, looking over the loungelike arrangement of couches and tables set between the still-used bar and the stone fireplace. Slack-faced people were strewn everywhere, all of them smeared in blood. Some were in skimpy evening wear, others in utilitarian uniforms. It was a free-for-all, everyone-welcome-no-one-leaves blood orgy. As Jenks had said, they still breathed, but it was obvious they were stupefied with either blood loss or blood indulgence—or both.

Where is my pack?

Ivy draped her scarf over her mouth and went in. Heart pounding and looking for something to shoot, I followed. It got worse as my eyes adjusted. Blood smeared the floor, furniture, and skin, but there were no large pools of it. People I hardly recognized wearing my dandelion tattoo looked as if they might have resisted at first, Cormel's children in skimpy attire—not so much. All dripped blood. No one was tending the satiated or depleted, which was not the norm—if any of this could be considered normal. It smelled like stale alcohol and dead things by the side of the road.

"Where's David?" I whispered, and Jenks hummed back from the fireplace, his trailing sparkle the only clean thing in the room.

"He's not here," he said, expression grim. "Downstairs, maybe? That's where they would've taken Nina this close to sunrise. Everyone's aura looks okay. No one is going to die. Today."

David wouldn't voluntarily leave his people like this. I tucked my splat gun away, my anger growing. All of them had taken my hurt for me, and I didn't even know all their names. I wasn't going to let this go, and someone was going to answer for it.

White-faced, Ivy crouched beside a big man with bulging muscles. "Dan," she said, giving him a shake, and the man snorted, eyes fluttering. "Dan, wake up. Who did this?"

Please don't say Nina, I thought, knowing Jenks was thinking the same thing as he sat on the banister and sifted an unhappy blue dust.

"Ivy?" The man smiled, then winced as pain etched his expression. "Don't move me. Oh God, don't touch me. Are they gone?"

Ivy took her hand away. With overindulgence, the undead left their victims with a very low threshold to stimulation. Even the breath of their assailant could register as unbearable pleasure, and the effect lingered for a time. "Danny. Who did this?"

"That bastard Cormel has been keeping in the basement," Dan breathed. "It was the Free Vampires. They got him out. The Weres showed up, following them, and things got out of hand. He pulled us all into it. They tried to get him to go with them, but he wouldn't and they finally went away. Left us as we were." His breath came in a staggering hiccup as he tried to sit up. "My God," he said, eyes unfocused but brilliant. "I'd die for him. He's like liquid fire."

Felix was here. The Free Vampires weren't. And Nina was with Felix.

Ivy didn't move when Dan gripped her arm, and the ragged tear in his flesh began to fill with blood. "Where is he?" he begged, his legs twisted at an odd angle. "I . . ." Confused, he looked at the vampires around him as if only now remembering. "Where is he?"

Ivy knelt, her katana within reach as she moved his hand off her and he moaned in pleasure. "Shhh," she soothed, yanking a throw from a nearby couch and tucking it under his chin. "Go to sleep. Rest."

"No," he said petulantly. "I need."

She nodded, her expression soft and caring. "I know. Go to sleep."

Dan stared up at her, panting as she gently brushed the hair on his forehead, and I shuddered as he fell unconscious.

Ivy's expression was tight with a hard anger when she rose, her grip white knuckled on her katana. "It's not supposed to be like this," she whispered, eyes black.

But it often was.

I followed her into the kitchen and the small elevator just off it that led to the lower rooms. Half the industrial ovens had been removed to make space for a big, comfortable table that could seat twenty people. Vampires were homebodies, keeping their "children" close and fostering a dependence that was attractive and felt safe. But it was a lie, and the danger usually came from within the same walls. "We're taking the elevator?" I asked, though it was obvious.

Ivy hit the down button and the doors slid apart, the car having returned to the surface to rest. She strode inside, her katana in hand and her hair pulled into a ponytail as she put herself at the back of the lift. Arms crossed, she waited for me. The elevator looked awfully small.

"I'm taking the dumbwaiter," Jenks said as he saw her black-eyed, tense state.

Seeing me balk, Ivy tried to find a less aggressive pose, and with my thoughts on finding David, I got in. Jenks hovered at the closing doors, darting away as they slid shut. "What's your plan?" I said as the lift descended.

Ivy's posture tightened. "Felix dies, Nina lives. That's my plan."

Yeah, I had a similar one. "You can't kill him," I said, knowing she wouldn't like that.

"You don't understand," she almost snarled.

Angry, I made a fist and hit the stop button. "Don't you *dare* tell me I don't understand!" I whispered, getting in her face and backing her up a step. "Not three years ago I came over here looking for revenge after Piscary blood raped you. I let him live, and you will *not* kill Felix!"

Even if they've killed David? a tiny voice whispered, and I couldn't answer it.

Her clenched jaw eased, and she dropped her eyes.

"Felix is the only undead vampire awake," I said, backing off before she found her anger again. "We need to find out why and if that's the only reason they're interested in him."

Ivy's chin rose. "I'm here for Nina. I don't care about Felix or Free Vampires."

"If you kill him, Nina will spiral out of control."

Ivy lurched forward to hit the button to make the lift move. "Nina is fine," she lied through clenched teeth.

Heart pounding, I smacked the stop button again. "She is *not* fine," I said, and then pity cooled my anger. "I'm sorry," I said softly. "The only way Felix could take control of her like that is if Nina let him, which means she's been allowing him access behind your back." Head down, Ivy pulled away from me. "You said it yourself that she was doing better than you expected. Well, it's because she's been sipping the blood of the dog that bit her. She's still tied to him."

"Nina doesn't need him!" she shouted.

My shoulders slumped. Hope died hard, and the lie was easier to bear. "Two steps forward," I said softly, and Ivy's jaw tightened again. *One back,* echoed in my thoughts. I knew Ivy was thinking it too. She'd been where Nina was now, and she balanced on the edge every day.

"If you kill him, she goes with him," I said, and Ivy nodded, tears making her eyes blacker. "Probably at the wrong end of a gun. If we get her back, we can keep taking two steps forward until she can let go. She's strong. She'll make it." God, I hoped she made it.

Ivy nodded, wiping her tears as if surprised to see them. "I won't kill him."

I could almost hear her unspoken "yet." It was the acknowledgment I needed, and I pushed the button to continue. Ivy exhaled, and then the elevator dinged. My chest hurt. What the undead demanded of their children was hell. But at least she hadn't been involved in the madness upstairs. There hadn't been enough time.

"Stay behind me," Ivy whispered, ghosting out, her balance perfect and every motion one of grace as she looked first to the ceiling and then to the sides. The large room seemed empty. She beckoned me forward, her gleaming katana dipping in a show of nervous tension. I edged to the door to look out and keep the elevator from closing.

Still holding her sword, Ivy flung a chrome and white leather chair to me. I lurched to catch it and wedge it between the doors. The elevator protested and whined, then went silent. Our access to the surface was open, but no one would be coming down that way.

Eyes scanning, I slowly explored the spacious room as Ivy padded from door to door, listening. Cormel had done little to change Piscary's underground apartments: pillars, white carpet, high ceilings, fake windows with long curtains, and one of those huge vid screens that let him safely see the outside during the day. It was expansive, decorated sparsely but with taste, and my eyes went to the informal dining nook placed before the vid screen where I'd beaten Piscary into unconsciousness. Anger still lingered at what he'd done to Ivy, and the vampire was long dead, really dead. Ivy's former lover, Skimmer, had killed him. I understood Ivy's fear, her frustration. I'd loved Ivy. Still did. Letting go had been the right thing to do.

My hand went to the small of my back, and I pulled my splat gun. I reached out a sliver of awareness, touching a line. We weren't too far underground. Piscary had liked his magic.

Ivy turned from the last pair of tall oak doors. "They're not in this room," she said, but it was obvious. My brow furrowed. Dan had said Felix had refused to leave. They were down here somewhere.

As if my thoughts had drawn him, Jenks hummed out of a hallway, looking out of place among the carpet and drapes. "Are you sure Piscary didn't have a second way out of here?"

"They aren't gone," Ivy said. Vampire fast, she strode into a corridor. My heart pounded as I jogged after her, being careful to look for attack since she wasn't. "They're in the safe room," Ivy said as she stopped before a formidable door. It was old, made of wood, and had been hacked, burned, and dented in the distant past, the damage under at least two clear varnishes by all appearances. No attempt had been made to erase them. Badges of honor, perhaps, or trophies?

"Piscary's safe room?" I asked, wondering where the electronic safeguards were when Jenks dropped down and wedged his sword into the keyhole.

"It's his bedroom," she said, fidgeting as Jenks worked. "The safe room is somewhere in it. I think I know where, but I'm not sure." Her eyes met mine, black and beautiful. "He never trusted me with it. I'm surprised Felix found it."

"Got it!" Jenks sang out, the dust spilling from him turning a bright silver.

"But the undead tend to think alike." Ivy waved us to be quiet and I retreated a good eight feet back. Seeing me ready, Ivy opened the door just enough for Jenks. I listened, ears straining as Jenks flew in, inches above the floor.

"It's empty," he called, and Ivy flung the door open. "It's just a bedroom," he said, shrugging as I followed her in. "A really freaky bedroom. You want me to do another sweep?"

I shook my head. Slipping a frustrated brown dust, he

hung at the doorway to watch the hall. *Freaky* was the word, and I edged in, my feet silent on the thick rugs with patterns of faces in the flowers. It looked like an Egyptian bordello, maybe, with palms and pillars, and gauzy drapes falling from the ceiling to enclose the heavy-looking circular bed holding court in the center of the room on a raised dais. There was only one other door that I could see, and it led to a bathroom as evidenced by the tile and fixtures. A chandelier, yellow with age and almost as big as the bed, hung to the side, casting a faint light.

"I told you there's no one in . . . there," Jenks said from the doorway, his last word faltering when Ivy pointed her katana at him to shut up.

"Help me move the bed," she said, and I tucked my splat gun in my waistband.

"There's a secret room under the bed?"

Ivy had put herself at the headboard, and she nodded as I came up the wide, shallow steps. "I think so," she said, and Jenks snorted, arms over his chest as he hovered in the doorway. "I've never seen it, but I once found his room empty when I knew he hadn't left. There's either a room or a way out of here, and the bed is the only thing that could hide it."

The bed was substantial, and I tried not to think about Ivy splayed across it in a blood-induced stupor as I grabbed the frame and lifted the foot. At least, I tried. The thing weighed a ton. It didn't move even a hairsbreadth, like trying to move the fountain at Fountain Square.

Ivy gave up before I did, frowning at the ceiling and the gauzy drapes. There were cords wrapped in velvet at the four corners, and with a dark expression, she plucked one. It was suspension-bridge tight. My eyes ran from the ceiling to the bed. Were they designed to lift the bed? Someone could go down, then replace the bed and no one would be the wiser.

I looked for anything that might control them, spinning back when Ivy grunted and a sliding sound broke the stillness. She was ending a power-filled strike with her katana, the rope before her snaking up into the ceiling as if being pulled by cheetahs. The cord vanished into a hole with a snap. Faint through the walls came the heavy thump of a counterweight falling.

"That's slicker than snot on a frog," Jenks said in admiration, and Ivy slashed the others, a thin sheen of sweat showing. It was fear, not exertion.

"Again," she said as she took up her place at the headboard, and this time, the bed moved when I steadied myself and lifted. Oh God, it was still heavy, but we managed it. "There," she gasped, looking toward the bathroom, and we slid it right down the dais's wide, shallow stairs.

It thumped halfway down and stopped. *So much for stealth,* I thought, but the falling counterweights would have given us away already.

Ivy was already halfway down the hole in the floor. "Wait," I whispered, renewing my hold on the line and making a globe of light. I couldn't touch it lest I break the charm, but Ivy and Jenks could, and the pixy flew it to her. Shadows made her face harsh with fear and uncertainty as she took it. My heart thudded, and she turned back to the stairway. It was a vampire's safe room; I was scared to death. But there was no way I was going to let Ivy go down there alone, and as Jenks took a last look in the hall and followed her down, I pulled my splat gun again.

My light in Ivy's hand was a comforting glow, and our steps were silent. There was another door at the bottom of the stairs, and I looked up at the dim square of light. Too many doors. There were too many doors between us and the sun, and I strengthened my hold on the ley line.

Ivy motioned for me to stay back, but Jenks was tight to her ear when she pulled the door open. In a hum of wings, Jenks darted inside.

"I-I-Ivy-y-y!" he shouted, and with a small moan, Ivy ran inside. The stairway went dark but for the thin slice escaping past the slowly closing door. Heart pounding, I reached out and stopped it. Inside, my globe of light rolled about the floor of the small room, making weirdly shifting shadows.

"She's okay!" Jenks was shrilling as he hovered over Ivy as she frantically felt for Nina's pulse, the blood-smeared, pale woman in her black nightgown slumped out cold in a lavishly embroidered chair. "Ivy, she's okay. Pick her up and let's get out of here!"

Someone had put her down here and left. I wanted to get out before that someone came back. Slowly I retreated to the stairs, taking in the room with its fainting couch, small table, and bank of monitors. Most showed the predawn sky and peaceful streets of ten minutes ago, but two showed a slightly brighter sky with FIB vehicles and ambulances. Stretchers holding vampires and handheld IV bags of blood were being carted out. Apparently Jenks had missed a few cameras. A pile of bedding, sundry clothes, knives, and what was probably blooding toys had been shoved in a corner, and the head-size hole in the floor had an obvious function. For all its lavish furniture, the room reminded me of the room under Cincinnati where we'd found Ivy's old I.S. boss and Denon. It was a place of hiding, of last stand, and it felt like a trap.

"She's okay," Ivy said, her voice almost a sob.

"Let's go," I said, making motions to get the hell out of here.

Jenks hovered over that pile of clothes, dusting heavily as Ivy hoisted Nina over her shoulder. Blood from unknown vampires smeared the both of them, and Ivy tossed her head to get the hair from her eyes as she stood. "You going to take Cormel out of here, too?" Jenks said, stopping me cold. "We got ten minutes until sunup. They probably got light-tight bags up there."

"Cormel?" I whispered, seeing the pile of clothes in a new way.

"Ivy?" Nina murmured, and Ivy's breath came and went in a frustrated sound.

"Get her out of here," I said, my insides knotting as I shoved the bloodstained, torn clothing aside until I found the round-faced businessman who had once run the entire free world.

"You think you can carry him?" Jenks said, hovering close.

"No." Tossing blankets aside, I unearthed Cormel, the well-dressed, somewhat short vampire, pale and unresponsive. "Wait for me outside this hole." *Please don't leave me here . . .*

Jenks's wings hummed. "Go," he said to Ivy. "I'll stay with her."

I gave Cormel a smack. He wasn't a huge man, but I couldn't lift him. He made no response. Ivy still hadn't moved, and I frowned at her. "I said take her out," I said, and Ivy let Nina slip to the floor, her expression pained. "Ivy!" I cried out as she elbowed me aside and shoved her sleeve up to her elbow.

"Hitting him won't help," she said, and I gasped when she calmly picked up a knife from the pile and cut the inside of her arm where it wouldn't be as noticeable. "He's starving. Look at his pallor."

That's what Al had said, and I felt ill as she squeezed her fist and a trace of blood dripped from her elbow. Her expression was empty as she dribbled it into his mouth. Most of it ran down his chin, but then his lips opened. A tongue pushed out, becoming red, and Cormel's face bunched up in distaste.

"Cormel!" I shouted, then looked past Jenks at the monitors and the ambulances. They couldn't get down here with that chair holding the elevator doors open. *How long?* I wondered. *How long would they search?* "Cormel, wake up!"

Ivy dribbled more into him. Still unconscious, Nina mewled like a cat as she smelled the blood, and my fear redoubled. The sound penetrated Cormel's haze where the blood hadn't. A shaky hand rubbed his mouth, and he stared at the blood repellently. "Ivy?" he whispered, his eyes hazy. Jenks was dusting her cut, and it immediately clotted. "Rachel?" he added, seeing me.

I gave him a shake as his eyes closed again. "Cormel!" I hissed, and one eye opened. "Have you seen David? Get up!"

"Who? Go away," he moaned, his tongue red with Ivy's blood flashing. "Let me sleep."

"How can he not be hungry?" Jenks asked. "His aura is almost not there."

Of course he hadn't seen David; he'd been asleep. "You think maybe a direct transfusion might snap him out of it?" I asked, but they must have tried that already.

Ivy frowned. "It's not the blood the undead need. It's the aura they take with it."

Frustrated, I slapped him, and Cormel's eyes flashed open. "Get up!" I shouted, tugging at him. "Felix is the only undead vampire awake in Cincinnati, and if we don't get you out of here, you might not live to see the next sunset."

"Felix?" Cormel muttered, eyes drooping, but with me pulling, he managed to push himself up on an elbow. Ivy watched, torn as Nina began to sob, but she left her there, taking Cormel's other arm and giving a yank. Like a drunken businessman in the gutter, Cormel rose, weaving on his feet between us. Ivy let go, and I struggled to hold him on my own.

"Where am I?" he breathed, again wiping his mouth of Ivy's blood and looking at it in distaste. Blinking, he looked at Ivy as she hoisted Nina into her arms. "Nina . . ." he said, then looked at his hand in wonder. "I see it, but the thought of blood is repellent," he whispered in awe, and I shivered when his gaze traveled to me. "What have you done to me?"

Jenks zipped up the stairway and back down. "Can we do this moving?" he said, making motions to get up the stairs. "The sun waits for no vampire."

Holding Nina in her arms, Ivy easily took the steps. Adrenaline gave me strength as I tucked a shoulder under Cormel. "Waves of wild magic are passing through Cincinnati causing magical misfires and the undead to sleep," I said, breathing deeply as vampiric incense poured over me, smelling sour somehow. "Except for Felix. Why?"

"Elves are killing vampires?" Cormel said, head hanging as he staggered.

My lips parted at the possibility, then I got us moving forward up the stairs. The light grew brighter, and the feeling of a trap lifted. "No, it's Free Vampires. Why is Felix the only one awake? What makes him different?"

Cormel shook his head as we emerged, orienting himself. "I didn't know this was here."

"Cormel. Why is Felix awake?" I asked again. Ivy was already at the door, Nina in her arms and katana on her hip as she looked first one way, then the other. Nina was crying, but I didn't think she was really aware yet. I let go of the ley line light spell, and a surge of energy lifted through me until it faded.

"I do not hunger," Cormel said distantly, and I suddenly found myself holding him upright, staggering under his weight.

"Cormel!" I shouted as he fell down the dais's shallow stairs. Cursing, I followed him down. His eyes were shut, and grabbing him by the lapels, I lifted his head and gave his face a smack. "Wake up!"

Cormel's eyes flashed open. "If you keep hitting me, I'm going to lose my patience."

"The I.S. is falling apart," I said, trying to get him to stand. "You have to stay awake!"

But his eyes closed, and I looked at Ivy helplessly. We couldn't leave him here.

"Smack him again!" Jenks said, and Ivy shifted Nina to a shoulder and a fireman's carry.

"I'll take him," she said shortly as she came forward, and my eyes widened. She wanted to carry both of them? "Go before me and make sure everything is clear," she added, and I watched, amazed, as she crouched with Nina on one shoulder, taking Cormel on the other as I got behind him and managed to get him somewhat upright.

Groaning with the weight, she staggered to a stand, reminding me again that she was more than human. Fear had given her strength, her fear not for Felix, but for Nina. She'd seen the hell Nina was in, been in it until my love for her had pulled her clean from it, as if a sword annealed in quenching waters. We had to get out of here before Felix realized what we were doing and dropped into Nina like a glove.

Ivy shuffled to the hallway door. Jenks darted out. I reached for my splat gun, giving it a shake to make sure the splat balls would flow freely from the hopper. Cormel's eyes opened as I passed him, and he fixed an upside-down, black-eyed, dead-doll stare on me. "You have to save us, Rachel," he whispered, and my spike of fear brought both him and Ivy to a brief, alert state.

"I do not!" I hissed, then shoved past Ivy and into the hallway. I was already trying to save their souls. I did not have to save their decaying bodies as well.

Jenks was a hovering spot of sun at the end of the hall. "Ladies . . ." he said, gesturing for us to hurry. Felix was down here. I could feel it. I jogged to Jenks, Ivy moving more slowly behind me, just managing the weight of Nina and Cormel.

"Take the vanguard," I told Jenks, and he darted off for the great room. We were almost there, and my pulse quickened at the first hints of possibility. *Stay quiet, Nina,* I thought, not wanting her to draw attention to us as she slowly became aware of what was going on.

The great room was silent as we entered, Jenks first, then Ivy, then me. My splat gun was out, and my pulse pounded. The open elevator beckoned clear across the room, less than fifty steps away. "How long until sunup, Jenks?" I said, knowing he was better than the weather service.

"Three minutes."

Ivy's eyes looked pinched at the corners. Just enough time to get Cormel into a specially lined body bag, but just.

Gun in one hand, I jogged ahead and pulled my phone out. "Okay. Go on up, Jenks. Find an I.S. agent. Get a shadow bag ready at the top of the elevator."

"You got it," Jenks said, and then he was gone, darting presumably to the dumbwaiter.

"And tell them not to shoot us!" I whispered after him, remembering the overabundance of FIB vehicles outside.

We were almost at the elevator when Ivy met my eyes. The relief in her expression was almost palpable. This time, there would be a happy ending.

"I can walk," Nina said before I could pull the chair from the doors, her voice clear and precise and holding a familiar, uneasy cadence.

Fear slid through me. Ivy gasped, then dropped both Nina and Cormel. *Felix.*

My gun swung, but Ivy was in the way. Heart pounding, I sidestepped. Three minutes. We didn't have time for this!

"Nina, no!" Ivy exclaimed, grabbing the woman's shoulders, but it was too late, and I saw Felix's persona slip in behind the woman's eyes and take over.

"You little *bitch*!" Felix/Nina shouted, spittle flying as she slapped Ivy. "Nina is mine!"

"Move, Ivy!" I shouted, gun pointed and trying to find a better angle. But then Nina looked at me and smiled. I froze, lips parting at the evil satisfaction pouring from her.

And then my breath was knocked out of me as someone hit me from the side. Gasping, I slid across the carpet. My gun went off, and my grip tightened on it, refusing to let go. Friction burned until I stopped. Struggling to breathe, I looked up to find Felix—the real Felix—on top of me, his long fangs bared and his beautiful, young face hard with a domineering need.

"Get off!" I snarled, bringing my gun to bear on him, and he knocked it aside. I wouldn't let go of it, and pain burned in my wrist. Blood covered him; none of it was his. I could hear Ivy crying as she grappled with Nina, the woman out of her mind as she fought for her right to go beautifully insane.

"Nina is mine," Felix said, his weight pressing into me as he pinned my hands to the carpet and leaned in to breathe on my neck. "I need her to do my daylight work. *Why* do you keep interfering?"

"Because she's not yours," I said, the words punctuated by my gasping breath.

My gun was pinned, but I could still defend myself; he snarled in pain when I pulled a ley line through me and shoved it into him, twisting and bucking until I broke his hold. I spun away to a kneel, gun aim wavering as my wrist burned, but he was eight steps back, pacing. The propellant would send it that far, but he wouldn't be there when it landed.

"I'm sorry," Ivy said as she grappled with Nina, and her face wet with tears, she put her hand over her fist and loggerheaded Nina with her elbow. The vampire's eyes rolled to the back of her head and she dropped. I looked at the huge clock above the elevator. The sun was up. Cormel was stuck down here. *Unless we could bring the FIB to us . . .*

"You can't have her," I said as I stood up, aim shaking. I moved, not watching my feet as I went to Ivy. She was standing over Cormel and Nina, her expression numb.

And still Felix circled, hunched and beautiful, like a jungle cat. "Did you not see Cormel's children?" he said softly, and his voice echoed in my mind like velvet, circling, numbing as he tried to bespell me. "I tried to work through another. Their minds are too weak. I need Nina. She knows me. I know her. Ivy has made her strong. Leave her, and I'll let you live."

Ivy was panting, and I reached for her when she fell to a kneel, fighting the pull in his demand. "We're not leaving . . . without her. You bloodsucking . . . bastard," she whispered, and I quailed at the reminder of what a master vampire could do, could call forth.

"Ivy . . ." Felix whispered, his hand held out to her. "Come to me."

"Ivy, no," I said, knowing not to touch her when she moaned, eyes closing in anticipation of a numbing pleasure. His summons to submit had permeated the room, and I wondered if I was going to have to down her with a splat ball. She'd be pissed, but she'd thank me later.

"You need to take a nap, Felix," I said. "Everyone else is sleeping. Why aren't you?"

Felix looked away. Behind me, Ivy took a heaving gasp of air as his hold broke. "They sleep because they feel no need," he said, his tone derisive. "I'm always hungry. Take Cormel if you want. He'll be dead in three days. All of them will. Nina stays. And Ivy."

Fear slid down my spine, and I tightened my grip on my gun. "Not happening."

"Then you will die so I can get on with living," he said, and with that as my warning, he jumped at me, his hands bent into claws.

"Rachel!" Ivy screamed, but instinct took over, and I braced myself, taking his momentum and flinging him into a pillar.

Felix twisted in midair. His shoulder took the blow instead of his back, and he sprang to his feet before I could shoot, eyes alight. "I've never had demon blood before," he said, eyes flicking behind me, and I felt Ivy's presence slide up to mine.

"That's not going to change, dirt nap," I said, drawing on the ley line until my hair floated.

Howling, he jumped again to kick my middle. My air exploded from me, and I found myself flung backward, skidding across the carpet until I hit the wall. My chest hurt. Eyes almost shut, I struggled to breathe, helpless as Ivy screamed and attacked. Fists a blur and shouts chilling, she forced him back from me. She seldom scored, but he was on the retreat. If he'd been trained in the arts, she wouldn't have had a chance. If he thought we might be able to best him, he wouldn't be playing with us as he was. If he noticed Nina crawling to the elevator to pull the chair away and send the lift to the surface . . . he might not be smiling, enjoying himself and the anticipation of our blood in his mouth.

But he didn't.

My gun shook in my grip. He was too far away. The propellant was only good for about twenty feet. Screaming in outrage, Ivy landed a side kick that sent Felix falling into a roll. "Why do you fight me?" he said as he regained his feet. "The Free Vampires will destroy the undead. All of them. I can stop them, but I need Nina," he coaxed, his hands spread in innocence.

Ivy retreated to stand beside me. "Do it without your slave," she said, panting. "You won't have her."

He knew about the Free Vampires? Then it was them after all? They were trying to kill the masters. The misfires were just a side effect. My grip on my gun grew steady, and with a soft wing hum, Jenks hovered between us, his satisfied smile making Felix hesitate. He was back. The FIB and I.S. were on the way. *Oh God, I hope they don't shoot me.*

"Your ass is staying under the grass, blood bag," the pixy said, and Felix's eyes became black as he looked at the elevator and Nina slumped beside it. Weak, she cracked her eyes and flipped him off as it dinged.

"You stupid bitches," he snarled, and then he dropped to a kneel, hands laced behind the back of his head as the doors slid apart and angry, yelling men in ACG gear and bulletproof vests ran into the room.

It was an excellent idea, and I held my hands up, gun dangling. I hated it when the good guys didn't recognize me. But then again, I *was* covered in blood. None of it was mine. I think.

"Don't shoot the women!" Jenks was shouting as he wove between Ivy and me. "Tink loves a duck, you're dumber than a troll's dildo! Don't you know a runner when you see one?"

"Ivy?" Nina cried in fear when a well-meaning man dragged her into the elevator.

With a quick palm thrust, Ivy snapped back the head of the man trying to cuff her. She bolted to the elevator, grabbing a gun from a second scared officer and throwing it across the room. "Don't let him in!" Ivy cried out, falling beside Nina and grabbing her shoulders to make her look at her. "Nina, I'm here. We can get through this. I won't leave you!"

Her cry brought everyone up short, and I could have

smacked Felix's face clean off when he watched, soaking in the emotion and relishing the pain and fear he was creating.

But he wasn't trying to take Nina over, and I absently handed my gun to the man demanding it, having to lean around the flood of angry officers in order to see Nina and Ivy. Felix was being cooperative, which was more than a little disconcerting. Mad men do not submit.

"I don't feel good," Nina said, her complexion becoming decidedly green.

"She's going to blow chunks!" Jenks warned, and I winced when she began to throw up great gouts of black vomit. It tended to clear a room out fast, and everyone gave her space as Ivy held her hair out of the way. Felix, the bastard, seemed amused.

"Sure, laugh now while you got the chance," I whispered, and he turned to me, clearly having heard.

But the elevator opened again and more FIB and I.S. guys poured out. "Edden!" I called as I saw his balding head among the rest. David was with him, looking an odd mix with his long duster and borrowed FIB hat, and a knot of worry eased. He was all right. He must have escaped the chaos upstairs and gone for help. Seeing me, his lips curved up in relief and I knew we were okay.

Felix was smiling despite his hands being cuffed behind his back. As the only awake undead, he might be able to turn this around, especially if he kept acting cooperatively. But I'd seen the madness behind his eyes. He wouldn't take Nina with him—not if I could help it.

"She's been attacked," I heard Ivy snarl at someone. "Get away from her."

"I'm good?" I asked the man checking out my ID, and he nodded, handing my gun back. "Edden! David!" I called, and David touched Edden on the shoulder, leaving him with two officers as he started to me. Tired, I leaned against the back of a couch, getting nasty, icky blood all over it.

"I know I said I'd call you," the Were said as he closed the gap. "But they did an end-around and took my scouts by surprise. I went to the church, but you were already gone—Hey!"

I pulled him into a hug, breathing in the complex scent of woods and gunpowder. "I thought you were upstairs in that mess," I said. "I was so mad." Leaning back, I looked at his grinning, sheepish face. "I still am mad!" I said louder. "Damn it, David. You've got to be more careful!"

Jenks wreathed us with a silver dust. "She was ready to *avenge* you," he said, laughing. "I've never seen her aura like that, all silvery with the need to do mean justice."

"I was not," I said, embarrassed that some of the officers were listening. "Okay, I was," I admitted. "So I take it you found some Free Vampires. Is everyone upstairs going to be okay?"

He nodded. "They are, though I might have to watch a couple of the younger ones for a while to make sure they don't need some extra help avoiding addiction." He leaned in, whispering, "They'll be fine. The focus is stronger than any residual vampiric pheromone bonds."

That was a relief, and I gave his shoulder a last shove to show how much he meant to me as Edden finished up with his officers and came forward. "You could have called," I said.

"They took my phone." There was a swelling on his face, and he wasn't standing with his weight on both feet. Clearly he was hurting, and David shifted to make room for Edden.

"Rachel," the older man said as he rolled to a stop, hands in his pockets as he ran his eyes up and down me. He didn't look much better than David, and I wondered when was the last time he slept. "This looks familiar," he added as he took in the mess and the officers trying to make sense of it.

"Ah, we need an lightproof bag from the I.S.," I said as I looked at the two guys trying to wake Cormel up. "Cormel needs protective custody. I don't care if Felix is acting sane, he isn't."

Head bobbing, Edden crossed his arms over his chest. "You got a few minutes to give a statement?" Edden asked, and my eyes narrowed.

"You got a few minutes to answer your phone?" I shot back, and he ducked his head, rubbing a hand across the back of his neck.

"Sorry."

It was the best I was going to get, and I pushed off from the couch, leaning on David as we limped to the elevator. Nina and Ivy were in it, and Ivy held it for me when she saw us coming. "Thanks for getting here when you did," I said to David and Edden. "I think we can safely say the Free Vampires are trying to rid Cincinnati of the undead, and they don't care how many people they hurt doing it."

Edden winced, looking at David. "That's what he said, but seriously?" he said, still not believing it when David nodded. "They're nothing more than a cult. A not-well-funded one at that. Where are they getting the magic to control the waves?"

Elves? whispered through me, and I banished the thought. Trent would know, wouldn't he? He was their unofficial leader, their Sa'han. "I don't know, but it's not the demons," I said as the doors slid closed and the lift jiggled into motion. "Al said the waves are being collected before they can leave the area. I think Cincinnati is a test case. One of the vampires upstairs said they came here to get Felix, probably because he hasn't fallen asleep like the rest. If you give him enough rope, they might come find him again, but I want protection for Ivy and Nina."

"We'll be fine," Ivy protested as she held Nina upright, gaze falling when I looked at her. The memory of my pack members taking my punishment was too new.

"I'll see to it," Edden said as the lift lurched to a halt and opened. Mustache bunching, he held the door so we could all limp out. The huge clock in the small room off the kitchen stared at me. Only fifteen minutes had passed. It felt like more.

"We need to find them like now," I said, everything hurting. "If we can't stop them from pulling wild magic out of my line, the undead will be dead by week's end. They're starving to death, Edden."

Edden sighed and held the door from the kitchen to the old dining room open. The come-and-go of radios and the chatter of FIB officers became louder, and the air fresher. "Happy Independence Day," Edden said softly.

Below us was blood, and violence. Before us, the blood-strewn room was now empty of people and looking like a macabre painting. Felix had been more vampiric than any other vampire I'd ever seen. Happy Independence Day indeed. "Someone has a sense of humor," I said, shuffling from the kitchen, and Edden grunted his agreement.

But it wasn't funny. If the master vampires were not around to control the living, then who was going to do it?

And were the elves behind it? Somebody was funding them. HAPA was down and disorganized. Same for the men-who-don't-belong. Witches wouldn't jeopardize their own magic like this. Demons would love the mischief, but wouldn't use wild magic to do it. Elves . . . maybe.

Lunch with Trent tonight was suddenly sounding a lot more interesting.

Twelve

Rachel? Hot dog or ribs?"

I cracked an eye, gut clenching at the thought of ribs slathered in sticky red: no ribs—not after wading through Piscary's blood-drenched upstairs this morning, not after spending fifteen minutes scrubbing it out from under my fingernails, not after the innocence of Trent's and Quen's girls putting a ballerina Band-Aid on my skinned elbow.

"Hot dog." Trent's eyebrows rose, but he dutifully passed the request to Jonathan before ambling back to the long teak table under the canopy where the two men from the elven religious sect sat deep in discussion about how Free Vampires might harness wild magic. I had yet to bring up the possibility that the elves were behind it. *Diplomacy, you are my middle name.*

"Ray! No! Mine!" Lucy shrilled, and I smiled as I settled myself deeper into the cushy lounge chair at the extravagantly landscaped pool. My eyes were shut, and I drank in the world through my ears: the hiss of the grill burning away the sugar sweetness, Ellasbeth's admonishment that Ray share the toys, Trent's musical, muted response, the sound of water tinkling in the kiddie pool. Family had never sounded so good.

But my smile faded at Bancroft's grating southern drawl,

his words indistinct but the emotion clear. The faint chill in the air from the setting sun seemed to cascade over me, and I shivered. Bancroft was *the* official of Trent's religion, dressed the part in a long purple robe I wouldn't expect in Ohio, no-nonsense shiny dress shoes poking out from underneath. I'd talked to him briefly before he grabbed his assistant, Landon, and retreated to a quiet room. He was back now, and I'd come to the conclusion that as polite as he was, he really didn't like me. I knew it wasn't anything I'd said or done. It was *what* I was, and it bothered me I hadn't had the chance to show him how nasty I could be before he wrote me off.

Smirking, I settled deeper into the cushions as Jonathan dabbed sauce on the ribs and they flamed up. It was blissful here, but the trip out had been a nightmare of roadblocks and checkpoints. A terrified world was watching Cincinnati now that the misfires were on the decline and the vampire violence rising, most people demanding a lockdown until it could be determined who was causing the undead to slumber. I'd be going home by ley line if they cordoned off Cincinnati and the Hollows. It was becoming a distinct possibility. I'd seen too many ambulances today, heard too many sirens, witnessed too much grief. My mind drifted as I began to fall asleep, twitching at the flash of memory of the blood-smeared bodies at the tavern. *Felix is awake because his age-born disease makes him always hunger. Why is that significant?*

The sound of beating wings fluttered, and the dream of purple blinking eyes lifted through me. They were taking Ivy from me, and the purple eyes became vampire black and angry.

"Don't wake her." Ellasbeth's voice slid between my dream of silvery wings, and the wheels with eyes faltered.

From right over me, Quen's voice said, "Her hot dog is done."

"Aunt Rachel is napping. Shhhh," Lucy said brightly, and

the last of the wings beat at the eyes, smothering them until they were gone.

I pulled myself awake, smiling at Quen as I sat up. He had two plates of food, and I thought it funny that they were paper. It was almost as odd as seeing him in casual jeans and a polo shirt. "I'm not asleep. I was listening to everything."

Knowing it for the lie it was, Quen handed me a plate. I took it, needing to sit up even more. I couldn't help but wonder if Ellasbeth had been being nice or if she simply hadn't wanted me taking part in dinner. Ribs, hot dogs, macaroni salad, baked beans, and chips. Who knew? Maybe they were practicing for the Fourth.

"Lucy," I said, seeing her sitting on Trent's lap as he continued to discuss some small point of religious belief with Bancroft under the canopied table. "Did you know that you can hear everything better when your eyes are closed?"

Ellasbeth eyed me from the inflatable pool set beside the fenced-off pool. She looked fittingly perfect in her swimsuit and light pullover with her feet in the water, Ray between them as the little girl watched the water run off her hands as she lifted them, then reached for more.

Lucy, though, settled onto Trent's lap with a little bounce. Sitting with a new stiffness, she closed her eyes, the picture of stillness for all of three seconds before opening her eyes and sliding down her father's legs. Wearing a wicked grin, she jumped into the pool. Water hit Ray, and the little girl started crying as Lucy splashed harder. Wailing, Ray clutched at Ellasbeth, and the woman lifted her up, admonishing Lucy to settle down as the dark-haired little girl pouted and glared, clutching Ellasbeth for security. I ate a chip, thinking Lucy had better stop tormenting her sister or she was going to find worms in her hair before her second birthday.

Then I looked up, surprised to see Quen still standing over me. "Can I get you anything else?" he asked, and I glanced at my plate. I wasn't used to being waited on, and not by someone who could flatten me with magic or martial arts.

"No thanks. I've got my iced tea."

"Mind if I sit down?" he added, his attention on the chair beside my lounger, and I put my feet on the patio and sat all the way up.

"Sure. Go ahead." I eyed my dog with all the trimmings, then Jonathan. Maybe I'd just stick with the salad.

Quen gracefully sat, the love in his eyes for Ray obvious as he watched Ellasbeth dry her off and help her into a robe. Lucy had taken over the pool, and Ray made her determined way to Trent with a rubber duck in her grip. It was an odd sort of family but it *was* a family, and I was grudgingly impressed with how Ellasbeth had endeared the girls to her. I hated to admit it, but she seemed to know what she was doing.

Landon came out with two more bottles of wine. Our eyes met, and I looked away, uneasy. Bancroft's assistant seemed to focus on the very things Bancroft didn't like about me, making me nervous in his analyzing. Landon was blond, as most elves were. His ears were docked, but he had an earring, giving him a decidedly devilish mien. Dressed like Bancroft, he had the added distinction of a multicolored sash. Jeans and tennis shoes showed under his hem. He was younger, too, his face clean-shaven where Bancroft had a tidy beard and wrinkles. Landon's accent was midwestern newscaster, every word pronounced with a perfect blandness.

Noting my mistrustful scrutiny, Quen forked a bite of meat off his ribs, his eyes never leaving mine.

"So the goats don't have to die to be considered sacrificed?" Trent asked as he pulled Ray up onto his lap and the toddler helped herself to his macaroni salad, eating it one shell at a time.

"No." Bancroft reached for one of the wine bottles Landon had brought out. "It's permissible to give them to the dewar. The intent of a sacrifice is to deny yourself a wealth or courtesy, and giving it to the church will accomplish that end."

And put a little jingle in the coffers, I thought sourly.

Shunning the hot dog on the principle that Jonathan had made it, I focused on the chips. *Church, temple, holy place.* Leave it to the elves to name their church after a flask used to store precious gases. Bunch of hot air.

The snick of a knife leaving a sheath brought my head up, but it was only Bancroft, and I watched him use a ceremonial foot-long frog sticker to open the bottle of wine by running it down the bottle's length and snapping off the top. *Show-off.*

"Thank God," Ellasbeth said, busy toweling Lucy's hair, the little girl staring at Trent's salad. "I couldn't stomach the idea of Trent slitting some poor goat's throat."

Probably with the same sword Bancroft was tucking back in his robes, I thought. Trent, though, was grimacing. I wondered if it was at the thought of killing an animal with his bare hands, or the question of it really being a sacrifice if someone other than the Goddess benefited from it. Recalling Jenks telling me about how Trent had slit the throat of an attacker, I guessed it was the latter.

The ice was long gone from my tea, and I wondered if I went to get more if I could trash my hot dog with no one the wiser. I went to stand, dropping back at Quen's quiet clearing of his throat.

"I wanted to thank you for giving Trent the space he needs to focus on his duty," he said, his melodious voice reminding me of earth and shadow.

Focus on his duty? Was that elf-speak for ignoring that Trent was making the biggest mistake of his life? Leaning back, I stabbed a couple of macaroni. "You're the one who asked me to watch him."

"Thank you for that, too."

He was nervous. It wasn't obvious, but it made me wonder if he knew about Trent's and my "date." Probably. Trent didn't keep much from him. I concentrated on my salad, stifling a shiver as the memory of that kiss we'd shared blossomed. Newt's warning echoed in me, and I ate another chip. What did it matter anyway?

"So, he and Ellasbeth getting along better?" I asked, smiling when Lucy finally broke from Ellasbeth. Running to Trent, she begged to be picked up. Last time the girls were here, he could have managed them both, but now they were too big.

"Yes, but it's mostly her efforts to change. She's not an unkind woman."

I looked at Ellasbeth rising up in her skimpy bathing suit and cover-up that didn't live up to its name. She was smart, sexy, and everything a man would like, and I suppressed an unexpected flash of jealousy. "She's peeved at being asked to do something she doesn't want to do. I get that." The salad tasted flat, and I set my fork down. *How far should duty rule a person?* I asked myself as Ellasbeth went to the table and took both Lucy's and Trent's discarded plates. They worked well together, and knowing Trent, duty was everything.

My eyes met Jonathan's. The nasty man had turned the grill off and was setting everything on a tray to take inside. He smiled evilly at me, and I smiled evilly back. As proper looking in his white-and-blue-striped cooking apron as he was, there was no way I was eating that hot dog now. Too bad, because it looked perfect with chili, mustard, relish, and even a sprinkling of parmesan.

Sighing, I set my plate aside, and as Ellasbeth gracefully took her seat at the large, canopied table, Trent beckoned me over. "Here we go," I whispered, both eager and dreading Bancroft's pronouncement.

"Let me help you with that," Quen said as he took my plate, and I reluctantly passed it to him. I'd get rid of the hot dog somehow.

"Thanks." Feeling awkward, I crossed the patio as I tried to decide where to sit. There was an empty place beside Trent, but that was out of the question with Ellasbeth smiling thinly at me. The chair beside Bancroft was not a good option. Neither was the chair beside Landon.

"Here, Ms. Morgan," Landon said as he stood to pour out the wine, and my choice was made for me.

"Rachel, please," I said as I sat down and pushed my empty wineglass away to make room for my iced tea. "We're being so informal today."

At least some of us were, I thought, glancing at Ellasbeth in her swimsuit. Trent was business casual, as was Quen. I didn't know what Bancroft and Landon were, but they seemed professional. And I, of course, was trying to impress everyone with how businesslike I could be with my black slacks and white top. Boring, boring, boring.

Quen silently slid my plate with my untouched hot dog before me, and I winced.

"Are you perhaps vegetarian?" Landon asked as he set the bottle down. "And no wine?"

My eyes flicked over the table, embarrassed that I'd telegraphed so much. "Just not hungry. And the sulfites in the wine give me a headache."

"A demon with a sulfur intolerance?" Bancroft said in disbelief, his dramatic drawl temporarily stilling Lucy's babbling.

Trent reached across the table to take my plate and hand it to Quen to remove from the table. "Rachel is not your usual demon," Trent said with a smile, and I felt a wash of gratitude. His eyebrows rose almost imperceptibly in question, and I glanced at Jonathan. Frowning, Trent held Ray closer as he watched Jonathan take his apron off. Ellasbeth's jaw was clenched at our silent communication, and she forced a smile when I noticed.

"What a shame!" Landon pushed back with his glass of red wine and eyed me over it. "To not be able to fully enjoy the fruits of the earth. You must make up for it in other ways."

His words were innocent enough, but the way he said it made me feel as if I were naked.

Bancroft harrumphed as he settled himself. It was nearing dusk, and the outside lights flicked on. "I appreciate your unique insight into recent events, Morgan," the man said as he took his cylindrical hat off and set it aside.

"I showed you mine. I'd appreciate if you'd show me yours," I said, and Landon snorted into his wine.

Bancroft ran his hand over his sparse hair to smooth it. "I beg your pardon?"

I leaned forward, wanting to hurry this up so I might get home before they closed Cincy. "The wave is wild magic. Do you really think vampires have the skill to pull it from my line and then catch it so it doesn't circle the globe? Just what are they doing with it, anyway?" Bancroft's expression went closed, and I drummed my fingers. It was going to be like that, eh?

"Wild magic is always leaking from the lines," Landon offered.

"Not like this it isn't," I said, offended they would try to snow me like that.

Stretching, Trent snagged the pitcher of iced tea. "I've found Rachel to be circumspect. She knows the value of information and works best when she has it. All of it."

"She is a *demon*," Bancroft said, staring at me. I refused to look away, even when Trent refilled my glass and the ice tinkled to the top.

"She is my associate in this matter," Trent said, the soft threat in his voice making Ellasbeth sniff. "If you don't explain the workings of the Goddess, I will."

Bancroft thought that over as Quen silently cleared the table. It was Bancroft who looked away first, and I drank my tea like a victory draft. *Point to me.*

"The Goddess is both one being and a thousand," Bancroft said sourly. "A communal mind. Usually she's in concert with herself, but as I prayed in Cincinnati this afternoon, I sensed a division. She is two. The subset of mystics being held from her is beginning to separate and take on a new personality. She's beginning to become insane."

"I think *insane* is a somewhat strong term," Trent said, and a flash of annoyance crossed Landon's face, fleeting and almost not there.

"She can't be balanced anymore," Ellasbeth said dryly,

leaning back in her chair with her glass. "Think of a group of people marooned on an island. In a few generations, the lack of genetic diversity begins to show itself."

"Just so," Bancroft reaffirmed, reaching for more wine. "When an elf petitions for attention and help, he—"

"Or she," Ellasbeth interrupted, gently bouncing Lucy on her lap.

Bancroft inclined his head politely. "Or she," he consented, "is not communicating with the entirety of the Goddess, but only the parts of her that are sympathetic to the petitioner's aims. The more the prayer resonates with the Goddess, the stronger the connection."

So the more the Goddess agreed with you, the more likely you were to be heard? "That doesn't sound very fair," I said, fiddling with my drink. "What does this have to do with wild magic leaking from my lines?"

"I'm getting to that," Bancroft said, and Landon coughed dryly. "We call her individual thoughts mystics. They roam freely in reality, leaving her by way of the lines and bringing ideas and concepts back to her, though not usually in the concentrations you've been witnessing lately. Several species host them in minute amounts, such as pixies, leprechauns, and Weres. It enables them to access their magic naturally without a connection to a line. It's the concentration of them in the wave that is unnatural, not their presence."

I nodded, remembering Jenks once telling me that he was "magic, baby!" I bet it burned the elves' cookies that they weren't hosts to their own Goddess when pixies were. It was starting to make sense, and I tapped the table in thought. "Then the wild magic is what's in the line that witches, elves, and demons get their strength from?"

Either warming up to me or the wine he was slamming down, Bancroft raised a hand for patience. "Only elves can access it directly from the Goddess. Energy collects between spaces naturally, sort of pools up. Witches and demons siphon it off through ley lines."

As long as I didn't think about it too hard, it made sense.

Little bits of sentient energy combining into one mega Goddess, the entirety of Inderland magic running on the energy she gave off, much like vampires existed on the energy given off from the soul. "Seems like a lot of trouble for such a tiny bit of energy."

Bancroft fiddled with his glass, watching the red wine swirl. "The amount in the waves is tiny, but it can be used to great destruction. It's like the sun. In space where it belongs, it warms and protects, but even a half-second burst on earth is devastating."

A sudden thought broke over me, and I sat up. Ellasbeth started at my quick motion, but Trent was smiling. "Newt!" I exclaimed. "That's what she was doing yesterday."

"Ah . . ." Bancroft said as he and Landon exchanged worried glances. "Newt? She's the insane demon, right?"

"Not all the time. She was catching mystics," I said, looking at Trent for confirmation. "Remember? Right before that last wave we got caught up in."

"She was decidedly not!" Bancroft huffed.

"She was! I have some in a jar on my windowsill."

Trent leaned across the table, almost shouting to be heard over Bancroft's loud and continuous denials that anyone could catch the Goddess in a *jar*. Lucy was right there with him, shouting and banging as she sat on Ellasbeth's lap. "You kept it?" he asked, his eyes alight.

"Duh. You think I'm going to trash anything Newt gives me? The woman is crazy, not stupid."

Bancroft shut up when he realized no one was listening to him, and I gathered my hair back and let it go in thought. This had possibilities. "Do you think we can talk to the Goddess directly?" I asked, and Ellasbeth gasped. "Maybe tell her what's going on so she can maybe, I don't know, stop parts of herself from wandering off?"

Bancroft's face was white. "It would take a huge fraction of the Goddess's attention to even attract her awareness of you. You can't talk to her as if she was a . . . a . . . person. And you can't catch her in a jar!"

"Someone is," I said, and the man put a hand to his chest, sputtering. "The same group of people pulling them out of my line," I added. Trent glanced at Quen, and the man stood, quietly taking Ray and then Lucy. "Otherwise the mystics would be circling the globe."

Bancroft stood, the cuffs of his robe shaking. "You cannot capture the Goddess! Who told you that?"

"A demon," I said flatly, ignoring his conniption fit. I was tired of arguing with people who couldn't see over the edge of the box they lived in. "The FIB—a human-run institution—figured out how to monitor for the waves yesterday. It's how we got the misfires under control. Someone is collecting them."

Spinning, Bancroft threw a hand up into the air. Beside me, Landon was still in thought. Trent was massaging his forehead, and Ellasbeth looked as if I'd spit on the Goddess, not offered up that she was real and touchable. My God. To actually talk to the divine?

But I'd already done that. I just hadn't believed.

"This is appalling," Bancroft spouted, face red. "I do *not* have to tolerate this!"

Trent shot me a look as he stood, but had he seriously expected me to sit here with my mouth shut? "Bancroft. Please. Rachel's theories often draw on a multitude of practices—"

"They are outrageous and counterproductive!"

And they usually get the job done, I thought, taking a sip of iced tea.

"And because of it, they have a tendency to appear outrageous, but they often lead to flexible solutions," Trent finished. "Please. Nothing she's said is false. Don't end the discussion because you don't like it."

I couldn't help but feel good that Trent had stuck up for me, but my smug smile vanished when Landon noticed it. Bancroft finally sat down, grumbling as he tugged his ceremonial robe straight while Trent opened a new bottle of wine and filled Bancroft's glass.

"Thank you," Trent said, adding a drop to his own glass

before giving me a tired look. "We've determined that the waves *are* attracted to Rachel. She's not a mystic magnet. It's simply because she made the line that they're escaping from and her aura resonates at the same frequency."

Still Bancroft frowned, his arms over his chest as he refused to take the drink Trent had topped off. From inside, I could hear Lucy singing, loudly and off-key.

Trent met my eyes and looked away. "I suggest that there's a high likelihood that the Free Vampires knew that Rachel created the Loveland ley line, hence their choosing it and Cincinnati as their test case."

Seeing Trent do his boardroom shuffle was kind of cool, and I tried to look more professional. "Which brings up something that you have all avoided like the emperor's new clothes. Would a vampire faction risk humanity freaking out and attacking *all* vampires just to further their belief that the undead existence is a blasphemy to the soul? The stuff the living are doing right now without the masters to curb them is as bad or worse than what the masters do themselves. I'm not buying it. Free Vampires are involved, but they don't know how to work with wild magic. Someone is helping them, and it's not the witches or demons."

Bancroft took a long swallow of wine. He looked up, and I could see the first hints of inebriation in his rummy eyes. He was tired, and I couldn't tell what he was thinking as he played with the stem of his wineglass.

"Meaning . . ." Trent said into the silence, taking Ellasbeth's hand above the table and giving it a squeeze when she reached for him in worry.

"The elves would benefit greatly from an end to the vampires," I said, point-blank. *And when diplomacy fails, you shoot first and run like hell.*

Bancroft's gaze darkened. "I don't see that at all."

"I do," I said, and Trent shifted uncomfortably. "You're balanced on species recovery, and taking out the vampires would solidify your foothold tremendously." I sipped my tea, ignoring Ellasbeth's shocked stare. "It's no secret you met the masters dollar for dollar in the economic arena when you were hiding and almost extinct. The undead worked hard to make the 'almost' part go away on more than one occasion. The waves are putting those pesky witches in their place, too."

Bancroft was incensed, sputtering like a boiling pot, but it was Landon's cool lack of expression that struck me as being dangerous.

"Rachel," Trent said, caught off guard and trying to keep things together. "I'm a loud voice in elven matters. If it was us, I'd know it."

Would he? I wondered, looking at Ellasbeth's utter disregard and wondering if it was her hiding knowledge or simply her dislike for anything that came from me.

"Elves would gain nothing from an end to vampires," Trent said with a light laugh, but it was for Bancroft and Landon, not me, and I could see a sudden concern trace like a ribbon of muddy water behind his eyes. The thought had occurred to him, too.

Fine. Lips pressed, I pushed back from the table and crossed my arms. I'd aired my beliefs. Any disaster that happened from here out wouldn't be because I'd played it safe and kept my mouth shut. "Perhaps you're right," I said sarcastically as Landon's grip on his wineglass tightened and Ellasbeth frowned at me to be polite. *Polite never saved anyone's ass.*

"Rachel," Landon said, voice low and coaxing . . . and raising every caution flag I'd ever had. "I'd be very curious to see one of these FIB devices in action. To be able to track the thoughts of the Goddess would be a marvelous step in finding out who is really responsible. If they are indeed trapping mystics, then all we have to do is follow the trail to where it ends."

Oh, if it were only that easy. "You don't think the FIB tried that?"

"I have two," Trent said suddenly, surprising me. "Edden asked me to put them on the outskirts of my property as part of their early detection." His eyes went to Bancroft. "I'd be more than happy to show you how they work."

"A pair?" Landon said, the scent of cinnamon growing stronger. "That's even better. With two, we can ascertain if Rachel's aura is glowing from repeated contact with the waves, or if she collects them simply walking about."

"My aura is glowing?" I said, stiffening, and Trent raised a soothing hand.

"Not like when a wave hits you," he said, but I didn't feel any better. "It's just got this silvery haze it usually doesn't."

Bancroft squinted at me. "Has your aura always had that black sheen? Or did that come with the mystics as well?"

Nope. Still didn't feel any better. Ellasbeth made a little noise, telling me she hadn't noticed till now. I took a breath to comment, then smiled as I felt a soft expanding of my awareness. The ley line running through Trent's compound seemed brighter, more scintillating, and I exhaled as the chiming purity of the lines in the greater Ohio area became clearer. Bis was nearby.

"It came with membership to the demon collective," I said, turning to the pool as, with the sound of sliding leather, Bis dropped out of the darkening sky, his red eyes wide and his pushed-in smile showing his black teeth. Ellasbeth gasped, and Bancroft choked on his drink. If the kid hadn't been smiling, I'd be worried. Jenks had probably told him I might need a jump home.

"Bis. Everything okay?" I asked as Landon rose, going around the table to crouch beside Bancroft as the man whispered something to make Trent unhappy.

"The Hollows and Cincinnati are locked down," he said, eyes darting between the people behind me. "I came to jump you home when you're ready."

I stood, wanting to introduce him. "Thanks. I think we're just about done here anyway."

Bis made the short flight to my shoulder, his bird-light weight hitting me just as I erected a barrier around my mind so I wouldn't pass out from ley line overload. His lionlike tail wrapped round my back, tucking under my armpit for a secure hold that was a hundred times better than wrapping around my neck. He lifted his wings, touching their tips together in greeting as he looked at Trent, and the man smiled, helping Ellasbeth to her feet. "Mr. Kalamack. Ms. Ellasbeth," he said with a formal stiffness, and Bancroft rose as well.

"Good to see you, Bis," Trent said. "I'd like you to meet Bancroft and Landon. They study the Goddess."

Bis nodded. "The lines are singing in step, but the music has changed," he said, and Bancroft pressed close, intrigued. He could talk to any gargoyle if he cared to try, but getting them to talk back was harder.

Landon stuck out his hand, and the adolescent gargoyle giggled, ruining the solemn air as he carefully shook it. "Pleasure," the younger man said. "Do you have some time? I've often wondered about the symbiotic relationship some of your people have with demons."

I was kind of curious about that myself, but I was more concerned about getting home to Ivy. She was watching Nina like a hawk on cheese . . . or whatever.

"You're welcome to stay the night," Trent offered.

"Yes, please stay," Ellasbeth echoed, and I quailed under her insincere smile.

Fidgeting, I looked back at my lounge chair where I had left my shoulder bag. "Ah, thank you, but no. I'd really prefer to be home tonight. Nina needs all the support she can get."

Ellasbeth's bristly mien softened. "Oh," she said, expression closed. "Of course."

"Nina?" Bancroft asked, and I went to get my bag, crouching carefully so Bis wouldn't become unbalanced.

"She's the unwilling scion of the only undead awake in the Cincinnati area," Trent said.

Ellasbeth looped her arm in Trent's to look like the perfect executive's wife. "Rachel's roommate is trying to break the vampiric addiction he has on her." I glanced sharply at her. A delicate flush colored her, and if I didn't know better,

I'd say she thought it was a noble endeavor. "Rachel, is there anything we can do? Trent's research is a hundredfold more sure now. Do you think she'd be willing to chance a reduction in her virus count?"

Shocked, I scrambled for words. "Ah, I'll ask her, but she's a living vampire. I don't think it would help. But thank you. I'll tell her you mentioned it."

His arm still in hers, Trent looked sidelong at her in surprise. Ellasbeth was stiff, making me wonder. She seemed to understand, and that was . . . totally unexpected.

"Well," I said, wishing the girls were still out here. "I'd better get going. Give Lucy and Ray a hug for me," I said, and Trent nodded. Behind him, Landon and Bancroft were discussing something intently, their backs to us and the words flying back and forth fast enough to make me nervous.

"Thanks for coming over," Trent said as he edged me away from Ellasbeth for a private word. The memory of our last kiss flashed through me, and I flushed, feeling guilty with Ellasbeth watching, but damn it, we hadn't done anything! "I'll see about getting your car to you tomorrow."

"I'd appreciate that," I said, seeing Ellasbeth watching me with a long face. "Dinner was great," I added, waiting until Bancroft finished arguing with Landon before popping out.

Smiling, he ducked his head and Ellasbeth came close, asserting her presence. "Sorry about the hot dog."

I made a snort of laughter, and Bis's tail tightened. "I'm sure it was fine."

Behind him, Landon took on an aggressive stance as he talked to Bancroft. "I think it worth finding out. When will we have another opportunity like this? It's my risk, not yours!"

"Fine!" Bancroft exclaimed. "I'll ask her!"

Ellasbeth took Trent's arm and leaned in. "Was there something wrong with the hot dog?"

"I'll tell you later," Trent muttered, then turned to include

Bancroft and Landon as they approached, the former slightly soused, the latter having a quiet urgency I didn't trust.

"Morgan," Bancroft drawled firmly. "Would you be willing to assist us on a matter?"

I could tell it was just about killing him to ask for my help, and I touched Bis's clawed feet, his toes carefully spread so he didn't pinch me. "Depends. What do you want?"

Bancroft glanced at Landon, then back to me. "My assistant wants to determine if the mystics currently coating your aura are from repeated contact with the waves itself, or if you're picking up free-ranging mystics, and if that is the case, if they're crossing the line to find you."

Landon pushed forward. "If they are, then a simple way to end the waves and wake up the masters would be for you to temporarily maintain a presence in the ever-after."

My first impulse to deny, avoid, and ignore swirled into simply avoid and ignore. I kind of wanted to know myself, but to voluntarily stay in the ever-after? "How?" I asked suspiciously.

"Ahh . . ." Bancroft hesitated, and Landon jiggled on his sneaker-covered feet.

"Rachel," Landon blurted. "I'd like to take twin readings from, say, here to Cincinnati? One meter in reality, one in the ever-after. We could go cross-country and avoid roads."

"At night?" Trent exclaimed, and Ellasbeth's eyes widened.

"In the ever-after?" I said, as appalled as her. "Do you know what happens after sunset?"

"Demons." Landon's eyes were unreadable, but his voice held a thread of challenge.

"Sometimes, sure," I said, tugging my shoulder bag higher. "It's the surface demons I'm worried about. I know most of the demon demons, but surface demons are like big, smart, hungry rats. You walk anywhere for any length of time, and they'll find you."

Trent was shaking his head. "Bancroft, I see your reasoning, and I agree the information would be invaluable, but Rachel is right. I've been there after sunset, and if you're not prepared, it is like, well . . ." He looked at me. "Like summoning a demon without a circle. It can wait until morning."

"Twelve hours might make a huge difference," Landon said, undeterred. "You have two meters. One team could travel through the ever-after, the other in reality. We'd take readings all the way, determining natural levels, her levels, and if the mystics will cross realities to find her."

Bis's grip on me had tightened, and I touched his foot again.

"Whoever is doing this is unable to collect one hundred percent of them," Landon said persuasively. "The entire Cincinnati area is simmering with untapped energy. If nothing else, it would give a tremendous insight into how the Goddess sees, ah, magic practitioners."

Yes, I was a demon, but a slow slog home through the ever-after wasn't my idea of fun.

"I volunteer to be on the ever-after team," Landon said, and Trent looked thoughtful. "If we go by horse, we can outdistance a surface demon, and if the team in reality is on horseback, they can evade the roadblocks."

It was starting to sound marginally reasonable, and Ellasbeth made a sound of negation as I looked at Trent for his opinion. "Trenton, this is not acceptable," she said firmly. "You have a family, children, responsibilities."

A fiancée, I added silently as he grimaced.

"The risk is minimal if I'm on the reality-based team," he said, and Landon's green eyes brightened in the dimming evening. "This has merit."

"Quen can go," she protested, and Trent took her hands, forcing her to look at him.

"Ellasbeth. This is my job. This is what I do. Let me do it."

My lips parted as his words fell from him, firm as he pleaded for understanding and acceptance. It was exactly what I had told Kisten, Pierce, and Marshal.

She dropped her head, defiance in her as it lifted. "Ellie,

this will foster goodwill if nothing else. And I'm curious myself." Letting her go, Trent turned to me, and my heart seemed to skip at his look of anticipation. "Rachel?"

The ever-after? On horseback at night? With Landon? I looked at Bis, and he lifted his wings in a shrug.

"Sure. Why not?"

Thirteen

The cheese was tangy, rich with flavor and clearly minimally processed. The bread was even better, with a crackling crust and the body textured and soft. Leaning against the rack of saddles, I wiped my mouth with a pinkie, the last bite of the sandwich still in my hand. I didn't think I'd ever had a cheese sandwich until just this moment. "You sure?" I said into the phone, and Ivy's sigh came back to me.

"It's easier at the safe house," she said, the background noise unfamiliar. "Nina's condition is common enough to have people who know what to do. It's okay."

She was already there, which made me feel both better and like I'd let them down. "I should be there," I protested, but there was little to nothing I could really do.

Landon, dressed now in jeans and borrowed boots, walked by with Ceri's old horse, and I felt a twinge of sadness. She'd been happy that morning. I was glad my last memory of Ray's real mother was of her in the dappled sun, content and crabbing at me to be true to myself.

"We'll be fine," Ivy said, and I stifled a pang of guilt. "Rachel, they just put Felix in charge of the I.S. The sooner you get someone else awake, the better."

"Felix?" I yelped, and Landon looked up from where he'd tied off his horse, brushing the animal out as he waited. It might be to give Felix enough rope to hang himself with, but he could hang the rest of us in the meantime. "The I.S. isn't coming after you, are they?"

"Not with everything else going on, but that's one of the reasons for the safe house."

This sucked. I really needed to be there, and I tugged my borrowed coat tighter about myself. I was eating gourmet cheese sandwiches and gearing up for a midnight ride when Ivy was hiding from the I.S. with an emotionally compromised woman. "You want me to send Bis back?" I said, looking at the last bite of sandwich glumly. He was waiting for us out on the cupola, snagging bats for his breakfast.

"Rachel, stop," she said loud enough that Landon could hear her. "Do what you need to do. Get someone else awake before Felix makes himself king of the world."

I sourly ate my last bite of sandwich. Trent went past, an English saddle in his arms. "I'll call you when I get back to the church." I chewed and swallowed. My eyes narrowed as I realized Trent was in with Red. He wasn't riding Red, was he? The horse had been trained for the track, not field. "Be careful."

"You too," Ivy said, and I looked away from how Trent's shoulders moved as he brushed the horse out. "If I don't hear from you by sunrise, I'm summoning you home."

I couldn't help my smile. "Thanks," I said softly. Home. She had said home, not the church, and that felt really good. "Ivy, tell Nina that it's all worth it. I promise."

"Thank you."

The click was loud, and I noted the time before I closed the phone and tucked it into a pocket. I liked Trent's stables. The air was always sweet smelling from fresh hay, and the air circulation was top-notch. Concerned, I pushed up and away from the saddles. Maybe Trent was just brushing the horse out.

"Red, right?" I said as I came forward, emboldened when the young horse flicked a friendly ear my way.

Trent smiled at me from inside the large box stall. "Right. Come on in."

He was wearing the same corporate-logoed coat I was, having changed into boots, jeans, and a thick shirt. There was a knit hat on his head, and I watched the horse, not Trent, as I lifted the latch, and Trent dipped under Red's neck to stand on her other side.

She was even more magnificent when close up, and I couldn't help but touch her, feeling her warmth and guessing at the speed she must be capable of. "My God, she's beautiful," I said softly, and Trent smiled at the horse—not me—freeing me to study the way his eyes crinkled.

"Isn't she? I'm riding her tonight." He smiled, patting her shoulder. "You can ride Tulpa. Your English seat has gotten good the last couple of months."

"Yeah, but—" I hesitated. "You were training her to race," I said, and then what he had really said sunk in. *He's going to let me ride his horse?*

Trent lifted a shoulder and let it fall, the brush making a soft hush of sound. "Ceri was right. She's not meant for the track, and she's not seen one since the afternoon Ceri . . . was taken. I'm going to give her to one of the girls when they get older. Ray, maybe, but Red's got a lot of bad manners to unlearn before then. Carlton's been working extensively with her to shift her signals and she's responding well, though she still explodes when given her head."

Nodding, I flipped part of her mane to the other side. "I didn't think you could switch a horse from track to western."

"Carlton can do anything," he murmured.

"And I'm on Tulpa?" I asked, and I pursed my lips when he nodded. The horse was friendly enough, but he was Trent's familiar. "Can't I just ride Molly?"

"Molly!" Trent eyed me over Red's withers. "You were the one who said I never gave you a horse you could win with. Besides, Molly hasn't been desensitized to the lines. Grab a brush, will you? Red's a big girl."

Flustered, I looked over the stall until I found one. The wood was smooth in my grip, the bristles stiff. Red flicked an ear when I gently brushed her, and emboldened, I pressed harder.

"You don't think you can take a horse through the lines and not freak them out of their flaky horse skulls, do you?" Trent said, a faint blush on his pointy ears. "After riding down Ku'Sox, I realized how big the hole in my security is, and since then I've been training my coursers to ride willingly through a line. Tulpa won't spaz out under you. Red, though . . ." He lifted a shoulder and let it fall. "She's young."

And flaky to begin with, I thought, and from down the hall, Landon snorted, turning it into a cough. Peeved, I gave him a dark look, having forgotten how well elves could hear.

For a moment, there was silence as we worked. Trent finished his side and tossed his brush across the hall to a basket. "Is . . . Tulpa okay?" he asked. "I can put you on another horse if you're unsure."

The hesitance in his voice caught at me, and my breath came fast.

"Trent!" came faintly through the stables, and Trent's smile faded at Bancroft's voice raised in annoyance. "I need some help with this wicked beast!"

But I was still lost in the thought that he wanted me to ride Tulpa. "Tulpa is fine."

"Good." Trent slid out of the stall and latched the door behind him. "Because Bancroft hardly knows the front from the back. I'll get him ready for you. Can you saddle Red for me?"

He trusted me to saddle his horse, and knowing what that meant, I nodded.

"Thanks." Smiling, Trent walked away, and Red's ears pricked as he shouted to Bancroft that he was coming. Landon watched him as he went by, and I wondered at that sly look of his. "What a baby you are!" I exclaimed softly to Red as I fondled her ears. "Such a sweet thing. I don't blame you for snapping at the nasty little men with their nasty little whips and caps." She snorted, matching my pitch, and I fell in love with her.

"Whips and little caps not your thing?"

Landon's voice startled me and Red nickered. "Hi." I put a hand to my face, then dropped it.

He brought his eyes back from the empty corridor, Trent's voice still echoing down it. "I appreciate you agreeing to do this. I know you have other obligations."

His mood bothered me, and I took up the currycomb and brushed Red some more. "No biggie. My previous obligations are settled and I've got the time." Red was picking up on my unease, the high-strung Thoroughbred bobbing her head. Trent could probably ride her just fine, but not me. I knew my limits.

"Can I ask you something?"

A warning flag rose when he came into the stall. Red backed up, and I went with her. I'd been around powerful men before, men who believed they were above the law either by birth, gender, or position, and something in his tone told me he was going to ask something that was probably none of his business, asking my permission so he could feel justified in being offended when I refused to answer. *Slime,* I thought, then reined in my emotions. This wasn't high school, and he wasn't Bob, Joseph, or Mathew. "Sure."

But I didn't like that Red kept flicking her nose up, warning him off.

"You meet with demons on a regular basis?" he asked, moving to Red's other side, right where Trent had been. My eyes met his, and his smile became predatory. "I only ask because your aura holds more smut than I've seen on any free person."

Is that so? "Not that it's any of your business, but I work to increase my proficiency just like anyone else with a skill. It leaves a mark."

"Mmmm." I looked up as I set the brush away. "Then you admit to practicing black magic on a regular basis."

Affronted, I checked Red's saddle pad for sticks or twigs. It was clean. I knew it would be, but I didn't like where this conversation was headed. "Smut is a show of created imbalance. It's not an accurate measure of morality."

"And you haven't answered my question."

I stared at him, the expanse of Red's back between us. Was he serious? "Yes," I finally said, because it was public knowledge. "I meet with Al. He's a demon. Some of what he teaches me are curses, but none of them are black." *Mostly.*

"Curses are black by definition."

"Then the definition is faulty, created by fearful men and women relying on hearsay instead of fact." Peeved, I put Red's saddle on her. It was a comfortable heaviness, and Red blew out her breath as the weight hit her. She was eager to run, and I cinched her loosely, planning on tightening it later.

I knew Landon was reading my "shut the hell up" signals just fine, but he had another question in his eyes when I turned around. "Then you admit you conscientiously apply yourself in learning black magic?"

Ticked, I reached for Red's bridle. "No. I don't. Excuse me, you're in my way."

He moved, but not as far back as I would've liked, and I unclenched my jaw, trying not to telegraph my mood to the horse. Red took her bit easily, and as Landon reached to do the strap, I jerked my hand back before we could touch. "Your aura is covered in smut. The mystics attracted to your aura can't hide it. Don't lie to me that you don't know black magic."

I yanked away, telling him to back off with my eyes as I finished the buckle.

"And you're tainting Trent with it," he continued, brow low. "When was the last time you did a black spell, Morgan?"

I looked at him, pissed. "Smut is imbalance, not a mark of evil. Most demon magic causes it, but not all demon magic is black, smut or not, and if you and your holier-than-thou religious zealots would pull yourselves out of your collective asses and actually look at it, you might figure that out!"

But he reached forward as I went to flip Red's reins over her head, and I started as a dart of ever-after shocked through me, hazing me like a second skin for a brief second.

"Hey!" I yelped, shoving him back, and he fell into the low wall of the stall, eyes smoldering. Red snorted and backed up. "What in hell are you doing?"

He wrung his hand as he got to his feet, expression dark. "Taking a detailed reading of your aura. You might have fooled Kalamack, but the dewar believes what we see, not what we wish, and you are black, Morgan. Back off from Kalamack. He's already lost the support of half the enclave because of you."

What? A widening of awareness expanded in me, and Red tossed her head as Bis swooped in, landing among the saddles across the corridor. His pushed-in face was tight in anger, and his feet clenched his perch hard enough to make the wood creak.

"I am not a black witch or a black demon," I said, rigid in anger. "Demon magic makes smut, and I don't do the bad stuff. Ask anyone in Cincy or the Hollows who does, and you'll get the same answer. Now take your white-bread ass out of Red's box before I throw you out."

A soft scuff drew my attention to the end of the hall. Trent stood there, and my face warmed. Had he lost political power because of me? Because I *worked* for him?

"Landon?" Trent's voice sounded icy cold and angry. "Would you help me with Bancroft. His balance is chancy."

With a final warning glance, Landon nodded. "Absolutely." He turned to me as if to say something, changing his mind when I pulled on the line in a silent warning to not touch me. He was lucky all I'd done was shove him. Seeing my hair beginning to snarl under the line's energy, he nodded, as if I'd confirmed his claim, and left.

I backed up to soothe Red, though to be honest, I was the one who needed the soothing.

Trent watched Landon go past him in search of Bancroft, and I shook my head when he wordlessly asked me if he wanted me to intervene. Mood bad, Trent followed Landon, and I busied myself with Red. Damn it, I could have probably handled that better.

"You okay, Ms. Rachel?" Bis asked, and I closed my eyes in a long blink.

"Fine," I said, my hand brushing Red. "Sorry. I didn't mean to bring you in here."

Bis shifted his feet. There were dents in the heavy wood. "He's a jerk. Forget him."

But I couldn't. He wasn't just a jerk, but one with the power to cause a lot of trouble. I'd known my working as Trent's security was going to raise eyebrows, but he hadn't seemed to care. He'd probably care now; the enclave was the political house of the elves, and therefore important. "He shouldn't have touched me."

"I know. That's why I came to check."

He was a good kid, and his ears pricked as the soft voices of Trent and Landon became more obvious. "You okay now?" he asked, and when I nodded, he stretched his wings and looked at the nearby open door. "I'll be outside when you're ready to go," he added, and Landon's horse tied to the door shied when he flew out like a huge bat.

Trent's voice raised, his anger clear as he said, "I didn't ask you here to test her morality. I asked you here to help solve a problem."

"I think she *is* the problem," Landon said, not a hint of remorse in his voice. "She is covered in smut. Smut caused by demon magic. She admits it."

"She admitted to doing black magic?"

"No, but that's the only place smut comes from."

What part of our conversation weren't you listening to? All of it? I wondered, feeling icky as I strained to hear

Trent say, "I watched her use a demon curse this week. It created a ball of light. It hurt no one, not even herself, and it caused smut. It was not black. Your logic is unsound, Landon. And I will stand in the enclave and say the same thing. Back. Off."

But my relief was short-lived. "Sa'han, if I may be candid, the reason the dewar is insisting on this marriage is because of your continuing association with demons."

"Rachel is—"

"Not a demon? Yes, she is, and you can't pull her back once you have pushed her across that line. I've seen all I need. Drop this association or you will lose what little support you still have. Marrying Ellasbeth is no longer enough to maintain your standing, living heirs or not."

Shocked, I slipped back into the stall as I understood what he was saying. Trent was being forced into this marriage because of me. To maintain control of the enclave and elven society, he had to marry Ellasbeth. He'd helped me survive, and I helped him in turn, and now he was going to lose everything.

"Landon!" Bancroft bellowed, and Red stomped, wanting to be out in the night.

"Your master is calling," Trent said, tone collected, but I could hear his anger.

I turned my back as the sound of Landon's boots went faint, not moving until the clop of another horse's hooves pulled me back around. Trent stood with Tulpa, the big animal watching Red with pricked ears. Trent's face looked as frustrated as mine, serious in dismay. I wasn't a black demon, but all the masses saw was perception, not truth.

"There's been a change in plan," he said, and I cinched Red's saddle tight and led her out. "I'm going with you, not Landon."

"Fine with me," I said, handing him Red's reins and swinging up onto Tulpa as if I'd ridden the huge animal every day of my life. I gave him a nudge, and he leaped for the door, his sudden burst of speed breathless. Trent was

right behind, and we took the fence at the end of the pad-
dock together, the wind in my hair and the darkness spilling
through me as we ran for the hill, oblivious of everything as
my thoughts churned.

Three months ago I might have simply shaken Trent's
hand and walked away. Now . . . it wasn't that easy.

Fourteen

Tulpa was a sweet, biddable horse, and I gave the old stallion a little pat as Trent came up beside us. Both horses shunned the tall, whispering grass, already having sampled it to find it as distasteful as everything else in the ever-after. The harsh landscape had a dusky red sheen, the nearly full moon nearing the western horizon. It was just shy of midnight and we'd been riding for hours. I could tell Trent was tired, but he didn't say anything as he brought his binoculars up, looking like a thief in his black pants and jacket with a matching black knit hat, scanning for a landmark that might be mirrored in reality where we could take simultaneous readings with Landon and Bancroft. I didn't really know why we were doing this anymore, except that if there was a chance that me parking it in the ever-after might wake the masters up, I'd do it.

Grit ground between my fingers as I wiped my face. A lot had changed since I'd traveled the ever-after that night with Trent. I glanced at Trent's closed expression—a lot hadn't.

Surface demons had found us almost as soon as we'd gotten the horses snorting and prancing across the realities. They had to be interested in the horses because Trent and I were clearly able to protect ourselves and surface demons preyed only on the weak.

"Where do you think we are?" Trent said, his expression lost behind the binoculars.

I shrugged, forgetting he couldn't see, then took my foot out of the stirrup to push Tulpa away from Red. He was making eyes at her even though she wasn't in season. "The industrial park, maybe?" I said. "That rise is probably in reality."

Trent's binoculars shifted to it. A rock clinked behind us, and he dropped them to rest on his chest. Expression grim, he nudged Red into a tight spin so we could watch each other's back. The horse's nostrils widened as she breathed in the scent of the surface demons. They were close—and becoming bolder.

"Bis?" I called, and the little gargoyle dropped to a nearby rock jutting from the surface. Red shied, but she calmed almost immediately under Trent's hand.

Bis's eyes seemed to glow in the shadow light, his black teeth glinting as he smiled. "You've six surface demons trailing," he said, and Trent's frown deepened.

"How close?"

"Not close. Not since I dropped a rock on one." Bis chuckled, which sounded like rocks in a garbage disposal. "They're curious about the horses, I think."

Curious, or hungry? We had to get moving. "Bis, could you tell Bancroft we want to take a reading on that hill?"

His wings opened, and Red snorted at Bis's rapid flapping and sudden liftoff as he made the short jaunt in mere moments. He hovered over the hill until I waved to tell him that was the spot, and then he winked out of the ever-after.

"Ready?" I prompted, and Trent spun Red around, neck arched and wanting to run. Bis would take Bancroft and Landon to the hill in reality, and then pop back so we could all take simultaneous readings. Trent was working the meter, but I was writing the results down as well.

We went to the hill in a slow canter, Trent fighting Red all the way. The mare was showing an increasingly dangerous alarm at what scuffed, trilled, and clinked. Once at the top, we settled in to wait, looking out over the wide expanse of basically nothing.

Before us and to the left were the remains of Cincinnati. The ever-after wasn't altogether real, and definitely not its own identity. Buildings rose when a new one went up in reality, but they broke even as they ghosted into existence, which was why the demons lived underground where their caverns remained untouched by what we did in the real world. The ever-after was a shadow of reality, populated by surface demons who were not demons at all.

I'd once believed the tall, skinny wraiths were the ancestors of elves or witches who had refused to flee the ever-after and had since been damaged by the ever-after sun. Now I wondered if they were really the shadows of people in reality, with their torn auras and malnourished state, but that didn't fit, either. Unlike the surface structures, they clearly had an independence from anything in reality. Al wouldn't talk about them, which made me wonder if they'd once been demons, now caught in an elven charm, destined to live in limbo forever—or at least until the two worlds collided.

We didn't have anything to do until Bis returned to tell us that Landon and Bancroft were in place, and I gave Trent a glance. He wasn't a big talker to begin with, but the more something bothered him, the less he was likely to talk about it . . . or anything else. Since Landon had given him the dewar's ultimatum, he hadn't said much of anything. "Trent, what does elven history say about surface demons?"

Somehow his expression became even more closed. "Nothing," he said, his voice clipped. "Rachel, I'd like to apologize for Landon."

A stab of alarm cut through me. "There's nothing to apologize for."

Brow furrowed, he looked past me to the horizon. He looked odd with that knit hat on, fair hair poking out from under it. "You have every right to file assault charges. He searched your aura, yes?" he said, flushed in anger. "What he did was appalling, and I apologize."

"I'm more worried about what he said than what he did. Trent—"

"I keep the company I wish, and no one is going to dictate otherwise."

"But—"

"I don't want to talk about it, Rachel."

He didn't want to talk about it. Fine. But this wasn't over. I liked him too much for him to sacrifice everything just so I could go on more dates thinly disguised as his security. "Ivy told me that they put Felix back in charge of the I.S."

Frowning, he looked over his shoulder at the shattered remains of Cincinnati as if it was a premonition. "I heard that too."

"He's not sane."

Red's nostrils were flaring, and she was trying her best to find something to spook at. "When are any of the undead?" he said, calming her. "They need a figurehead, and maybe he'll lead us to the Free Vampire faction. Is Nina okay?" he asked, surprising me. "I heard she was involved in an incident at Rynn Cormel's."

That was a nice way of putting it. "No. It was a big setback," I said, shoving the ugly images away. "Ivy's not giving up. She's proof that you can escape them."

"Love is strong that way," he said as he brought Red back from the edge with half his attention. Landon had threatened him, but I couldn't believe that his giving the elves viable children was worth nothing. *Unless they believed it was through me. Through demon magic.*

Red finally gave up trying to bolt, and Trent settled into the saddle. The last couple of months with Trent had been . . . interesting. With Ellasbeth threatening to stay, I was seeing things in the light of "last time" and I was shocked to realize I didn't like it, especially not with Landon's threat. If not for the different tax bracket thing, or that he was going to be engaged, or that because of me, he'd lose everything if he didn't marry Ellasbeth . . .

Good God. I need to just walk away.

Trent's grip tightened on the reins. Fearing surface demons, I spun to look down the hill, but there was nothing. Turning back, I froze as I saw his angry determination from under his bangs. "Al warned me off you yesterday. While you and Newt had your tea party," he said, and my shoulders stiffened. "I find that amusing," he said bitterly. "Five thousand years, and everyone is still fighting their damned war. And the elves are no better. The enclave's questioning of my status is based on an ancient law that limits my voice should I wed a barren woman. No children means no voice."

"But you have a child," I said, then bit my tongue.

"It's an excuse," Trent said. "Someone wants the progress I've made between the demons and elves stopped, and silencing my voice is the easiest way to do that."

"Oh." Embarrassed, I fiddled with making Tulpa's reins exactly the same length. But then I flushed as a new thought niggled and twisted its way deeper. He wasn't upset because of an archaic tradition equating children with power. He was upset that the dewar had told him it was Ellasbeth and power, or me and nothing. And he wanted both. Trent didn't take no well.

"There's no reason—" he started again.

"I understand," I said, not wanting to talk about it as the soft feel of Bis in my thoughts became obvious. He was searching me out. "It doesn't matter."

Lips a thin line, he hid himself behind his binoculars, scanning the path behind us. "It does matter."

"Not when there's no other choice," I said, meaning about three things, and I gave Tulpa a thankful pat, glad I was on him and not flaky Red. "Bis is coming."

Trent dropped the binoculars as the gargoyle popped in to startle the horses. "They're almost on top of you," Bis said, landing awkwardly on the ground since there weren't any rocks nearby bigger than a softball. "Take your reading."

Red stared at Bis, legs like posts, and the concerned gargoyle shifted his skin color to vanish against the red earth. She didn't like that either, and for a moment, Trent concentrated on keeping her from rearing as he danced her back and forth. Honestly, she was a little fruitcake.

"Zero point five hundred naught seven," Trent said, snatching a look at the meter. "You got that?"

"Bis," I pleaded, and the kid flashed back to his normal pebbly gray skin and pointedly walked away. Finally Red calmed, and I wrote the reading down on a scrap of paper. Trent wasn't happy about my casual regard to science, but the number was clear and precise.

"Maybe we should get moving," Trent said as he tucked the handheld meter away.

"I so agree," I said, sending Tulpa down the hill in a jolting, uncomfortable motion.

"That way?" Trent pointed to the towering slumps of rocks, and when I nodded, we took off at a fast canter across the wide flat plain full of rocks and dips. A frustrated howl echoed, and we turned. Behind us, three surface demons stood under the open sky, unable to keep up. Bis laughed from overhead, but I wasn't happy. The horses were vulnerable. This might have been a mistake, and from the look on Trent's face, I could tell he felt the same way.

"I know this place," he said loudly, and we slowed to a jolting trot.

"Rail yard?" I guessed, seeing a deep gully cut across the landscape. It was flat here, but across it were the dips and slumps of broken buildings.

Trent pointed to a substantial road spanning the ravine. "I don't like how close the surface demons are. Let's get across before we take a reading."

"I'll find a good path for you," Bis said, and Red snorted when he flew ahead, hovering over the broken bridge before dropping down to check out the underside.

Tulpa went first; if the ground gave way under him, the older horse would react better than Red. The excitable mare was becoming more and more agitated, testing Trent's implacable cool as our hooves echoed and we skirted the gaping holes. If we were to be ambushed, it would be here. I breathed easier when we finally made it across, but I couldn't shake the feeling we were being surrounded.

"This looks good. Bis?" I said, just wanting to get a reading and move on.

The gargoyle stood on a pile of rock, wings held tight to his body as he tried not to scare Red. "It might take a while. You wouldn't believe the cops on the other side," he said, and then he sort of sidestepped into nothing. *Wow, the kid is really getting good.*

I wanted to get down from Tulpa but didn't dare. I glanced at Trent. "Thanks for doing this with me."

Trent looked up from the meter. "I wasn't about to leave you alone with Landon." A wry smile showed in the dusky light. "I know you better than that."

Tulpa had sidled up close, and Red seemed to appreciate it. "I hope you can get home through the blockades," I said. "But with your pull, it probably won't be hard."

"Shouldn't be, but things change." Eyes squinting, Trent kept looking at the moon, estimating the remaining light, maybe. Red nickered when a sliding rock clinked not four hundred yards away, and my expression blanked when a tall surface demon slowly pulled himself up from behind a boulder to look down at us. The gritty wind pulled at his tattered clothing, making it seem as if it were his aura fluttering, ragged and torn.

"He's a bold one," Trent said, his voice just as calm as before, and I knew the surface demon heard him when he hissed. We had to leave. Science day was over.

Trent turned in the saddle. His expression was grim when he spun back to me. "I don't think we're going to get any more readings. Where's the nearest line to get out of here?"

My pulse pounded. We weren't in any immediate danger, but the horses were. "Ahhh, the university?" I said, wincing as I realized the surface demon had vanished. "Or Eden Park." Neither of them were good choices, the first too far away, and the second up an impassable hill. "Oh!" I said suddenly, and Tulpa snorted, stomping his foot at nothing I could see. "There's one just across the river. I keep forgetting the river is empty here. We can just run across it."

Red whinnied. Tulpa's ears went back, neck arched and tail up like a war horse. Trent pulled Red up short, and she spun, barely under control. "There!" Trent shouted, and Red danced sideways as a huge slump of building slid into the empty tributary we'd just crossed.

Surface demons scrabbled out, howling and brandishing rocks like the long dead. Red kept backing up, rising up on her haunches as Trent yelled at her. Tulpa finally broke his cool, and I struggled to bring him around to face the demons as I pulled heavily on the nearest line.

Squealing, Red dropped to her front feet, taking the bit between her teeth when the reins went slack—and then she bolted.

"Trent!" I shouted, giving Tulpa his head as she ran, almost going down as her feet skidded in the scree. Her eyes were wild with fear as she found her balance and rose, Trent still on her. A surface demon howled, and Red lunged to escape, taking a tiny opening and clattering onto a wide boulevard. My heart pounded as I followed. The shadows of the buildings seemed to hold a hundred eyes as we thundered past.

"Rachel?" Trent shouted as we caught up, but Red was totally out of control. Leaning, I reached for her bridle, and the horse lunged ahead. She had been teased, tormented, and frustrated by Trent's dubious training techniques. If there was a trick, she knew it.

"I have to let her run it out!" he cried, and I dropped back. Out of control or not, we were headed for the river.

She is a damn fast horse, I thought as Tulpa began to slowly lose ground.

And then a soft boom turned into a building slowly crumbling down before us.

"Look out!" Trent shouted, managing to get Red slowed enough that Tulpa barely took the lead. Out of her stupid horse mind in fear, Red followed him, making a hoof-sliding turn to the left behind us. Trent looked pissed as he struggled to bring Red under control as we galloped down the ruin of Cincinnati's streets, the way remarkably clear. Unusually clear. *Not good.*

"We're being forced somewhere!" I yelled, and Trent's jaw tightened. "We have to get across the river!" I called out, my heart pounding at the sudden silhouette standing atop a building, watching us. "Trent—"

Howling and waving a stick long as a broom handle, a surface demon rose up right in front of us. Tulpa screamed in anger, and I fought to keep him from charging. Red squealed in terror, the stupid mare spinning in useless circles. Surface demons were dropping from the surrounding buildings like spiders.

"Tulpa! Stand!" I shouted, and the old stallion screamed at me again, but finally halted, lungs heaving and sweating as I gathered a wad of energy and forced it into my hand. The surface demons circled us, all of them reaching for Red. "You will not touch her!" I exclaimed, and with a huge pull on the line, I shouted, *"Detrudo!"*

The curse exploded from me in a visible wave, blowing the surface demons back like leaves and sending them head over heels into the shadows. Red screamed in terror, rearing up and teetering backward. Trent gave her her head so she wouldn't fall, and with that bare hint of control, she dropped to four feet, lowered her head, and bucked him right off.

"Trent!" I screamed, and Tulpa lurched to him as Trent sat on the ground, struggling for air as Red's horsy ass quickly vanished into the dark and down the open path between the buildings. Hooting, the surface demons flashed into a flailing motion after her. In five seconds flat we were alone, the sound of Red's hooves and the howling demons fading.

"Ow," Trent said softly, his alarm hesitating as he got up and felt his backside. "She bucked me off," he said as if in awe. "That flaky horse dropped me!"

"It happens to me all the time," I said, fear tightening my shoulders at Red's distant whinny. "Come on. Get up!" I extended my arm down to him as if I actually knew how to lift a person onto a horse like that, and Trent took it, somehow managing the leap as if we'd done it all the time. Thank God I'd learned how to ride English. It made stuff like this easier.

He settled in behind me, Tulpa spinning as Trent gripped me around the waist. Without warning, he shouted, "Hiiiee!," and Tulpa bolted, Trent's heels and seat pushing him forward.

I might be holding the reins, but I wasn't in control, and a shiver went through me as Trent screamed the word, his anger, desperation, and fear all rolled into one decisive action. The wind whipped my hair, and breathless, I held on as Tulpa shifted direction, cued by Trent's legs more than my reins. Behind us was a wild howl of frustration. "I thought you said Red was desensitized to magic," I said, shouting so he could hear me.

"Magic, yes. Explosions, no!" he shouted back, his lips inches from my ear to make me shiver again. "Where did you learn how to pull a rider up like that?"

"The movies?" I said, and he made a sound of disbelief.

We rose up a small hill, easily seeing over the damaged buildings. The wind lessened as Tulpa's pace eased, and Trent brought him up short as we came to a drop-off. It was the dry bed of the Ohio River, and I stared as Tulpa stood and breathed hard. Down below and about half a mile ahead, a horse raced down the smooth expanse, a dozen surface demons chasing her.

"My magic won't work that far," I said, guilt and fear making my stomach churn.

Trent's weight shifted, and Tulpa took the slope. Trent slid into me, the jostling motion jarring until we found the bottom and he settled back. Again Trent shouted, and Tulpa stretched into a gallop. I hunched low, Trent pressed close. The scent of wine and cinnamon poured over me, and the wind was a wall. I could feel Trent's tension, and the horse under us beginning to tire. Tulpa was not young—but he had heart.

Heart, though, would not catch Trent's best mare, not when she ran unfettered with the hounds of hell chasing her.

We weren't going to catch her, and I could have cried when Trent sat up, murmuring softly to Tulpa to bring the horse down into a slower pace until we stopped, watching Red again become faint with the dusky red and distance.

"Trent, I'm sorry," I said as Tulpa hung his head and heaved for air under us.

"I'm less than useless," he said bitterly, turning to see me. "I'll get off. You can probably catch her if I'm not dragging you down."

"You!" I exclaimed, then gasped at the sudden and sure tug on the line. Both our eyes shot to where we'd last seen Red. A huge dome of energy had risen, tainted with red and the black of smut. The flailing outlines of surface demons flew through the air. "Newt!" I shouted as I saw her silhouette, arms raised as she screamed defiantly at the surface demons, and then the bubble of energy was gone, the shadow of Red rearing up before she found her feet and ran.

"Newt . . ." I mused, feeling as if Red was going to be okay as I saw Newt run after her. Newt wouldn't let surface demons touch her. Not if that had been any indication.

"My God, that horse can run," Trent said, his bitterness tempered with pride. But silver eyes had turned to us, and I stiffened when I realized they were the very demons that Newt had tossed aside. Behind us were even more, and Tulpa was tired, burdened by us.

"Ah, Trent?" I said, pointing, and his expression grew resolute.

"Not quite done, Tulpa," he said, leaning around me to pat his horse's neck, and the old stallion made a soft sound as if to say he was up to it. "Nearest line?" he asked me, and I sent out a quick thought, relieved when I found it.

"Up there," I said, bringing Tulpa around and nudging him into a fast walk. The approaching demons tightened their formation. Tulpa noticed it, too, voluntarily picking up the pace. "I think that's a path," I said, and the massive animal lunged forward into the climb. Trent's arm had gone around me again, and I was increasingly aware that he smelled really, really good despite the burnt-amber stench that permeated everything.

"It's going to be close," he said, words a warm breath on my neck.

I snuck a look behind us as Tulpa scrambled up the last of the hill. The surface demons had packed up, but as I watched, they split again, half deciding to run after Newt and Red, the other coming after us, taking the slope as if it was nothing. "You aren't kidding."

If I died here, Jenks was going to be pissed. Awareness searching, I found the line again and nudged Tulpa in the right direction. The slumps of rocks were fewer, and the grass more prevalent on this side of the dry river, tall enough to hide a surface demon in the moonlight. Trent's arm around me tightened. I wanted to kick Tulpa into a run, but the horse was exhausted, head bobbing as he walked fast. His ears kept flicking behind us, listening for pursuit.

"It's a pretty big line," I said, trying to ignore the sensations that were plinking through me as I sat before Trent. "I'm going to walk the length with Tulpa. I've never shifted three auras before. This is going to be tricky without Bis."

Tricky, but not impossible, I thought as I closed my eyes and brought my second sight up. A sigh of relief went through me as I saw the line. But the grass was moving contrary to the wind. Tulpa noticed too, and the horse snorted, his feet lifting a little higher. If we could just get across, the church was only a few blocks away.

"Ah, Trent?" I said.

"I see it . . ." he said tersely. "You sure you can't do this at a run?"

"No?" I squeaked out, heart pounding as the line took us. The surface demons hooted, and I closed my eyes, desperately shifting all three of our auras to the resonance of the line. Tulpa nickered, and a shudder passed through me. The awful wind died, and I took a breath, my eyelids cracking open when Tulpa stopped. The howling of the surface demons muted, dulled, and then renewed into the more mundane alarm of a cop car. We were home.

"Thank you," Trent breathed, and the tack jingled as the horse dropped his head, nosing the mown grass as if wanting to roll in it. We'd made it back, but we'd lost Red.

We were in someone's backyard, fenced on two sides, with low shrubs separating it from the yard over. There was an inground pool, the soft lights making reflective patterns on the undersides of the trees. It belonged to a witch, I was guessing, by the flowers arranged in an antihex circle by the back door.

"Good boy," Trent said as Tulpa clip-clopped over the decking to get a drink. "Lots of treats for you tonight."

Feeling icky, I looked up at the sky. It was just as red as the ever-after, the low clouds hiding the moon and reflecting the emergency lights and fires in the Hollows. The scent of burning furniture had replaced the acidic bite of burnt amber. It was quiet here, but a street over I could hear someone on a bullhorn shouting half-heard demands and the dull thumps of a drum. All hell was breaking loose. Inderlanders didn't take well to being cordoned off.

"Let's get to the church," I said, reluctant to dismount, and from inside the house, a light flicked on. Tulpa lifted his head, prickly lips dripping. A door slammed open, and a dark silhouette showed, a wand at the ready. An outside light blossomed, and I squinted at the bright white light, my night vision completely ruined.

"What the hell are y'all doing in my yard?" a man asked, his anger dulled by the incongruity of a horse, no doubt.

"Leaving . . ." I prompted.

"Thanks for the water," Trent called. "Sorry about the bushes."

"My bushes?" the man asked, but Trent had reached around me to take the reins and wiggle his heels into Tulpa. My eyes widened as he sent the horse at a dead run toward them. They were only three feet high, an easy jump, but Tulpa was carrying two and was exhausted.

"Ohhhh noo!" I called out, a thrill running through me as Tulpa crashed through them.

Head up, Tulpa pranced into the street—his hooves tatting out a merry beat as the man shouted at us. I didn't understand Trent's mood. He'd just lost the end point of ten years of careful breeding—the foundation for the next generation—and he was laughing as a spotlight from a cop car turned to find us.

"You!" a magically enhanced voice boomed out, and the world was suddenly cast in a white-light relief. "Yes, you on the horse," the cop shouted when Trent pointed at us. "You're breaking curfew. Put your hands up. Both of you!"

"Ah, if I let go of the reins, the horse is going to run away!" Trent said from behind me, and then softer, to me, "I don't particularly want to spend the night explaining things, do you?"

"No. Church is that way." I pointed with my chin, and when the cop demanded that we dismount, Trent gave Tulpa his head and shouted something elven.

Tulpa sprang into motion. I gasped and thumped back into Trent. His arm went around me, and grinning, I inched myself forward again.

"Ah, shit! They're running. Hey! Come back here!" the cop shouted, and Trent urged Tulpa into a faster pace, shifting him up onto the lawns to dodge kiddie pools and bikes as we trotted through the Hollows, the cop car following with his siren blaring.

"Ms. Rachel!" came an urgent call from overhead, and Tulpa's ears flicked when Bis darted through the trees. "I saw what happened," he said, his skin a dark black as he flew alongside. "Thank the scrolls that you made it to the line."

"Stop! Or I'll shoot!" the cop shouted, and outrage shocked through me when a pop cracked through the air. *They're shooting at us? Are you kidding me?*

"Damn," Trent said, sending Tulpa pacing through a side yard to cut to the next street over. "It's not any safer over here."

But he was wearing that weird smile I couldn't figure out when I leaned to look. "That way!" I said, and Tulpa shifted on a dime. "Go!" I shouted when the cop car skidded around the corner, going full tilt the wrong way down a one-way.

We were only two blocks from the church, and Tulpa took a low fence as we crossed another row of houses. From the street we'd just left, the cop revved his engine and backed up, sirens wailing.

"We aren't getting over the fence at the church," Trent said, his words a tingling sensation on my cheek. "I'll slide down to open it. Just get him through."

"You're the better rider. I'll get it!" I said, and then we both ducked when Bis buzzed us.

"I'll get the gate," he said, then darted away.

Tulpa's feet skidded on the hard pavement as we found the next street, and I breathed in the scent of wine as we trotted for a block—until that cop showed up again, spotlight searching. "Hurry!" I shouted. I could see the church steeple. We were almost home.

"What the Tink blasted hell are you doing?" Jenks shrilled, dusting when that cop car whooped his siren, spotlight searching. "You're on a horse? Seriously?"

"Jenks, help Bis with the gate, will you?" I said, laughing as Trent pushed Tulpa into a soft canter, staying on the sidewalk to hide the prints. Bis had the gate open, and Tulpa snorted at the sudden flash of pixy dust as Jenks's kids found us. I waved them off, telling them to dampen their dust as Tulpa walked into the garden, head up and his nostrils flaring. We were home.

"You guys stink," Jenks said as I slid off Tulpa, right after Trent. Knees aching, I hobbled to the gate, closing it and standing on tiptoe to watch the cop car drive past. The cop's radio was turned up loud, and I ducked down as the searchlight played over the carport, then the church. A slice of it made it through the fence, and my whisper to stay quiet was never spoken as I saw Trent.

He was standing beside Tulpa, holding the big animal's head in his arms to keep him quiet, lovingly rubbing his fuzzy ears. His clothes were covered in ever-after dust, rumpled and dirty. He looked nothing like himself, and seeing me looking at him, he pulled the black cap off, leaving his hair in complete disarray. His eyes smoldered with the memory of our race. I took a breath to say something, finding no words.

And then the spotlight moved and he was a shadow.

"Nice. Really nice," Jenks said as Bis sat on the fence, clearly worried as his feet put new dents in it. "I've got a horse in my yard. Ivy is going to freak out."

"Ah, Bancroft and Landon are in custody," Bis said, his eyes squinched apologetically. "That's what kept me. I'll tell them you're okay."

"Bis, wait," I said, but he had already launched himself. Jenks scowled as he hovered before a captivated Tulpa, but he was probably more angry that I'd been in trouble than upset about a horse in his backyard.

"Maybe you should stay the night," I said to Trent. "If they put Bancroft in custody, they'll probably lock you up just for fun."

"I agree." His voice was soft, and his eyes were on the sky. "Ah, I'm sure the couch will be more than adequate."

My bed is softer, I thought, then pushed down the thought.

Jenks looked between me and Trent, his dust shifting to an odd silver pink. "We can do better than that. Wayde's cot is still up in the belfry."

"Belfry?" Trent loosened the cinch and pulled the saddle from Tulpa, pad and all.

"It's surprisingly nice up there," I said. "He fixed it up. Real windows . . . lock on the door." *Lock on the door? Had I really said lock on the door?*

Trent turned with the saddle. "Capital. Thank you, Jenks. Can I use your phone? I should tell Quen where I am, and the towers are down."

Again? Frustrated, I reached for Tulpa's reins. "I'll cool him off," I offered, not wanting to go inside yet. My thoughts were churning. I had no right to be looking at Trent like that. None.

"You sure?" Trent asked, and I started back to the graveyard, horse in tow. The pixy kids were playing with Tulpa's mane, and the patient horse was taking it well, making me wonder if Trent had a few pixies he didn't know about in his stables.

"You'd better call Quen," I said, almost walking into Ivy's grill. "He and Ellasbeth are going to be worried sick." A sudden thought stopped me, and I reached into a pocket. "Ah, here are the readings. They'll probably want them, too."

"Thank you." Trent didn't move as I extended the paper and he took it. He wanted to talk to me. I couldn't do this, and I turned, pace fast as I led Tulpa deeper into the graveyard.

"My God, you stink," Jenks said to Trent, his voice becoming faint. "I've got some clothes from when I was your size, but you're going to have to shower before you put them on. I don't want them ruined. You really smell."

"Thanks, I'd appreciate that."

Jaw clenched, I stopped in the darkest, most secluded spot in the graveyard. The daydream of Trent in my shower rose back up, and I quashed it. Pulling my borrowed jacket off, I began to wipe the sweat from Tulpa with it. Was it cowardice if there was no way?

My mind said no, but my heart said yes.

Fifteen

The sheets were light atop me, and I languorously stretched a foot down, jerking when it slipped out of its warm spot and into the cold. Feeling fuzzy headed, I looked at the sunlight on my ceiling. It was morning, or early afternoon, maybe. I could hear pixies past my stained-glass window propped open with a pencil. Rolling over, I looked at my clock. The radio was on in the kitchen. It was turned to the news. That was weird. Ivy never listened to the news in the morning.

Trent.

Heart thudding, I sat up. He was still here. Had to be. He wouldn't just leave, would he?

I lurched out of bed. My blue robe wasn't going to happen, and as the muted sounds of the announcer droned, I did the hop-scuff into a clean pair of jeans and slipped into a fresh camisole. My hair was a mess. There was no way I was going to go into the kitchen without a stop in the bathroom first; perfume didn't cover morning breath. It was almost eleven. Trent had been up for hours.

Breath held, I cracked open the door. The smell of coffee dove deep into me, alluring.

"It's God's retaliation against the wicked," a masculine voice said, his vehemence dulled by the radio speaker. "Cincinnati is being visited by *God himself* in the guise of a blood-borne virus. It will sweep away the undead and leave the clean!"

"That's dumber than tits on a man," Jenks said, and when Trent chuckled, I ran to the bathroom for the detangler. My bare feet were silent on the cold oak, and I winced when the door squeaked.

The radio dulled to nothing, and I stood just inside the bathroom, breathing in Trent's wine and woods scent. There was a water glass on the sink, and one of the toothbrushes Ivy and I had bought for Jenks when he was human-size. The wrapper was in the trash can, and a set of towels, clearly used but folded up, were on top of the dryer.

Trying to be quiet, I got ready for the day. I'd seen Trent's bathroom. It was bigger than my kitchen and had a closet of equal size attached. I was just finishing my teeth when Jenks slid in under the door, his dust a cheerful silver. "'Bout time you got up," he said, hands in his pockets instead of on his hips as he hovered such that his reflection was easier to see than him.

"You mind?" I said, spitting in the sink. Trent's glass was sitting there, and after hesitating, I used my hands to get some water as I always did. Yep. No social grace at all.

"Wow, I don't think I've ever seen your hair like that before. You going retro eighties?"

Dismayed, I looked at the snarled, frizzy mess. "It's called going to bed with your hair wet," I said as I sprayed detangler and tried to comb it. I had a charm in the kitchen . . . but it was in the kitchen. Frustrated, I finally put it in a scrunchie and called it good. The man had seen me in sweats and in a hospital bed. *I shouldn't care. I don't care.*

"You should have Trent over more often," Jenks said, his wings transparent with motion. "It's nice talking with someone without having to wade through all that estrogen."

"I'll get you a puppy." Trying for a cool attitude, I gave myself a last look, adjusted my camisole, and headed out. Jenks darted before me, his dust trailing behind like vanishing crumbs in the forest. Trent had his head in the fridge when I came in, and my heart gave a thump. My eyes went to the windowsill and his ring, still under the water glass with Al's chrysalis. *Crap, he probably already saw it. He's going to know it's important to me.*

"Morning," I said, arms swinging awkwardly, and he pulled himself up and out. He was wearing Jenks's sweats from when he was human-size. And stubble. *Whoa.* The slight haze threw him into an entirely new category of yummy, and I stood there, blinking like an idiot as he rubbed his face, clearly knowing it had caught my attention.

"Morning," he echoed, glancing at the clock to confirm it was still before noon. "Are you hungry?" He stood at the fridge, tugging at his sweats as if uncomfortable.

"She's always hungry," Jenks said. "You should see how this woman can eat!"

"Don't you have something to do, Jenks?" I said, wondering what Trent would look like with a real beard. *Stop it, Rachel.*

"What . . ." Jenks complained. "I like a woman who eats." Wings clattering, he went to the sink to check on his kids in the garden. "None of this prissy 'Oh, just a salad. I'm watching my waistline.' Hot dogs and milkshakes, baby! Give you energy for more important stuff."

I shot Jenks a look to shut up before he could enumerate, and when he took a deep breath, I threw the dishcloth at him. Trent looked up at the noise, and I stuffed my hands in my pockets. "What looks good?" I said, trying for nonchalant as I went to stand at the fridge beside him. *His stubble was reddish blond. Cool.*

Trent's eyes met mine, and suddenly unsure, I backed up, deciding to get some coffee. From the counter, the radio was running a list of closings. There were a lot, from social events to entire businesses. "I was thinking about French toast, but it has eggs in it," Trent said, and I poured myself a cup of long-brewed coffee.

"Most days I can handle that much without a problem." I leaned against the counter, a safe five feet between us. The mug was warm, and the coffee tasted as good as it smelled. I let a swallow slip down, waking me up. It was a good day, bright and sunny. It didn't jibe with the serious tone of the announcer talking about the riots at the closed borders, and I wondered if Trent might go running with me sometime. He had the build for it. Then I frowned. Why would he want to go running with me? He had an entire private woods to run in where he wouldn't have to dodge strollers or dog crap.

"Good coffee," I said, and he came out of the fridge with a carton of eggs and milk.

"Jenks said you liked it dark," he said, and then my head snapped up as Edden's voice came over the radio.

"Hey, listen!" I said as I reached for the knob, and Jenks got over his dishcloth-induced sulk, coming to sit on my shoulder as we stared at the radio as if it were a TV.

"Let me say again," Edden's smooth voice said over the click of cameras. "The rumor that Cincinnati and the Hollows are closed due to a biological threat is false. After expert analysis of data gained last night, we can definitively say that the magic misfires and the inability of the undead to wake is *not* biological, but a calculated attack on the undead by a fringe organization called the Free Vampires. Outside help is being obtained, but until we resolve this, Cincinnati and the Hollows will remain locked down with no entry or exit. We don't want those responsible for this getting out of our jurisdiction."

The reporters shouted questions, and I looked at Trent, knowing Inderlanders would respond badly to being fenced in no matter what the reason.

"Listen to me!" Edden shouted, and they all shut up. "I know this isn't popular, but we are confident that the people responsible are still in Cincinnati or the Hollows. I'm asking everyone to calm down and be cooperative, and for God's sake, don't go targeting your neighbors because they have fangs. We've got a hotline set up if you think you have something we need to know, and I'm confident—"

I turned the radio off, arms around my middle. And the day had started so nice, too. "Edden told them," I said, surprised. "They must be out of leads."

"Either that or they were worried about a panic that a new virus was killing the undead. You know how sensitive everyone is about that." Catching back a snort, I nodded. He was looking at my bare feet, and I tried to hide one under the other. "It was Bancroft's idea to break the news," he said as his gaze rose to my spelling pots hanging over the center island counter. "I phoned the data to him last night. He says thank you."

Bancroft? My suspicion rose. "Always glad to help," I said, watching how Trent's hand entirely encompassed the bottom of my smallest spelling pot as he gently lifted it free of the hook, but my notion to tell him not to cook with it slipped away as I remembered seeing him last year, wet from the shower, a towel around his hips and his hair clinging to his face. His abs had been beautiful, his waist trim, and his skin taut as he moved. "And?" I said, hiding behind my cup.

"Moving you to the ever-after won't solve anything."

"Oh, thank all that is holy," I said, slumping. "Ah, not that I wouldn't have."

He smiled, and I slid to the side so he could throw the shells away. Jenks was using both hands to work the twist tie on the bread bag, and I belatedly got a plate down, feeling like a fifth wheel.

"Thanks," Trent said. "I hope you don't mind me using your exercise bike. I needed to stretch out after last night. I've not ridden like that in a long time."

I dropped my eyes before they caught his. His mood was pinging on my subconscious. Something was on his mind other than breakfast. I had a feeling I knew what it was, and I didn't want to talk about it. "You used Ivy's machine? It's a good one, isn't it."

From the sink Jenks's wings hummed in discontent. His kids must be up to mischief. "Hey, I owe you, cookie man,"

Jenks said as Trent found a fork to beat the eggs with. "It would have taken me all summer to move those rocks."

"I said I'd help you with that," I said, and Jenks's dust shifted to an annoyed orange.

"Like I said, all summer," he said to make me feel guilty. Trent, though, was all smiles.

"My pleasure. I don't count us even, yet. Moving rocks isn't payment enough for your help last year."

Stealing his daughter, I thought, wondering if it had really only been a year. "Can I help with anything?" I asked, needing something to do so I'd stop thinking about stuff.

"No, I've got it," he said as he took a pan from under the counter and set it on the stove.

"I'm not used to people making me breakfast," I said as I sat at the table. Jenks was watching me as if I was doing something wrong, and I made a *what?* face, switching back to a bland smile when Trent came up from eyeing the flame under the pan.

"I hope you don't mind I just hung out here this morning. Ivy wasn't back yet and you were sleeping. I didn't want to simply leave." He touched the inside of the pan once, then again, clearly dissatisfied with the temp. "I like your church. It's quiet, but in a good way. Not lonely."

Jenks frowned at me, and I had no idea why. "Excuse me," he said, his tone almost caustic as he flew out the kitchen.

Whatever. "Thanks," I said as Trent crossed his arms and stifled a yawn. It was nearing noon. Time for all good pixies and elves to siesta. I wasn't all that rested myself. Sleep had been hard to find, and fleeting. There was an unfamiliar laptop and a mug of coffee beside me, and I glanced at Ivy's spot at the table. The laptop was shiny enough to be hers, but she'd just gotten a new one. "Yours?" I asked.

Trent held his hand over the pan and pulled back. "Quen had it couriered over. Cincy is locked down, but there're a few ways in and out of the Hollows yet if you know the back roads. Oh, that reminds me," he said as he almost danced to the table and picked up a set of keys and jingled them. "Your car is in the carport."

"Thanks!" I said, stuffing them in my front pocket. My car wasn't just a car, it was my freedom, and he knew it. "At least now you know you can get Tulpa home," I said. But then guilt hit me, and I set my mug aside. "Trent, I'm so sorry you lost Red—"

Head shaking, Trent reached for the egg mixture. "It's my fault. Carlton said she wasn't ready. I disagreed. He was right. Ten to one Newt has her."

"Even so, she's still lost. She must be worth a fortune."

"And then some," he admitted, face grim. "I can't *believe* I fell off her."

"I'm really sorry. If Newt does have her, I'll see about getting her back."

Head down over the egg mix, he sighed. "I'd appreciate that."

I eased back in my chair, an odd feeling rising through me. I'd heard Trent say those words half a dozen times a day, and every time he meant it, but this time it was about something he couldn't buy or fix, and he knew I'd offered because it was important to him and I just wanted him to be . . . happy.

I'm not doing this! I thought, panicking even as the warm feeling born from caring about someone suffused me. Beyond the walls of my church, all hell was breaking loose. I didn't have time to fall in love. "I can't tell you how long it's been since anyone made me breakfast," I said, almost whispered, really, as I tried to get a handle on this. "Thanks."

"My pleasure." The snap of the nutmeg top was loud. "I can't tell you how long it's been since I've had anyone I've wanted to cook for. You look content in the early light."

My thoughts swung back to Landon's threats, and I made myself rise to get more coffee. "Seriously?" I said lightly. "I've not even been able to get through my hair yet. Burnt amber seems to bring out the worst in it."

He was coming over to me, and I backed up, my spine hitting the counter. "I like it like that," he said, not looking at me as he pulled open a cupboard and took down a large plate to soak the bread in. "All out like a lion's mane. Comfortable. Wild."

Wild. He liked my hair. My heart pounded, and my stomach felt funny. "Trent," I said softly, and his eyes fixed on mine. He was so close the light caught in his stubble and the scent of him drifted through my awareness.

"You kept my ring," he said. "Why?"

"You want it back?" I was flushing, and he caught my arm as I reached for it. Tingles fed upon themselves, rising to find my core where the sensation settled in to grow.

"I'm glad you did." He set the plate down, and I held my breath. His grip on my wrist was tight but not imprisoning.

"Trent, maybe Landon is right. You have responsibilities and I understand that." *What am I doing?* "So do I."

Still, he moved closer, and my heart pounded when he looked at my lips. "Landon who?"

My eyes widened when his long hand slid across my cheekbone as he leaned across the space between us and brazenly kissed me. "Mrent," I mumbled, shocked, but he pulled me to him with a sudden tug. A spike of desire dove through me, fueled by the demand of his hand on my waist. His lips moved against mine, and the scent of him plinked through me. My eyes closed, and I leaned into him, little drops of feeling sparking wherever his fingers touched, wherever my hands found him. His stubble was prickly, and the newness of it was thrilling.

Oh God, it was the best kiss yet, and my toes pressed into the floor as I leaned into him. His hand slipped behind my neck, the slight hint of a tightening grip bringing my fervor to a sudden and unexpected pitch.

It took everything I had to pull from his lips, and even as I did, I felt a new desire layering itself over the old, soaking in where it would linger in my thoughts. I could say nothing, the long length of our bodies touching, his hand at my neck and back, mine at his waist. The heat of desire was in his eyes, and I could hardly breathe, imagining what it would be like to have him—have everything. *Right now.*

"I enjoyed last night," he said softly, the words making me shiver, though it might be the sensation of his fingers hinting at pulling me back to him. "Riding," he added, a gentle pressure building between us. "You before me. I'm glad you stayed on this time." He smiled.

"Me too," I whispered. "I wish . . ." His fingers eased their pressure, and I looked away. "I wish things were different," I said, then held my breath as I looked up at him, regret tightening the corners of my eyes. "You have *everything* waiting for you. I don't want to ruin that."

Trent's expression became empty, and I pulled away, hating myself.

"Please don't close up," I begged, but his hands had fallen away, and I took them in my own. "Talk to me."

Exhaling, he looked up from our joined hands. "No, you're right." His focus blurred at the sound of a motorcycle at the curb. "I should listen to the people whose experience I value. I don't want to hit the ground again. Excuse me. Quen is coming in about an hour with a horse trailer. I'd like to be showered by then. Do you mind?"

There was no regret in his tone, no accusation. Nothing. "No, go ahead," I said, and he nodded and turned away.

My throat was tight as I looked at that damn skillet on the stove, now radiating heat waves. The door to the bathroom clicked shut, and hunched, I turned to the window. My stomach hurt, and I held it. The passion of that kiss still rang through me. Stopping it had been the right thing to do. *It had!* I was not going to be his mistress. I was better than that.

"You are a blind fool, Rache," Jenks said from the archway to the hall, and I spun, wiping the hint of moisture from my eyes.

"And you're a Peeping Tom," I accused when the shower went on and Trent couldn't hear us. His beard would have grown in soft. I could almost feel it on my fingers right now.

Jenks flew in, the greenish-purple dust telling me he was pissed if his scowl wasn't enough. "I am not. I like happy endings, and you're ruining it!"

"Whose happy ending?" I said as the church's door opened and a pixy sang out a cheerful greeting. "Not mine."

"Rache . . ." Jenks rose up, his expression pleading as his dust hit the pan and sparkled. "I can't believe I'm saying this, but you're perfect for each other! You irritate people, and he smooths things out. You have good mojo, and he only thinks he does. You're broke, and he's rich. You've got those weird feet of yours, and he's got them cute ears."

"Stop it!" I whispered, not wanting Ivy to hear. "It was a mistake going on that date, and I won't jeopardize his future with Ellasbeth and the girls."

"Rachel?" Ivy's voice lifted through the church. "Why is there a horse in our backyard?"

I gave Jenks a look to shut up, and he flipped me off. Her footsteps sounded closer, and I went to the stove and turned the flame down, pretending to be busy.

"Who's in the shower?" she asked as she came in, looking refreshed in her black slacks and tailored jacket.

"Trent," Jenks said. "And Rachel is dumber than Tink's little pink dildo."

"Oh my God!" Ivy said, eyes wide. "You didn't!"

"No!" I shouted, my frustration coming out as anger. "I didn't!"

Ivy's expression went wide-eyed. "But . . . he spent the night?"

Jenks frowned, hands in his pockets. "That's what I'm telling you. She didn't. Biggest mistake she's made since quitting the I.S."

"Shut up, Jenks," I said, tossing a piece of bread into Trent's egg mix and pushing on it until it accidentally tore. "We didn't. He slept in the belfry."

Wings humming, Jenks went to sit on the sill. "Dumbest

thing I've ever seen," he grumbled, and Ivy set her purse down. "Him up there staring at the ceiling, her down here staring at the ceiling."

"I'm having a hard time sleeping with the vampires out of control," I said back to them as I cooked the French toast. "Is Nina okay?"

"About what I'd expect." Ivy sat before her computer, but she was eyeing Trent's laptop as she typed in her password and everything came alive. "I can't believe they made Felix the functioning head of the I.S. You heard Edden's announcement?"

"Up to him asking for everyone's cooperation. I think *functioning* is the key word there. We have got to find these jokers before the vampires start targeting one another. You want one or two of these?" I pointed to the pan so she'd know what I meant.

"One is good." Concern pinched her brow as she looked past me to Jenks, but the pixy was smiling insincerely when I turned to him. "I'm kind of surprised they named names, to tell you the truth."

"Trent says it was to squelch a rumor of a biological attack."

"Still, to say it was Free Vampires?" Ivy tapped a pencil against her teeth. "Every living vampire out there is going to be hunting them."

"Maybe that was the intent. Keep them so busy they can't make more trouble."

"I swear, you can lead a horse to water, but you can't make her drink," Jenks said loudly, and I threw the fork at him. "Pixy pus!" he yelped, darting out of the way when it hit the window screen and bounced into the sink.

"Leave her alone, Jenks," Ivy said as I stomped to the silverware drawer for a new one. Jenks hovered over the sink, darting back when I threatened to bop him with the stainless steel. A cell phone began tinkling, half heard and almost ultrasonic, and I turned my back on him to flip the French toast.

"Towers are back up," Ivy said, and when I ignored it, she added. "It's not mine."

"Well, it's not mine," I said. "Jenks, if your kids can't leave my phone alone—"

"Why do you blame my kids for everything?"

"Because everything is usually their fault." Agitated, I turned the flame down and went into the back living room to check. "They're as nosy as their dad."

"Hey, I'm just pointing things out," he said, but I'd skidded to a halt, staring at the black-and-silver phone tinkling out its little song on the coffee table. It was Trent's.

"Rachel?" came faintly from the bathroom, over the sound of the shower. "Can you get that for me?"

Slowly I picked up his phone. That was kind of intimate. What if it was Ellasbeth?

Jenks hovered over my shoulder, his dust making the screen blank out. "If you don't, he might come out all naked and dripping to get it himself."

"Rachel?" Trent yelled as it rang again, the sound clearly reaching him through the walls.

"Got it!" I yelled back as Quen's name popped up.

"Lucky," Jenks said, and I waved him off.

"Hi, Quen," I said with a false cheerfulness.

"R-Rachel?" the older man stammered.

"Trent's in the shower," I said, hearing the sound of traffic in the background. "Apparently I'm his secretary this morning."

There was a hesitation. It was heady with questions, but I didn't say anything. Trent could talk to him about this morning. I sure as hell wasn't going to. "Ah, okay. Will you tell Trent that we have a problem that needs his immediate attention. Bancroft is at the top of the FIB building."

Jenks's wing hum bobbled, and I went back the kitchen. "You mean, like the top, top? Why? Is he threatening to jump?" I said sarcastically.

"It's hard to tell," Quen said, and my eyes met Ivy's. *Holy shit!* "Landon says Bancroft tried to contact the divided mystics this morning and convince them to go back to the Goddess. I'm guessing something went wrong, seeing as he's blown out the entire top floor."

Blown out? I turned to the bathroom, a niggle of fear growing.

"The news is keeping the deaths of those who fell quiet until the next of kin are notified, but they haven't been able to search for survivors. He's raving incoherently and threatening anyone who gets close. Even Landon can't get through to him."

My chill deepened. Edden worked in that building on the Inderland-related crimes. *Bancroft blew out the top floor? We didn't have a wave come through, did we?*

"Rachel, I'll be there in about half an hour to pick Trent and Tulpa up."

My head jerked up. "Trent's not going out there if Bancroft is throwing people off the top of the FIB tower."

"He's not throwing them off the top floor. They fell during the initial blast."

"Yeah? You said he's threatening anyone who gets close. Let the I.S. handle it. It's their job."

"In the FIB building?" Quen said, then exhaled heavily. "Rachel . . . Trent is the only person Bancroft personally knows in Cincinnati. The man is the head of the elven religious sect. They can't just shoot him. Maybe all he needs is an understanding ear."

Hip cocked, I fumed. "Fine, I'll tell him." Ivy was watching me, the rim of brown around her pupils shrinking. "But I'm going with you."

Quen, though, had already hung up, and I closed Trent's phone with a snap. From the bathroom, the water turned off. Maybe Trent's hearing was better than he let on.

"He tried to talk to the Goddess?" Jenks said, landing on my shoulder and sending a worried red dust down my front. "As in, 'Hi, how you doing, babe. Got any threes?' "

Ivy went back to her e-mail. "Sounds like God answered him back."

"Or he found out something that he didn't like and is having a tantrum," I said, feet slow as I went to knock on the bathroom door and tell Trent I was coming with him. If Landon thought I was a black demon, that was his problem. Maybe it would take a demon to keep Trent safe from his Goddess, much less a pissed-off priest who could blow out the entire top floor of a city high-rise.

Sixteen

"W ell, do your best," Trent said into his shiny phone as he flipped my car's tiny visor to block the sun flashing irritatingly through the building-lined Hollows street. He looked tired, overdue for his afternoon nap. Apparently the holes in the Hollows blockades had been closed, and much to Trent's disgust, the Kalamack name wasn't opening doors like it used to.

The shadow of the bridge shaded us, and I slowed my little car as we wove past the unattended BRIDGE CLOSED sign. Jenks's dust shifted to a concerned orange and he shrugged, feet drumming the rearview mirror. I'd left a message for Edden that we were coming in, but if he hadn't gotten it, I didn't know how we were going to get past the manned blockade.

"There's a few days' pasture at the church before he eats it all," Trent added, and I slowly crept down the bridge at a meek forty miles an hour. The empty bridge looked odd. One would think that if both Cincinnati and the Hollows were closed, they could be closed together.

"He's not going to hurt me," Trent said, giving me an uncomfortable glance. "The man was there at my birth. Quen, Rachel has this."

Which was why I'd jammed my splat gun and several

other nasties in my bag before we left. Yesterday, while eating hot dogs and ribs with the man, I wouldn't have thought he'd swat a fly, much less destroy an entire floor of the FIB. It would've been major news if it hadn't been shoved below the fold by the rising violence between various vampire gangs and Were packs, all of them looking for Free Vampires.

It was bad and getting worse, and now that I was out of my church, I couldn't ignore it. Misfires were one thing, but possible vampire-on-vampire violence was far more dangerous. My worry for Ivy layered over everything, and I slowed to look at a damaged pylon. Were graffiti was scrawled among the broken pieces of plastic and cement chunks in clear warning. Six different packs at least.

It had been in the news, but the visual confirmation that Weres were becoming more aggressive in the face of feuding vampires was chilling. Maybe that's why the blockades between Cincy and the Hollows. The trains, too, weren't stopping anymore, blowing through the usual stops at eighty miles an hour, horns screaming a klaxon warning. I knew David was working with Edden to find the Free Vampires, but I'd not heard from him since yesterday, more reason to be concerned.

"As soon as I know," Trent said tersely. "Thank you." He closed his phone, twisting to tuck it in a pocket. Expression grim, he stared out over the river. The wind brushed through his hair, and I wanted to touch it—to bring him back to me. I'd seen Trent quietly lose his temper before, but seldom when it involved Quen. The passion from our kiss, hardly an hour old, flashed through me and was gone.

"Anything I can do?" I offered as the cop just past the end of the bridge flagged us down. There were four of them, but only one seemed interested.

Trent exhaled, using the motion to hide his frustration. "No. Thank you, though."

Experience told me he wouldn't say another word about it, and I put the car in park as the cop came to my window. Jenks darted out of the car, immediately lost in the glare.

"Ma'am?" the officer said, black glasses reflecting me as he pushed his cap up. "Turn your car around and go back, please. The city has been closed. No one in or out."

It wasn't a request, and I reached for my ID, already pulled out of my shoulder bag. "Captain Edden asked us to come down," I said, stretching the truth as I handed it over. I was sure if he knew we were coming, he would have cleared us. "I'm Rachel Morgan." I turned to Trent. "Give him your ID," I prompted, then smiled at the cop again. There was no way we were getting in. I could see it already. They'd even diverted the interstate.

"ID?" Trent hedged, and then he brightened. "You know what? I think I have it on me."

The officer's eyes were lost behind thick sunglasses as he compared my name to the list on his clipboard. Jenks was hovering over his shoulder, and he shook his head when our eyes met. "Ah, sorry, ah . . . Ms. Morgan," the cop said as he handed it back. "No one gets over the bridge unless they're government food or fuel trucks."

"What about them, huh?" Jenks said, startling the man. "Rache, tell him your name is Dr. Margret Tessel. *She's* on the list."

"Found it," Trent said, and I held out my hand for his ID, but he leaned across me, flashing a professional smile as he passed it to the cop. "Officer, the man at the top of the FIB building is my friend. I think I can talk him down. Can you please let us through?"

The cop's stern expression suddenly became wide-eyed. "Seriously?" he said, turning into fan-boy as he looked from Trent's license to Trent. "Mr. Kalamack?" His glasses came off, and he got that weird smile people have when they meet their idol. "Wow. This is so cool," he said, shifting from foot to foot. "I got a scholarship because of your dad. It made the difference in which side of the jail cell I was on."

"Good to meet you," Trent said, and I pressed back into the seat when the cop stuck his hand in to shake Trent's. I gave Trent a pained look, and he barely lifted a shoulder in a shrug. "I understand you have your orders, but my friend has information about the misfires. I have to help get him down."

Clearly torn, the cop looked out over the river, then behind him at the barricade and the three other cops trying to stay cool in their cars. "I think we can make an exception," he said as he handed the ID back. "Just promise me you won't start a riot," he kidded.

I snatched Trent's ID before he could, blinking at the bad picture he'd taken. His eyes were wide and his smile quirky.

"I was in a hurry that morning," Trent said as he twitched it from my grip, clearly peeved.

"Open it up!" the cop said, whistling three times in quick succession to get the three other men moving. "They're cleared!" The man looked back at us. "I hope you can talk your friend down, Mr. Kalamack."

"Thank you. I'm sure my father would have enjoyed meeting you."

"If you need a place to stay, give me a call," he added, then fumbled for a card, handing it in. "The hotels are full and you're kind of stuck here now."

"I'll do that, thank you."

"Tink loves a duck." Jenks darted back in. "Guys give you their number too?"

Trent shrugged, but the cop was waving us through, and I rolled my window up so I wouldn't have to talk to anyone else. "That was nice," Trent said, and a tremor passed through me as the barrier scraped back in place behind us. We were in, and it felt wrong.

"How so?" I asked.

Bringing his arm in, he rolled his window up. "Lately, it's not always good when I've been recognized out on the street."

I thought back to Limbcus. The "them and us" animosity probably wasn't entirely new to Trent, but finding it in a public setting was. "It happens to me all the time," I said, leaning to see around the corner before we made the turn into the city. My unease was thickening. The entire city felt wrong, and it was more than the graffiti.

Traffic was almost nil, but the city *was* closed. Those who were out were driving with little regard for traffic signals, going too fast and treating reds like flashing yellows if no one was coming. In contrast, both of the stadium parking lots were packed.

"There's no game today," Jenks said as we passed them.

"They're using it as an emergency shelter," Trent said, pointing at the marquee. "I didn't want to believe it was this bad. How are they keeping a lid on this?"

Apart from the stadium, there was little foot traffic, and those who were out walked furtively fast. Were graffiti was everywhere, covering up and mutilating the new FV symbols. Shops were closed with hand-lettered signs in the window, some of them tagged with territorial graffiti. It reminded me of the chapter on the Turn in my fifth-grade history textbook—the one titled "The Decade's Darkest Hour."

"Crap on toast, look at that," I whispered when I tried to make a right turn to get to the FIB's tower, only to find it cordoned off. Beyond it, the street was littered with chunks of cement and glass, the cars at the curb covered in debris. The scent of dust and smoke hung in the air like a haze of sun, and a uniformed man was directing people with FIB business elsewhere when the sign saying to take FIB matters to the arena didn't do the trick. My eyes flicked to the top of the tower, seeing the damage. Hands clenched, I drove past, not wanting to be noticed by the news vans.

"Jenks, you want to do a quick look-see?" I said as I lowered my window, and he whizzed out.

"I don't understand how they are keeping this out of the news," Trent said as I turned down a side street looking for somewhere to park. Bits of cement littered the road, and an ambulance was parked illegally in a cordoned-off alley. "There's a spot beside the ambulance," Trent said, pointing, and I stomped on the brake when he reached for the door, not waiting for me to stop before getting out.

"Trent!" I protested, but he was lifting the caution tape, eyeing the street behind me as he gestured for me to get through. I leaned forward as I slowly drove under it, carefully sticking to the curb and parking out of sight beside the ambulance. The front door to the FIB was just a block away. We'd never find a better spot.

"Trent, wait up!" I said as I fumbled for the FIB sign under the seat and shoved it on the front dash in the hopes it would be the difference between being towed and left alone. Grabbing my shoulder bag, I got out, trying to be quiet as I shut the door. It was eerily silent between the two buildings, and the air had an unusual musky vampire scent under the increasingly familiar scent of burning furniture.

Trent was scanning the damaged top floor as he came forward with two hard hats and a clipboard from an abandoned front-end loader, clearly here to get rid of the chunks of building. "It's strange how we need the very thing we fear," he said as his eyes met mine.

"Beg pardon?"

"The undead vampires."

"Tell me about it." I took the hard hat, the glare diminishing as I dropped it on my head. "How do I look?" I asked as we started up the alley, and he gave me a sidelong glance.

"I'd suggest the front door," he said, his words coming from the back of his throat, and I warmed. Maybe he had a working-girl fetish. My flush deepened as he touched the small of my back, ushering me forward as he lifted the tape for me. Trent was always touching me, but after that last kiss, it felt different. Seeing him in Jenks's jeans and silk shirt along with that hard hat and the thickening stubble of a workingman wasn't helping either.

I breathed easier when his hand fell away. Arms swinging, we strode down the side street to the front, picking our way through the chunks of concrete and glass. Jenks's wings gave me a breath of warning before he landed on my shoulder. "I hope Edden got your call," he said. "I've been inside, and they aren't letting anyone up there but emergency people. It's creepy, Rache. The entire building is empty."

"He promised he wouldn't ignore me!" I almost hissed as we slipped in behind the man directing traffic; Trent's small wave and our hard hats said we belonged. Even the news crews didn't notice us.

"Tell them you're Margret Tessel. She's the hostage negotiator," Jenks said.

"He's taken hostages?" Concern laced his voice as Trent reached to open the door for me.

Worried, I went inside, the sudden calm and coolness of the air conditioner making me shiver. The very emptiness was shocking. There was trash on the scuffed floor, and the orange chairs were empty. The front desk was unmanned, and the metal and magic detector abandoned. Nearly out of sight, three uniformed FIB officers and one plainclothes were helping get a stretcher and an ambulance crew into the elevator.

"Hey!" I called, striding forward and ignoring the beep of the detector as my boots clicked unusually loud on the tile. "Hold the lift!"

But it was too late. The elevator doors closed, leaving only a single uniformed officer and the plainclothes still there as informal gatekeepers. "Top floor, right?" I said, breathlessly as Trent and I halted before them and I pushed the call button, making the plainclothes frown. "Edden is up there already?"

"Ah, who are you, ma'am?"

"Ma'am?" Jenks snickered from my shoulder. "He called you ma'am."

I tried to turn my grimace into a charming smile with mixed results. "Rachel Morgan and, ah, Trent Kalamack. I called Edden this morning. He was supposed to clear us."

"Oh yeah!" the uniformed man exclaimed, eyes wide as they shifted from Trent to Jenks and then me. "I heard you came in Wednesday." Heads down, they both looked at the list on the clipboard. "Neither of you is on the list. Mr. Kalamack, I'm sorry, but I can't let you up there."

I sighed at how fast Trent became the governing force here, but he *had* once been on the city council and was a major benefactor to the FIB's and I.S.'s pet charities as well as half a dozen others. They knew me only because I caused trouble.

"You should have told them you were Margret Tessel," Jenks said in a soft singsong.

"I'm sure we can work something out," Trent was saying, his political voice in top form.

Behind us, the elevator whined to a stop and dinged. I didn't have time for this. "Is that the latest report?" I said as it opened, and their heads snapped up when I took the papers right out of the man's hand. Smiling, I backed into the elevator. His head ducked to hide a smile, Trent quietly got in beside me. Jenks hovered at the opening, and I frantically pushed the door-close button, my smile never wavering.

"Ma'am. Mr. Kalamack. Please get out of the elevator," the plainclothes said, his hand twitching as if to reach for his cuffs, and Jenks's wings hummed, stopping the man dead in his tracks when he made a motion to reach in and pull us out.

"Do me a favor," I said, holding the door-close button down and smiling. "Tell Edden I'm on the way up? My calls don't seem to be making it through lately."

Finally the doors started to move. The cops reached to hold them open, jerking back when Jenks buzzed them. The pixy darted back in at the last moment, and I exhaled, falling back against the elevator wall with a loud sigh. Trent was smiling as Jenks hung in the middle of the elevator in satisfaction, a pool of dusty sunshine growing under him.

"You can do bold," Trent said in admiration, and I pulled myself straight, my worry for him flowing back. Why was I working so hard to get him up there? Bancroft had flipped his lid.

"You haven't seen anything," Jenks said as he landed on the railing, feet pedaling to stay on when they slipped and his wings caught him before he moved a hairsbreadth. "I've seen this woman push her way into—"

"Jenks!"

Grinning, Jenks shifted to Trent's shoulder. "Ask me later."

But Trent wasn't even listening, intent on the report that I'd taken. "This doesn't sound like Bancroft," he said, brow furrowed. "Hostages?" He flipped a page, eyes widening. "Oh no."

I leaned to look and Jenks whistled. It was hard to tell with the fuzzy, enlarged photo, but it looked as if a third of the walls of the entire top floor had been blown out to make a sheltered cave at the top of the sky. "Tink's little pink rose-buds," Jenks breathed, hardly louder than his wings. "How much magic did you bring, Rache?"

"Enough?" I said, not sure as I tugged my shoulder bag up. I didn't have anything that would let me fly, and we were more than thirty stories up. "Is he making any demands?"

Trent flipped through the pages as the elevator dinged. "Not . . . yet."

His words trailed off as the silver doors parted and the unmistakable scent of fresh air and broken concrete poured into the elevator and down the shaft. Almost immediately the doors began to close, and I put a hand out, stopping them. All three of us looked out into the alien-seeming, broken building as the wind pushed my hair back. The walls between us and the horizon were gone, and though there was still a ceiling, the Cincy skyline spread before us in magnificence unimpeded. Fluorescent lights, some on, some not, hung from the ceiling in a once-regular pattern. Desks and office equipment were shoved into haphazard piles. In one corner by the edge, a huge pile of stuff stretched to the ceiling. It had to be at least forty feet in diameter and was made of desks, pieces of wallboard, and twisted rebar. It looked like a nest.

Bancroft did this? "Maybe we should keep the hard hats on," I whispered. Between us and the clutter was a much more modest barrier of desks, and behind it with their backs to us crouched two officers and Edden. Almost at our feet and clearly waiting to be taken down were two ominous, coat-covered bodies. The ambulance crew and stretcher were nowhere I could see, but the second elevator was going down.

They're removing bodies, I thought, inching in front of Trent.

"I don't know if I've got enough magic for this," Trent said, and Edden turned, still in a crouch. When I gave him a little wave, he frowned and gestured brusquely for us to join him.

"You think?" Jenks darted out, immediately lost in the wind and glare bouncing into the open floor from the nearby building.

"Get over here!" Edden all but hissed, and we jolted into motion, hunched as we half ran. Rebar and wallboard littered the carpet squares, and cool air still flowed from the air ducts. Bancroft's voice was coming from the weird "nest," shouting about the sun and having to go deeper.

"Oh, thank God," Trent breathed when we got closer. "There's Landon. He looks okay."

I pulled my gaze away from the covered bodies. Okay was a matter of interpretation. The young man was sitting on the floor, jaw clenched and eyes darting. *Doctor Tessel?* I wondered, eyes going back to the bodies by the elevator. Not good.

"What took you so long?" Edden demanded as I stepped over the thick extension cord snaking through the rubble to power the monitor the two officers were staring at.

"Took us so long?" I said, peeved as I sat on a prone file cabinet. "We had to romance our way over the bridge and bull our way up the elevator." Miffed, I sat hunched over on the cabinet to stay hidden. "I swear, Edden, if you keep ignoring my calls—"

"I told them to let you through!" Edden said, and the two officers fiddling with the equipment shrugged as if it wasn't their fault. Immediately my anger vanished, and seeing it,

Edden sighed. "Mr. Kalamack, it isn't safe up here. I understand your relationship to Bancroft and I appreciate the offer, but I'd feel better if you'd go back downstairs."

Trent gingerly sat beside me, checking to see that his head was below the level of the piled desks. Reaching out across the space, the two men shook hands. "I've known him all my life and I think I can help." But doubt was creeping into his eyes as he followed Bancroft's voice over the demolished floor open to the wind on two sides. I was starting to have serious doubts myself. The man sounded nuts.

Landon stirred. Stubble shrouded his face, thicker than Trent's and somehow ugly. "I can't believe you brought her," he said, his voice flat and his eyes malevolent. "Are you intentionally being contrary, or is this the famed Kalamack pride I'm seeing?"

Trent's expression darkened, but it was Edden who shoved between us, his face red as he exclaimed, "Landon, you're here as a courtesy! One more word, and you go down with the next body. Got it?"

The elevator dinged, and everyone looked as the plain-clothes man and two of the officers came out of the second elevator. Lips tight, Landon averted his eyes, his show of contriteness just that. "Sir?" the man from downstairs asked as he looked at me.

Edden's frown deepened. "Just take the bodies down," he muttered. "And someone post a memo that Rachel Morgan can see me any time the thought enters her head, okay?"

Mollified, I eased closer to Trent, watching Landon closely as Edden took his hard hat off to run a hand over his hair. He looked tired as he put it back on and turned to the nest. Behind him, one of the bodies was lifted onto a gurney and taken downstairs. "I don't know what you think you can do, Mr. Kalamack. We brought in Bancroft and Landon early this morning for breaking curfew, releasing them once we realized they were collecting data about the waves. We didn't know Bancroft was, ah . . . an elven holy man."

It had been hard for him to say, and I understood. How do

you easily acknowledge a religion that's been in hiding for two thousand years?

"I thought that was the end of it, but I came in this morning to find they went to the top floor to take more readings." Edden gestured at the destruction. "And then this happened. There should be thirty people up here handling this, and I've got two. I was lucky to get the dogs up here to look for survivors." Softer, he added, "Most of our resources are at a gymnasium full of high school kids being detained by vampires because some idiot kid yelled 'Free Vampires rule.' I'm running out of lies, Rachel, but the truth will ignite forty years of hidden hatred and fear."

"My God," I whispered, thinking of Ivy, and Edden held up a hand.

"We've got it under control," he said, but I didn't feel any better. "The I.S. has a couple of agents over there helping us defuse the situation, but eventually someone is going to do something stupid we can't come back from." He looked over the pile of desks and chairs to where Bancroft shouted. "It was a mistake to name the Free Vampires as the reason for the masters being asleep. I don't know why I went along with it except that everyone is afraid of a plague, and only half the population is afraid of vampires."

My eyes slid to Landon, who was ignoring me with a stiff-jawed determination. I could tell by the slant of his shoulders that he'd pushed for it. My frustration deepened, tinged with fear for Ivy. We had to find these guys and get the master vampires awake before the vampires started staking each other first and asking questions later.

Trent's feet shifted, the thick grit soundless between his feet and the flat carpet. "Edden, can I talk to him? Something triggered this. Maybe I can find out what."

"You're not going closer," I said, glancing up at what used to be the ceiling. "Jenks?"

"I was thinking more along the lines of a bullhorn?" Trent said as the pixy dropped down.

"Rachel is right," Edden said as he gestured for one of the officers to hand it over. "It's unclear if he killed the negotiator intentionally or not, but I don't like his talk about goats. Newman, call and stop the ambulance crew from coming back up. I don't want any misunderstanding."

Goats? Trent took the bullhorn, and I put a hand on his arm, stopping him. "Hold on a sec. Jenks? What does it look like in there?"

The pixy's face was screwed up in a puzzled expression. "It's as weird as a troll living in his mother's basement, Rache," he said, and the officers working the monitor turned to him. Even Landon was watching, and knowing it, Jenks's dust shifted to a nervous pink. "That pile of stuff is a big hollow ball, with lights inside everywhere making it brighter than day."

"Hostages?" Edden asked.

"No. Just him."

Clearly relieved, Trent rested the bullhorn on the top of the uppermost desk. Landon was watching him with an unnerving intensity that tightened my suspicion. The elf knew something. He just wasn't saying. Frowning, I toyed with the idea of asking Edden to beat it out of him before his silence killed us. Instead, I inched closer to Trent and renewed my grip on the ley line.

The bullhorn popped as Trent thumbed the circuit open. "Bancroft?"

"Too bright!" Bancroft was shouting, his voice muffled. "Need to be higher, higher than the light. Must get between it where it's dark. Stop looking at me, you damn harlots!"

Trent's brow furrowed, and I edged even closer. "Bancroft, it's Trent."

"Trent?" Bancroft's tirade cut off. From the pile in the corner came a sliding crash. "Trent! Did you bring your goat?"

The officers swore as Bancroft stumbled out. He was ragged, his face stubbled and his cylindrical hat sitting askew. His hands hid his eyes as if the light pained him. "Trent, we were right," he said as he tripped over the debris, seemingly oblivious that he could walk around them. "The mystics have splintered, gone insane. I can hear them. They have to be freed so the Goddess can make them whole again."

Jenks's wings hummed. "He's nuts," he said. I agreed, but when the officer next to me rested a long-range dart rifle on the desktop, I turned to Edden.

"You're going to dart him?" I said, appalled.

"Easy now," Edden said, his eyes on Bancroft. "It can take thirty seconds to work. I don't want tomorrow's headlines to read 'Elven Holy Man Jumps from FIB Tower.' Wait until he's away from the edge."

"He's not an animal!" I protested, and Edden's eyes flicked from mine to Trent's.

"The last person who tried magic on him is dead."

"Well, thanks for the heads-up," I said sarcastically, seriously thinking about dropping the line, but I didn't. A protection circle was fairly innocuous. My skin was prickling. Bancroft had stopped moving and was tugging chairs and chunks of wallboard into a circle around him as if instinctively starting another nest.

"Rache, something wicked is coming," Jenks said as he tucked back in at my shoulder.

I stifled a shudder as the feeling of cat feet walked through my soul. "I feel it too."

"It's coming from Bancroft," Jenks said, and Trent swore. "Use your second sight," the pixy suggested. "That's what your aura looked like, Rache. Right before those waves hit us."

My lips parted when I pulled up my second sight to find Bancroft's aura was a harsh white, flaring as if his soul were on fire. *A wave?* I wondered, and Jenks shook his head at my unspoken question. He was just covered in mystics.

"Is he close enough?" Trent said, and the man with the rifle shook his head, his gaze never shifting from Bancroft as the man dropped a monitor on top of a new wall of trash. Trent tightened his grip on the bullhorn. "Bancroft? We can get you some help."

Bancroft patted the broken monitor, pleased with where he'd put it. "Help? Nothing can help me. I hear her eyes. All the time. Whispering, prickling through me," he said, and a chill dropped through me when he looked up, his eyes reflecting the light like a cat's. "I'm hers," he moaned, weaving on his feet. "I'm her chattel," he said, heedless to the tears making shining tracks through his stubble. "It's too bright. Too bright," he chanted, and then he wiped his eyes, his face becoming crafty. "She's coming. I have to be free of them or she'll kill me to get her eyes back!"

The man with the rifle shook his head, still not having a clean shot.

"Bancroft! Wait!" Trent shouted, but the man was climbing over the broken ceiling and walls back to his larger pile.

"Not enough goats," the man was mumbling, picking up a ream of paper and dropping it on the pile. "Not enough goddamned *goats*!"

"Give me the gun." Trent shoved the bullhorn at Edden. "I can get closer than your men."

My stomach clenched and Jenks's wings clattered.

"With all due respect, Mr. Kalamack," Edden said. "No."

My heart thudded, thinking first of Trent, angry and unafraid, and then what I'd risk to keep him from doing something dangerous. "I'll do it," I said, voice sounding hollow.

"Rache," Jenks protested, and Edden shook his head.

"Who do you have that's better than me?" I said. "A splat ball will drop him instantaneously. I'd do it from here, but my range sucks."

"I'll do it," Landon proclaimed as he stood. "Give me the gun."

Like that was going to happen? Edden's expression twisted into a sour mess. "Get him downstairs," he said, gesturing for one of the officers to take him, and Landon protested, head high and eyes wild. "Second thought, we can't spare the man. Lock him to a pole."

"You don't have to lock me up!" Landon demanded, but there was already a zip strip around his wrist making him pretty much helpless. The officer knew what he was doing, carefully manhandling him to a fallen emergency sprinkler system and cuffing him to it.

"Trent?" Bancroft shouted, and a billow of smoke poured out of the nest. "Did you bring your goat? We can stop this now if you brought your goat."

Jenks's dust turned gray as he hovered. "What the pixy pus is he talking about?"

Rambling about goats, Bancroft shoved and tripped his way out again. The man with the rifle put him in his sights, and my heart pounded as I found my splat gun. I'd have to get close, dangerously close. It didn't help that the old elf already distrusted me.

"If you kill your goat, the Goddess won't become any sicker. We can mend her. You and I. It would be a great thing. Good for publicity. It would bring the unbelievers back to the fold and solidify your standing in the enclave. The Goddess needs *adherence*!" Bancroft exclaimed, then hesitated as he looked at the small circle of stuff he'd laid out as if not remembering having done it. "She needs *obedience*. Are you pious, Trent? Your mother was a poser."

My motion to inch out hesitated as Trent's hands clenched on the bullhorn.

"She didn't believe, and the Goddess killed her." Bancroft staggered to a broken table, almost falling as he set it legs up on the pile. "Her eyes are whispering to me, how your mother asked for guidance and strength and then refused when the Goddess demanded payment."

Trent's expression became tight, and I crouched, waving him to stay back. Jenks's dust was a silver white, the sparkles looking like the beginning of a migraine.

"The Goddess destroyed her," Bancroft said, oblivious to Trent's anger. "Drew her forth with promises and abandoned her when she needed her most. She's a proper bitch, she is. The Goddess, not your mother. We shouldn't be punished for our weaknesses. She gave them to us."

My feet found a careful place in the rubble as I eased behind a file cabinet. The papers stuck to it fluttered in the stiff wind, blocking my view. Almost close enough . . . If I had more than one shot, I would have taken it.

But then Bancroft's eyes found mine and I froze, half hidden, half not. "You brought your goat! Good man!" he shouted. "Bring her to the fire and we'll slit her throat together."

"Holy crap!" I exclaimed, bringing my gun up when Bancroft lunged toward me, motions jerky as he fumbled for that huge knife of his, up to now hidden in the folds of his clothes. Jenks was a haze of dust between us, and I pulled the trigger. Like a villain in a fantasy flick, Bancroft waved his hand and the ball exploded three feet from him.

Gasping, I ducked back to avoid the splattering hot spell. Quickly I jammed the gun in the file cabinet before he burst the rest of the spells in the hopper and put me down with my own weapon. Trent was shouting, and Jenks inked when I suddenly found myself pulled backward, falling into the FIB's shelter.

Eyes wide, I stared up at Trent.

"Take it!" Edden exclaimed from over me, and then I surged to my feet when the dart gun went off with a little pop. Breath held, I watched Bancroft roll to evade it.

"Unbelievers!" he shouted, clearly not hit. "You will twist and die under her power! She comes! She comes!"

"Oh my God . . ." I breathed as Bancroft ran to the edge, a stark silhouette against the bright light, arms spread wide as he faced Cincinnati. He was going to jump!

"She comes!" he screamed, and in the distance, a siren started, then another.

Trent's face was pale, and Edden frowned as he stood over the man at the keyboard. "Just what we need," the man grumbled. "A wave. At least we know it's headed right for us."

Because it's coming for me. Chilled, I looked past Bancroft to the horizon. More sirens were lifting into the air, joined by church bells. "She comes!" Bancroft shouted, his robe falling to his elbows as he shook at the edge of the drop-off.

"Captain, can I move forward for a better shot?" the man with the dart gun asked, and Edden nodded. Immediately he slunk forward, stealthy with urban guerrilla tactics.

Trent rubbed a hand over his face, starting at the feel of his bristles. "Rachel, I don't know what he's going to do if that wave hits him."

"He's going to kill himself," Landon said, and I spun, having forgotten the nasty man cuffed to the fallen sprinkler system. "Pray that whoever is pulling mystics from your line catches them before they reach Bancroft, or he's going to take us with him."

My gut clenched. If I used magic, I'd kill us faster.

"He tried to rescue them," Landon said, chin lifting to indicate Bancroft. "He was going to put them back in the line so the Free Vampires couldn't use them to put the undead asleep. But it went wrong. They won't leave him, and now he's insane."

"Here!" the crazed man shouted. "We're here! Join us!"

"I told him it wasn't a good idea," Landon said, but the thread of satisfaction in him made me think he was lying. "You can't talk to the divine and survive."

But I had.

"Trent!" Bancroft shouted, spinning to us. "Bring your goat! It's your destiny! You must make amends for what your mother refused to do!"

Excuse me?

Eyes on Bancroft, Trent took my elbow. "Don't even think about using this as a way to get near him," he muttered.

Cackling, Bancroft spun back to the opening, dancing a weird shuffle with his arms waving over his head as if he could fly. "She's coming. She's coming!"

"Rache, look at that!" Jenks exclaimed, and my lips parted. Beyond Bancroft was a sparkling cloud. It drifted below us, just over the tops of Cincy's buildings. Beneath the distortion were little flares as magic misfired, but the sirens were minimizing the situation. I'd seen that cloud before on the bridge, and my fear tightened to a hard pit. Mystics.

Edden chewed on his lower lip, eyes on Bancroft at the edge and his man inching closer. "Edden, call your man back," I whispered, face cold. "If Bancroft does any magic under that wave, it will misfire! I can protect us, but not if he's way over there. Get him back here. Now!"

"Stand down!" Edden shouted, gesturing frantically. "Newman, get back here!"

"Dust!" Bancroft shouted, spinning to the opening as the first of the wave sparkled over him. "Oh God! Make it stop!"

He wants to kill himself, I realized, and as Newman ran for us, I yanked Trent closer. "Go to ground, Jenks!" I shouted, then bubbled everyone I could reach before the wave hit us, feeling my power lick up and around the running officer as I fell to a knee and the circle invoked. A molecule-thin barrier swam up, bisected by a hundred cords, a hundred ways in to those who knew. I prayed that the mystics didn't.

"Make it sto-o-o-op!" Bancroft howled. And then a sparkling lilt seemed to lift through me with the sound of wings as the wave hit us. My skin prickled, and Trent looked at me in shock. I knew my aura was sparkling with them. The Goddess's eyes, her mystics, were on us.

"I'm so sorry," I whispered, not knowing what for, and then I cowered as Bancroft's own spell misfired. He screamed, his high-pitched cries cutting off with a gurgle when his lungs melted, and I covered my ears, trying not to hear him.

Wild magic beat at us, crawling over the surface of my circle for the way in. My heart thudded when it found a resonance in my chi, and the first feelings of tendrils sought me out. *Please no,* I thought, feeling that same something that was digging through my circle quiver awake—already inside me. A thousand eyes spun, rising up in anger as they recognized me.

Stay out, I begged, knowing it was my aura they were following, tricked into believing I was the way back to her. To take them in would draw Bancroft's spell into my circle, and they lingered, intensifying his charm as they refused to move on. Fire danced over us as the world burned and the air grew warm. Sparkles skated over the layer of ever-after protecting us. *Please, please, please, see us not,* I thought as the floor burned, and from inside me—the way made open from the resonances between me and my line—I heard a mocking laugh.

For now, the Goddess taunted, her voice clear as water in the chaos of my thoughts.

Trent yanked from me, mouth open and shock in his eyes. Then he jerked his head up as the insane wild magic darted away, drawn by the sensation of something brighter than my aura.

Panting, I let the bubble drop. For a heartbeat there was silence, and then came the hissing shush of the sprinkler system flicking on. I looked up, glad now that the ceiling was a twisted wreck and we were still dry. The scent of wet carpet rose, thickened, and began to purge the reek of burning skin.

"What the devil was that?" someone said, and I fell back, hiding my face as I sat on my butt and held my knees to my chin, rocking almost. The scent of burning plastic was slowly fading, and I could hear the men moving about in the superhot, increasingly moist air. Whether she was divine or simply a force of nature, it was obvious that the Goddess was real. Her mystics had opened a channel. I'd heard her again—in my head as her mystics sought me out. Trent had heard her too.

Trent's touch shocked through me, and he pulled back as I started. He looked haunted, and ash covered his hands where he had touched something. It was on me now, and I thought the black smear was fitting as it marked me. "Rachel? Did you just . . ."

He couldn't say it. I didn't blame him. "I think so," I said dully.

Dropping down to me, he peered at me in concern. "Are you okay?"

He was tucking a strand of hair behind my ear, and closing my eyes, I tilted my head so I could feel his hand on my cheek. It sang through me, tingling with the last of the wild magic, and I had no right to it. "I don't know."

"You are a *demon*!" Landon shouted, expression vehement and stumbling when his cuffed hand brought him up short. "How dare you speak to the divine!"

Numb, I could do nothing as he struggled to reach me, finally working his cuff around a bend in the piping and running at me. The two officers, finding something they could cope with, tackled him.

"Get off!" he shouted from under them. "Get off me!"

Edden lowered a hand to help me rise. "Great. I think he's got it now."

My hand was trembling as I put it in Edden's and stood. Bancroft was a pile of twisted, blackened bones in the middle of the charred top floor. His rings were still on his cooked fingers, and I wondered about the shackle on his ankle, up to now hidden behind his robe.

"Get him out of here," Edden said, and I flinched when Jenks's dust hit me and burned with wild magic. Bancroft had said mystics lived in pixies. Why had I never felt it before now?

"That could have gone better," Trent said, and Jenks landed on his shoulder instead of mine. Landon's tirade cut off as the elevator door closed. The sudden silence broken by the hiss of sprinklers was somehow worse.

"At least he didn't jump." Fingers fumbling for his phone, Edden looked at Bancroft's remains and sighed. "Mr. Kalamack, I'd appreciate it if you could give us an hour of your time at your earliest convenience. Rachel, you too. There's going to be an inquiry. I can feel it already."

"Sure." *I hate reports.* I turned away, shuffling to the edge of the dry spot to watch the cloud of insane mystics sparkling in the sun as they continued on toward the Hollows. Sirens heralded their progress. The arena was right in the way, and my gut clenched at the thought of all those people huddled in fear as it passed over.

I'd like to think that the mystics had moved on because of the Goddess, that she'd driven them off, but the truth of it was they'd left because they'd felt a magnet stronger than my aura, a brighter light. Somewhere down there in the streets, someone had called the mystics away, called them to be collected, and with that, the wave would end. Slowly my numb stupor evolved into a tight anger. We had to stop these people.

The sound of Jenks's wings was loud, but I felt his dust first, like the soft prickling of wild magic. "That was some freaky shit, Rache. You okay?"

I nodded, watching the cloud go faint in the sun as I took off my hard hat. Dropping it, I grabbed someone's scarf, glad the file cabinet I'd stashed my gun in was in the dry zone. Using the scarf like a potholder, I opened the drawer. Sure enough, my cherry-red splat gun was coated in busted charms. Depressed, I wrapped the scarf around it and tucked it in my bag. The heat might have destroyed the charms' potency, but I doubted it.

"David!" Edden said loudly, and I spun to the elevator, but he was on his phone. "I can't bring the wave any closer to you than that. Did you get a fix on where these bastards are?"

"David," I whispered, striding back to Trent. "You're talking to David? Give me that!"

"Alone?" Edden said loudly, holding me off and grinning all the wider. Jenks, eavesdropping at his shoulder, gave a thumbs-up. "Rachel and Mr. Kalamack are with me, and I do believe they can get there faster than that."

"David?" I exclaimed, knowing he'd hear me. "You found them?"

"Will you be quiet?" Edden said, hand over the speaker. "I'm trying to talk to David."

Frustrated, I dropped back to my heels. "You know where they are?" I asked when Edden ended the call with a terse "We're on our way." But I knew the answer already by his smile, both satisfied and predatory.

"That little coffee shop a few blocks down," he said, gesturing for us to head for the elevators. "He's got them pinned down but he's alone. I don't know if we can get there before their reinforcements arrive."

Junior's, I thought, my mood sobering as we passed the last covered corpse, still uncharred under my protection bubble. Of course.

Seventeen

I pulled up short as I strode out of the quiet FIB lobby and into the bright sun. It wasn't the sudden wind that stopped me, but the cry of recognition and the surge from the newspeople. They'd seen the explosion at the top of the tower, and they knew Trent's face, even stubbled as it was.

"Whoa! How we going to get through that?" Jenks said in disgust, his dust like needles, holding an unexpected energy as the bright sparkles slid through my aura.

Sighing, I rocked to a stop, unwilling to push through the crowd. "I can't take you anywhere," I muttered, and Trent looked up from his phone conversation with a frustrated acceptance. The call had started in the elevator, and I was amazed at how he was able to keep his cool when everything was falling apart. But that's what made Trent, Trent.

"I am so sorry," he said to me, then "Make it work" to Quen before ending the call.

Edden was craning to see over the heads to the car he'd called for, but the reporters had converged, ducking under the plastic ribbon and overwhelming the few officers out front. Backup was at least half an hour out. It would be over by then. Hell, it would be over in ten minutes! We didn't have time for this, and I caught Jenks's eye.

"Go tell David we're on our way," I whispered, lips barely moving. "Do what you can."

"You got it," he said, and I watched enviously as he lifted off, unnoticed as he flew over the tops of everyone.

Trent was watching too, a touch of melancholy in him. "I am so tired of this," he said softly. Knowing it was a bad idea, I sent my fingers to find his, and he started at the tiny squeeze, returning it full force. But he didn't let go, and I froze at the memory of that last kiss.

"I'll go first," Edden said, eyes narrowed. "Stick to no comment. I don't know what kind of a spin I have to put on this yet."

I took a deep breath as the somewhat squat man began waving his arms, dropping down the last few steps to the sidewalk to force a path. My hand slipped from Trent's, and he touched the small of my back, making me go next. I stifled a shiver, something in me rebelling, another part enjoying the sensation I knew I had no right to call mine. Head up against the shouted questions, I fell into place behind Edden. We got about three steps.

"Captain Edden." Shoved and harried, a woman with her hair pulled back into an unusually informal ponytail fell into the squat man, forcing him to recognize her. "Sorry about that," she said as she found her feet and gave him a winning smile. "Can you comment upon the most recent explosion and destruction of the top floor of the FIB building?"

Ignoring the mic shoved at his face, Edden kept moving forward. "Not at this time."

"Captain Edden!" a man at the back shouted, his mic held up over the heads of everyone. "Cincinnati has been closed as well as the Hollows. Give us something, or we're going to start making things up!" There was a light titter, but it wasn't much of a joke.

"Mr. Kalamack! Can you comment on what you and Ms. Morgan were doing at the FIB today? Was that demon or elven magic?"

"We can make stuff up about that, too!" someone else said, getting a more certain laugh.

The cameras were snapping; I wasn't the only one who liked Trent's new look. He took a breath to speak, only to be cut off by Edden. "Another wave is passing through Cincinnati," the captain said tersely as he tried to get us moving again. "The alarm system is working. I'll make a statement at the arena as soon as we've been over the data."

"Or like never," someone muttered. The crush of people was oppressive, and I stifled a surge of panic. Trent's hand landed on me, steadying me with his calm as if I were one of his horses.

"Captain Edden! Any progress on finding the Free Vampires?"

Another officer had reached us to force a path, but it wasn't enough. The sound of pixy wings zipped through me, and Jenks darted down.

"Is David okay?" I said as he landed on Trent's shoulder, and he held up a hand for me to wait, out of breath as he put his hands on his knees and his wings hung flat. We were surrounded by hundreds, but I felt alone. "Is he okay?" I asked again.

"Yeah, but you gotta move," the pixy panted, and Trent's brow furrowed, having heard him as well. "He's got them pinned down, but he's alone. The pack is at a good old-fashioned Were and vampire riot at the arena. Edden's men are out, too. Whoever gets there first wins."

Crap on toast. How was I going to get through this? Trent looked over the crowd, knowing as well as I that we'd never get out of here in time. Finally one of the other officers got to us, face pale as he whispered in Edden's ear. I watched, alarm pooling in me as Edden's expression became even grimmer.

"It never rains but that it pours," Edden grumbled, starting to push his way through again, our pace faster now that we had help. "We lost everyone headed to the coffeehouse. There's a riot at the arena, which leaves just us. Damn it! We're going to lose them!"

Frustrated, I took Trent's arm as someone jostled us. "Rache . . ." Jenks whined, waiting for direction.

One of the reporters saw me holding Trent's arm and I let go when her eyes lit up. "Mr. Kalamack?" she said, turning her back on Edden and elbowing herself some room. "Tammy Gavin from the *Hollows Gazette*. Are you and Morgan officially a couple?"

Like flowers to the sun, every single face turned from Edden to us. There was a moment of silence, and then the questions started up again. Trent's confusion vanished as he put a hand to my shoulder to give me a gentle shove back the way we'd come. "Go," he said between his unmoving, smiling lips. "I got your back."

"I got her back, not you," Jenks said irately.

"What?" I said, and Jenks took off from his shoulder like a shot.

"It's your job," Trent said, almost hiding the hint of bitterness as he stepped between me and the crowd. "Go."

Heart pounding, I edged backward as Trent eased forward, drawing the crowd around me and away. "Tammy, was it?" Trent said brightly. "Ms. Morgan is my security. Who better than a day-walking demon to keep a person safe?"

Jenks was a bright spot of sun in the shade of the building across the blocked-off street, and I took a step back. Trent stood alone surrounded by the cameras and mics, the sun dusty in his hair—and I felt a pang of loss. *He'll be okay,* I told myself, but it was harder than I expected to take another step back.

Seeing me slipping away, Edden began to follow me. That is, until Trent turned to the reporters, smiling as he said, "A wave-induced magic misfire took the life of Sa'han Bancroft this morning." Edden jerked to a horrified halt, and Trent added, "He was attempting to contact the entity we believe is trying to communicate through the wave. He died a hero's death."

"Ah, that's not confirmed," Edden said, but the reporters loved it.

"Sahhon Bancroft. Is that with one H or two?" a reporter asked.

Trent became solemn. "That's Sa'han. Capital S, lowercase A, followed by an apostrophe and then lowercase H, A, and N. It's a nongender-specific elven title commensurate with sir or madam, not a given name. Bancroft was the highest authority in the study of ancient elven religious beliefs, and his wisdom will be sorely missed."

I was clear of the crowd. Tension vibrated through me as I hitched my bag higher, my head down as I walked for the shadows.

"Then that was elven magic?" Tammy asked, and Edden started waving his hands to get Trent to shut up.

"You know your elven history, Ms. Gavin," Trent said, beaming.

"Elves have always fascinated me, Mr. Kalamack," the woman flirted, and I was gone.

The shadow of the building covered me. I felt guilty for leaving Trent behind, but I didn't look back, striding forward in a near run. *Jenks* . . . I thought, then caught a sparkle of pixy dust from the traffic control box at the nearest crosswalk. I quickened my pace. He didn't have to watch for traffic, but I did, and just before I reached the crosswalk, the light suddenly changed.

Horns blew as drivers already distracted and nervous slammed on brakes. There was a sickening crunch of plastic, and I didn't slow down, crossing the street as someone's radiator began to leak and the accusations flew. I swung my hair aside as Jenks joined me, wings a satisfied hum. "You just ruined someone's day."

"I'll write them a haiku in apology," he smart-mouthed back. "Mark has cleared the place out but for David and the two guys he's got pinned. They're vamps, all right. Both short, both in military anticharm gear. One's blond, one's brown haired. Other than that you guys—"

"All look alike to you, I know." The potency of his dust

spilling over me was easing, but that unfamiliar tingle worried me. God, I hoped my aura wasn't glowing.

But even as I hustled down the sidewalk toward Junior's, my thoughts were on Trent, not the probable firefight waiting for me. He'd willingly stayed behind, a *distraction* so I could do what we both wanted to. Why? I knew this was what he wanted to be.

He said it was my job, I thought, meaning it wasn't his. He was trying to be who everyone had told him he was—and I didn't like it. I didn't like it a lot.

Deep in thought, I strode down the empty sidewalk, listening to the thunderous booms of antimagic deterrents and mundane tear gas going off at the arena, my mind on Trent's anger when Bancroft had said his mother was a poser, his disbelief and anguish that it might be true. And then his shock when he heard the echo of the Goddess in my mind when Bancroft's magic misfired. I was starting to believe *all* demons could do elven magic but shunned it on the principle of belief. Al was going to be pissed if he ever found out I'd talked to the Goddess.

I jerked, startled when Jenks flew up in my face. His first flash of annoyance turned into suspicion, and he flew backward as I realized we were almost there. Honestly, why did everything seem to happen at Junior's? It was almost as if it were a crossroads to a time continuum or something.

"You'd better get your lily-white ass in there," Jenks said as he flew backward before me. "They're getting itchy."

My heart gave a quick pound. Adrenaline was a cool stream behind it, spilling through my muscles and clearing my mind. David needed me, and I wanted to talk to some Free Vampires and find out why they were messing with the undead. Not to mention what in *hell* they thought they were doing imprisoning mystics.

"Thanks, Jenks," I said as I yanked the door open and the bells jingled against the glass. His dust was an eager silver as the door closed behind us, sealing us in a shop smelling of spicy Were, angry vampire, and really good coffee. Junior, or Mark, rather, was pale as he stood behind the counter in an uninvoked circle he'd had etched in the floor. Trouble followed me like a puppy, and he knew it. But apart from that, the place was empty. *Thank you, Mark.* I'd impacted his life enough for him to know the drill.

David stood almost in the middle of the store, and I sauntered to him, surprised that he was in a suit, albeit a rumpled one. The Were was the model alpha with his dark wavy hair slicked back into a ponytail and his face holding a bare hint of stubble. The expensive fabric mirrored his pelt as if he had been on four paws instead of in a pair of designer dress shoes, the black-and-silver smoothness a definite contrast to his hard expression.

"Sorry I'm late," I said, but never looked from the two men he was holding unmoving at a corner table at the wrong end of a sawed-off shotgun. It was his favorite, a vamp killer. He could hit both of them with the barest shift of barrel at this distance, and though Free Vampires promoted a quick second death, I didn't think any of them were in a hurry for it. Anyone else would look wrong with the ugly thing tucked atop their arm, but not David.

"What took you so long?" David asked, shifting to make room.

Jenks's blade was catching dust, making a steady stream fall from the tip in threat. "We ran into the press," the pixy muttered, clearly still peeved about it.

The black-eyed vampires shifted, and David lifted his gun. Slowly they eased back, hands on the table. I couldn't help my smile. The confidence needed to stand against two living vampires wasn't small, and feeling the pheromones tingling over my skin like silk, I wasn't sure even David would've been able to best them if he hadn't had the power of the focus shimmering just behind his eyes. "Press?" David questioned, and I tapped the nearest line, wishing my splat gun wasn't covered in sleepy-time charms.

"Trent took care of it," I said, eyeing the tissue-box-size

device in the dark-haired vampire's grip. *Mystics?* I wondered, deciding it had to be for the strength he held it with. Two vampires, three of us. It wouldn't be easy, but we could do this.

"Good," David said, the slant of his lips catching my attention. I knew he didn't trust Trent, probably because a possible friend had committed suicide in Trent's lockup rather than divulge the location of the focus, the same curse now residing happily in David.

I tightened my grip on the nearest ley line and put a foot on a chair, shoving it to a nearby booth. Both vampires jerked, telling me they were versed in the arts of security, not the bedroom—if their uniforms hadn't given it away. "I wish you'd get off Trent's case," I said as I sent the small table to join it. I wanted room to work, and dodging around tables and chairs slowed me down. "He's not as bad as you think."

David glanced at me, a weird light in his eye. "You mean he's not that bad anymore. You probably saved his life, you know."

"Today?" I blurted, and he shook his head. There was one last chair between us and the two vampires, and they began paying attention when I shoved it to join the others.

"No . . ." David pulled his rifle up to keep them unmoving. "Last year or so. His morals were becoming nebulous. You forced him to make a decision. I wasn't going to make my generation live through another Kalamack."

"Seriously?" Jenks said, altitude fluctuating. "Dude, I gotta tell Trent."

"No you don't," I said as I tossed my shoulder bag to land next to the counter, hopefully out of the way. If I was lucky, one of them would try to search it and knock themselves out with the spilled sleepy-time potion. "You. Blondie. Where are the mystics you just stole?" I asked, and the blond vampire's eyes widened, lips parting to show his sharp canines.

"Shut up," the other snarled, eyes black as pits.

"Frank, it's that demon witch!" Blondie said, clearly shaken.

"I said *shut up!*" he said again, his gaze darting to the windows, and I stood with my feet placed for balance, breathing in the growing scent of angry vampire. Their heavy slacks and long-sleeved shirts were coated with a charm retardant, and their boots were made for running. *Military?* I wondered, knowing you could get them at any outlet, though I personally wouldn't trust the anticharm glaze anymore. Their hair, too, was cut close to their skull, and my lips curled. Military vampires were just asking for trouble. They were too pretty for that and often strayed from orders.

"Are they in there?" I said as I looked at the device, and he pulled it closer.

"We will be free of them," Frank said, his voice taking on the cadence of the misled. "They use us and trade us like dolls." His head came up, eyes cold with hatred. "They don't deserve life!"

"You had me until that last one," I said, fingers moving in a charm to harness the line's energy into my tingling fingertips. "Look, I understand about wanting to change society, but this isn't how to do it. You're hurting people."

"They killed my sister!" the vampire shouted, and when he stood, I released my spell.

"Dilatare!" I yelled, the ball of light exploding in the light hanging over the table.

Glass shattered. Jenks darted to David, hiding behind him as his rifle blew a hole in the ceiling. Teeth clenched, David leaped at the blond vampire, rifle poised as a club.

"Not the ceiling!" Mark shouted from behind the counter. "Damn it, Rachel! I'm still making payments!"

Dust rained down in a cloudy mix of pixy sparkles. David and the blond vampire were on the floor, crashing into chairs and tables. The other lay dazed, slumped in the booth, and I watched as the device fell from his grip to hit the tile.

"Got it!" I shouted, diving under the table.

Awareness flashed across the dark vampire's face, and with a savage grin, he dropped down under the table to meet me.

I couldn't stop. I slid under the table, slamming into

him. Thick and heady, his scent struck me, diving deep as I gasped and struggled to pull back from under him. Snarling, he reached for my shoulder, teeth bared. Adrenaline sang, and I kicked wildly at him, my head thumping the bottom of the table as I wedged the device out from under his foot.

"Get off!" I screamed, flooding him with ever-after, and he howled, flinging himself back and hitting the wall.

Scrambling, I tucked the mystics to me. A hand clamped on the back of my shirt and pulled me out. My butt slid on the tiled floor as I spun in a dizzying circle, landing almost in the center of the room again.

But I could breathe, the oppressive feel of the air under the table washed away. "Thanks, David!" I panted, then froze, the mystics pressed against my middle. It hadn't been David.

"You!" I said, scrambling up and backing away from that same vampire I'd seen on the bridge. My pulse pounded at the absolute confidence and anger in his blue eyes. The room had gone silent, and my first impulse to blast him choked into dismay as he shook his head and held up a little lantern that was anything but, seeing as Jenks was in it, the pixy as mad as a wet banshee, the tip of his sword pressed into the corners as he looked for a way out. *Shit, he'd caught Jenks.*

I kept backing up as the dark-haired vampire crawled out from under the table, his lips pressed tight and eyes black as he dusted himself off. Mark was hiding behind the counter, and David had the blond one pinned to the floor, rifle at his chest.

"That belongs to me," the Kisten look-alike said, soft with threat and promise. My heart pounded. His voice was higher than Kisten's, and his face narrower. His hair, though, looked naturally fair, not dyed, and he smiled as he saw me look at it.

"Who are you?" I said, not expecting an answer as I backed up until a survivable eight feet separated us. I knew for a fact that Kisten didn't have a brother, but vampires played with their children's bloodlines as if they were Thoroughbreds. The man before me had probably once belonged to Piscary, discarded or traded like a duplicate card when Kisten showed the proper balance of domination and submission the master vampire preferred. No wonder they hated them, even as they were conditioned to love and die for them.

"Give me the mystics," he said, hand shaking slightly and pupils slowly widening.

I shook my head, imagining Jenks among the broken shards, his dust slowly fading.

"Give me the mystics!" he screamed, and I jumped, startled into pulling on the line and making my hair float.

"Back off," I whispered to David. "Give him back his man."

In a sliding sound of fabric, David pulled back from the man on the floor. I'd made the newly arrived vampire lose his temper, and clearly that bothered him as he flipped his hair out of his eyes. Shoulders back, he took several cleansing breaths. Maybe it was his temper that had made him unsuitable, because by God, he looked perfect. Perfect and untouchable.

"I'm Ayer," he said, voice creeping over my skin and raising goose bumps. "If you want *this* back alive, give me my mystics." He gave Jenks a shake to make sure there was no question.

"Okay." I stood up straight, looking to buy some time. David was limping as he joined me, wiping the blood from his cut lip and scowling. "Tell me why you want them," I said, and a hint of bitterness stained Ayer's perfect beauty.

Motions slow, he went to help the blond vampire up, setting Jenks on the table before extending a thin hand to his friend. "I hear you almost lost your life trying to save Ivy," he said as he tugged the vampire's shirt.

I nodded, glancing at the empty parking lot. *Edden, where in hell are you?*

"Then you know why. The masters use us like things. It has to end."

"By killing them?" I said, looking past him to the streets

emptied by fear and the vampire and Were graffiti mixed like continuous acts of aggression. "We can't survive a second Turn."

"We can't survive without it," he said, and my eyes flicked to his arm, only now noticing the long burn visible in glimpses through a tear in his shirt. His clothes, too, were dirty, making me wonder if he'd been involved with the mob at the arena. "Give them to me. I'm not going to ask again."

"I agree the current system sucks," I said, wondering if I could break the lantern without cutting Jenks to shreds. "Putting them to sleep isn't helping. Or haven't you bothered to take a look past your carefully constructed blinders?"

"Blinders!" I jerked when Ayer shouted, and David warned him off with the rifle. "You saw what they did to Ivy. How can talk about blinders when I know she's ripped them from you? Look at me!" he bellowed, shocking me with his shift from calm to furious. "I was bred like an *animal* to someone's specifications, abandoned when another pleased him more!"

And jealousy will make him more dangerous. "This isn't about Ivy. This is about you murdering the undead!"

His teeth clenched, but with a visible effort he calmed himself, leaning back against the table and crossing his ankles to look relaxed. I knew he wasn't; I could almost see the pheromones rising from him and prickling along my skin. Behind him, the two vampires were exchanging worried looks. "It isn't murder if what you kill has no soul," he said softly, his hand going atop Jenks's prison to block the pixy's view, and suddenly the container was full of a black dust. "Give me the mystics."

He picked up Jenks, and David grabbed my arm, keeping me where I was. "Look, those waves you're pulling out of my line aren't simply powering your lullaby," I said as I shook David off. "You've divided a communal mind, and she's looking for them!"

"Energy isn't alive!" he barked, but I'd clearly hit a sore spot. He knew, damn it. He knew! And he didn't care.

"She's not energy, she's sentient," I said. "And you've made her psychotic. You're in over your head and lost control. Let them go, and maybe she'll go away."

Ayer looked me up and down, and from behind the glass, Jenks's wings were a blur. "You know a lot more than you should."

"That's because it's my line you're pulling them from. The wave is following me around like a puppy." Ayer's soft fidgeting ceased, and I squinted at him. "You didn't know that, did you?" I said, and his eyes went entirely dark. "My God, you didn't even know why the wave patterns were shifting."

Table creaking, he stood, turning to look pointedly at the two men nursing their hurts behind him. Beside me, David leveled his shotgun. Ayer hadn't said a word, but he'd just told them to be ready to act. "We do now," Ayer said, and I stiffened when he held Jenks at his middle, long fingers caressing the glass. "Interesting that they like you, Morgan."

"Let go of my partner," I demanded, setting the device on a nearby table in a show of exchange. It made David cringe, but Ayer didn't even look at it.

"You've talked to her, haven't you?" he said, his voice low with the holding of secrets. "They follow you like puppies, you said. You can control her."

"No," I said, fear sliding through me as I remembered Bancroft, driven mad by them.

But he only smiled, chilling me. "Either you're lying to me, or elven magic *is* more powerful than demon—as he said." He leaned in until my skin tingled. "Which is it?"

"Elven magic isn't more powerful than demon," I said, affronted. "She's nuts, and she'll drive me nuts too!"

"I can live with that," he said, a slight eye twitch giving me bare warning.

"Rachel!" David shouted, but I flung myself backward, gasping as I tried to stay out of Ayer's reach. Hitting the floor, I rolled and kept rolling. Again the shotgun blasted, and the scent of gunpowder overtook the stench of angry vampire.

"Rachel! Here!" David cried, and I sat up, eyes widening as he threw the mystics at me. I caught the device almost in self-defense and held it close.

"Get her!" Ayer shoved David's head into the counter and the Were slid to the floor. Fire and darkness in his eyes, Ayer strode toward me, but I was already moving, slamming my palm into the nose of the first man to touch me, then grabbing the arm of the next to pull myself up. My knee hit his chin, pulled down within easy reach, and he groaned and fell away.

Panting, I spun in my cleared space, the mystics making a tingling in my hand. I was alone, ringed by three vampires, two bloodied by me, the other just pissed. Mark had pulled David to safety, and I felt a twinge of relief when the witch invoked the circle he had back there. They were safe.

Me, on the other hand . . .

Ayer paced before me, knowing better than to try to take me by force while I could tap a line. "You will talk to the splinter or die," he said, his face ugly as he held the lantern as if to drop it.

"You want them, you can have them," I said, then threw the mystics at him.

Snarling in rage, he flung Jenks at the wall.

It was too far away. Heart breaking, I leaped for the lantern. Desperate, I made a circle to catch Jenks for the half an instant I'd need. Eyes widening, I held my breath as my feet left the tile, watching as Jenks crashed into the inside of my circle, rolling down it end over end until my outstretched hand hit the edge of the bubble. With a surge of tingles, the circle fell.

But I had him, and I pulled him to me even as my back slammed into the floor, knocking the air out of me. I couldn't breathe, but I almost cried as my shaky fingers gripped the lantern and held it close. It hadn't broken, and the small prison was thick with a gray dust. Two little hands pressed the glass, and a faint swearing filtered out.

"Oh God! Jenks!" I wheezed, trembling as I undid the

latch and he came boiling out, a beautiful flow of pixy swearing rising up with him.

"About time!" the pixy snarled. "What were you waiting for? God to say go?"

Shaking in relief, I sat on the floor as Jenks's dust wreathed me in sparkling tingles. But it wasn't over yet, and I slowly got up to reassess the odds. Three vampires against a demon, a pixy, and a Were. Sure, two of the vampires weren't going to do much—one unable to see due to his broken nose, the other because I think I'd fractured his jaw—but David was out and I was a wreck. Besides, they had the mystics. All they had to do was run.

But they didn't, and I watched, numb when Ayer tossed a zip strip at me. It slid to a halt at my feet, and I ignored it. "You're going to have to kill me first," I said, not having any right to be so cocky—except I could see something he couldn't.

News vans, three of them, were pulling into the parking lot. Ayer didn't turn at the sudden sound of the engines, but the others did, their moods becoming hesitant when men and women began getting out. Mark stood up from behind the counter, sweat stained and shaken, but his relieved expression told me David was okay.

Trent got out of the largest van, and something in me twisted when he extended a hand to help a woman to the pavement. His eyes met mine through the glass, and my heart gave a thump at the relief he hid behind a cheerful, half-heard banter.

"You have the luck of the damned," Ayer swore, turning on his heel and heading for the back door.

"I guess you'll get me next time," I muttered, and Ayer hesitated, giving Mark a dark look before running his gaze over me once—and then following his men out the back as the front door opened with a cheerful jingle. They had the mystics, and I didn't care.

Head down, I limped to David, not believing that I was glad to see reporters as they poured in with their cords, cameras, lights, and noise—all of them waving their hands before their faces and commenting loudly on the vamp pheromones and fallen tables. "You okay, Jenks?" I asked.

"Yeah, I'm fine. I must be getting old. He caught me in a net. Like a three-year-old."

I gave Mark a thankful look and got a trembling thumbs-up before he shuffled to the counter to take an order. He was shaky, but he looked okay. He'd know to keep his mouth shut, too. Smiling in relief, I helped David to his feet, the blinking Were looking decidedly sheepish. "How about you?" I asked. "You hit the counter pretty hard."

"I have a thick head," he said, rubbing it as he turned his back on the cameras. "You mind if I . . ."

"Go," I said, knowing he wanted to check on his pack—our pack—at the arena riot. "But will you call me tonight?"

"Call?" He touched my arm, very aware of the watching people. "You'll be lucky if I don't sleep on your doorstep. That vampire is crazier than Goldilocks on bane."

Smiling, I gave him a quick hug. David headed for the door, righting a table before he slipped unnoticed out the front door, now propped open to air the place out. Unnoticed that is, except by Trent, and a weird feeling slipped through me at the silent look they exchanged before he limped away. *I'd saved his life, eh?*

"There she is!" Trent said brightly, as if he'd discovered the *Mona Lisa* in a scavenger hunt, his mask already back in place. "Rachel, I promised them an exclusive with you about what it's like to be my security. Over lunch, perhaps? Now that you got your coffee?"

"Sure. Coffee," I said as I limped to my shoulder bag. He was here—not for lunch and an interview, but to save my ass. My smile wasn't faked, but the distance between us felt larger than the four feet he stopped at, his hands behind his back and a false lightheartedness to him. The ending would have been different if he'd been with me, but I wasn't going to tell him that. Not when he was finally doing the right thing for his girls and himself.

"I thought perhaps Carew Tower?" Trent eased up beside me, noting my slight tremor. "We can have a quiet interview there. Unless you want to do it here?"

"Carew Tower is great." I was tired. Tired and hungry. Crap on toast, I hadn't eaten yet.

"Capital!" His hand slipped behind me as he pulled me close, playing to the cameras but supporting me in a way that looked like he wasn't. "They're closed due to the curfew, but I know one of the cooks and she said she'd come in." He brightened as he led me to the door. "Shelly, perhaps we could simply carpool over there in your vehicle?"

"Yes, of course!" a blonde with a hundred-dollar hairstyle said, beaming as she shoved her cameraman out the door ahead of us. "Well, make room!" I heard her tell him as we followed. "Get a cab! Mr. Kalamack wants to see the inside of my van!"

Jenks landed on my shoulder to tend his torn wing, and Trent's fingers at the small of my back almost lifted. "Are you okay?" he asked softly. "What happened? Was it the Free Vampires? Did they have the mystics?"

"Yes to all, and I'm okay," I said, and his shoulders relaxed. "If you hadn't shown up, it would have gotten ugly. Thanks."

"It was the least I could do," he said, words holding a tinge of frustration, but it wasn't aimed at me. Thankfully he beat my reach for the door, and I kept my mouth shut as he guided me out of it. It was like a party behind us as everyone enjoyed the lingering pheromones, and I squinted as we came out of the noise and into the sun. Shelly was at the van, yelling at her camera guy to make room for us.

"What did you find out?" he asked, and I met his eyes, letting him see my worry.

Besides them wanting to force me to talk to their Goddess splinter? "They're using the mystics to intentionally kill the masters. Maybe they think the living will toe the line once they realize there won't be a second life waiting for them."

"Mmmm." Focus distant, Trent helped me to the van.

"That's what I was afraid of. It still feels odd to me that vampires are doing this, but even so it's unacceptable and will be curtailed."

Curtailed? I'd prefer crushed into a paste, myself. But I couldn't help but wonder. Would he have cared six months ago? Or simply adjusted his long-term goals accordingly. "This guy, Ayer, is nuts. He thinks that because I can't control her that elven magic is stronger than demon."

Trent said nothing, and I looked up, another layer of worry coating me. "It is?" I prompted, and he grimaced, his grip on my elbow tightening as he helped me into the van.

"Mmmm," Trent whispered again, his breath tickling my ear. "Why do you think the demons tried to exterminate us?"

Swell. Just swell. No wonder Al didn't like him.

Eighteen

A depressingly few spots of light glowed in the graveyard, flitting about at the edges and looking like lost souls. Jenks's kids were down to a bare handful. I honestly didn't know how he managed to maintain his hold on so big a space, unless it was because Jumoke and Belle both were ruthlessly savage with intruders. That, and Jenks was arguably the oldest pixy on the continent and perhaps his reputation was keeping both the pixies and fairies at bay.

The soft snuffing of Trent's horse was soothing, rubbing out tension caused from the occasional siren and the ominous red glow on the bottom of the clouds over Cincinnati. Curfew was in effect, so of course everyone not human was outside dodging cops. It wasn't as if the I.S. or FIB could stop them. Tomorrow's Fourth of July fireworks had been canceled, but the occasional rocket went up in a show of defiance in bright sparkles and noise. Sleep was impossible, and I was in the garden with Bis brushing out Tulpa.

The rhythmic motions and the sound of the bristles on the stallion's coat were soothing, and I'd continued long after what little dirt I'd found had been brushed away. The horse seemed to enjoy the attention, not minding Bis on his back making braids in his mane. The gargoyle's wings were out for balance, clawed feet spread wide. His long, dexterous gray fingers were almost the same color as the horse's mane. I'd caught him once at Ivy's computer, and the kid could type as fast as a career secretary.

A howl three streets over brought Tulpa's head up. Ears pricked, he nickered a warning. "Easy, Tulpa," I soothed, smiling that the big animal had already claimed the small patch of grass as his own. "Trent will get you as soon as the ban is lifted."

As if understanding, Tulpa nosed the bowl I'd brought the brush and hoof pick out in, both purchased at a local farm and feed store along with an ungodly expensive bale of sweet-smelling hay. It was a small spot of calm after a morning of chaos and fear, and I was reluctant to leave it.

"I don't think he approves," I said as Bis finished his braids.

"He likes it," Bis said, his low voice both gravelly and high. "He told me."

"Told you, eh?" I kidded him, and Bis flushed a dark black to blend in with the night. The grass was tickling my ankles, and I ran a hand down a leg, giving Tulpa a shove to shift his weight so I could lift it. The hoof was fine, and I set it down with a pat, running my fingers up his leg along the contour of the muscles. My thoughts wound back to seeing Trent pull his shirt off as he stood at the back of Ivy's mom's car. I slumped, imagining what it would be like to run my fingers over the lines in his back, feel the tension under them relax at my touch. *Stop it, Rachel.*

Lunch at Carew Tower had been both a pleasure and a trial—pleasure because not only had I gotten to eat a specially prepared meal, but I'd also embarrassed Trent with impunity, regaling Ms. Shelly with the humorous stories I'd collected over the last three months, and a trial because Trent was his expected Teflon self for the reporter, polite and proper even as his occasional embarrassed smile pegged my meter. That Cincy was falling apart under us didn't help, slowly turning as we ate until we saw every smoldering fire, every closed bridge, every torn-up park and blocked roadway the Free Vampires were serving up in their effort to make the world a better place.

Sighing, I dropped the hoof pick into the bowl and gave Tulpa a push to head out to the graveyard. He had a few days' feed there, and now I wouldn't have to mow it. Jumoke already had plans for the piles he was leaving behind.

Bis moved to a nearby tombstone, and we watched Tulpa flick his ears and huff at the pixies arrowing to him. I hadn't liked Trent's noncommittal answer when I'd pressed him again about elven magic being stronger than demon. Sure, humans had been summoning and containing demons for centuries, but containment was not control. Those slave rings, though . . . They had been the ugliest things I'd ever touched.

A dim spot of gold edged in blue circled Tulpa, driving the rest away so the horse could stand and watch the fire-glow from Cincinnati in peace. It evolved into Jenks as the pixy darted to us, circling once before landing on a tall Queen Anne's lace. "You look better," I said as the plant swung and bobbed and slowly settled, and Jenks shrugged.

"I taped my wing but it still itches like hell," he said sourly.

Bis rustled his wings, his red eyes blinking eerily in the dark. "Well, tell her," he prompted, making me wonder what was up.

Jenks pulled his gaze from his kids tormenting Tulpa. "Bis," he complained, unusually whiny. "It doesn't matter."

"It does," the cat-size gargoyle prompted.

"But it's not her who I need to apologize to," he said, and my thoughts darted to Jenks caught in Ayer's lantern.

"Bis, we all get tagged sometimes," I said, as uncomfortable as Jenks. "It happens. We work around it. No big deal."

"That's not what he needs to apologize for." Bis shot Jenks another dark look. "It's a big deal, and you need to say the words. To her. Now."

Jeez Louise, I thought, pushing up from the monument I'd been leaning against and heading for the church. Something had gotten Bis's knickers in a twist. "It can't be that bad," I prompted, trying to make light of it, whatever it was.

"Ah . . ." Jenks hesitated as he landed on a shoulder, and I started when Bis landed on my other one and bopped Jenks with the tip of his lionlike tail. "Okay! Okay!" Jenks protested, a thin slip of silver dust falling down my front. "I'm sorry for the way that I've been treating Trent," he said, almost belligerent.

Trent? Confused, I looked at Bis, his ugly, pushed-in face inches from mine. He was leaning forward to see around me, his grimace clearly saying he was waiting for Jenks to say more. "Why are you apologizing to me?" I said, thinking that Jenks and Trent had a great relationship, then thinking I never thought I'd ever think that—not in a million years.

Bis cleared his throat, and Jenks's wings tickled my neck. "Because it involves you," the pixy said. "I misjudged him. I thought he was all talk, no action. Just a, ah, piece of pretty elf ass. And he is! But . . ."

I stepped over the low stone wall separating the grave-yard from the backyard, being careful not to dislodge either of them. *Piece of pretty elf ass?* "But what?"

Jenks took to the air, hands on his hips as he glared at Bis. "Why don't you go away?"

"Soon as you say it," he shot back, his tail wrapping across my back and under my arm.

I stopped where I was, not wanting to go into the church and involve Ivy. Jenks fidgeted in midair, a dull spot of gold in the night. "Don't say anything until I'm done, okay? Just hear me out." I nodded, and he added, "Ah, he's an okay backup."

Ah-h-h-h . . . Finally it began to make sense. Trent had said he had my back, and Jenks told him it wasn't his job. I took a breath to protest, holding it when Bis pinched my shoulder.

Jenks's dust grayed. "He has some inabilities that might get you killed, sure," he said, and Bis cleared his throat in warning, "but he's doing okay."

"Inabilities," I prompted, glancing at the shadows moving in the kitchen. Ivy, probably, seeing as Nina was zonked out on Brimstone to keep Felix from taking her over.

"You know." Jenks fidgeted. "Jumping to the wrong conclusion, overreacting. Kind of like you used to be." He looked up, flashing me a sick-looking smile. "I'm *sorry* for doubting your ability to pick a good . . . uh, work partner on your own. Okay?" He made an ugly face at Bis, flipping him off as he flew backward.

"Whoa, whoa, whoa!" I said, hand waving in protest. "I can pick a good work partner? Jenks, you're my backup, not Trent. That's not changing."

Jenks's nasty expression softened, becoming both full of pride and sorrow. I'd seen him look at his daughters like that, and something in me hurt. "Yeah, I know," he said. "Good luck with that. Can I go now, you stinky piece of bat flesh?"

That last had been directed at Bis, and looking as satisfied as Buddha, he nodded. Immediately Jenks darted off. Tulpa was snapping at his kids, ears pinned and tail swishing.

"Jenks?" I called, faltering when Ivy came to the back door. "We're going to talk about this later," I muttered at Bis, and the first hints of unease stole over his softly pebbled features.

Ivy stood behind the screen door, arms over her middle. "What was that all about?"

I slowly climbed the stairs, the weight of three sleepless nights heavy on me. "I don't know. How's Nina?"

The screen door squeaked, and Ivy held it for me. "Zonked out and afraid of the dark," she said, and I thought it one of the most wrong things I'd heard all week—and it had been a week full of wrong. "Landon's here. He wants to talk to you."

"Landon?" I jerked to a halt just inside the church. "I thought he was in the hospital."

Ivy nodded, a dark look in her eye. I'd told her what had happened at Trent's stables and the top of the FIB tower, and seeing as I'd taken care of it in a suitably positive fashion, she was content to let me handle it. But now he was here in my church and I wasn't sure how I felt.

"What does he want," I muttered, and Bis hopped to the back of a chair when I leaned to brush the horse dirt off me.

"You want me to get rid of him?" Ivy asked.

Shaking my head, I went to the kitchen for a drink. The lights were high in the sanctuary, and I could hear a pixy buck talking to Landon. The elf wasn't talking back. "No," I said as I took a couple of sodas from the fridge. Hesitating, I held one up to Bis, and when he nodded, I grabbed a third. Soda. Landon had watched his boss commit magical suicide and I was going to offer him a pop?

"Want to listen in?" I asked Bis, handing him the three bottles one by one to open for me with one of his long claws.

"Yeah," he said as he gave me back the first two and kept the last. "I don't like him."

"There's something about him I don't like, either," Ivy muttered, her long hair swaying as she leaned to look down the hall.

"That makes three of us," I said, then wedged off my shoes. Ivy had been looking at them and I didn't want to track the graveyard through the house.

Ivy made a low noise of discontent as I passed her, and knowing she'd stay out of sight but not out of earshot, I ambled down the dark hall to the bright sanctuary, bottles clinking. Landon was sitting on the couch as I'd seen countless clients, depressed, afraid, perched on the edge of the cushions with his elbows on his knees and his head in his hands. His expression when he looked up at Bis gliding in behind me was about the same, too, sort of a desperate, you're-my-last-hope kind of a thing, and I shoved my rescue impulse down deep.

Though scrubbed clean from the hospital, he looked out of sorts in a slightly too-large pair of overalls and boots too big for him. His hair was flat, and his eyes red rimmed. A paper grocery bag with EAT RIGHT FOOD emblazoned on it sat beside him, the top rolled down to a ridiculous shortness.

"Hi," I said as I sat in the chair across from him. Bis had perched himself on the back of his overstuffed chair, the one he'd found at the curb this spring. Magazines were piled on it since the cushion was blown out, but Bis had a tendency to ruin furniture and it didn't matter.

Landon's expression was numb as I held the pop out. "You have pixies in your church," he said as he took it.

"And a gargoyle in the steeple," I said, nodding toward Bis. The gargoyle was slugging his soda in one go, and I hoped he would contain himself in the coming belch. "They're part of our security," I added. "You remember Bis, right?"

Landon hardly looked up, his gaze unfocused on the bottle in his hands. "May your updrafts all be warm."

"And your downdrafts few," Bis belched, earning a titter from the ceiling.

Nice. I wished they'd all leave so I could tell Landon his problem wasn't going to become mine. "I'm sorry about Bancroft," I said, thinking I could manage civility, holding my expression bland at the memory of his charred bones.

"He died a hero."

I waited for more, and in the silence, I took a sip of cola and set the bottle down. The soft clink seemed to stir Landon, and he took a deep breath. "You're probably wondering why I'm here," he said as he set his bottle down untasted.

"No, not at all," I said lightly. "I just figured you're on a walkabout. It must have been hard getting across the river with the bridges closed."

Grimacing, he wiggled his fingers to indicate magic. Across the table, Bis had his bottle angled high, a long, sinuous black tongue reaching all the way to the bottom for the last drops. "I came to apologize," Landon said, hesitating when he noticed Bis.

Wow, an apology, I thought sarcastically. I hadn't trusted him before, and this only strengthened my suspicion that he was up to something. A man like Landon didn't cross security lines to make apologies unless he wanted something.

"For what I said earlier," he said, eyes flicking up to mine. "Just because your aura is black doesn't mean you're immoral. I shouldn't have taken a reading without your permission."

Thank you, I thought, but didn't say it. With the crack of snapping glass, Bis took the top off his bottle, jaw moving sideways as he ground it to a pulp. It was a show of aggression intended to cow Landon, and it seemed to be working.

"It was inexcusable and . . ." He hesitated. "I need your help."

"Uh-huh." I was so not surprised. I could set aside my dislike for him in order to see an end to this, but I didn't know what he thought I could do.

"You talked to the Goddess," he said, his eyes unable to hide his anger even as he tried.

Oh. That. "Who told you? Trent?" I asked, peeved. That was rather personal information, but perhaps, again in the name of seeing an end to this, he'd deemed it acceptable.

"I was wrong." Landon's gaze flicked to Bis when the kid took another tinkling bite of glass. "It isn't blasphemy for you to commune with the Goddess. If it was, you wouldn't be able to do it. I was jealous she chose to speak directly to you." His lips twisted, and the scent of hospital drifted to me, a tantalizingly familiar scent of electronics and dust just under it. "You don't even believe."

Not trusting the soul-searching truth spilling from him, I leaned back with my cola. "Who told you I don't believe?"

"Then maybe *I* don't believe," he said, but I wasn't buying it. "It came too soon," he said as Ivy scuffed to a halt in the hall, listening. "They want me to take his place. I can't tell them I don't even believe!" Angry now, he met my eyes. "Where do you get your faith!" he demanded. "This isn't even your religion!"

This was not at all comfortable, and I looked at the night-mirrored windows as I picked my words. As much as I distrusted him, he was an elf skilled in a magic that I wasn't familiar with. "She's not a goddess," I said, watching his mood evolve. "She's a communal mind that ancient elves deified, like the Egyptians deified the sun. Even so, I'm not going to try to talk to her. Even when she's all together, she's insane."

Insane wasn't quite the right word. Oblivious to her impact on others, perhaps. Or adhering to a standard that didn't apply to creatures of flesh and a limited life.

"But you have to!" Landon exclaimed, and I crossed my knees, tuning him out. Bis turned a threatening black, and Landon drew back, stymied. "Rachel, it's your aura the straying mystics look for. It's your amplified aura resonance they're being lured into captivity with. You can talk to her. Please," he said. "We have to stop this. If you can talk to her, the sane part, not the divided portion that broke Bancroft, maybe you can convince her to not send any more out through your line."

It made sense, but seeing Bancroft crazy from just a splinter of her was a heavy warning. "No, I'm sorry," I said, and he fell back into the cushions, looking not defeated but annoyed.

"Landon, can I call someone for you?" I said, wanting him out of my church. "Trent has a helicopter. He can get you out of the Hollows, wherever you want to go."

"I can't leave," Landon said indignantly, and Ivy came to stand just inside the sanctuary like a soft and certain threat. Landon's brow wrinkled and the hospital scent thickened as he became more determined. "You can end this. The waves, the sleeping undead, everything. If they wake up, your room-mate and her girlfriend will be safe. Isn't that what you want?"

Ivy's tight expression made it obvious that that was what she wanted. She wouldn't ask me to risk my sanity for it, but I might risk everything for her shot at happiness. No vampire should be afraid of the dark.

Something didn't feel right, though. He was too eager and not enough afraid. Unsure, I looked at Bis, stray bits of glass that had fallen to his skin sparkling in the artificial light. "Let me call Trent," I said, and Landon stiffened.

"No!" he said, then lowered both his voice and his eyes. "No," he reiterated, easing back in the seat. "He'd interfere. Ruin it."

Trent doesn't know Landon is here. My eyes narrowed in suspicion.

"We don't need him," Landon said as he reached for that bag. "I can do the ceremony right here. I have everything I need."

Even the goat? I wondered, but Ivy wouldn't have let him in here with a knife.

Ivy slipped closer, her long hair draping down to almost touch me. "Want some help cleaning the living room, Rachel?"

I held my breath, not wanting to take in the pheromones she was kicking out. "You really think I can—" I started, and Landon pushed forward to the edge of the chair, eyes alight.

"Yes!" he exclaimed. "You've talked to her before. She recognizes you."

His jealousy was obvious, and I felt a flash of pity. It was hard when someone achieves without apparent sacrifice or effort that which you've strived your entire existence for, doubly so when the person never even wanted it. "You think she'd listen to me?"

"It's worth a try." With a renewed enthusiasm, he pulled the bag closer, eyes flicking to Ivy when she sat where she could see both of us. Bis, too, seemed to settle in, and the pixies flew out, probably to tell their dad. "And it isn't difficult," Landon said as he set a clear crystal and etching sand on the table. "We do it all the time. Usually we only get a hint of a response, because all anyone can attract is a bare fraction of her attention. It's only lately, when the waves have concentrated her thoughts, that we've actually gotten a real and irrefutable connection."

Like the one that made Bancroft insane? "You know

what? I'm going to call Trent," I said, reaching behind me for the phone in my back pocket.

"No!" Landon blurted out, then bowed his head submissively when Ivy's eyes darkened. "I'm sorry. He'll turn it into a committee decision, and I simply want this to go away."

Jenks hummed in, his garden sword hanging from his belt. "I think you need to go away," he said, landing on the table with his feet spread wide and hands on his hips.

Landon's face scrunched up in compromise. "What if I do the summoning? Will you just watch? Tell me maybe what I'm doing wrong? If we could get her to stop sending her thoughts through your line, the waves would end and the masters would wake up."

Ivy and I exchanged questioning looks, and Jenks's dust pooled under him, fanning out when he rose. "I don't like this guy," he said, and I noted Landon's brief second of hidden anger.

I didn't like him either, but I'd risk a lot to bring an end to this, to end Ivy's heartache. "What does it entail?"

Exhaling, Landon put on his spelling cap and ribbon. "I'll show you."

Jenks walked, no, strutted, across the table, poking the tip of his sword at the bag of scribing sand. "It looks like the same stuff you used to use to summon Al."

Nodding, I sat back in my chair. More proof that demon and wild magic had a common source, perhaps?

Moving quickly, Landon scribed a plate-size circle on the coffee table, the sand hissing down with a smooth motion that spoke of years of practice. A triangle went around it so that the edges touched in three places, and then a second circle around that, nesting the three glyphs together. The clear crystal went into one of the spaces between the outer circle and triangle, a knotted bit of hair in the centermost space. If it was like demon magic, he'd probably want to put something in the tiny space above it.

"Ah . . ." Landon looked up, hesitating. "I need something that just died. The fresher the better."

"I take it back," Jenks said. "This is nothing like summoning a demon."

"You want a corpse?" Ivy said, aghast.

"No!" Pointy ears reddening, Landon grimaced. "A bug. A fly. Anything that was once living. She needs something to animate. Unless you want to volunteer to be a vessel?" he said. "That's what Bancroft did."

My chin lifted. No wonder Trent hadn't wanted to talk about it. Using dead things was usually black magic.

Jenks took to the air, his dust an eerie green. "Jumoke killed a hummer at sunset. I'll be right back."

Okay, I really wasn't liking this. "Your goddess converses with you through zombies?" I said, and Landon scowled, ignoring me as he used a magazine card to fix the sand that Jenks's wing draft had displaced. "I said, your goddess converses with you through zombies?" I said louder, and Jenks came back in, saving him from answering.

"It's been dead for about an hour," the pixy said, dropping it with a tiny thud.

"Perfect. The neurons will still be active."

I watched, distaste growing, as Landon casually moved the tiny thing to the top of the triangle, setting it inside the larger circle, but outside of the smaller one. "And you questioned my morals?" I muttered.

Bis resettled himself, and I wasn't surprised when I felt Landon's tap on my ley line out back. My nose wrinkled. It really wasn't my line, but no one else ever used it. It was Newt's, actually. My unease grew when Landon's eyes found mine with a fevered intensity, the spilled sand lines seeming to ripple into themselves as he murmured, *"Ta na shay. Ta na shay, enmobeana. Ta na shay, mourdeana. Ta na shay, eram. Ta na shay."* His breath whispered the words into nothing, but the awkward rhythm he was tapping continued, sort of a three-beat, two-beat, three-beat, three-beat.

Shoulders stiffening, I twisted my lips as something not altogether unpleasant slowly crept through me.

"Ah," Jenks said as he hovered beside Ivy. "Should your auras be glowing like that?"

"My aura is glowing?" I said, panicking.

"Yes," Landon said, the rhythm never hesitating. "That means it's working. Quiet. *Ta na shay, enmobeana.*"

I jumped when Jenks alighted on my shoulder. "His is glowing too, Rache. I think it's okay. Oh. Hey, it quit!"

"Yeah?" I squeaked, feeling something sort of peel off me with the pinch of a scab lifting away. The mystics, probably. "Look at that!" I said, pointing at the crystal. It had hazed purple. "Dude, it's the same color as her eyes!"

The tapping hesitated. "You've seen her eyes?" Landon asked bitterly.

I really needed to learn how to keep my mouth shut. "Ah, in a dream?" I said, and he resumed the tapping beat, jealousy making his motions fast.

"Ta na shay, mourdeana," he said, sounding almost vindictive.

Jenks's wings fluttered, and I shuddered at the feel of them on my neck. "Whoa. Anyone else feel that?" he asked.

Ivy gasped, and my eyes shot to the hummingbird. It lay on the table, wings moving but never taking to the air. A quick look with my second sight showed it was flaming with a white aura. Landon's eyes were wide, his cheeks flushed as if he hadn't thought this was going to work. "Rache . . ." Jenks whispered. "This don't feel right."

I was tending to agree with him. Landon was sweating, and we all jerked when the hummingbird lurched into the air, never leaving the tiny space in which it had been placed. The head wasn't quite level, and it truly didn't look alive.

"It's working," Landon whispered. "My God, I've never seen this strong a connection."

My eyes dropped from the bird, now leaking blood from the wound it had died from, to the curled and knotted hair in the center. It was a place of honor. My jaw clenched. There was no way you could put a person into a glyph this size, but hair was often used as a bridge.

"Landon," I said in warning, and his smile became ugly.

"Ta na shay, eram!" he said, his anger and jealousy spilling over into his voice.

I gasped as a scintillating flow of mystics poured through me, my defenses as effectual as a sieve as they danced through the spaces around them with the sound of wings and spinning wheels made of purple eyes. I wasn't connected to a line. I *was* a line, the living energy existing in the spaces between mass, chiming to the sound of my aura.

"Oh shit . . ." I breathed, and my hands clenched on the cushions as the bird's wings stilled and it hit the table.

"Rachel?" Ivy said, leaning close, but I couldn't see her, my vision unable to process anything as something seemed to play with my aura, caressing it.

You've come home. The alien thought lifted through me. *Become. Tell me what you've seen.*

"No," I whispered, feeling the presence begin to pull me in, the edges of my awareness become fuzzy. *No,* I thought, and the whirling eyes of the Goddess's thoughts turned to me, purple feathers shedding from it at my defiance to leave it unblinking.

"Get out!" I screamed, shifting my aura sideways until the mystics sort of stepped left and were gone.

I took a huge breath, head snapping up to see Bis atop the table, the spell scattered as he hissed at Landon, wings spread wide. The man was scrunched in his chair, facing down a very pissed Ivy and Jenks. "I'm okay!" I said, and Ivy turned, the relief in her overwhelming. "I'm okay." But my hands were shaking, and I didn't think I'd ever be able to sleep again.

"It was an accident!" Landon was saying. "Look, she's okay."

Jenks hovered before him as Ivy came to look into my eyes. "I might be a pixy, but I know enough magic to know that you used her hair! You *meant* to do that!"

"No. No I didn't. It's never worked before!"

Shaky, I stood up. "You need to leave."

"But you called me. *Ta na shay, eram,*" a high-pitched voice said, and I spun.

"Holy shit!" Jenks swore, and I stared, Landon forgotten, at the little boy standing before me. He was in a hospital gown, ashen and thin with that ugly ID band on his wrist and pale-rimmed holes in his skin where the IVs once were. His hair had been lovingly arranged, and I recognized the amulet pinned to his coat from the morgue. He wasn't alive, and as I tried to figure out what to say, he shuffled forward, no expression, no nothing. My middle ached, as if something was being pulled from it.

"I remember this dream," the boy said, head down. "There you are," he lisped, shuffling three steps before falling over and hitting the floor with a thud. Ivy reached for him, her face pale as she drew back. "It's time to become," he said to the floor.

Horrified, I scrambled to put the chair between us. Holy crap, it was like the night of the living dead in my living room! Jenks was on my shoulder, and Bis flew into the rafters, hissing.

"Rachel?" Ivy said, eyes black and freaking out. "Where did he come from?"

I'd kicked the Goddess out of my mind. Apparently she'd found another, one who couldn't stop her, and jumped it here. "Ah, the morgue? I think it's okay," I said, coming out from behind my chair. Landon was no use, huddled as if he'd never seen a zombie before. Hell, I knew I hadn't, but I was used to things like this. Leaning over the boy, I carefully flipped him over and stared at his unseeing eyes. *Sort of.*

"I think she thinks I'm one of her mystics," I said, and the boy stared sightlessly at me. Either she didn't know how to work the eyes, or the optic nerve was already dead.

"You are," the boy said, gaze vacant. "You're my thought. Come home."

Okay, I could handle this, and I moved so that his eyes might find mine. "I'm not," I said, creeping out. "My aura is the same is all. Listen. Your mystics slipping from my line are damaging reality. Can you not use that line for a while?"

"Line?" the boy said, his motions to try to get up faltering to nothing. His eyes met mine, and I froze, pulse hammering. "You're not my dream," he said suddenly, and Landon began chanting half under his breath. He sounded terrified. I knew I wasn't all that happy. "You're the solid everything lives within. What are you?"

"Rache!" Jenks exclaimed, and my eyes widened as the Goddess suddenly tried to slip into my thoughts again. Breath hissing, I bubbled myself, shifting my aura, then shifting it again. If not for my practice holding my own against demons, I might have been lost. *No!* I demanded, and my face burned where Jenks's dust touched me as I felt her soak into me, layer by layer, as if absorbing the chemicals and synapses in my brain and reading them like memory. *I'm not you! I'm Rachel. Get out!*

Again I shoved her away, and panting, I stood in the middle of the sanctuary, shaking. Landon was crouched by the boy at my feet, and he looked up as I took a gasping breath of air.

"Who is that?" I said, and he shrugged.

"She forgot to breathe for him," he said. "And with a lack of oxygen, the biological processes fall apart very fast under motion. When the brain quits functioning completely, she can't stay."

"Then it's over?" Jenks said from beside Bis in the rafters. The gargoyle looked totally freaked out, a pale white beside Jenks's green dust.

"Good." Ivy cracked her knuckles, her eyes dark and her fear of the dead obvious. "Get out."

But a jerk on the ley line brought my head up, and I dropped back as a man in a hospital gown was suddenly standing in my church.

"You're not singular," the man said, clearly more animate than the boy, making me wonder if he had perhaps just died and he had a larger number of neurons and synapses still working. "You are a complicated dream . . ."

"Tink's little pink dildo! We got us another one, Rache!"

"I am not a dream!" I shouted, amazed at how quickly my horror could turn to annoyance, and I swear the Goddess almost focused on me. "I'm another entity. I'm . . . a singular," I said, trying to use words she might understand. "I exist in the mass that creates spaces. We all do. Now will you listen to me? Someone is stealing your thoughts. I'm trying to help."

The man listed as he shambled forward. "They're stealing me?" she said, the first hints of real emotion crossing her, and Landon backed to the hallway at the end of the church. "Errant dreams are holding them?" I backed up too as the dead man suddenly lost control of his feet and fell to his knees. "They take them for their own? They are mine! Mine!"

She was angry again. I was losing what little ground I'd gained. "If you could—"

"You know where my thoughts are." The man's head slumped, and he fell forward, his body shutting down. "I see it in you, errant singular," she said, facedown on the floor.

Taken aback, I hesitated and looked at Ivy. It was hard to be afraid of something that kept falling down.

"You're complex," the Goddess said, face still planted in the floor, and Jenks dropped down, his dust glowing like a second aura. "How do you not become? Perhaps you exist. Perhaps not. You will be my thought. My thought with . . . independent movement in the mass between spaces."

Huh?

"You need direction," she added, and the man collapsed, the strings utterly cut.

No! I screamed, but that fast, she had me, the Goddess learning the electrical impulses of my body in a flash of insight. My eyes flew open, and I felt a surge of shock and pleasure as she saw the world through me, her first spike of confusion vanishing as she dipped through my brain and found out how to make sense of it, learning what a corpse could never teach her. She was in my soul, wild, bright, dark, all things.

"Rachel?" Ivy said, squinting at me in concern. Jenks watched, horrified, as she iced through me, seeing the world through her thousand eyes. I opened my mouth to speak, but the Goddess's attention was upon the pixies as she calculated the flow of dust by taking in the air currents and heat patterns. Struggling, I tried again. Landon had crept back out of the hallway, smiling wickedly. Feeling my surge of anger, the Goddess fixed on him.

"You're a wicked trickster," I said, but it was the Goddess speaking, and Jenks moaned. Through her, I could see Landon's betrayal, see his thoughts like the aura spilling from his soul. It had been my hair in the charm. He'd done this knowing she'd eventually take me over, destroy me like the splinter had destroyed Bancroft. *He'd convinced Bancroft to do this same thing,* I thought, remembering that same glint of satisfaction in him at the top of the FIB building. *He murdered Bancroft as surely as if he had slit his throat.* God, I had been stupid!

It was Landon, I suddenly realized. Landon was the one helping the Free Vampires eliminate the undead. Landon was a master of wild magic, and he was using them to kill all the master vampires. Bancroft. Trent. All of us were pawns in his game.

"Rachel?"

But a pawn could become a queen if she reached the end and came back again.

Wavering slightly, I turned to Ivy, feeling the Goddess's attention fracture a hundred different directions to leave me free to breathe and speak. "Um, maybe?" I whispered.

Jenks darted up, frantic. "Rache, she's in you!" he said. "Kick her out!"

But I couldn't. She had dug her claws in deep, enjoying seeing mass in a way she never dreamed was real.

You are as I, she thought. *But so small. A single iden-*

tity that holds thousands of thoughts instead of a thousand thoughts holding a single identity. Mass can't do this.

Her grip on me loosened more, and I took a breath, then another. Jenks's wings clattered, and I looked at my hands. They were shaking, but I felt the awe of the Goddess in me. They were beautiful in structure, diverse in intent. I'd never noticed.

"I don't believe it," Landon said, and my head snapped up. His hatred was etched into his features, and I felt a tiny shock as the Goddess only now linked the facial expression to the emotion. He'd expected me to be taken as Bancroft had been. He'd expected me to be snuffed, destroyed, my single identity holding a thousand thoughts ended—and that pissed her off.

"You're not wicked. You are ill," the Goddess said through me.

He opened his mouth, and I smacked him.

My hand met his face in a resounding crack. A burst of ever-after struck him, and he was flung backward, slamming into the wall between two stained-glass windows.

Bis dropped down to Ivy, and Jenks took to the air. I knew my aura was wrong. I couldn't feel Bis anymore. Unable to stop, I walked to Landon cowering under a window. The Goddess's eyes were whirling in me, in the line, in the spaces between. The feel of the wood against my feet was exhilarating, and I could feel the pressures shift as my weight was pulled into the earth. It was glorious, and only a fraction of the Goddess's eyes were on Landon as he gaped at us.

Us? the Goddess thought, a fragment of her awareness seeming to enfold upon itself at the concept of two individuals acting as one.

"You are an ugly dream that should be dreamed no more," I said, then cocked my head, delighting in the sound of my voice coming back from the rafters. *Like errant thoughts,* the Goddess mused, finding common ground in how sound moved between empty space and solids.

"Rachel, no!" Jenks cried out as I reached for Landon,

and I managed to pull my hand back from the Goddess's reach to throttle him. "Please, let her go," he pleaded as he hovered before me.

"You are a worthy dream," the Goddess said to Jenks, forgetting Landon as I turned to Ivy. She was crying, and I'd never seen her so beautiful. "And you," the Goddess said through me, and Ivy blinked fast, catching back a sob. "Us. I like us," the Goddess said aloud, and I felt a smile grow.

"You're a trickster singular, Rachel Morgan," the Goddess whispered aloud so she could hear her words come back from the ceiling. I was starting to sound crazy, and Bis had gone chalk white. "Your purpose is to make balance. Mass has meaning through you. I will dream this further and will find my errant thoughts."

No! I thought. But it was too late, and the Goddess had yanked not only my thoughts but my body into the line.

Suddenly I existed only as a thought, one eye among thousands, but a thought that could think a thousand more, unique and alone, able to be I, and us, and we. Around me was the Goddess, her trickster thoughts aligning within me. She knew how to end dreams that were unworthy of being dreamed.

She'd let me help.

Nineteen

I was both in the ley line and not, and there was no protection bubble to mute the sensation of energy flowing through the spaces in me. Around me were the collective thoughts of the Goddess, emotion being the easiest thing to comprehend. Oh, I could hear her thoughts, thousands of them all at the same time fluttering at the edges like purple wings, but comprehending a single voice was like picking out a single note in a full orchestra. Emotions were easier, broader sweeps of feeling—and most of the Goddess was pissed.

But parts of her are frightened, I thought as a blossoming of her fear gathered closer to me as if drawn by my own unease. Suddenly it became easier to pick out single frightened thoughts, mystics perhaps, fragments of a collective mind. Doubt, fear, anger, they whispered until I felt sorry for her.

Like a failing tide, the Goddess's fear fell away, replaced by her own thoughts of compassion for the small dreams that she'd been dreaming, lost and alone. The sudden switch from fear to compassion was a shock, and as soon as I realized it, her compassion fell away, replaced by the Goddess's own thoughts of amazement that something could exist outside of her, that unlivable mass had found a way to support independent thought.

Suddenly I realized I was attracting the parts of her that resonated with my current mood. The thought to use that to my advantage crossed me, and I wavered as the Goddess's own crafty thoughts of trickster wish fulfillment coated me in an unreal slurry. Reeling, I felt as if I was caught in a roller-coaster nightmare and couldn't get out. It was like trying to walk through a morass where the ground kept shifting.

Here! the Goddess thought suddenly, and when her eyes turned from me, I clawed my awareness out from under it all. *My thoughts!*

But the Goddess's elation too soon mutated into confusion. *They can't hear me,* rose a thousand laments. *They can't hear me!*

Struggling to think through her noise, I scraped together the thinning remnants of the Goddess's resolve. She wasn't thinking three dimensionally, but four. *I need to have mass,* I said, trying to impress upon her that her straying thoughts couldn't hear her because they weren't in space, but mass. *We have to leave the line as they did.*

Line, line, she lamented. *There is no line, there is only . . .*

I shifted my aura and left the line, praying we weren't underground. The Goddess felt me slip from her, and I shuddered as little claws of thought dug into my awareness. With a wrench that tore me, I felt her extrapolate from where I was, modulate what I could not, and as easy as breathing, felt myself become solid. Sort of. She was with me still, in the spaces inside me.

Surprise, elation, and understanding filled her, spilling over into me. *There is a line,* the Goddess thought, her conviction growing as she saw, understood, and accepted. And then she began to play with it, shifting my aura in and out, tasting what it was like to go from solid to thought, and back to solid.

Enough! I shouted. Heart pounding and lungs starved for air, I phased back into existence, the Goddess firmly embedded within me as I dropped to one knee. My hands clenched into a thick, yellow shag carpet. It was the best feeling ever, even if it was matted, and I took a moment to simply breathe. I had a tiger by the tail, and I didn't know if I could survive a thousand thoughts-not-mine racing through me.

Not so much! I begged her. *Fewer thoughts. I can't . . . carry all of you . . . at once.*

Denial met me, and I stared at the carpet, demanding that she look at it, absorb its intricacies of chaos and how they manipulated the mass around space with color and texture.

A huge chunk of her finally did, finding delight in it, and I could breathe. My connection to the ley line was unbreakable, and it flowed through me with the roar of a fire. I could hear the sound of clicking keys and low, muted voices. I stared at my sock foot, and the Goddess thought it was amazing how something solid was used to cover living mass. *I am in a mass that is sentient,* she thought. *Impossible. Only energy can be sentient.*

"Oh my God!" someone exclaimed, and the clicking of keys stopped.

I wanted to look up, but I was afraid to move, and I wiggled my big toe.

"Ah, Ayer?" a masculine voice said, and I cringed.

"What the hell?" Ayer said, and I wrestled for more control, forcing the Goddess into the background where she focused on my lungs and the bits of matter I needed in order to keep from dying and snuffing my thoughts born from organized mass. After the two corpses in my front living room, I thought it might be important.

Living, dying, so small a shift, so big a difference And it hinges on . . . this little bit of mass? she thought, only now understanding why her previous vessels kept failing her.

"Yeah," I whispered, glad I had enough command to speak again as I slowly pulled control of my body back to me.

"Nothing registered on the auratoscope, Ayer. She just . . . appeared."

"That tricky elf came through," he said, and I got my head up, my attention flitting briefly over the two banks of electronic equipment staffed by men and women in military garb before going to the dark windows. I was in a large, high-ceilinged living room, an entire wall of windows looking out over the Hollows, the Ohio River, and Cincinnati beyond. The land spilled out before me, breathtakingly beautiful with the lights and fires of the living. Fifty years ago, it had been prime real estate. Not so much anymore, being too far from the city center and in the wilds.

The Goddess fastened on it, drawing understanding from me as I filled in the blanks of what she was seeing. Shag carpet, sunken living room, and top-of-the-line electronics that didn't go with the seventies vibe the sunken living room and fire pit were giving me. And of course, the Free Vampires playing army.

New concepts spilled through the Goddess as I took control and rose, thoughts of balance and mass and the sensation of gravity—an unseen presence that grew from mass itself. Heart pounding, I stood facing them, my fear muting to anger as the Goddess gathered her rage at her missing thoughts.

"I don't believe it," Ayer said, motioning at two men at the outskirts. "Take her."

I remained still as they reached for their weapons and made an uneasy semicircle around me. I didn't really care. *Like they could hold me?* I thought, the Goddess agreeing. "You might want to rethink this," I said, and Ayer blinked in surprise. His eyes were so much like Kisten's it hurt.

"Sir, she's not dead," a frightened man in fatigues and a buzz cut said as he held a readout to Ayer. "She's coated in them," he whispered, eyes going black. "What do you want to do?"

Ayer looked down, then back to me. "Landon said the

Goddess can't inhabit the living, only the dead. Get me a different reading. That's impossible."

"No, just really uncomfortable," I said, squinting at the ceiling. "She's focused on the light photons right now, but I suggest you give her the mystics you've captured."

"She?" Ayer waved the men to stand down. Reluctantly they did. "My God, you didn't go crazy. She's in there? With you?"

His avarice caught the Goddess's attention, and together we focused on him, comparing the electricity in the wires in the walls to the electricity in his brain, all jumping about in a chaotic perfection. "Singular who stole my thoughts," I said, but it was the Goddess speaking through me. "Give them back." My hand went out palm up, the Goddess having sifted through my thoughts and finding the gesture appropriate.

Shock crossed him, and he backed up a graceful step. We breathed in the scent of frightened vampire, relishing the way it made our skin sparkle like the space between mass.

"Yes, she talks," I said, wishing I could force her to put my hand down, but I was picking my battles and was glad I had control of my mouth. "Go on. Explain to her why you're stealing her thoughts. I'm curious myself."

Suddenly I was moving forward, struggling for control. "I did not dream you," the Goddess said through me, my accent unchanged, but her anger now coloring it. "You're therefore singular. And fragile."

Weapons were cocking, and fear iced through me. *Stop!* I demanded. *I'm fragile too!* And she did, though I don't know why. Maybe my fear pulled all hers together to one spot and made the danger more real.

"Singular?" Ayer took another readout from a white-faced woman with a gun on her hip. The Goddess tasted my fear, weighed it against her own, and dismissed it as incidental. *How can a small bit of mass projected from a dead object end you?* she wondered, but doubt seeped into her confidence when she dug deeper and found the answer.

"Singular," I echoed, answering Ayer. "As in not a part of

her." But the Goddess's outrage was growing. "Ah, I suggest you let them go!" I said, gaining a smidgen of control as I took another unwilling step toward him. "Please!"

"Ayer!" someone shouted as I tried to stay still and failed. "What do you want us to do!"

"Stand down!" he shouted, backing up out of my reach. "I want her alive!"

Swell, he wants me alive? "Listen to me," I said as I got my feet to stop moving. "I know you think Landon is helping you, but once the masters are dead, he's going to turn on you. You've got to stop this. Now!"

Behind him, I saw uneasy glances and guilt, but Ayer studied me calmly, noting the Goddess inside. "I know Landon lies, but that doesn't mean he's not useful. My original aim was smaller. A personal choice limited to a building or a room. With his help?" he said, a graceful hand shifting to encompass the entire city. "We can end the suffering of all our people. I agree it's less than ideal right now, but as soon as all the masters die, the living will submit, faced with a true death and no second chances. Landon doesn't control us. *I* control us."

Again there were downcast eyes. The Goddess saw it, and I told her what it meant. Ayer had gone beyond what his people had wanted. There was a schism. There was a chance. "Yeah?" I shuffled forward a step, trying not to. "What makes you so sure you can outfox him? He already set you up. Told the FIB it was you all along."

Ayer smiled, beautifully oblivious. "He lost his faith, and without that, elves are easy to control. That, and he wants to see you dead."

"My existence is singular," the Goddess said through me, and Ayer's focus sharpened as he heard the difference. "I cannot die. I can only become. And you can't make me."

"She's completely nuts!" someone whispered.

"No. She's got a god in her," Ayer said tersely. "Are we in the green? Run it."

I spun. The Goddess didn't understand my alarm as a

man flicked a lever on a panel and the lights dimmed. Far away, I heard a thrum, and a thump shifted the air.

Elation not mine pulsed through me. It was the Goddess, and she strengthened inside me until I staggered and fell to a knee. It was her thoughts. Her missing self. She'd found them!

"No!" I cried out, even as she forced us upright and staggering to the center of the room before the windows, arms outstretched as she searched.

"Don't touch her!" Ayer bellowed, and I wrestled just enough control from the Goddess to make a circle. She was oblivious as bullets zinged and ricocheted.

"I said leave her alone!" Ayer screamed, yanking the weapon from the nearest man. "I will drop the next man who touches a trigger! Use the darts!"

The Goddess's dismay cascaded over me, heady and unending. *They refuse to become!* she wailed, and I floundered, trying to get her to listen to my one single thought that it was the machine that held them captive. Destroy the machine, and they'd be free. *Would I survive it?* I wondered, but the Goddess's grief was my entire existence, and I'd do anything to make it stop.

"The machine?" the Goddess exclaimed through me as she finally listened, and I felt ill with the sudden rise of emotion. "They're caught in the . . . In that?"

Together we looked at the machine, and with an odd twist, I felt myself see with her awareness, feeling the tiny space the machine created to hold thoughts born and existing in the space between. I stared at it, my awe coloring her outrage. It was a tiny bubble pulled out of time, created with wild magic and science. Landon had created a new everafter, but one so small it could be lost on the head of a pin. It was all they could muster, but it was enough to hold a Goddess's thoughts.

"We're good!" someone shouted, and her outrage flamed as the Goddess finally realized what they'd done. She shook within me, and as I struggled to maintain the circle. *They're blind to me,* she thought. *I hear them singing, and they sing the wrong song.*

"Release them!" I screamed, but I wasn't sure if it was me or the Goddess.

"Ready . . ." Ayer said as they backed up, and I saw the circle of wire they'd put about me. "Now!"

My eyes widened as a man at a bank of equipment shoved a thick lever up. Lights dimmed, and the thrum pounded through me. A scream ripped from my throat as a wave of pure wild magic cascaded from my soul to my fingers, outstretched in pain. It struck the machine full on, and I cowered inside as the Goddess stood firm, arcs of electricity dancing in the suddenly dark room, waves of black energy surging back and forth between the walls, now bowed out and cracking ominously.

And with a bang that echoed in my soul, the bubble of time popped.

No . . . I thought as suddenly the air sparkled. Wild magic. It was everywhere, and a cloud of freed mystics hazed the air. I felt them inside me as I breathed, blinked them from my eyes like tears. But the Goddess gloried in them, her thoughts bright with power as she called them to her, waiting to bring them home to become with her again.

"Get up! Get up!" someone was screaming, the faint glow from the sky the only light in the room. "Divert power! Increase flow. Take them! Take them all!"

The room was both pitch-black and bright as day as mystics glowed in my mind's eye. Madly moving silhouettes between me and the glass darted, and the Goddess danced within me.

That is, until the first few thoughts of her failure reached me. The mystics were not responding, even the ones she'd just sent out to bring the others in.

"Increase it!" Ayer shouted. "Get out of my way. I'll do it myself!" he snarled, shoving the dazed man out of his chair and taking his place. I couldn't see him in the dark, but I knew it was him by the sparking of neurons in his brain. "I want all of them!"

Elation dimming, the Goddess seemed to hesitate. *They're not my thoughts,* she said, turning inward to me, her sole guide to this madness of mass. *They won't become!*

The rapid shift of emotion was draining, and I staggered, going down before the windows. "I told you they were changed," I whispered, and she snatched control back.

"They corrupted and stole my thoughts," she said aloud through me, and Ayer met our eyes in the emergency lights now flickering on. He was pleased. His mystics had escaped, and he was thrilled. Something was wrong, but she wouldn't listen to my one thought among her thousand. "These singulars will no longer be dreamed!" she shouted with my voice, and I found myself standing, unable or too sick at heart to stop her.

"You will die!" she raged, my body shaking with her anger. "I am all! Everything! You are one singular! You can't make me become!"

This is a mistake, I thought at her, but with a primal scream, she drew her thoughts of anger into one point and exploded the room.

"Now!" Ayer shouted, and I gasped as the room flashed white.

"No!" I screamed as the Goddess's power was pulled through me, out of the spaces and into their control.

"Secondary storage full!" someone exclaimed. "Third online!"

Stop! I howled into my thoughts, but she didn't hear, continuing to funnel her frustration and anger into one act of violence that Ayer pulled to him like a master taking in a soul. With an unheard shatter, the windows blew out. I fell, my hair hiding my vision—but I could see it all from a thousand different angles as her eyes filled me.

"They are mine!" the Goddess raged, my throat becoming raw.

Looking alien in the emergency light and the smoke, Ayer smiled. "Do your worst," he taunted. "I'm going to bleed you dry, bitch."

Wild magic sang in me, heartbreaking in its singular intent of revenge and justice. I could only watch as the Goddess filled the room with her intent, not listening to me, ignoring my single voice among her outraged thousands.

They're killing you. I begged her to listen as I felt the sensation of being sucked up from the inside. *Stop! Just stop!*

I . . . I . . . She faltered, only now noticing that she was failing, that we were slumped to the floor, the acidic bite of smoke stinging our eyes. *I am . . . failing?* she thought, a new idea born. She found my own memories of loss, and pain, and failure, learning from them, and I took a deep breath as the sting of a dart found me.

What . . . she seemed to mumble as I plucked it away, but it was too late.

"I told you not to do that," I said, muscles going slack.

But inside me, the Goddess abandoned her new emotions of failure, fastening on an old one. *You knew this would happen!* she accused me. *You betrayed me!*

I curled into a ball. I could hear fire extinguishers and smell the outside. Wild magic pricked my skin, but it was the escaped mystics. "It was Landon," I whispered, eyes clamped shut. "Not me. I tried to warn you! You didn't listen."

Your thought was too small! she said as men whispered in fear over us. *Only thoughts with many agreements should be followed.*

"Not when they come from a singular," I whispered. The drug was taking hold, making it easier to think as the Goddess began losing her grip on me, and I moaned at the wild magic they pulled through me, lessening her bit by bit. "My single voice is the sum of a thousand thoughts. Listen to me!" I said, and another dart hit me. "You have to leave," I breathed, eyes closing. "They're destroying you. Go!"

But you have only one voice, she thought, trying to understand. *How can it be correct?*

"Storage unit three full, Ayer."

"Go to four. I want everything this bitch can dish out."

And with a sudden implosion of understanding, she understood. Making a sob that would make angels cry, she vanished.

"Wave complete!" someone said, and I gasped at the sudden silence in my mind.

Oh God. She's gone. It was what I wanted, but I felt awful. Bleary from the drug, I turned my head, my cheek sliming in my own drool. Hands fell from me, and I welcomed the stark emptiness of nothing.

"Sir!" It held the confidence of a battle won. "Entity is gone. We tripled our density, but there are a few clouds condensing in the immediate area. Do you want us to mop them up?"

Heavy boots crossed the room, tripping on something in the dim light. "Go. Yes," Ayer said, and I focused enough to see him bending over a glowing screen. "Don't let them out of the area. I don't want them increasing the isolation zone."

I was empty, and as the drug took hold, I felt as if I was dying. I could no longer feel the sun pouring through the earth. Even the circling thoughts of the undead, revolving like lighted tops in the night, were missing. Numb. I was numb and empty. I shook, alone on the floor, ignored as nothing. What if she came back? She thought I'd betrayed her. She'd kill me, make my dream no more.

A toe nudged me, and I did nothing. "If she can survive the main entity, she might be able to draw all of them in," Ayer said. "We don't need Landon anymore. Cut him loose."

"Sir."

"Wrap her up," he added. "Put her in the chair. As soon as the ranging cloud is collected."

"Now?" someone new blurted. "She's almost dead."

"Which is why you're alive," barked Ayer, and I groaned when he flipped me over with his boot, my arm flopping to hit the floor. "She's a demon. Treat her like one or you'll be someone's toy. As soon as the ranging mystics are collected, I want her hooked up. We get them talking, and that bitch will come back."

Swell. I couldn't even move my fingers as they bundled me up. All too soon I was being lifted, and the rattle of a gurney intruded. My breath came out in a gasp when they dropped me onto a rolling table and the disconcerting feeling of motion made me dizzy.

"Nicely done, Morgan," Ayer whispered, and I felt the sudden lurch of an elevator. "You survived. Not what Landon promised, but I'm flexible. You're going to bring the mystics right to me. Very efficient. You moved my timetable up two months. Let's see what another minute or two connected to the divine will do."

I cracked an eye. There were three men in the elevator with me, but I could do nothing. *Wrap her up. Put her in the chair.* Better and better. "That's what she does, you know," I said, and Ayer stopped the nervous man from darting me again. "She gives you what you ask for. And you pay for it in the end."

Ayer grunted, eyes on his watch as he took my pulse. I couldn't feel him holding my wrist, and he looked so much like Kisten it hurt. Between the drugs and my failure, I couldn't help my eyes tearing up. How was I going to come back from this? I was so alone.

But then a tiny whisper of tingles sparked through me, shocking me. Mystics. There were some in me, resonating to my feelings of loss and grief. Eyes fixed open, I stared at Ayer counting my pulse, seeing my hand dangle limply in his. She'd left behind what she didn't want to think about, and now her thoughts of betrayal and loss added to my own, almost crushing me.

"Are you sane?" I asked them, words slurring, and Ayer dropped my hand.

"History will judge me, not you," he said, thinking I was talking to him, and he pushed me into the hallway when the doors opened.

But I was focused inward toward the abandoned mystics. Pitying the tiny new thoughts she'd left behind, I took them in, wrapping them up in my own pain, giving them a place to exist within me until I could return them to her. She'd probably want these back. God knew I didn't want them.

Twenty

Tingles of returning circulation stabbed my legs as the gurney hit a corner. The dart was gone from my thigh, but the drug was clearly in force. I could do little as I was trundled down a corridor. The lack of an echo and the ornate wall sconces led me to believe we were still in someone's residence, probably someone with severe light restrictions by the feel of it. The outward-looking faces of the three men above me held a wide span of emotion: unease, dismay, concern, excitement. That last was in Ayer's eyes, barely beating out his avarice. I was a thing to him. A way to up his time-table, and it scared me.

"You're making a mistake," I said, glad the Goddess was gone and it was just me in my skull again. "Bancroft was trained in dealing with the Goddess, and your splinter was too much for him. I don't know if you heard, but he left this world from the thirty-ninth floor this morning."

The gurney slowed at a door, cracked open about a foot or so. "You misunderstand," Ayer said, his voice oily. "I fully expect you to go insane. That's what will bring the Goddess in, and then we will sop her up like spilled milk."

"You want me to go crazy?" I said as the gurney stopped at the open door.

Crazy? came a thought-not-mine, and I choked as the alien fear lifted through me. It was a mystic. *Is that different from loss?*

The question hung in me, and shocked, I realized that mystics were able to change their purpose, in essence, evolve, when exposed to the complex matrix of sustained thought of a living system. Perhaps that was why they had gone wrong in the prison the Free Vampires had made. They couldn't grow *or* return, so they'd became erratic—spinning in the same repetitive circle like the thoughts the undead made—alive but static.

There was a spate of muffled noise down the hall, and Ayer's brow furrowed. "Can she move yet?"

"If I could, you'd be dead," I muttered, then winced when one of the gurney guys lifted a lid and shined a light in my eye. "Ow?"

"No, sir," he said, continuing to breathe normally despite my wish to choke off his air.

"Get her strapped in and wait for me," Ayer said tersely. "Wait for me!" he shouted, taking one of the men and heading toward the noise. "And don't take off that zip strip!"

"Yes, sir!" the remaining man shouted, eyes rolling as he backed out of the hall and into a quiet room, dragging me behind. "I know how to handle magic users," he grumbled.

More circulation prickles washed through me, or maybe it was wild magic, but I was able to shift my head as they wheeled me to a stop. It was a bedroom, underground and decked out with too many pillows and a chandelier that screamed undead vampire. A thick bundle of wires snaked in from the hallway and prevented the door from being shut. Two living vampires were waiting, a woman sitting at an empty card table and a man standing at the bank of equipment the cords were feeding. Both were in military garb complete with little caps; both had pistols on their hips; both had them unsnapped. Neither looked happy.

The chair was where my eyes landed and stayed, though; the thing looked ominous with its straps and head brace, and my heart pounded. Why couldn't they have just put me in a cell for a few hours? But no—let's hook her up now!

"That's her?" the woman said, and I tried to get the drool back in my mouth.

"Category five," the man who wheeled me in said as he unstrapped me. "Though you wouldn't know it to look at her. Keep that zip strip on her. She completely trashed the control room."

The woman flicked a piece of broken glass off my shoulder, leaning to stare at me with her black eyes. Vampire filled my world, and my skin tingled. "I'm not touching her. You do it."

I felt sick as the two men worked together to sit me up. The woman had taken up a handheld scanner, and her lips parted, showing her tiny canines, when she looked up from the reading. "Shit," she whispered. "She's already covered in them. Can you feel it?"

"No . . ." one grunted as I hung in their grip. "And you can't either, Annie. Some help here, maybe?"

The scanner clattered as it hit the card table, and she turned the chair so they could just drop me into it. "This isn't a good idea," I said as I eyed it. Damn it, it even had ankle straps. "You think maybe you could just sort of let me go? I'll tell them I hit you and everything."

"One, two, three, shift!" the guy to my right muttered, and they moved me, very professional and with little wasted movement.

My heart pounded as they backed off. Two watched with pulled weapons as a third strapped me in to keep me upright. "Please," I begged as they fastened my hands to the chair's arms. "He's going to kill all the undead. Is that what you want? All of them dead? Free Vampires are all about personal choice, right? This isn't choice, it's murder!"

"Shut up!" the man nearest me said, and I gasped when his hand smacked my face.

"Hey!" I shouted, and he grinned, leaning in to eye my exposed neck, my flash of anger triggering his bloodlust.

"Back off, Snaps," the other man said, and Snaps, apparently, eased back, a new, sultry grace to him as he enjoyed his little daydream.

I couldn't help but notice that the woman's eyes had fallen in guilt. But then she dropped down to tighten my ankle straps and I felt my chance slip away, even as the rising tingle of mystics hazed me. Their curiosity finally outweighed their fear as they lifted from me like a second aura, drifting away in search of an answer I couldn't give them.

The lack of their faint background voices was a blessing, and hoping they were gone for good, I slumped in the chair as the three people clustered between me and the tower of machinery with its lights and dials. A second bundle of cords punched through a rough hole in the wall, and I wondered if the entire place was designed for capture and containment, sort of like a huge dish. They were whispering over the readout of the scanner, and Annie looked scared. "There's a lot of them already in her," she said. "And he wants to add to it?"

"As long as he doesn't hook me up, I don't give a shit," the one who'd hit me said.

Ivy, I thought, remembering her last look at me. And Jenks. They'd look for me. Bis, too. But if Bis could find me, he would have already, and as I watched the woman preparing an injection, I didn't think anyone would find me in time. The memory of Bancroft screaming at the top of the FIB tower filled my thoughts, and I tried to breathe faster, willing the drug out of me.

A soft thump followed by men shouting jerked through me. My eyes widened as the ranging mystics flowed back into me without warning, frightened and bringing half-realized impressions.

Oh God, they were back, and I panted, so full of their fear that I . . . couldn't . . . think . . . Dizzy, I tried to focus but the images they brought were confusing. What in hell were they doing back with me? I couldn't help them.

Sensation was returning to my hands, and I curled my fingers under, the smooth feel of the chair grating across my nerves. A strap holding me pulled, and a mystic wondered why I didn't move through the spaces in the strap and become free.

Slowly I walled them off, ignoring them until I could breathe again. My head rose when Ayer came in, his pace satisfied. I let go of my fist when he noticed it. "All set?" he said loudly, and Annie backed away from the machine, her eyes black in fear. "Glad to see you regaining your small motor skills, Morgan." He turned to Annie. "Do we have the last of them contained yet?"

The man by the door stiffened. "Yes, sir. They're being brought down right now."

"Good. Good. Try to make it a good fight, Morgan. You last long enough, and we'll have enough mystics to be out of Cincinnati tonight."

They were going to take this madness on the road? "Just because I'm strapped down doesn't mean I'm helpless," I said, feeling . . . helpless.

Annie was at the machine, her shoulders hunched. Still smiling, Ayer swung the folding chair around and sat in it, the length of the table between us as he leaned back and put an ankle on his knee. A tingle of wild magic went through me, driven by a flash of fear as Annie went to the door to take the little box from the man standing there. Snaps left with him, leaving just the three of them—the three of them and that little box that held a world.

Annie hesitantly set it on the table, then dropped a mess of wires and little skin pads beside it. Shit, they were going to hook me up. *Make* me talk to the splinter. My heart thudded at the softly glowing lights on the containment device. It was identical to the one I'd seen at Junior's, and Ayer gently touched it. "Please don't do this," I whispered, looking at the leads on the table. "She's going to kill me."

Kill! echoed the mystics, their feelings of loss taking on the tint of mistrust, and then a sudden, heady desire to crush everything that threatened them. My skin tingled with wild magic, unfocused and unusable.

"Demons beg?" Ayer said, pushing Annie aside to untangle the lines himself.

"Please!" I exclaimed as he attached the first pad to my temple, needlessly grabbing my chin to make me look at him. The zip strip kept me from tapping a line, but the thinnest thread of wild magic seeped through me, maddeningly present but too little to even lift a feather. My heart thudded as the last electrode was fastened to my wrist. Ayer watched, arms over his chest in mistrust at my sudden silence, and Annie gathered the cords and started to plug them to the machine itself.

"This is wrong," I said, feeling no change as the connections were made one by one. There was probably a button to push or something. "I know the masters are a pain in the ass. I know they're abusive and move on cronyism and backroom deals, but killing them to make the rest behave isn't going to happen. You're just going to piss them off and start a street war! The more vampires that die, the more undead there will be. You're killing yourself!"

I wiggled, caught in the chair as the last wire was connected and Annie stood back, her eyes wide in indecision. The drug had worn off, but now I was caught by straps and Velcro. The man waited at the tower of machinery as if for a signal. A single wire went from it to the box on the table, and then to me. How could something so small hold something so powerful?

There is lot of space between space, a handful of mystics said, feeling my fear but not understanding how it could come from a box.

Again a soft thump shifted the air. Over the bed, the chandelier jingled. The man took his hand off the machine and put it on his pistol. My breath came fast, and I held it. Ivy? Jenks? *Trent?*

"Go see what that is," Ayer said, and the man jogged out the door. Immediately Annie took his place at the bank of machinery. "We will be free of the masters," Ayer said as he stood, moving to where he could watch both me and the door. "We will break the curse for good."

"Do you even hear yourself?" I said as Annie flicked a switch at Ayer's direction, and a warm feeling echoed between my ears. Within me, the mystics swirled, agitated but unfocused. "You're killing them to make others afraid!" I looked at Annie, trying to play on her guilt. "You're killing innocents!"

"The masters are not innocent!" Ayer shouted, his face reddening. "It's not murder if they have no soul!" He strode to the bank of machines, and the woman backed up, scared. "Is it ready?" he barked.

"Yes, sir," she said, and Ayer reached in front of her and flipped a second switch.

Energy washed into me, thousands of voices circling in madness. A harsh moaning grew until I realized it was me and I choked the noise off. My head pounded, and I tried to stand only to fall back, bound to the chair. Insane mystics poured into me, swamping the meek and frightened ones I'd grown accustomed to. They rolled my thoughts upside down, tumbling them like waves spinning a swimmer into the rocks.

Wild magic was a flash behind them, and I grasped it, shoving everything else away and using it to ground myself, building a bubble about me to numb the force, but it did no good.

"Sir, it's pegged!" Annie shouted, and from somewhere outside myself, I felt my hands digging into the hard chair. "It's going to kill her!"

"Leave it where it is! Shoot her if she gets free!" he said, and fear rolled about my mind, jumping from one mystic to the other like an electrical storm until fear was all I was. I hung my head, trying to find one tiny space where I could catch my breath. The insane splinter ate away at me, their wild magic sparking through me in painful pings. It demanded an outlet, demanded action. But I had no control, and it simply became harder to bear.

"God, make it stop!" I heard myself moan, heart thudding. But I couldn't escape. I was going insane. It would be easier that way. One by one, my barriers began to crash, the loud bangs echoing in my head.

"Down! Get down!" someone yelled, and I realized the thumps were real. Something was happening.

"Edden?" I whispered as the squat but powerful man spilled into the room, his eyes alight and a bellow of outrage coming from him. With the sound of a thousand wings, the splintered mystics rose up from me.

At least I thought it was Edden, and I stared, my head lolling as the splinter hazed the room. He was head to toe in black, little half-moons of charcoal under his eyes. A cap with no insignia was on his head, and a clearly non-FIB-issue rifle was in his hand.

"Get away from that machine!" he shouted, and a little sob escaped me. Confusion rose among the splintered mystics, and I felt a shift, a tiny bit of control.

Ayer had his own weapon pointed. "The FIB?" He laughed. "Are you serious?"

"I'm not FIB tonight," Edden said grimly, and I could hear David shouting in the hall. "I'm running with the pack."

Ayer's confident motion to bring his pistol to bear hesitated as Annie shoved the barrel of her weapon into his kidneys. "Sir," she said, and Ayer froze.

Betrayal! the mystics screamed, recognizing Ayer's emotion. I gasped, head dropping as I tried to calm them. "Get this off me!" I cried, but no one moved.

"Annie?" Ayer put his hands slightly up and away from his body. "They killed your father. You're going to let that happen again to another innocent?"

"This isn't right," she said, nervous but her hand steady. "It's a choice everyone makes. You can't make it for them."

"Put your weapon down!" Edden said as he edged closer to me. "Now!"

I gasped as Edden jerked one, then another of the electrodes from me, eyes never leaving Ayer, muzzle never wavering from the vampire. But it made no difference. There was enough splintered mystics in me that I'd become a battlefield. The savage need to survive sparked from one to the next—and like a tree catching on fire, I was suddenly fighting the desire to destroy every thought but my own. Problem was, I couldn't decide who I was anymore.

Wild magic prickled along every nerve. It hurt to breathe, and I held my breath—eaten alive as the mystics looking to me tried to mend the splinter I'd taken in, calming them with the elasticity of my own thoughts and turning their circling into growth and change. But it wasn't enough.

Ayer breathed deeply, his eyes flashing black as he took in the fear of the room. "You can have my weapon when you pry it from—"

"Your cold dead hands," Annie finished for him, digging her muzzle into him a little harder. "It ends here. You said we could leave any time we wanted. Consider this my notice."

Panting, I hung my head. I could see my feet. I was in socks. *I am in socks?* That seemed important, and I concentrated on it, letting the mystic noise roar in the back of my head. *I,* as in singular. *Am,* as in existing. *In socks,* meaning I had feet. I was solid. I was real.

"Put the weapon down!" Edden shouted. "Now!"

"Hold on, Rachel," someone whispered, and I felt the last of the electrodes being plucked from me as the spicy scent of Were sparked a memory of David. *I. Am. Real.*

I breathed. Groaning, I tried to move, my hands unresponsive since they were still bound to the chair. David was at the machine flipping levers with a reckless abandon. I felt the thrum of the air shift, and the ache of wild magic began to pull from me, lifting like a fog, most of the mystics drawn away by a brighter light than my own. The insane splinter was flowing past my awareness with the coldness of a January moon. Slowly my confusion abated.

Kneeling, Ayer put his weapon on the floor.

"All the way," Annie demanded, and he lay down, gaze never breaking from mine.

"I think that's it," David said, thumbing off the power and turning to me. He looked anxious as he dropped to kneel before me. "Rachel. Are you okay?"

I was tied to a chair, but yes, I thought I was okay.

"Rachel?"

He touched me, and I twitched. Mistrust flooded me, born from the mystics. *It's David!* I hammered at the ones who had ignored the pull of the machine, demanding that they heed my single thought. But he'd seen my fear, and pain had filled his eyes. "I'm okay," I said, not moving as he undid the straps. Still in the chair, I rubbed at my wrists. It was hard to focus. Remnants of the wild magic lingered in me, spinning like purple eyes. I was afraid to touch the line—the air already crackled with a lingering cloud of mystics.

Within me were more mystics than before, most tainted with the quick bite of insanity, but the ones I'd saved were circling, trying to absorb them like a white blood cell absorbs a virus. The confusion I felt wasn't mine, but it was still real, and I sat and breathed as it slowly eased and abated. "I'm okay," I said again, wanting to believe it.

"Can you move?"

Looking at David, I was shocked with how angry he was. His hands had been so gentle. Somehow I managed a smile. "Yes." Edden was standing over Ayer. The man was face-down, his gun kicked away and his hands on the back of his head as Edden recited the Miranda. "How many people did you bring with you?" I asked, hearing noise in the background that couldn't be good. "It will take many singularities to end his dream."

Aghast, I put a hand to my mouth.

David straightened, exchanging a nervous glance with Annie standing guard over the Ayer. "Thanks for your help. I'm sorry, but we're going to have to cuff you."

"Use mine," Edden said, reaching behind himself for his cuffs.

"Look out!" I shouted, falling back into the chair as Ayer lurched from the floor, grabbing Annie and yanking her to his chest.

"Resignation accepted," he snarled, and my heart sank at the sudden twist and snap of her neck.

"No!" David shouted as he dove for Annie, now falling as Ayer ran for his weapon. She was dead dead, the second death. I couldn't tell you how I knew, but the energy from her mind was suddenly not there. I hadn't even realized I could sense it until it was gone.

She shouldn't have trusted the singular, the mystics thought, most of them siding against me. *Many outweigh the one,* they scolded me. *You will become and do as the majority say.*

I'd had enough. *Give me that!* I shouted in my mind, taking control of the wild magic still spinning through me. *"Rhombus!"* I screamed as Ayer's stretching finger touched his gun and pulled it to him as he spun to aim it at me.

My bubble rose up, dismaying the mystics until they realized they could go through it with impunity. Their delight quickly turned to thoughts of outrage as Ayer sprayed us with a hail of bullets, all of them harmlessly bouncing off.

"No, wait!" I cried, reaching out as they turned their thoughts to gleefully dealing out death. *Not so much!* I protested as they spun control of the wild magic away from me and a blast of white-hot wild magic exploded from my fingertips.

"Stop!" I cried out, knowing it was his death, but Ayer had leaped out of the way. Magic hit the wall and passed through, effortlessly dissolving the matter. Glowing, the leftover energy fell in on itself and vanished with a hiss. *Crap on toast, I'd made a hole in the wall.*

Edden stared at the new four-foot hole before turning to me. David looked up from Annie to Ayer, more anger in him. "You killed her!" he exclaimed, furious. "Twice!"

Weapon in hand, Ayer reassessed the situation, hole in wall included. I couldn't help my smile as the wild magic brushed over my skin with the feel of feathers. Maybe I should kill him. Then I wouldn't have to decide if it was right or not. *End him,* the mystics demanded, the urge strengthening as myriad voices became one, louder than my own. *End them all!*

"Right," Ayer said, then dove through the hole in the wall, fleeing.

I couldn't help myself, and I stumbled after him as the mystics took control. *You will stop!* I demanded even as I felt my feet pulled out from under me. Snarling, I spun as I hit the floor. Edden's shocked expression flashed over him as I raised my hand to strike him.

"Enough!" I shouted at the mystics as he let go and fell back. Groaning, I curled into a ball. It took all my strength to keep from killing him, from killing them all with a blast of wild magic. Panting, I huddled where I was, but the mystics refused to believe that some people were worthy of trust and others weren't, that people were different, not the same.

"We have to go," David whispered, and I pulled my head up. They were both looking at me, and nodding, I shakily got to my feet.

"Sorry," I said, giving the hole in the wall a last look. *Edden is my friend,* I tried to explain to the mystics. *David, too. I trust them with my life.*

End them, the mystics clamored. *End all of them. Every single last one.*

"You will not," I whispered, ill as the wild magic they were giving off turned my stomach. What if they got back to the Goddess? They might give her the idea to end us all.

"Rachel?"

It was David, and I waved his reaching hand away. "Don't touch me," I panted, afraid the mystics would misunderstand. "I'm okay. Let's go."

Dark face sorrowful, he nodded. He gave Annie one long glance before turning and going out before us, the alpha in him making him graceful and resolute. *He has left the dead before,* I realized, not bothering to explain to the mystics the emotions I was feeling. It wasn't fair. Hell, it wasn't even just.

In the distance was the noise of battle, and I wondered how many people they'd brought—that, and where Ivy and Jenks were.

Ivy and Jenks? the mystics wondered, and I had to explain it since the once-splintered mystics outnumbered the handful of voices that had a grasp of friendship. Understanding bled through them like water, and slowly the confusion eased.

We crept into the hallway, and I thought my sock feet looked odd on the flat brown carpet. "We can't go the way we came in," Edden said tersely.

"Garage is that way," David said. "I've got three packs out there ranging about. We get out of here, we'll be fine."

"Which way? These hallways all look alike to me."

David made a face. "It's that way," he muttered, pointing and getting us moving again. "I can smell garage."

I felt small between them, even with the thousand voices echoing between my ears, numb as I was pushed along like a leaf in the wind. "Rachel, stay behind me," Edden said as we paused at the fire door.

David put an ear to the door, listening. "I think we're good." He opened the door a crack and looked through. Silence and darkness met us. Behind came the pop of guns. They'd lost their meaning, but my unhelped slash of alarm brought the mystics awake.

End their dream! a slew of voices insisted suddenly.

Be still! another, smaller faction insisted, and that was the one I upheld, turning the tide though we were outnumbered. I couldn't tell who was who anymore. They were all mixed up, all of them driving me crazy.

I can't do this forever. Confusion seeped up from the corners of my mind as David beckoned me through and into the dark. I could feel an open space, hear an echo from their shoes, and grit scrunched under my sock feet.

"Let me find the light switch," Edden said, his voice drifting away. It was an undead vampire's garage, and the best were usually lightproof. This one was no exception.

Found it, I thought, the mystics in me reading the patterns of electricity in the unseen wall. With a thought, I flipped the energy flow and the lights came on, flicking eerily until they warmed up. Dust coated a row of cars, and Edden pulled his hand back from the light switch, never having touched it. Seeing his unease, I shrugged. "Thanks."

Pace increasing, we shuffled for the small door at the end of the room. There had to be at least half a dozen, all small and fast. A thump shook the floor. Edden looked at David in question, and the younger man shook his head.

"Ah, can you do any magic?" David asked, not knowing that I'd switched the light on.

"The trick is to keep from doing it," I said, thinking the jet-black car we were passing was beautiful—sparking a mystic conversation in me about why I used mass to move through more mass instead of just moving in the space between. I had to get rid of them before they drove me crazy.

Uneasy, David gave me lots of room as he reached for the door. My head came up as it opened, the scent of burning city a balm after the stuffy, vampire-incense-rich air. The mystics picked up on my desire to be free, bolstering my need to be outside. I practically bolted out, coming to a shocked stop at the three men in the bushes. Fear blossomed as I slid to a halt, gasping at the surge of wild magic. Vampires.

End them! the mystics raged, and I gaped at the three men in horror as wild magic coursed through me, my not-mine desire to destroy them burning bright.

You will listen! I shouted into my mind, staggering into David as I struggled for control, beating the thousand voices back, demanding that they heed my one. *You will listen to me!*

"It's okay! I've got them cuffed!" the Were in the borrowed FIB hat exclaimed as I fell back in apparent terror. "They gave themselves up."

"I never agreed to killing masters," the vampire in the

raggedy T-shirt said, his hands indeed pulled tight behind him, but if they were FIB-issue cuffs, they wouldn't hold.

"Is that the woman Ayer has been going on about?" the other vampire said, and I hunched into a ball, my feet in the gravel and my hands clenched and breath held as I tried not to kill them. The scent of my cotton shirt filled my nose, and I focused on it, picking the details of the aroma apart to distract myself. *Dusky, dry stones in the sun.* "It's okay, ma'am. Ayer's crazy. We won't hurt you."

David pulled me to my feet and drew me past them into the shadows. "She's not scared. She's trying not to kill you," he muttered. "Let's go. Where is everyone?"

The man with the FIB cap pushed the vampires into motion. "Tailing them. They had a back door we didn't know about, and most got out that way." He hesitated. "Is that Morgan?" he asked, his voice holding disappointment as I stumbled, head down and not watching where I was going.

"It's been a bad day," David said, his hand still on my elbow. "Edden, where did you leave the car?" he asked, and Edden pushed his mustache out as he scanned the long-abandoned streets. Behind us, something exploded in a harsh pop.

"South," Edden said, and we started up the crumbling abandoned roadway in the dark. I didn't know why the mystics accepted David's touch when everyone else was considered a threat, but I needed it, and I lagged, head down, as the mystics demanded I follow the splintered majority and wipe everything clean. It was a bad day, indeed. "Help me," I whispered, and his grip tightened. "Don't let go."

"We'll get you sorted out," David said. "Try to numb it," he suggested, thinking it was battle rage.

But that would only make things worse. If I numbed myself, the mystics would overrule my single voice and take control. Heart pounding, I refused them any sway. I moved under David's hand, not seeing the abandoned homes or the cracked, potholed street. The sky was red, low clouds reflecting the light from the fires burning in the Hollows, and slowly I began to think again as the mystics became bored and drifted away.

"Is she okay?" Edden questioned, looking back at us.

"Ask me later," I panted, leaning heavily on David, dizzy as the mystics darted away from me and back, bringing to me confusing visions of what they saw. There was a rustling about us, a wind that wasn't born from rising air or lowering masses.

"Where's the van?" Edden said in affront as we halted at an abandoned gas station.

David's wide shoulders slumped. "You lost the van?"

Edden spun. "I left it right here!"

"We're in the wilds! You can't leave a working car in the wilds!"

Most of the mystics had left me, and my head came up, daring to believe that I might be rid of them altogether. "There's a bus stop. You want me to see what the schedule is?"

"They don't run buses out here," Edden said, reaching under his cap to scratch his head. The soft glow of a screen shone, lighting up his face, showing the worry wrinkles around his eyes. "Give me a second. I'm not getting a good signal."

"Because they don't put towers out here either!" David muttered, peeved as he turned his back on us, watching the dark as we stood under the gas station awning. In the nearby distance came a rustling in the weeds, and I staggered as a hundred different mystic perspectives of the same view hammered at me. I wondered if I looked that ill or if it was just my imagination. Nauseated, I shoved away all views but the one coming from my eyes. The mystics buzzed over it, clouds of them following the electrical impulses through my brain to analyze how I put it all together. My head hurt.

David's concern was obvious when he turned back to us. He'd heard the rustling as well. "We need to keep moving. Who are you calling?"

Mood somber, Edden put the phone to his ear. "Ivy."

"Ivy?" Mistrust surged, and I banished it with a vengeance.

Edden smiled. "She's downtown, under the streets with Jenks looking for you. Bis, too. Apparently your aura has shifted and he can't find you. Ah, Rachel? I don't want to know about those two cadavers in your front room, but they'd better be gone tomorrow. Okay?"

Nodding, I turned away, blinking fast. The memory of Ivy's last expression passed over me, confusing the mystics and prompting a flurry of discussion over I, us, and we. Ivy and Jenks were looking for me. I knew they would, and I felt loved.

Edden pulled the phone from his ear, ended the call, and hit Jenks's number instead. "Half the city is looking for you. The only reason we found you first was because of Trent."

Trent? How had he known where I was? And why hadn't he come to get me?

Betrayed, the mystics hummed, and I shoved it aside. Trent hadn't betrayed me. He'd told Edden how to find me, and that was more than he really needed to do.

No, betrayed! a single mystic screamed, and I spun, hearing a new meaning in the rustling from the dark. An image of glowing eyes burst in my thoughts, ignored until now.

"It's them!" I shouted, wild magic a sudden, painful pulse.

"Down!" David shouted, falling on me.

I hit the ground, watching as the two surrendering vampires with us fell, groaning. The soft retort of twin shots echoed an instant later. Swearing, David shoved my head down and crawled to them, Edden joining him with a frantic haste as they jammed whatever was handy onto gaping wounds that glinted wetly in the dark.

We were under attack and I could do nothing, struggling with a splinter of a Goddess bent on revenge. "Not this time," I gasped, wrenching control back. "Make a circle. A circle!"

I gave them an outlet, and a circle sprang up around us, humming with an unreal but familiar sensation. I wasn't connected to a line. It was as if I had a direct line to the divine, my every wish granted. Even the ugly ones, if I wasn't careful.

"Damn, Rachel, you're glowing," David said as he glanced up, his hands bloodied, and I looked at myself, scared. I was, the mystics' energy leaking out of my pores.

"Don't tell anyone, okay?" I said as I got up. It was better. Somehow it was getting better, and I wavered only slightly as David and Edden rose as well, standing beside me and safe in my circle.

My lip curled as Ayer sauntered out of the dark with about twenty men, all dressed alike with those damn little caps. How could I have ever thought he looked like Kisten? Ayer's soul was ugly. He was nothing like Kisten. *Careful,* I thought, not wanting to get the mystics riled up and out of control, but a small part of me was halfway to letting them have their way. Humming, the mystics darted in and out of me with little zings of power. We'd found common ground. I didn't understand why, but they were finally listening to me.

The Free Vampires stopped eight feet back with Ayer coming a few feet closer. He motioned for his men to start laying a thick electrical cord in a circle about us, and I stifled a shiver. We were safe in my mystic-born circle, but it was a trap. I'd managed to gain control of this small fraction. I'd lose it if he took them from me.

"Looks like you've got a handle on it, Morgan," he said, and I tried to flatten my hair. Trent's hair floated when he did magic. I'd always thought it was because of the ever-after energy, but maybe it was mystics.

"Then you'd be wrong," I shot back.

He turned. "Bring her down," he said as he walked away. "Kill the rest."

"Sir?"

"You want them to talk?" he shouted, clearly disgusted. "Kill them!"

Edden shifted his weight, his hand on his pistol. "They can't do anything if we're in this circle, can they?"

A howl split the night, bringing Ayer's expression to a frozen stiffness. "That was supposed to have been taken care of," he said, and the man next to him fidgeted as David began to smile.

"We got the mystics out, but Smith hasn't checked in, sir."

More howls, this time closer. It was my pack, a fact I knew for certain thanks to a wandering mystic bringing me back an image of my tattoo.

"This was supposed to have been taken care of!" Ayer raged as his men began retreating, one by one and in pairs. For all their bloodlust, vampires did not make good soldiers. Shaggy hunched shadows were padding out from the abandoned homes and rusted cars, pushing them along. A low growl and a bark made one man fall, and he scrambled to his feet, backing up fast.

"I never thought I'd be happy to see a mob of Weres." Edden drew closer as a thin man in jeans and an open shirt eased confidently out of the dark. No gun, no weapon, and tattoos everywhere, he came up to Ayer with a confidence that couldn't be faked.

"Leave, or you will have to fight for your life," the man said. Behind him, the sound of harsh panting became obvious.

Ayer moved, and suddenly his last few men were surrounded by not panting wolves, but snarling ones. "Some of us will fall, but all of you will die," the man said, without even a glance at me, but David was grinning, eyes bright in pride. "Leave. Now."

"Look what's in his back pocket," Edden whispered, and I relaxed. It was a wilted dandelion.

I think it was my relief that turned the tide, and with a snarl, Ayer took three steps back, spun on a heel, and stalked off, looking neither to the right nor the left, passing within feet of the snapping Weres without flinching. His men followed with less confidence, almost running to keep up.

David exhaled, and the alpha male smiled at me before turning to a Were on four paws. "Follow them. Don't let them back into that house. Get them out of my hills."

The Were huffed, tail waving as he padded off.

I dropped my circle. The mystics were slipping from me again, but since they weren't trying to kill anyone, I let them. It was the caps the Free Vampires were wearing, I suddenly realized. They'd focused on the caps as a signal of who to trust and who not to.

Suddenly shy, the thin male who had spoken to Ayer fumbled for the dandelion, extending it to me as he minced across where the circle had been as if it were holy ground. Two gray Weres descended upon the downed vampires, whining. "It's a pleasure to meet you," the man said, nodding to David. "Both of you. Can we be of any help?"

"I told you half the city was looking for you," Edden said, and I took the flower.

"Thank you," I said, thinking I didn't deserve this. "Does anyone have a phone that works out here?"

Twenty-One

The heavy weight on my feet vibrated, the audible growl of discontent becoming obvious as it gained strength. My eyes opened, and I stared at the familiar patterns of dim light on my ceiling. Ivy was talking to someone at the front door with the terseness she reserved for news crews and siding salesmen. I was betting it was the former.

"Get off my stoop, or I'll send pixy kids to play in your van," came faintly, and the rumbling at my feet ceased.

My head rose and I smiled at David, even as I shoved at him to give me more room. I hadn't been pleased last night when he'd insisted I wasn't to be left alone, but you don't argue with two hundred pounds of wolf—you make room.

"Let's go," an unfamiliar voice said. "We can get what we need with the telephoto lens."

"I wouldn't," Ivy threatened them. "I really wouldn't."

The door thumped shut, and I sighed. Head flopping over, I looked at the clock. Eleven. I should be rested, but I wasn't. Sleep had been elusive and so mixed up that I wasn't sure it had happened. After the initial confusion over dreaming, most of the mystics had left, returning periodically to color my dreams with what they'd seen, giving me a skewed vision of what had been happening within the nearest ten miles or so. I hoped much of it was simply my imagination, because what the mystics had been bringing back for me to decipher was dismal.

Ivy's steps were soft as she padded by my door. "Jenks, go send your kids to do something bad, will you?" she said.

"Sure, why the Turn not? Jumoke?" Jenks said, and then their voices became quiet—apart from the ultrasonic cheer that seemed to go right through the walls and into my head.

Maybe if I just rolled back over, I could catch a few more Z's.

Z's have to be caught? a mystic asked, and a handful of others drowned it out with their superior knowledge that Z's were dreams, which only caused more confusion that some dreams were not sentient and an uproar ensued in the back of my head.

Yeah. I was awake. Stretching, I ignored them as I got up, tugged my nightgown in place, and looked at David smiling wolfishly at me. "You didn't have to stay the night. Especially not *on* my bed."

David yawned to show me his teeth as if to say nothing was going to harm me when he was around. Either that, or he wasn't about to sleep on the floor. Hopping down, he padded to my door. I knew he could handle the doorknob himself, but why get his slobber all over it? "Go on. Get out," I said as I opened it. "I want to talk to you when you can answer me back."

Nails clicking, he trotted out. "David!" Jenks said, and I reached for my robe. " 'Bout time you got the princess of perpetuity up."

My hair looked like an eighties music video, and wincing, I caught it back in a scrunchie. When I'd gone to bed, new waves of mystics had been flooding Cincinnati almost hourly, and by the faint sound of emergency sirens, they still were. None were apparently making it across the river, Ayer probably soaking them up as fast as they came. Either he was calling them out or the Goddess was out of control, looking for her missing thoughts. I wasn't sure which would be worse, and the effect was probably the same.

Not wanting to talk to anyone yet, I hustled to the bathroom. Most of the mystics were still ranging about, making me feel almost normal, and I carefully tapped a line.

Mistake.

In a terrified flood, they raced back. I staggered as the twin sensation of the line and the wild magic they brought with them raced through my synapses, tainting the clean energy with thoughts of fear, danger, and alarm. Visions of Cincinnati bombarded me in no order. Groaning, I collapsed.

"Rache!" Jenks shrilled, his dust suddenly blinding me.

Reeling, I dropped the line. It did no good. Wild magic took its place, and I cowered, hands over my head as I sat on the floor and tried to control the terrified mystics.

"I'm okay!" I moaned, talking to all of them, but their combined voices were too much, and they refused to listen to me. *You're okay! Back off!* I shouted into my thoughts. *I was just tapping a freaking line for the hell of it!*

"David!" Ivy shouted, and I felt her cool arms enfold me, pulling me from the hard floor. "Rachel just collapsed." My head lolled as she sat me up. "Jenks, what happened?"

Vampire incense poured over me and I breathed it in to pull memories of Ivy to the surface. It worked. Distracted, the mystics' fear and alarm damped like water turning a towel darker.

"I don't know!" Jenks was upset, and his dust warmed my face. "One minute she's trying to get to the bathroom without anyone seeing her, and then she falls down!" I cracked open my eyelids to see a worried dust slipping from him. "Tink's a Disney whore, her aura is white again," Jenks said as he dropped to within inches of me, hands on his hips as he hovered. "Jeez, Rache. How many you got in there?"

"Go calculate the rate of your dust falling," I said, dizzy, and Jenks darted back in alarm.

"You were supposed to watch her!" Ivy accused him. My

fingers were tingling, and slowly the wild magic began to abate.

"I did! I watched her fall down! Tink's tampons. What do you want me to do? Catch her?"

It was better now, and Ivy's eyes met mine. Damn it, I was cowering on the floor like a victim. "Okay," I breathed, finding my voice. "I'm okay. Better now." I looked at the ceiling, feeling the mystics there, hovering. "Get out! Go learn something!" I shouted, and Ivy gave Jenks a worried look.

Jenks, though, was hovering backward, clearly pleased. "That's better," he said, his dust shifting to a bright silver. "There she is. Damn mystics. Get the hell out of my church!"

Exhaling, I looked up as David walked into the hallway, an afghan about his hips. "I'm fine," I said, trying to sit up. Ivy reluctantly let me go, worry clouding her black eyes. I didn't wonder why. This was a structured possession, pure and simple.

"Is she okay?" David asked, and I did a double take. Damn, the man had a nice set of abs. And pecs. I bet he had nice everything.

"Yes, I'm okay," I said sourly. "I tried to tap a line, is all." Ivy stood, hand extended to help me up. "It hurt?"

I wavered, hand on the wall. "Uh, no, it kind of felt good," I admitted. "But the mystics thought it was an attack and came back." I glanced at Jenks. "I think they brought friends."

He nodded, and I grimaced, finally letting go of the wall. It seemed to be getting better, but the reality was I was balancing on a fine line of control. The more mystics there were, the faster they were. What was saving my ass was that they seemed to be learning how to teach one another. The Goddess wasn't going to thank me, but maybe she shouldn't have left them in me to begin with.

"Ah, I'm okay. You mind if I . . ." I looked at the bathroom door, and they began to drift away, Ivy to the sanctuary and David back to the far living room and presumably a set of clothes. Clearly distracted, Ivy changed her mind, brushing past me in a wave of vampire incense to go to the kitchen instead. She didn't give David a second look, which I thought telling. She'd had a crush on him last year.

I hesitated, waiting for Jenks to back off. "David, thanks again," I said, and he inclined his head. A long slice of sun coming through the back door glowed on him.

"It was my pleasure. Everyone has been itching to do something, and it was a good outlet for the more aggressive packs. Got them away from the city center. By the way, you have twenty minutes until Edden gets here. Vivian couldn't get a flight in time, but she doesn't have anything to add, just demand, so we'll do this without her."

He vanished into the back living room. Suddenly my need to use the can took a backseat. *Vivian? The head of the witch council, Vivian?* "This? Do this what?"

David poked his head out. "Talk over the state of the city, of course."

My shoulders slumped, and Jenks darted off as Ivy shouted for him. Ah. Another one of *those.* The last time I had been to one of *those,* Al had shown up and Ivy's ex-girlfriend had killed Piscary. At least this time the city's problems weren't my fault. "Shouldn't Trent be here?"

David hesitated as if he wanted to say something, finally shrugging before he ducked into the back room and presumably a set of clothes.

A surprising spike of disappointment hit me. I ignored it along with the questions the mystics were raising over it. How could I explain when I didn't have an answer?

Standing at the sink, I pulled the scrunchie from my hair and rummaged for a detangle charm. I'd taken a shower last night, but my hair needed major help, and as I stood before the mirror and tried to make some order out of it, my mind drifted to last night: the relieved reunion with Ivy and Jenks, my thirty-second call to Trent that ended with me feeling brushed off.

Why isn't he coming? I thought as I gave up and let it be a lion's mane today. He was a mover and shaker in Cincinnati, but maybe he was being excluded because his religion was suspected of funding the faction trying to kill the undead.

Mystics clustered between me and the mirror as I brushed my teeth, liking the idea of personal hygiene. Maybe it hadn't been so much being brushed off as Trent being distracted. He'd clearly been glad I was okay. Hell, if he hadn't cared, he wouldn't have messaged over that finding charm to Edden. Perhaps he was simply distancing himself. My motions slowed, and I spit in the sink, refusing to admit that the idea depressed me. Distance between us was what needed to happen. It would make everyone's life easier, mine included. It was better this way.

But a feeling of tingles cascaded over me as I remembered the touch of his hand on my waist, firm with demand, a promise of more.

Us? A handful of mystics asked, their voice clear as they combined into one. *This is not us. This is . . .*

"Nothing," I whispered, wiping my mouth and staring at my reflection.

It is! they insisted, myriad conversations rising in the background. *This we is different.*

Whatever. Leaving them to figure it out, I shimmied out of my nightgown and found everything I needed in the dryer. Oblivious in their debate, the mystics left me alone as I got into a fresh set of jeans and a dark green camisole. Barefoot and feeling a chill in the air, I padded to the kitchen, hesitating at the threshold. Normal. It looked normal, and I wished it was mine to keep, to see again and again, like the slow repetitive feel of summer days until the fear was dabbed away.

Ivy was frowning at her monitor, Jenks sending a bright dust down her shoulder as he tried to help. Bis was asleep on top of the fridge, a red bandanna wrapped around his head like a street fighter's. Three pixy kids darted through the hanging rack, arguing over a seed someone had found. Dressed casually in jeans and a button shirt, David made the simple task of starting a second pot of coffee into an art. We'd had men in the church before, and they all had fit in as if they belonged. None of them had stayed, though, and it was starting to wear on me.

Pixies, friends, almost lovers, I mused, wondering if it would all amount to anything other than a good story. My head hurt. I needed a cup of coffee.

Lovers? a returning mystic asked, and it was swamped by the new debate over the different we's they had found.

The coffee smelled wonderful, and as it went chattering into a mug, I gave the mystics a memory of Kisten, the way he'd touched me, the way I'd felt, the emotions I could pull from him, the desire. Ivy looked up, the rim of brown about her eyes shrinking, and I shrugged. Shaking her head, she went back to her computer. The mystics were even more confused.

"It means nothing," I breathed as I sat at my usual spot, the cup of coffee warm in my hand.

Jenks was taking me talking to myself in stride, the visual clue of my aura flaring making it obvious I wasn't alone in my skull, but David and Ivy exchanged worried looks. I didn't care as I took another sip, eyes closing as it warmed me from the inside out and woke me up. I felt lost, even as the mystics gave me a sensation of the space around me as they darted through the room and garden like pixy kids coming back to me with their visions. The idea of David crossing the room lifted through me, and I started, eyelids flying open when I heard a chair being pulled out and I saw him in my mind as he sat down.

"Sorry, didn't mean to startle you," he said, and I turned, seeing him exactly where I knew he'd be.

This can't be safe, I mused, hiding my concern behind another sip of coffee. If the mystics didn't drive me insane, or the Goddess didn't kill me for polluting them with my "singular visions," Newt would, just for the crime of harboring elven wild magic. Al would beat them out of me or kill me trying. And Dali would sell tickets. I was on my own.

But as a handful of mystics flowed back to me with the idea that a woman was entering the back door, I set the cup down and smiled. I was on my own—with a lot of help. All I had to do was learn how to use it.

Jenks rose up in a wing-clattering alarm as the woman I'd seen in my thoughts appeared in the doorway, her Were-soft steps silent on both the steps and in the hallway. "Holy mother of toad piss!" he exclaimed. "Give a pixy a little warning, huh?"

I didn't know her, but clearly everyone else did, and I couldn't help but notice David's eyes light up. "David," she said flicking a glance at me that was neither subservient nor challenging, and I warmed when it lingered on my hair, frizzy and full—like a red wolf's mane. "I know the meeting is about to start, but that issue with the Black Sands has come to a head. You want me to facilitate an alliance while it might be still effective?"

David set his coffee down and stood. "Yes. Megan, come in and meet Rachel now that she's not delirious with magic."

Smiling, he gestured for her, and she eagerly strode into the kitchen. "It's a pleasure," she said, hand extended. "I saw you last night, but I was on paws and you were a little out of it."

She was wearing my pack tattoo, and I stood, feeling a flash of guilt the mystics buzzed over until I told them it was a task I'd failed to give the proper attention to. "I'm sorry," I said, taking her hand firmly. "I really should know everyone in the pack. I've been . . ." My words trailed off. Preoccupied didn't seem to cut it, but it was hard to be involved in mundane matters when the world needed saving every three months.

Megan let go of my hand, her smile widening. "I meant to get to that last pack meeting you were at, but my youngest was graduating from kindergarten. We've both been busy," she said, not a hint of recrimination in her voice. "In times of unease, alphas range far afield to shake danger to death. The pack is content. If it wasn't, I'd pin someone."

Pride crossed her, and I liked seeing it there. She was a good woman, and a second flash of guilt flickered and died.

The mystics currently within me pondered my immediate trust. Some liked her, others didn't, and a tiny, almost unheard faction shouted it was dangerous to like everyone just because they wore no cap.

I blinked, and David fidgeted as both he and Megan realized that I wasn't quite with them at the moment, but I think the mystics had made a joke. Oh God, the Goddess wasn't going to be happy. Humor?

Megan got an awestruck look, backing up a step. "When you get a moment," she said, eyes flicking between us, "there's a few things you need to know about. Nothing pressing."

David nodded, and I shoved the voices away. "You've got me all afternoon."

"It was good to meet you," Megan said, and I winced, realizing just how badly I was serving my pack. Sure, I was busy with other stuff that mattered, but that was no excuse. David needed a real alpha to help him. It had never been meant to be anything but us two, but now it was more, and I needed to let go.

"You're not staying?" I asked, and she halted, clearly uncomfortable when David winced. "I wish you would," I added, ignoring him. "Unless there's something you need to do."

Her eyes lit up. "No, I'll stay."

Her head a little higher, her hips swaying a fraction more, she headed for a cup of coffee. Ivy snickered from her computer, and I went to David to explain. "I thought you'd rub each other wrong," he whispered. "She has the bearing of an alpha."

Which was why he was attracted to her, I decided, inching closer yet, glad when a flicker of irritation crossed Megan's face, quickly squelched. "David, I'm not a Were," I said quietly to him, and his eyes flicked from her to me. "She's a capable woman, and I like seeing capable women doing important things. Besides, if she's doing my job, she ought to be able to have the same info you're getting."

He thought that over, the first hints of regret in the back of his eyes. The pixy kids trying to stay out of sight in the hanging rack flew out without warning, and from the front of the church came a familiar hail. " 'Scuse me," Jenks said, following his kids. It was Edden, and I ignored David's denial that nothing was happening between him and Megan as I looked for somewhere to go with my cup of coffee. It was going to get crowded in here, and I already felt cramped, what with the mystics and all.

"David. Ivy." Looking tired, Edden strode in with a wreath of pixy kids and headed immediately for the coffee. "Rachel," he said as he poured it in a mug with rainbows. "I like your hair like that," he said, making me touch it. "Where's Kalamack? Shouldn't he be here?"

Yeah, I kind of thought the same thing, but it got noisy as Megan was introduced and I was hesitant to bring it up. Setting my drink aside, I went to open the window. Al's chrysalis was still safe under its overturned water glass, and I wavered on my feet when every single mystic in me left to look at Trent's pinkie ring, trying to figure out how something solid could cause so much emotion.

Jenks was a sparkle at my shoulder. "You need to sit down, Rache?" he asked, and I shook my head, hesitated, then nodded, leaning back against the counter and levering myself up. I felt like a kid as I scooted back with my coffee until I hit the cupboards. Edden looked tired, which made me think I must look like hell if we were doing this in my church instead of the FIB building.

Trent helped Edden find me, but he didn't bother to come out himself, I thought with a flash of disappointment. *And that's a good thing,* I added bitterly. Trent was finally seeing how his actions impacted his daughters and his . . . fiancée.

Oh God, I'd actually thought the word, and I tried to find a pleasant expression as the introductions finished.

"So!" Edden said loudly. "I've got two more of these things this morning. Let's get a move on. Who's going to run it?"

Silence deep enough to bring the mystics to a quiet descended, and I realized everyone was looking at me. "Ah . . ." I hedged, and Ivy sighed, a new spate of typing taking over.

David looked at her screen, then moved to the doorway, effectively bringing all attention to him. "I'll start since most of you already know what I have to say," he said. "The threefold increase in wave action we've seen hasn't caused an increase in misfires simply because people aren't doing magic. Unfortunately the I.S.'s claims that the vampire violence has dropped as well is not true. What's happened is that it's shifted focus from vampire/human predation to vampire/vampire stalkings and attacks. As Edden feared, Landon's idea to blame the Free Vampires has started a schism that is being fought out on the street. The inability to use magic is making it harder to cap the violence. Either Ayer and Landon are getting ready to move as Rachel said"—David lifted his mug to acknowledge me—"or the Goddess is being more aggressive in her search for her missing, ah, mystics and Ayer is capitalizing on it. None of the waves are making it out of Cincinnati."

My eyes widened, and the influx of mystic thoughts took on an ominous feeling. "Can't you track them?" I asked. "Find them like you did before?"

Expression solemn, David shook his head. "We can, but the waves quit vanishing early this morning. They're circling."

"Cincinnati?" I blurted. Crap on toast, Ayer had all he needed. He wasn't drawing them out anymore—which meant the Goddess was looking for her lost thoughts. Looking for me.

"It's anyone's guess how long we have until they try to break the containment lines," David finished, and I stifled a shiver, pulling my knees up to my chin, heels on the counter.

Edden scooted his chair a little deeper into the room, arms crossed over his wide chest. "I've got some good news, bad news," he said. "I don't know how useful it is, but the Free Vampires who gave themselves up last night told us why the masters are sleeping. The high concentrations of mystics in the area are giving the effect of a soul or aura on the undead, which lowers their appetite. They sleep when their true aura levels drop below a threshold. As long as there're captive mystics anywhere in the city, the undead will not wake up."

And with the city closed, they couldn't evacuate the sleeping masters.

"They also confirmed that Landon gave them information and the technology to do this. Rachel, I'm sorry, but the elves *are* involved. We know for sure now."

My frown deepened. "Trent wouldn't do this," I said, and David shifted from foot to foot.

"Rachel, I know how you feel about Trent—"

"I'm telling you, he wouldn't sanction anything that resulted in the death of an entire demographic!" I said loudly, then calmed down before I accidentally blew something up. Damn it all to hell, he wouldn't! Not now. I had to believe that. I did.

"And you'd be right," came Trent's voice from Ivy's laptop, and my head snapped up.

Trent? About a dozen mystics dropped their discussion of the reflective surface of copper pots as a thread of adrenaline pulled through me, and my eyes widened when Ivy spun her monitor to face the room. It was Trent. On the screen. *Cool.*

Ivy frowned at her computer. "About time," she muttered.

"Sorry for being late," Trent said, the picture jerky but riveting. "The software wouldn't load. Rachel is right. I haven't heard of any such action being put into place, but I seem to have lost most of my voice in the enclave and I never had it in the dewar."

He looked tired. Behind him, colorful fish swam in a smaller tank. "Can he see us?" I asked, freezing when Trent seemed to look right at me.

"Yes. I'm glad to see you're recovered, Rachel."

His attention was on my hair, and I fumbled for something that wouldn't sound dumb—or interested in the slightest. *Singular,* echoed in my head, and I clamped a hand over my mouth before I could say it, warming as mystics began arguing over the logic. He was clearly not made of mass, how could he be singular, even if he acted singular. Everyone else was staring as if I had lobsters coming out of my ears, Trent most of all, and I forced my hand down.

"What have I missed?" he said, a slight red along the rims of his pointy ears.

"Nothing you've not heard before," Jenks said, shooed from the monitor when his dust blanked it out.

But Trent hadn't known about Landon, and I breathed easier as everyone backed off, accepting that as truth until he proved it false. Which he wouldn't. Looking back over the last three days, the conversations between Trent and Landon were making a lot more sense. It had felt wrong that Trent had lost his voice for something as stupid as not marrying Ellasbeth, when he was in fact being cut out because the powers that be knew he would've been able to turn the tide of events to a vote of no-action. The dewar had used our relationship to force him out, and we'd played right along with it until it was too late. God, it was irritating.

Edden cleared his throat. "Trent, Edden here," he said since he was probably out of sight of whatever camera was transmitting. "Ivy, are you sure we can't wake the undead? If it's the mystics, maybe a special room or something?"

"No," she said, her voice thick with worry. "There's not enough time. I've been in contact with several houses and they tell me they think their masters have less than twenty-four hours before they begin to die of aura starvation. They're showing the first signs." Her jaw clenched, and I remembered her mother was among the undead. "We need to evacuate them."

"They won't let me. They're worried about contamination," Edden said, and Ivy bristled.

"That's bull, and you know it," she growled. Her eyes had

flashed black, and as Jenks hummed a warning, I leaned to shove the window up more.

"Easy," David said, standing up and moving to get the last of the coffee. I thought it was more to be up and on his feet than any desire for caffeine. "We're just trying to figure out the best way to find an end to this." Megan, too, was watching everyone, and it made me nervous. "I've had no luck locating Landon or Ayer. Edden, can you spare anyone?"

Edden shook his head. "Three days ago, perhaps. The FIB and the I.S. aren't going to be effective in any capacity come sundown." He glanced at David, now at the empty coffeepot, and shrugged. "If I had the men. I just can't spare the resources to find them at this point. Fire, emergency, all public services are, for all intents, nonexistent," Edden continued, and I sucked on my teeth as I noticed Trent wasn't paying attention, busy with something on his desk. "So far, new medical emergencies are going to the arena, but if something big catches on fire, it's going to burn to the river."

Jenks landed on my shoulder, startling the mystics but not me. "And you can forget about any outside help," Edden said, his voice resolute. "Until the waves cease, we're considered quarantined. Vivian confirmed it."

My lips parted. "No government assist? What are they doing with my taxes?"

"Apart from a small advisory group arriving in a few hours, they'll help contain us only," Edden said. "No one in or out. Do you have enough feed for that horse of yours?"

"Ah, it's my horse?" Trent said, giving me a sharp look through the monitor, and reminded of Tulpa, I looked out the window, not seeing him.

"A few more days. I can take him down to a park, but someone might try to eat him."

Eat a solid? a mystic asked, its voice clear in the somewhat reduced amount of them in my head. *Consume a singular mass that can move on its own? This is acceptable?*

Not this particular one, I thought, distracted as Edden's

hands rose up only to fall back onto his lap in a helpless gesture.

"If we could get the waves to stop, we might have a chance," Edden said.

"What about you, Rachel?" Trent asked, and I jerked. "The elves will not help for obvious reasons, but demons are over five thousand years old. They might know something about controlling mystics."

The arts of war, I thought, my fear kindling a sudden rush of mystics back into me. I held my breath as they flooded in, and everyone jumped when a charm in my cupboard exploded, unable to take the influx of wild, unfocused magic.

"I take it you haven't discussed this with them," Trent said, and anger trickled through me.

"Me talking to the demons right now isn't a good idea," I said tightly. It was better to be angry than afraid. Even the mystics understood that. Why was he being such a jerk?

"The waves have to be stopped," Trent argued. "It's going to require the knowledge the demons have to either destroy the vigilante group or get the Goddess to stop thinking about her missing thoughts."

He was right, but I was afraid—afraid of the look on Al's face, afraid of how deep the scar went. "I'd rather not," I said.

Motion fast, Ivy shifted the monitor slightly. "Rachel said it wasn't a good idea."

Jenks darted to hover beside Ivy so Trent could see him as well. "She's got pieces of your elf goddess in her right now, cookie farts, making her aura glow. You think the demons are going to be hearts and roses over that?"

Trent's face went ashen, and a chill went through me. "No one told me that," he said quickly, almost getting up, sinking back down in agitation when he remembered he was on camera. "I talked to you last night, and you didn't tell me that."

"Well, if you hadn't brushed me off, maybe I would have," I muttered, and David exchanged a concerned look with Megan.

"Brushed you off!"

I leaned toward the monitor, hands on the counter beside my knees. "Brushed me off." I couldn't help but wonder if this was our first argument, but didn't you have to be a couple before you could have one of those? He had made his choice—the right choice—and I wasn't it.

Clearly upset, Trent looked off screen. "You didn't tell me she was harboring mystics."

"I didn't know, Sa'han," Quen's voice came faintly. "She appears to be handling it."

I ignored Ivy's uncomfortable look. The mystics humming through me made my fingertips tingle. Trent knew I was playing with fire. I had to get these things out of me for good—preferably before anyone in the ever-after saw me with them. There was a chance Al would help. It was thin, but money moved him, and turning me in would put his bank account in jeopardy. Besides, my decision to avoid him was based on fear, and I wouldn't let fear rule me.

"Rachel," Trent said tersely, his tone solidifying it.

"I'm fine," I said, and Jenks's dust shifted to an unhappy orange. "And the truth of it is, you're right. With Landon and Ayer dug in like ticks, I won't ignore the possibility we might not find them in time. As you say, the demons might be our best option. If we can wake up the masters, we *will* find Landon and Ayer. The vampire violence will stop, too."

"Rachel, I don't want you going to the demons," Trent said, and Edden threw his hands up in the air in disgust.

I looked at him, shocked at the emotion he was showing. Or maybe I was just able to read him better now. "It was your idea."

"Yes, but that was before I knew you had mystics still in you."

Choosing to be angry over afraid, I slid from the counter, knees shaking as I crossed the room. Megan pulled back, and even David looked discomfited. "You aren't here," I said, hands on my hips as I looked at his image; the little box next to it with my face looked wrong. *My God, is my hair really that strung out?* "You don't get a say," I added. "I'm making cookies, and whoever wants to go with me can go come sundown. End of story."

"Count me in," Ivy said, and a new worry surfaced even as I was glad for her help.

"Me too!" Jenks added, making it worse, but honestly, I couldn't stop them this time—and I needed help. I needed it bad.

"Cookies?" Edden muttered.

Jenks nodded knowingly as he hovered beside Edden. "Al loves cookies. It will buy her at least five minutes."

"Why sunset?" David asked. "It's hours from now."

"Because Jenks can't be in the ever-after until sundown, and Bis won't be awake until then," I said, heart pounding, and the pixy glowed a happy silver. "We can do this. We've done it before. And who knows? Maybe Al has a way to get them out of me." One that didn't involve a lot of pain, maybe—but I doubted it.

"Rachel . . ." Trent protested, leaning toward the screen, and ticked, I smacked the lid down to end the call, making Ivy jerk.

"Meeting adjourned," I said, heart pounding. Ivy was staring at me, and I turned to see that David, Edden, and even Megan were wide-eyed and silent.

"What?" I said, wondering why the mystics were all silent or gone. "Edden, if you can find Landon and Ayer before sundown, I'm all ears, but otherwise, I'm going."

Mass that interprets sound waves, a mystic said importantly, and the knowledge cascaded through the rest, starting a flaming conversation that I was more than ears, and was this insanity or a joke? I felt a hysterical laugh bubbling up, and I choked it off.

I'm going to go nerking futs, I thought, eyes widening as that made it all worse.

"You heard the lady!" Jenks said, dust shifting to an annoyed bronze. "Get going! Find the bastards. It takes me a week to get ever-after stink out of my clothes."

Edden brightened, eager to use the demon card and get back to normal. "That's it, then?"

David was nodding, extending a hand to escort Megan out. "Good. Edden, if all you need are eyes on the street, I can help. If we find these SOBs, Rachel won't have to talk to the demons at all."

"Worth a shot," Edden said. "Bring your people down to the arena and we'll give them a grid. Rose can tell you where I am better than me."

The phone was ringing, and Ivy's eyebrows rose after glancing at the caller ID. I shook my head, and she let it ring. He wasn't here. He got no say. We could handle this the way we did everything else. Together. But my heart was pounding and my knees felt wobbly as I told the mystics buzzing in my head to back off and let me think my singular thoughts.

David had his hand on Megan's shoulder, the two of them starting for the door with a pile of clothes in their hands. Seeing their casual, comfortable contact, I realized I couldn't procrastinate any longer. "David?" I called, waving my way through Jenks's dust. "Hold up. Can I talk to you for a second?" They both came to a halt, and a flash of angst went through me. I wasn't abandoning them. I was making things right.

"You sure you can handle the demons?" he asked, and I nodded.

"It's nothing we haven't done before." *Minus the deep-seated hatred.* "We'll be fine. David, I've been thinking."

Immediately his face darkened, and I pulled him aside so Edden and Ivy could slip by us. She touched my shoulder in passing, the simple contact starting a buzz of controversy concerning "we" in a few mystics.

"Ah, I've been doing some thinking this week," I said, raising my hand when he started to interrupt. "No, listen," I said, but he wasn't.

"Nothing has changed," he said, and Megan flushed as

Jenks left, joining the noise on the way to the front door. "I don't want—"

"You don't want," I interrupted, searching his eyes until I found the focus in him, so deep and entrenched that I didn't think it would ever leave him. I hoped it never would. "It's too late for what you *want*," I said, unhappy that this wasn't working out. Seeing him and his pack rallying together under a common goal made it very clear this wasn't working. "You need. You *need* an alpha who is there, focused on the same thing you are. Clearly I can't do it."

"Rachel."

"I'm not a Were," I said, interrupting him. "David, Megan needs the clout that goes with the job she's doing." *My job, the one I neglected so badly that I hadn't even met the woman doing it.* "Maybe if you were just an ordinary alpha this could work, but you're not. Not anymore."

"Maybe if you were just an ordinary witch," he said ruefully, and my shoulders eased as he began to understand. We were both being pulled in different directions. It was time to let go.

My throat closed up, and I braced myself against the questioning mystics. "Don't think this is easy," I said, and he nodded, taking my hand and giving it a firm squeeze. "What do we have to do?" Head high, Megan came closer, her breath held in hope.

David let go, his fingers finding hers, a new, eager look in his eyes. Yes, I was doing the right thing. "You're not leaving our pack," he said, and Megan nodded.

"No, but I can't be alpha." But I knew this was the first step out. I wasn't a Were, and to pretend so would only lead to more grief. I never should have tried in the first place. But who knew it would lead to all this? I looked at Megan, who was almost glowing. "We don't have to fight or anything, right? I'm really tired."

David ducked his head in a chuckle. "A handshake will do it. The paperwork is only for the registry."

A handshake. The mystics clustered close to my upper-most thoughts, trying to figure out why I was both upset and happy as I held out my hand. "Megan, all good things to you," I said as our hands met.

"Go shake death until you win," she said, and I sighed in regret. *Coulda, shoulda.*

"I'll do that. Thank you." I let go, and the mystics hummed their confusion.

I made her single voice count more, I thought at them.

A single voice can't have more merit than many voices, they thought in unison.

It can if that single voice sees more than others, I thought back, then caught my breath as a flood of them left me, fueled by the concept. I hid my sudden unbalance by giving Megan a hug. It was the right thing to do, and David was beaming when I rocked back. Steps silent, they headed for the front door, their soft words twined and falling over each other. It was good. I'd finally done something good.

"That's nice," Jenks said as he came back in and landed on my shoulder. "So you think cookies are going to keep Al from busting you up?"

I looked at Ivy's empty corner, relishing the new quiet of my kitchen. "No, but I think you, me, Bis, and Ivy working together can," I said softly, and the dust spilling down my front turned an alarmed red. "I just hope they find either Landon or Ayer before sunset. Al is going to be pissed, but he won't turn me in. He'd be broke."

Jenks's dust turned a dismal brown, and I exhaled. "Maybe Al can get them out of me," I said as I turned to the fridge. I was starved, and the last thing I wanted to do was fight demons on an empty stomach.

But as Jenks and I discussed the leftovers in the fridge and the likelihood of food poisoning, I wasn't sure I wanted Al to get them out. I was starting to become used to them . . . and the tingle of wild magic they brought to me.

Twenty-Two

Chocolate-chip-scented air rolled out, shifting my hair as I opened the oven door. They'd been frozen dough fifteen minutes ago, thawed by a charm Ceri had taught me and baked as a quick bribe to distract Al while I explained why he should think about his bank account before his pride.

This is so dumb, I thought as I set the pan on the counter and rummaged in the drawer for the spatula. I was going to end up in an ever-after jail cell for uncommon stupidity. If Al didn't go for it, I'd be spending the next precious twenty-four hours trying to explain to a bunch of demons why I was hosting bits and pieces of the goddess of the species who had enslaved them, warred upon them, imprisoned them in an alternate reality, and then cursed them so their children would be stunted shadows of themselves.

Maybe they had a point, I mused as I looked up, forcing a smile as Jenks darted in, a horsehair in one hand, his crying daughter in the other.

"Rache, tell her that horse is going to eat her," he said, frustrated sparkles sifting from him when he let go of her and darted into the utensil rack where he kept the wing tape. "I swear, I should just let the stupid animal snap your wing clear off."

"Tulpa did that?" I said, and he pulled the girl down to

stand on the counter where his dust pooled with hers in a beautiful kaleidoscope of silver, gold, and green.

"No, she snagged it when she darted away from him. Hold still. Hold still!" he exclaimed as his daughter awkwardly looked behind herself and held her wing so her dad could fix it. A tiny cut leaked silver dust, mirroring the twin tracks of tears spilling down her face. "Tink's little pink rosebuds," he grumbled as he finished and rubbed the sticky stuff from his hands. "Was it worth it?"

Beaming through the tears, she nodded, taking to the air and snitching the horsehair from the counter in passing. In half a second, even the sound of her wings was gone.

"Darn kids grew up so fast," he whispered, and I felt a flash of guilt for including him in my madness.

"Ah, Bis and Ivy will probably be enough help tonight," I said, and he spun.

"Bull," he said, taking a crumb from the counter. "Al doesn't scare me."

"He scares me," I admitted, and Jenks nodded, silent as he nibbled the pixy-size cookie crumb. "I mean it," I said, pushing a warm cookie off the spatula. "You and Ivy both. This might be too much for Al to stomach."

"All the more reason to come," he said, looking toward the street and rising up at the revving of a distant engine and a tinny horn. "Face it, Rachel. You're stuck with us." A second horn joined it, and then more engine, closer this time.

"Kids," I said, hoping that was all it was. "Isn't there enough going on without getting into an accident?"

"Ah, that's Trent's car," Jenks said, and I jerked upright, the cookie I'd just taken a bite from forgotten. "I mean, that's his horn."

"Trent?" A sliver of adrenaline sparked through me, pricking the interest of the nearest mystics, their attention diverting from the minute pigment shades in the paint to my rising flush. "How did he get into the Hollows? We're under lockdown."

A car door slammed, and Jenks rose higher. "You got me. That's him, though."

"Rachel? Rachel!" came echoing from the street. "I have to talk to you!"

Oh. My. God. He came to stop me, I thought, and the mystics hummed at my alarm, confused that it was not based on possible injury, but . . . embarrassment? Trent knew this was a bad idea. Hell, I knew it was a bad idea. But if he tried to stop me, I'd have to admit it, and then I'd have to do it anyway because, as he implied, there really wasn't another option.

"Crap on toast," Jenks said as a thunderous booming echoed in the sanctuary as Trent hammered on the door, and I winced. "I'll let him in before the neighbors call the cops. Not that they'd come," he finished as he flew off, his dust a bright sparkle.

Trent is here, I thought, my grip on the spatula almost white knuckled. This was my life, my decision. What he wanted didn't matter. That fact was very clear. Full of a misplaced anger, I dropped the spatula and snatched up the hot pad.

Grimacing, I opened the oven for the last tray of cookies. My brow furrowed at Trent's voice in the sanctuary, and I intentionally turned my back on him as he stomped down the hall.

"Why didn't you tell me you had mystics still in you!" Trent shouted. Shocked that he'd raised his voice, I spun, a tray of cookies in my hand. He was still in the clothes he'd been in earlier, his dress slacks wrinkled and the top two buttons undone from his shirt to show a wisp of hair. His sleeves were rolled to different heights and it made him look disarming, even as he glared at me, tips of his ears red.

"You want to say it a little louder, maybe?" I said as I dropped the tray clattering onto the counter. "I don't think they heard you two streets over."

He came in, disheveled and upset. A pen poked from his

shirt pocket, and I raised my spatula threateningly when he reached out as if to give me a shake. Mystics hummed, the nearest gathering into me, and sensing it, perhaps, he paused. His eyes dropped to the cookies, then rose to Jenks perched on the curtains over the sink.

"You haven't gone yet . . ." he started, and I shook my head, lips pressed into a line as I wedged a cookie off the tray.

"Not yet," I said, wrangling it to the cooling rack. "Ivy is settling up with Nina this afternoon, and I'm waiting until sunset so Jenks and Bis can come with us." Angry that I had to risk them all for something that they had nothing to do with, I used too much force, and a cookie went sailing off the tray and onto the floor. Frustrated, I threw the spatula down. "Why are you here?"

"You can't go to the ever-after with pieces of the Goddess in you! I know I said it was the only way, but we can think of something else. What if Newt saw you?"

The worry lines at the corners of his eyes pushed the anger from me, and my first biting response died. "We don't have time for anything else," I said, feeling numb. "Besides, if I can keep this between Al and me, it will be okay. He won't turn me in. He'd lose everything." But a smidgen of fear lingered. I'd seen Al's hatred of the elves. His emotion was not one filtered through generations but raw. The pain was his own, not a passed-down story.

And yet he had loved Ceri . . .

"It will be fine," I said as I picked up the cookie and threw it away. "And it's not any of your concern."

"That's not fair," he said, and I leaned over the counter to him.

"Yes. It. Is." I took a slow breath, ticked even though I knew he'd made the right decision. We both had. "Mr. Kalamack."

Shoes scuffing, he sat down with an almost imperceptible sigh. He was facing sideways to me, and I could hear pixies playing in the garden. If it wasn't for the sirens and faint scent of burning building from across the river, it might almost be a normal day. Slowly the memory of making cookies with Trent surfaced. Tension easing, I resumed moving the cookies to the cooling rack. The memory hadn't been real in the sense that we'd actually done it—seeing as I'd been trapped in my mind and he had been trying to free me—but he remembered it too, so perhaps it was real after all. The kiss afterward sure had been.

"Your aura is white," he said, still not looking at me. "How many?" His head turned, and my breath caught. "I can still ask that, can't I?"

I nudged a cookie to be exactly even with the rest. "It varies. If I tap a line, too many to breathe. Right now, not a lot. Just a few voices. They recognize you from the computer. Congratulations, you've been granted the title of trusted singular. I suggest you refrain from wearing hats."

"Ah . . ." His confusion was sudden and wary, and I managed a wry smile.

"They recognize you as an individual. They weren't sure from seeing you through the computer. They've been ranging about a lot, which makes it easier." Ranging about, then coming back with confused friends, bombarding me with images, thoughts, and questions about things happening miles away. It was lofty, godlike to know what was going on everywhere. *I'm going crazy, and I think I like it.*

Jenks's wings hummed, and he flew from the curtain rod to the cooling cookies. "If you're not going to fight, I'm going to go rescue your horse from my kids," he said, and then with a cheerful dust I didn't understand, he darted out into the garden.

Trent watched him go, looking frustrated as he turned his attention to the spelling pots over the counter. "I vowed I'd never tell you anything you wanted to do was a bad idea," he said, his low voice pulling at me. "But this isn't worth the risk. Rachel, look at me!"

I set the spatula down and faced him, cookies and a thousand words unsaid between us. "Why are you here?" I asked softly.

"You can't let the demons see you with mystics in you. Even Al," he said, and fear spiked through me. "You don't understand the depth of hatred they have for us. Especially now that there're a dozen Rosewood survivors growing up healthy. The demons know they exist. They're simply ignoring them until their neural nets are mature enough to play with."

"I said, why are you here?" I asked again, breath catching when he got to his feet.

"Rachel, your aura is white with mystics," he said, and I didn't pull away when he took my elbow. "They're not fools. They'll know. They will *remember*. They hate the Goddess."

"Then maybe they know how to contain her," I said, lifting my elbow away. "Getting help from the demons is the best option we've got. So it's the harder choice—why change anything now?"

Exhaling, Trent leaned closer, and the scent of cinnamon and wine crashed over me. "I want you to slow down," he said. "We can figure this out. Going to Al is not the only option; it's the easiest for everyone but you." A hint of fear settled into his strained expression. "I can't do easy anymore. It's too hard on my soul."

There was danger in his words, and I turned to set the empty pans in the sink. "You're getting married," I said, back to him. "You lost your say in what I do." Lips pressed, I turned around. "Why are you even here?"

"I came to talk some sense into you," he said. "And I'm not leaving until I know you're not going to do this."

My head hurt, and I looked down, thinking my feet were too long to be pretty. "What you *want* doesn't matter." I brought my gaze up, shocked to see how he looked in my kitchen, pleading at me to listen to him. "Trent, you worked hard to become responsible for the elves, and that goes both ways. You belong to them. You belong to Lucy, and Ray, and Ellasbeth. You belong to flipping Cincinnati and every elf east of the Mississippi. I work for you when I need the money, and I'm not doing it anymore. You made a choice. It was a good one and I support it, but you can't have it both ways. So go away and *let me do my job*!"

He stepped forward, forcing me back. "You're right. I made a decision. It was the wrong one."

Shit. I felt my face go white. Mystics clustered in me, looking for the source of my fear, amazed to find it again in emotion, not physical hurt. More gathered, fascinated and making me dizzy.

"When I heard you were taken by the Goddess, I tried," Trent said, noting his mismatched sleeves and rolling one up. "I did what I was supposed to do. I stayed where it was safe. I fulfilled my responsibilities by sending that finding charm to Edden. I told myself that he could find you, that you'd be okay. And you were. I did the right thing, what was acceptable and needed—and it worked. But it almost killed me."

He came close, and I backed up until I hit the counter. Watching me, he took my hand in his, bringing it up between us. I looked at it with mine, seeing the masculine strength in his long, graceful fingers. "I'm not going to work for you ever again," I whispered, wanting his fingers skating across my skin. "Don't ask."

Trent's eyes fixed on mine. "I told Ellasbeth to leave this morning."

My breath caught, and I held it, feeling dizzy. "What?"

His smile was faint and tremulous—unsure and confident all at the same time. "Right after you hung up on me. You were right that I had no voice in what you did if I married her, and I didn't like it. I told Quen to pack her things if she didn't. I told her to be out by tomorrow. I told her that she would have the girls three months in the summer, and that's it, and if she contests it, she will never see them again. I'm not going to marry her. Ever. I don't love her, and I never will."

His hand on me was trembling. My God. For once in his life, he was setting aside what was expected of him and following . . . his heart. "You can't do that," I whispered, scared. "Everyone expects . . ."

"I already did." His jaw clenched. "I don't want easy anymore. It's worthless and the shine doesn't last. But you already knew that."

This wasn't happening. I mean, I'd seen the signs, I'd seen them, and we had agreed . . . "Why are you doing this?" I said, a flash of anger coloring my words. This was unfair! We had agreed! Why was he dangling this in front of me when he knew it wasn't a real possibility? "You know who I am!"

His expression became serious, and his hand almost slipped from mine. "I've had a long time to think about it."

"This can't work!"

He looked down, then jerked his head up in frustration as his fingers tightened on mine. "I'm not asking you to marry me, Rachel. I just . . ."

My heart pounded, and he stepped closer, so close the scent of cinnamon and wine enveloped me.

"I like walking into a room and seeing your face light up when you see me," he said earnestly, the sun from the open window making his hair glow. "I like arguing with Quen over the wisdom of employing a demon to be my security."

My throat caught. This wasn't going to happen, but something in me was withering. I wanted more—and I knew I couldn't have it.

He touched my hair, and I twitched as he tucked a strand of hair behind my ear. "I want to wake up beside you, see your curls on my pillow. I want a chance at falling in love."

My breath came fast. That was what I wanted too, and it hurt more than I thought was possible to survive. "Stop," I said, hardly able to breathe the word. "I can't. Don't do this."

I couldn't help it, and a tear slipped out. His arms went around me, and I began to sob. His strength enfolding me felt so good, so honest. And it wasn't mine.

Why not? a mystic asked, and I couldn't answer.

"Please, just stop. Go away," I said, my voice weepy.

But he didn't. "I know you're scared," he said, rocking me so slowly it almost was no motion at all.

"I'm not," I said, head buried in his shoulder, touching him, being held, finding strength though it hurt even more.

"You are," he said, his words easing through me. "I want to love someone. I think I might already."

A small noise escaped me, and I shoved him away. *Love?* "You son of a bastard!" I exclaimed, and he blinked at me in surprise. "How dare you walk into my kitchen and tell me you might love me. You know it won't work! The elves don't want it. The demons won't allow it! We do this, and you lose *everything*!"

"Well, I'll be damned," he said, his shock evolving into an amazed wonder tinged with the bare hints of amusement. "I finally found out what you're scared of, Rachel Morgan, and why you keep spending time with men and women who can't give you what you need."

"I am not scared," I said, terrified. "I'm a realist!"

"You're scared," he said calmly. "And I'm going to prove it."

"You're . . ." I said, falling back when he paced to me, his expression intent. He was looking at my mouth. "Hey!"

His hands grabbed my shoulders firmly and yanked me across the few feet that separated us. "Trent, you, mmmph," I managed to get out as he stole a kiss, a wild, wonderful, passionate kiss.

His lips were heavy on mine, an erotic mix of demand and softness. My hands against his shoulders were set to push him back, but I couldn't, shocked at the sudden surge of desire that burst from my core, flaring through me like flash paper.

Eyes closed, my back hit the counter.

Emotion vibrated up through me. My hands clenched on him and my eyes opened. Heart thudding in my chest, I shoved him back and away. Oh God, it was a fabulous kiss. I could hardly think. "That might work on your secretary," I said, looking him up and down and imagining him naked. "But I'm smarter than that. Get out! Now!"

I pointed at the door, the mystics in me glowing, adding to my ardor.

Trent didn't move, eyeing me, reading my lie. "You *are* scared," he said, and the scent of cinnamon made my knees weak. "Screw them, Rachel. They don't matter. You are a demon, and I just told my fiancée to get out. Tell me you don't want to see where this could go. I am not going to live with regret for not having tried."

He stepped closer, and I retreated, wanting to touch him, wanting to run my hands between him and his shirt. I couldn't move as he slipped into my personal space, and I shut my eyes, pretending that if I couldn't see him, I wouldn't have to tell him to leave. I wasn't breathing, and vertigo spilled through me.

"Tell me you've not wanted to know for a long time," he whispered, and I quailed as his hand touched my shoulder. "Tell me that right now, and I will leave."

The memory of his expression when he found me beaten and struggling under the city swam up, his anger at someone harming me and his shared pain at my bruises.

"Don't. Don't go."

Trent's breath came in with a shaky sound. His touch on my shoulder changed, becoming less fragile.

"Please don't go," I said, eyes opening to see his relief. "I don't want to be alone anymore." How could something be so wrong and so right all at the same time? No, not wrong, just difficult.

He pulled me close, our bodies touching their entire lengths. "You've never been alone."

"But I have," I said, the tears starting up again. Damn it, I didn't want to cry, but it didn't seem to matter as Trent kissed me lightly, his lips never the same place twice.

"Don't go to the ever-after," he said. "We can figure this out."

The ever-after was the last thing on my mind, and I made a choking laugh. "I was hoping you would come to stop me. I really think I was."

He was smiling as I wiped my eyes, and still we remained where we were, pressed against each other. "Hell of a way to make a man put his priorities in order."

I tugged him closer, wanting to run my finger along a line of faint stubble. "What took you so long?"

My head pressed against his shoulder, and I felt his breath in my hair. "Scared, I think. I have so many eyes on me."

"I know what you mean." What had just happened? All I knew was my relief was overwhelming, a tired acceptance and a sensation that everything was going to be all right, no matter what. My hands traced the outlines of his shoulders, and I let them follow the lines of his muscles down lower, anticipation stirring in me as he tensed.

His breath came and went, moving my hair. And still we stood there.

"Where is everyone?"

His words sparked through me, a thousand feelings, only one question. A flash of passion flickered and settled into a steady, demanding burn. Trent was here. Everything was different. Nothing felt wrong. My hand rose back up, finding a new tension in his shoulder. But he'd asked me something.

"Out." I tilted my head and breathed long and slow in his ear. Once. Twice. Three times. Neither one of us moved. We both knew where this might go. My heart pounded, and finally I leaned my weight into him, stretching until my lips found his earlobe and I gently fastened on it, tugging suggestively. "All of them," I breathed, not letting go.

Trent shifted, and I suddenly found myself pressed up against the wall beside the archway. My eyes opened. Desire was hot in his eyes, and a faint smile crossed my mouth as I wondered if I'd find out if he'd taken Al up on that circumcision curse. "Mr. Kalamack," I said playfully, and he took my wrists and pinned them to the wall beside my head. There was just enough force in it, the demand tempered by passion, and it zinged through me, lighting me alive.

"I was kind of hoping you might not be a talker."

I ran a foot up his pant leg, then back down. "Then give my lips something to do."

His head bent toward mine again, and we kissed, lips moving against each other, testing, searching, his grip on my wrists edging into a new firmness. His body pressed into mine, and my fingers curled into fists, even as I held myself there, enjoying the hell out of this.

What am I doing! echoed in my thoughts, and I silenced it. I was kissing Trent, and doing a damn fine job of it.

But I wanted more. He let go at my slight hint of motion, and my hands dropped to lace behind his neck. Eyes open, I found his gaze. The light in them blazed through me. This was going to be good. I could tell already. It's the quiet ones you needed to watch out for. "We are going to be in so much trouble," I said, thinking it was funny, and he smiled back, eyes going to my lips.

"Then let's make sure it's worth being in trouble for."

The husky depth of his voice dove to my middle. Fear, passion, desire. God help me. I'd been wanting this for a long time.

I thought of my bed as I pushed from the wall, but his hands were at my waist, and I found myself sitting atop the table. This worked nicely, and I wrapped my legs around him, pulling him closer. Heart pounding, I went for his belt buckle. God, he had a slim waist.

His lips were on my neck, and I started as he found the last hints of the scar that Al had given me, the neurotoxins buried deep in the tissue flaming back to life, shocking me. They'd been dormant for so long.

"Sensitive," I gasped, then blinked as I realized he had undone the top three buttons of my shirt and I'd not noticed. I inhaled as he shifted my shirt open to my shoulders to show my chemise underneath, his fingers lightly tracing my outlines. My hands sprang to his hair, burrowing into his silky strands as he tugged my chemise free of my waistband.

God, yes, I thought when his fingers met my skin, and I shivered as he traced the lines of me up until he cupped a breast. His head bowed, and I tightened my legs around him as he kissed my shoulder, his lips becoming more demanding as he inched lower, lower.

There wasn't enough room, and I shoved Ivy's papers aside, arching back on the table, my legs wrapped around him as he supported me with one hand as he pushed my chemise up . . . his lips finding me at last, tugging, pulling, bringing me alive with a tingling sensation that went all the way to my curled toes.

Moaning, I looked at the ceiling, gasping when he pinched too hard, hoping he would do it again. Ivy's binder clips were in my back. There were better places to do this.

But Trent was working to get my pants off, and I sat up, breathless. I'd managed his buckle, and I let my legs fall away from him as I undid his zipper, pressing into him and biting hard just under his ear, one hand buried in his silky hair.

His motion hesitated, and he came back even more demanding. Smiling wickedly, I jerked his pants down, then shoved them even lower with a foot to tangle about his feet. The question of boxers or tighty whities was answered, and I smiled.

"My turn," he said, lips lifting from me long enough to pull me off the table to slide my pants down, his hands making a trail of sensation on the way back up. Thank God I was barefoot, and I kicked my pants off, scooting back up onto the table, much to his dismay until I again wrapped my legs around him, pulling him closer, my hands encircled about his neck and me pressed up against him.

I shivered at the cool air as my shirt came off, and I broke from him so my chemise could follow. Everything. Everything had to go, and a button popped as I tugged his shirt off. His eyes met mine as I pulled his undershirt, so proper, off him. It was all I could do not to sigh, and I tantalizingly traced his abs as his shirt hit the floor. His muscles tightened, and I leaned in and kissed his neck, feeling him respond, his fingers becoming demanding as they skated over me. The memory of his skin glistening in the shower flitted through me.

Pulling back, I eased my hold on him, my hands between us moving lower until I found his thighs, strong from his horsemanship. His fingers were at the base of my spine, and I sent my hands drifting inward until I found him.

His nibbles on my neck became rougher. Velvety smooth, I traced the length of him, imagining him inside me, and I shuddered, wanting it all. Wanting it *now*. It was just him. No ley lines, no magic, and it was . . . indescribable.

"Trent," I breathed, shifting closer, hands at the base of his back as my legs wrapped around him, tugging him to me.

I looked up, watching the emotions cascade through him as he pulled me closer and slowly slid into me. My breath caught, and I clutched him to me, shuddering. *Oh God, he was perfect.*

"Not yet, damn it," he whispered, thinking I was going to climax, and I looked up, lips finding him, moving against him, showing him there was more. We could find so much more before this reached the end.

"Couch," I demanded, and his hands on me tightened. "I'm not doing this on the floor of my kitchen."

I felt him move in me, and passion zinged a jagged path. He was looking behind me at the table, covered with Ivy's stuff.

"Couch," I demanded again, gripping him tighter with my legs, arms wrapped about his neck, my lips just under his ear. "Oh God, Trent. I can't touch you where I want to if I have to keep holding on like this."

That did it, and he shifted his grip, his hands lacing under me as he slid me from the table. "Hold on," he said, voice strained with more than my weight as he shifted back, carrying me in a slow, shuffling motion, his pants about his feet.

Arms wrapped around his neck, I nibbled his ear, knowing he was helpless to stop me, knowing he'd probably do something deliciously wicked to get me back for it. I breathed him in, smelling cinnamon and wine, feeling loved.

"Okay," he said as he found the couch. "If you hold on, I think I can . . ."

He could, and I held him still inside me as he awkwardly lowered us to the couch. The cushions eased up around me, smelling of vampire and warm to the touch. I eased my grip, letting him pull back as he rose over me. He was beautiful, his skin glistening, bare to the world. I ran a hand over his chest, his back, stretching to reach his thighs, finding the rise of his buttocks.

His eyes were doing the same to me, and a quiver went through me. "You are amazing," I said, hands exploring the tightness of his backside. Damn, the man had a tight butt.

"From where I am, you're the amazing one," he said, and I reached for his shoulders, protesting as he slipped out of me.

"No," I moaned, but it was only so he could send his lips over me, biting gently at my neck, leaving little spots of sensation at my breast, and dropping lower, making me gasp as he found my middle. My fingers could almost reach him, and with a desperate sigh, I found him, bringing him tense as he rose again to my breast, nibbling, pulling, tugging, driving me crazy until I moved my hips suggestively against him, luring him into finding a common motion.

He shuddered as my hands left him, but his lips gave way to the hint of teeth. My grip on his shoulders spasmed, and he bore down harder. Delirious with passion, I moaned, and he came within an inch of too much.

Legs wrapped around him, I reached to find him, guiding him to me, head thrown back when he slipped inside me once more, an instant of coolness dissolving into heat.

"Oh God, yes," I moaned, my hands making a soft pop as they hit his back. He found my mouth, and I almost died as we kissed, his hands massaging my breast and our rhythm becoming demanding. I could not . . . think . . . and with a groan, I felt the first hints of my passion climaxing. "Trent," I gasped, trying to let him know. It was too soon. I wanted this to last, but I couldn't help it. He was . . . he was . . . "Oh God, Trent!"

My eyes opened, lips parted as I felt him climax. "No," he groaned, clearly wanting us to share this, but it tipped me over the edge, and I cried out, clutching him to me as wave after wave crashed through us both.

With a guttural groan, Trent pushed deeper as ecstasy swept through us both, ebbing and flowing like the tides of ever-after until it was spent, leaving nothing but a contented shush of emotion.

Breath harsh, I realized it was over. I could hardly move. I didn't want to. He was warm on me, and it was the most content I'd been in a long, long time. I cracked open an eyelid to find my hair in my face. Trent was propped up over me, a masculine shadow through my curls.

I opened the other eye. Now I could see him, the sweat a sheen on his muscles, the lines of him all the way down to where we were still joined.

Oh. My. God. What had we done?

Trent grunted, jerking as I tensed under him. "Ow. Rachel?" he said, his calm voice flowing through me. "You can panic in a minute, but please don't move just yet." He winced. "Please?" I exhaled, embarrassment a brief flash.

I could still taste him on my lips. My heart thudded in my chest. I had just had sex with Trent. Really good sex. I sent my eyes over him, beginning to relax as I looked at the lines of his muscles. Well, of course it had been good sex. We'd both been thinking about it for almost two years. Arm lethargic, I raised it to touch his skin. His expression shifted, and he lost his pinched expression.

"That's better," he said, smiling as he leaned down to give me a tender kiss.

Not caring what happened next, I tilted my head up to return it. I was exhausted, but my mind was whirling. I didn't know what to think. The mystics were somnolent, quiet at last.

"Stop thinking," Trent demanded, his lips lightly touching me with his words. "Can this couch hold two?"

"Um . . ." He began to move, and I reached up to grab him, holding us together as he eased down to lie beside me. Slowly he lost his wince. I still hadn't let go yet.

"Yes, it can," he said in relief, finding a comfortable position to wait it out. He was smiling at me, inches away, and I suddenly felt shy. "Hi," he said, tucking a strand of hair back.

"Sorry about that," I said, eyes on the red mark I'd put in his shoulder. "It's been a while. Um, the better it is, the longer it might take." But he knew that. I was babbling.

"There's a compliment in there, I think." He was arranging my hair, delighting in it. "I see what you're thinking, and nothing is going to change unless you want it to."

But I was looking at his eyes, and I could tell that he wanted things to change. A quick stab of panic knifed through me, and I sat up, pinned between the couch and him.

"Ow!" Trent exclaimed as he pulled from me. "Rachel, we need to work on this timing thing."

Pressing back into the cushions, I dragged the afghan to cover myself. There was a horse looking in the window at us. "How can you say that?" I prompted, scooting an inch farther away from him, but seeing as he was between me and the floor, it didn't make much difference. "Nothing is going to change. You know that's wishful thinking. We just had sex, and I'm not going to say it was a mistake and pretend it didn't happen!"

Trent sat up, elbows on his knees as he collected himself. "That's not what I meant. And I'd hate to think you thought it was a mistake." He wedged his shoes off, then his pants. Leaning across the space between us, he put a hand on my neck, drawing me in to give me a reassuring kiss. "Everything will be fine."

I began to realize that Trent was sort of an all-or-nothing kind of man, and I apparently had slipped into the all category. I think he had touched me more—loosened up on his iron-clad calm distance—in the last five minutes than he had the entire last year. My slight headache began to dissipate. This . . . might work out. I needed to be touched, and he needed to touch someone.

"Sure," I said, more glum than angry. "Easy for you to say. You've got a big fence around your house. I've got news crews two streets off."

His hand trailing from me raised goose bumps. "And pixies pulling their transmission plugs," he said, head tilted to me. "God, you're beautiful. How could I have been so stupid? Thank you for waiting for me to smarten up."

I hesitated, my hand atop his as he touched my cheek. I thought about camp. Perhaps the seeds of understanding had been planted there.

He leaned into me, our heads touching. "You weren't the only one who was scared," he said, his lips inches from mine. "I don't like easy, but this might be the toughest sell I'm ever going to have to make." He pulled back, the determination I remembered slipping back behind his eyes. "Because I'm never going to let you go, Rachel. I don't care how much you push me away because you're scared. I'll just hold you until you get over it."

I put my arms around him and breathed him in. It was what I wanted. But he was right: we were going to have to fight for it. "What are we going to do?"

He sighed, the sound of relief in him a clear indication that he had heard the depth of my commitment. We were going to do this. It was going to happen. The only question was how much collateral damage we were going to leave behind. "Take it one day at a time," he said, making it sound easy.

We parted, the first hints of unease shifting about me as reality pushed out the glow he'd filled me with. I'd just lost a steady paycheck, because I couldn't work for him anymore. Damn it, I was going to be doing his security for free. "And today?" I asked, fiddling with the tassels on the afghan.

He turned, looking as collected and together as if he were in a three-piece suit. *Jeez, how did he do that?* "Today, I am stuck in the Hollows without my cell phone. Fortunately Jenks has a box of clothes."

I nodded. "In my closet. Top shelf. Help yourself." But he knew that already. He stood, and I looked up at him, trying to be polite but not doing very well. He was a beautiful, beautiful man. A smile crossed my face at the memory of what his skin felt like. It was all I could do not to touch him right now—now that I could.

Trent scooped up his pants and turned. Smiling, he extended a hand to help me up. I sort of fell into him, and tingles sparkled where we touched as he kissed me lightly, rekindling my passion, promising that it wasn't a onetime affair. "We will find a way to fix this without the demons," he said, and my current trouble came crashing back. "We just have to break it down to its smallest component and work from there. You want the shower first?"

My hold on his fingers tightened and I pulled him to the hall. "It's not as big as yours, but it can still hold two." I couldn't bear the thought of not being with him right now. I was afraid if we parted, even for a moment, that I'd wake up to find it was a dream.

He followed behind me, scooping up his shoes as he went and tossing them to the door. "That's good to know."

And then our talk turned to what we had in the fridge as I soaped his back and he lathered my hair, delighting in its length when it was wet and how the water turned it to a darker shade. This was either the smartest thing I'd ever done, or the dumbest. Trouble was, I wouldn't know until it all fell apart or we made it stick.

Please, God. I'd do just about anything to not be alone ever again, I prayed, and the mystics hummed, their thoughts unclear and walled off from me.

One thing I knew was one hundred percent sure was that he was right. Nothing had to change unless we both wanted it to. My toothbrush was staying right where it was, but as I looked at him and the way the water sheeted off the smooth lines of his muscles and the memory of his passion arced through me, I thought I might buy an extra one.

Just in case.

Twenty-Three

Trent? Never mind. I found one," I said, breezing into the kitchen with a legal pad I'd found stuffed in the back of my closet. Ivy had them, sure, but I was tired of looking like a pantser all the time. I could plan stuff, too.

Trent spun from the cooling rack, looking guilty as he rubbed crumbs from his fingers. "You're a three-cookie man, huh?" I said as I found a black marker, and he grinned sheepishly.

"Five, actually. Chocolate chip are my weakness." The cookie broke, and he lurched to catch it, looking totally accessible in the colorful silk shirt he'd borrowed from Jenks. The cuffs of his jeans were rolled up and he was barefoot, which all but pegged my meter. He looked different, but his mannerisms were as collected as always. In the background, the dryer was a contented hum. I didn't even care since it had his socks in it.

Smiling, I got a plate. We'd been sketching out our plans in the back living room since there was less chance of being spotted by a roving news crew, and I could use a couple of cookies myself. "Where *do* you put it?" I asked as I intentionally bumped into him.

"High metabolism." Ears turning red, he stacked cookies

on the plate. "Mmmm, these are good. No wonder Al likes them."

"They're worth their weight in spells in the ever-after." Content, I added to the pile. The world was imploding outside the stone walls of my church, and I didn't care. "Too bad they don't last more than an hour. Did you know that the demon who owns the coffeehouse connected to your dad's vault drew up a contract for a supply of reality-made coffee?"

"Really?"

I nodded, remembering having shoved it into my pocket before going to talk to Newt. Al had looked at it later, tossing it into his fire after pronouncing it grossly one-sided. Maybe I shouldn't have brought it up.

Sure enough, Trent was thinking as he leaned against the counter beside my dissolution vat of salt water. His ankles crossed, and I almost forgot how to breathe. Damn, he looked good. "The cookies get eaten that fast?"

"They pick up burnt amber that fast," I said, taking up the plate and snagging the legal pad on my way to the back living room. Trent followed, either me or the cookies. I didn't care which. He was here and it felt right—even if several mystics had just brought me an image of my human neighbor boarding up her basement windows.

It was the sight of our papers, notes, and scribbled plans wadded up and thrown into the black fireplace that brought reality crashing back. Between David's street force and Ivy's contacts, Edden had found Landon *and* Ayer holed up in a pre-Turn mortuary just inside the Hollows. They were twenty minutes, and a whole lot of planning, away. Edden and the out-of-state I.S. troops who'd been sent to enforce our quarantine were going to subdue Landon and Ayer shortly after midnight, but getting the mystics from there to the Goddess was up to me.

Or us, rather, I thought, feeling like I was a part of something important as I pushed aside the map of Cincinnati to make room for the cookies. I dropped the legal pad, accidentally blowing Jenks from my last scratchings. Grimacing, the pixy dropped down to stand on the paper and tap his sword tip against it in thought. After an afternoon of popcorn, cold cuts, and Trent's tart lemonade, we had a workable plan on how to get the mystic splinter from the mortuary to the Loveland ley line, but it relied heavily on Edden's ability to clear the roads. Trent's copter was out as everything had been grounded, and much to Trent's hidden dismay, his money wasn't buying what it used to.

"I don't know, Rache," Jenks said, tapping the paper, and I took a cookie before pushing the plate to Trent when he sat down across from me on Ivy's couch. "There's a lot of ifs there. I mean, first, you're relying on the I.S. and FIB to get us in."

"Assumption number one," I said, snapping a cookie between my teeth.

"We let the mystics out," Jenks said as he rose up a bare inch and hovered backward to tap the second line.

"Assuming they're there and we can do it," Trent said, pulling the legal pad closer.

"The FIB clears the streets and you run to the Loveland ley line trailing mystics." Scowling, Jenks tapped the number three. "And the Goddess takes them." Sword tip pressed, he tore a line under the last item on the list. "This is the best plan we got, but it still sucks."

"I'm not arguing with you," I said, not liking that Felix okayed the outside I.S. agency to come in and help. I understood not wanting the mess in Cincinnati to spill over into the rest of the state, much less the country, but we had this.

Scowling, Jenks put his hands on his hips. "I still say a small team has a better chance than a big one. People talk too much and committees make decisions slower than a troll in love."

Trent had his elbows on his knees as he looked at the map of Cincinnati Edden had e-mailed over. He was making notes, marking up the escape route Edden had indicated with a bright red line. "My biggest issue is this circular route around the city they want you to take. I understand needing to curtail as many misfires as possible, but the splintered mystics are hazardous. What if they catch up? You barely survived the last time," he added, pencil tapping.

"Sometimes you just have to trust," I said, and I couldn't tell you why arguing with Trent didn't feel like an attack. Maybe because he had yet to say no, just "convince me." That, and I was still glowing from earlier—literally, if Jenks was to be believed. "The entire city wants them gone, and once they get in the line, the Goddess will take them."

Wings a low hum, Jenks flew to the mantel to where he could keep one eye on the garden out the high windows. Trent kept studying that map as if trying to find a better way. I knew he liked this plan less than I did, but Ivy was on her way from the FIB and would fill in the gaps and turn it from one of my ill-thought-out schemes to one of her excellent strategies.

Trent reached across the space between us and took the bowl of popcorn as he said, "Speaking of trust, the Goddess doesn't like you anymore. I'm not so sure she's going to blindly accept them from you."

My shadow of concern pricked through the mystics in me, bringing them to a full awareness. Letting them figure it out on their own, I shrugged. "Perhaps, but she does want her thoughts back. Crazy or not."

Insane! a rising mystic in me cried out, and a slice of them swung around to the idea that we were in danger. Swallowing hard, I told them to chill. They were acting in concert a lot more. A hundred diverse voices I could handle. One determined developing Goddess complex was a lot harder.

Trent didn't notice the controversy echoing in my skull, but Jenks did, and I took a handful of popcorn and flicked a kernel at him to get him to keep his mouth shut.

"Okay," Trent said as he looked up at Jenks's muttered swearing. "Assuming we go with this very rough plan—"

"Ivy will buff out the corners," I interrupted. "It's not like we have to do this alone."

"We still need to figure out how to free the splinter," he finished. "Your magic is twitchy, and my resources are about to take a nosedive."

His Goddess-based magic, I mused, pulling my knees up to my chin until I realized it made me look scared. "I can do magic. The trick is to keep *them* from destroying everything once they're stirred up." I rubbed a spot on the coffee table, uneasy when a few mystics arrowed back to me with images of Ivy's bike weaving through abandoned dented and burned cars down a side street. They were getting better at recognizing her, and every time a wandering mystic saw her, it came back to let me know. If I could get them to individually grasp the concept of time, I might be able to tell how old the image was. "Besides, I saw the containment array yesterday, and it relies on electricity, not magic. Cut the power, and they're free."

Trent pushed back from his hunch over the table. Propping an ankle on a knee, he eased into the leather cushions. It lacked a little polish in that he was barefoot, but he more than made up for it when he ran a hand through his hair and stared out the window at nothing. "Maybe. A lot of those pre-Turn mortuaries have secondary power sources. We'd have to cut that along with their mundane connection to the grid."

"Right," I drawled, remembering. Mortuaries were the natural choice before the Turn to help move the undead into their next existence, in effect underground minihospitals with all the power needs that went along with it. I had to hand it to Landon. He'd thought this through. "If I didn't know better, I would think you don't like my idea," I said, only half kidding.

"I don't, but it's the one that impacts the fewest lives."

"See?" Jenks said from the mantel. "I'm not the only one who thinks the I.S. and FIB are going to mess it up."

"I have not said it's a bad idea," Trent protested. "Just that it's not a *good* one."

Jenks was laughing again. I would have gotten mad, but

Trent was staring at my mouth. If the table wasn't between us, I think he would have kissed me. The thought was almost as good as actually doing it, and my bad mood vanished.

"Tink's titties, you're at it again?" Jenks groaned.

We both turned to the sound of a bike at the front. Thanks to the mystics, I'd been watching Ivy approach the last few minutes, but Jenks darted out to see. Suddenly nervous, I stood. I hadn't aired out the church because it felt like an apology. Trent was lounging about in Jenks's old clothes. His underwear was doing the tango with mine in the dryer. She'd understand, but Ivy didn't handle surprises well.

"That's Ivy," I said as I went into the kitchen. "You want anything?" Yep, I was a chicken.

His head was over that legal pad again. Good grief, how much planning could you actually do for a run like this? "I could use another coffee," he said, and my bare feet padded on the linoleum. "It goes with cookies surprisingly well."

"It's just Ivy!" Jenks's voice echoed back.

"How on earth did she know that?" Trent muttered, and I smiled, pouring coffee into his favorite mug, then poured myself a glass of iced tea.

"Mystics," I said as I came back in as Ivy's boots sounded lightly in the foyer. "They've been bringing me back images of her the last five minutes."

Trent's eyes widened. "Are you sure you want to get rid of them?"

I extended his coffee to him, thinking he looked tired, but he *had* missed his afternoon nap. "Absolutely," I said as about half a dozen mystics combined their complaint into one loud voice demanding to know why ice floated and everything else that became solid due to temperature reduction sank.

Trent glanced at the sound of Ivy's boots in the hallway. "Maybe I should go. We can finish this later."

"There is no later, there's only now," I said, then hesitated, thinking I was starting to sound like Newt. Ice clinking, I stood where I was between him and the doorway. "She'll be fine," I said, looking at the empty hallway with a feeling of foreboding. "She knows I'm not hers, but vampire instinct will make her feel attacked."

"Like I said, maybe I should leave."

"Rachel? I'm home!" Ivy shouted, Jenks's voice lost in the sudden clatter of her boots. "You would not believe what the I.S. is trying to pull. Edden—"

Her words cut off, and I met Trent's eyes, wincing. *Surprise!*

"Uh . . ." she muttered, still in the hall. "Rachel? Did you and Trent—"

She jerked to a stop in the doorway, her pupils widening as she took in Trent sitting on her couch in Jenks's old clothes. They darted to me, and I tried to smile. I knew it must have looked kind of sick, but I kept doing it. "You're here," she said, meaning Trent.

"Yep!" Jenks said as he darted in, clearly having not told her. "They bumped uglies, did the horizontal fandango . . ."

A silver dust slipped from him as he gyrated. "Stop it, Jenks."

"Rolled in the hay, played train and tunnel, got their parking tickets validated . . ."

"Grow up, Jenks!"

Giggling like a twelve-year-old, he went to the mantel when I threw a handful of popcorn at him. "I'm telling you, Ivy, this is the best thing to happen to her since that boy band she liked got run over by a pack of migrating deer. Look how relaxed she is. Better than a spa day."

Ivy licked her lips, eyes darting to Trent as he put his feet on the floor and sipped his coffee. The rims of his pointy ears were a delicate shade of red, which made Jenks laugh more.

"Ah, hi," she said, looking professional and caught completely off guard.

Trent smiled up at her. "How is Nina? Felix is leaving her alone, yes?"

"For the most part." Her purse slipped from her shoulder,

and she set it on the coffee table. Her eyes flicked over the maps and lists, but she looked very distracted. "I think it's because he's been too busy to harass her."

This was going better than I had thought it would, and I set my glass of iced tea down, working my way around the coffee table to sit on the couch with Trent. "Your timing is perfect. We're working out how to free the mystics and cart them from Cincinnati to Loveland."

She started, her thoughts clearly jolted back to what she'd been saying when she came in. "Oh! Right. Has Edden called?"

My eyebrows rose, and Jenks stopped gyrating on the mantel. "Not recently. Why?"

Ivy took off her riding jacket and draped it over the chair I'd been in, clearly still trying to wrap her head around Trent and me. "Um, Columbus's I.S. took jurisdiction over the run," she said, and beside me, Trent softly swore under his breath. "They pushed out not only the FIB, but the local I.S. as well. Edden's lucky to be observing. I'm guessing he hasn't called because he's still trying to argue some sense into them."

"Or he's afraid," I said, and Trent exhaled loudly, a hand to his forehead. "Jenks, where's the phone?" I added, relieved in a way that we had something more important to talk about than my sex life.

"I was afraid of this," Trent said softly as he checked his watch.

"They can't kick us out," Jenks said as Ivy crossed the hall to go to the kitchen, and I slumped beside Trent. "It's our run! Who is going to move the mystics?"

"Apparently they are!" Ivy shouted from the other room. "Felix cut a deal with his old buddies, and with everyone else sleeping, there's no one to say otherwise. The Columbus I.S. agents working the case are going to keep the captured mystics, and Felix gets whatever he wants in exchange. Whenever he wants it."

Nina, I thought, my eyes finding Ivy's when she came

back in, not with the phone but her laptop. My God. He'd given the ability to control wild magic to the I.S., and therefore the undead, in exchange for Nina.

Looking scared, Ivy sat in my recently vacated chair. Her hair hid her eyes, but her fingers were trembling as she opened the computer and waited for it to come alive. It was her security, and it was going to come up short this time.

"Ivy?"

She didn't look up. Trent was fidgeting, but Jenks was mad enough for all of us, the pixy hovering in the center of the room, his dust spilling onto the papers until I thought I could smell smoke. "Whadya mean they get the captured mystics?" he said bitingly. "They *like* what's going on in Cincinnati?"

"As a matter of fact, some of them do," she said, her eyes holding intolerance. "Being able to put your rivals to sleep is something many of the undead would pay dearly for."

"They wouldn't!" I exclaimed as I pieced it together. Ayer had said his original idea had been a more personal choice, a building, a room—a single undead. They could parcel the mystics up. Sell them like miniassassins. Having trouble with your labor pool? Buy a city full and watch them toe the line.

Trent slumped into the cushions, his disgusted expression making it clear he'd figured it out immediately. "The I.S. having control of the mystics would be worse than the Free Vampires putting all of them asleep," he said.

Not to mention it would cause a legal blind eye to fall on Felix turning Nina into his belonging. This was three times wrong. "I say we go there, steal the mystics, and get them to the Goddess before they leave the I.S. tower."

"Yes!" Jenks said, exploding from the mantel in a burst of silver. "I never liked the idea of working with them anyway."

Ivy's relief was almost palpable, but Trent, not used to working with such a small, maneuverable ship, frowned. "You think we four—"

"Five," I corrected him, pointing to the steeple and Bis.

"Five," he continued, "can break into the mortuary, one they're probably already monitoring, cut the power, free the mystics, and run for Loveland all under the I.S.'s nose?"

I nodded, rising to go stand beside Jenks to form a visual alliance. His dust made my skin tingle, and I smiled as Ivy exhaled, her fear easing. "Yup. Welcome to my world, Trent."

"Seven," Jenks said as he hovered by my ear. "Don't forget Nina and David. We got an entire city of Weres to plow our road. They're out there already, and no I.S. agent can stop a Were on four paws."

"Seven, and a city of Weres," Trent said. "So how do we get in? It's a fortress. Lots of security. No easy way out once you get in."

"If it's pre-Turn, the security is all outdated," Jenks said as he flew silver-dusted wreaths around Ivy and landed on her shoulder. "I have yet to find the building I can't break into. Hell, if I can get Rache into your back office, I can get into a pre-Turn coffin klatch."

Flicking his hair back, Trent pulled his map of the city close. A shiver rose through me as I saw him fitting into my life in a way I'd never imagined, and then I stifled it, remembering the heat in his eyes as he lay atop me, the feel of his body against mine. *Why had I done the smart thing and waited so long?*

"You're not thinking like a pixy," Jenks said, seeing Trent's lingering doubt. "Four inches?" he said pointedly. "I only need a hole the size of a dime. Code requires adequate ventilation in those kind of facilities, and wire mesh is easy to cut."

"You can get in," Trent said, and I smiled when he propped his bare feet up on the edge of the table so he could use his legs as a makeshift table. "Which means *we* have an in as well."

"Jenks, how long would it take for you to whip up some pixy pow?" I asked, seeing possibility where there'd only once been doubt. It was the same plan, but we were in charge now, and it made all the difference.

"Hey!" he exclaimed, a bright flash of silver slipping from him in a temporary sunbeam. "Who told you . . ." He glanced at Trent, his wings slowing. "I can have enough to blow the steeple off the church by midnight. Sundown with some help."

Ivy hit a key decisively, and from the kitchen came the hum of the printer. "We'll only need a thimbleful to take out the redundant power system they have in there," she said, clearly in a better mood, though her fear for Nina was just under the surface. "I'll take out the main power. Jenks can get you in and shut down the internal system. By the time you're ready to run, I can be outside with a van. David plows the road to Loveland."

Why did it sound so much better when she said it? Beaming, I passed the popcorn to her. "Told you," I said to Trent, and he leaned back, eyeing us over his scribbled legal pad.

"You have amazing friends."

"I need them to stay alive through my *amazing* life," I said, and Ivy became almost sultry as she pulled herself together in her chair and smiled at Trent.

"Very well. But I'm still concerned that if everything goes as planned and the Goddess takes them back, she won't be able to master them and we'll be right back where we started." His eyes met mine, and my shoulders hunched. It was a possibility that we had no control over, no way to plan for, and it bothered me.

Ivy stiffened when the doorbell rang. "More news crews," she grumbled, gathering herself to stand, but Trent was faster.

"It's probably Quen," he said, glancing at his watch. "I asked him to bring over my phone and daily short list. If it's reporters, I won't open the door."

"If it's reporters, I'll sic my kids on them," Jenks said, taking to the air, and Trent jogged out, bare feet making tiny chirps of sound on the old oak flooring. It was a noise I'd never heard before in the church, and I ached that it might never sound again.

"I wonder how Quen got past the quarantine," I said, and Ivy cleared her throat. The dry sound of it caught my attention, and I stiffened. *Oh yeah. That.*

"I'm not calling what we did a mistake," I said defensively. "Nothing is going to change." *At least not where it showed.*

"It has already," she said faintly, and then her eyes fixed on mine, black and unreadable.

"I'm not moving out, Ivy." God! What did she think I was going to do? Go live with the man? I liked my church, even if Trent did have a pool the size of my house and a twenty-four-hour kitchen. "That would be my least favorite thing to do," I added, and her eyes dropped, making me wonder if she was the one who wanted out of this weird relationship we had.

Head down, she stared at her fingers, silent on the keypad. "Rachel? I . . . Thank you."

Surprised, I stood, not wanting to be sitting when Quen came in. "For what? Dragging you into this? No problem. I'll probably be doing it again before Christmas."

Her lips curled into one of her few smiles, surprising me even more. "Sort of. Three years ago?" she said, hand lifting to indicate the church. "I can admit now that you were my long hunt. I'm sorry, but you were, and you slipped me."

My lips parted, her bare honesty pulling through me like a heartache.

"But you proved I could help someone, even as messed up as I was. You helped me find a feeling of worth. Made me live up to my ideals."

"Oh God, Ivy," I said as she sniffed, and I went to her.

"I almost quit a hundred times," she said as she smiled at me, eyes beautiful and black. "But you thought I had it in me and I wanted to prove I was as good as you thought I was, and now Nina is in jeopardy and you're helping me . . ."

"Ivy, I'm so proud of you," I said, dropping down to give her a hug. "Nothing is going to change." My eyes closed, and I felt her arms go around me, the strength in them holding a frightening loyalty though we'd never be more than we were today.

And that was enough. "We will get Nina out of this," I promised, and she sniffed again, pulling back to wipe a tear away. "She's a beautiful person. A little crazy, but good for you."

Her head bobbed, and I scooted back to sit on the coffee table. "Do you . . ." She hesitated, jaw tightening, clearly determined to be out with it. "Do you think Jenks would be mad if I moved out?" My eyes widened, and she rushed to add, "Not right away. Maybe in a month or two?"

"Um," I said, standing up at the soft sound of Quen's shoes in the hall. "Honestly? Probably. But it's nothing he won't get over."

Why does she pick the worst times to do stuff like this? I thought, my mind swinging back to Quen as he walked in. He was not a dumb man. Even if Trent hadn't been up front about his feelings for me with him, the way Trent must have blown out of his estate without his phone or a way to reach him would not go unremarked upon.

Sure enough, Quen's expression was tight with a sour annoyance. I gave him a confused smile as I tried to wrap my head around Ivy's possibly moving out, feeling it slip from me at the man's hard stare—as if I should have known better. Trent had that same preoccupied, tension-filled expression I'd come to associate with him trying to handle six things at once. The folder in his hands was leaking papers, and he immediately sat down and spread it open.

"How did you get through quarantine?" I asked when Quen noticed Ivy's wet eyes.

"Rachel," he almost drawled. "Ivy," he said with a little more professionalism.

"You can get past the blockades any time you want, can't you?" I accused Trent, and a faint blush marred the rims of his somewhat pointy ears.

"For the moment." Trent leafed through the small stack. "Though I'm finding things have a tendency to change fast. Here." He held out a stapled group of papers. "You might be interested in this. I'll have a copy sent over every week if you like."

Jenks's wings hummed as he came to sit on my shoulder as I took it and sat down on the couch. Ivy shut her laptop with an accusing snap. "Ooooh, figures and data!" I said sarcastically, and then brightened as I flipped the page of chemical compounds, numbers, and graphs over to see a fussing infant. "Oh! The Rosewood babies!"

Trent was smiling when I looked up, and a warm feeling kindled in my middle. The infants' continued survival was the first decision we'd come to together, one that would need decades to see through. I knew it meant a lot to him, even if I'd chosen the path he hadn't wanted.

Seeing my expression, Quen slumped in exasperation.

"Don't start," Jenks said, his wings tickling my neck. "I think this is a good thing."

Did we have to talk about this? So we had had sex. So what? We'd been "dating" for almost three months. They all knew my track record. Where was the big surprise here?

"That's because pixies think with their hearts," Quen said, ignoring Trent's peeved expression. "This decision is already causing problems."

"Most warriors think with their hearts," I said, telling the mystics to back off and that I wasn't angry with anything they could crush or explode. "It's what keeps them alive through the crap they have to deal with to keep the rest of you safe."

For a long moment, no one said anything, then Trent cleared his throat. "The Rosewood babies are doing fine, both in development and security. So far, no demon activity has been noticed, but I think all of them have been marked. If you think it prudent, I'll move them again. I don't want to rely on good luck to keep them safe."

Good luck would be a nice change, I thought, which started a new line of argument among the mystics. I figured I was probably glowing like a friggin' lightbulb by the way Jenks was looking at me, but at least I wasn't speaking in tongues.

Trent reached for the papers as I nodded, and I handed them over. "Watch this one," he said to Quen as he flipped through and circled something. "I don't like his levels. Try that new permutation, see if we can't even out his metabolism a little more. If there's no dramatic shift, I want a detailed report in three months. If it works on him, it might boost self-repair in the others."

"Yes, Sa'han."

Trent handed it back to me, and I smiled at the pictures. This was much better than gravestones—until the demons came for them and I'd have to fight for every single one of their lives. My smile faded. Difficult future or not, it had been a good decision. Nothing would change my mind. Their parents would back me up.

"And here's the latest on the issue you wanted to move forward with," Quen said, pulling a sheaf of paper from the small stack. "Your groves in Madagascar have been overrun with a rare species of butterfly that have taken a liking to Brimstone leaves."

Trent's brow furrowed, making him charming in that silk shirt of Jenks's. "Oh. Very nice. Yes." His frown deepened. "Quen, there's coffee in the kitchen. Help yourself."

Quen put his hands behind his back and stared at the fireplace. "Without intervention, their larvae can eat an entire field down to the roots in two days. Since it's a rare species, we've been relocating rather than destroying, but if their numbers continue to increase, we'll have to resort to chemical warfare to maintain a minimal harvest."

Yep, my boyfriend was a drug lord, and I leaned to see if there was a picture, but it was all figures and data.

"Mmmm," Trent hummed, clearly preoccupied. "Maintain current suppression methods."

Quen nodded. "One last thing that arrived this morning," he said, taking an envelope from his jacket's inner pocket. "It's an enclave decree to desist from all contact with Rachel Morgan."

Shocked, I jerked my head up. "Beg pardon?"

"Seeing as she is a day-walking demon," Quen finished, handing it to Trent.

Ivy's incessant tapping ceased, and she looked up as Jenks rose on a column of silver sparkles. His dust left a glowing trail as he hovered over the paper Trent was now unfolding, and I watched the silver sparkles make a shadow where the watermark was.

"Well, I'll be Tink's Great-Uncle Bob. Lookie there, Rache. You're an undesirable citizen."

Trent finished scanning the letter and let it fall to the table. Leaning back, he steepled his fingers and stared at nothing.

"That is so unfair!" I said. "They can't tell you who you can . . . talk to!"

Trent's eyes flicked to mine, a surprising flash of pleasure crossing him at my outrage. "No, it's okay. I expected this."

"But how did they find out so fast!" I exclaimed, then flushed. This wasn't because we had done the horizontal fandango, as Jenks would have said. It was because Trent had walked away from his voice in their enclave to have a voice in my life. Not to mention I'd survived where·their highest authority, their grand pooh-bah of their religion, had died. They were scared. And Trent was the one taking the hit.

Quen jerked the paper out of Ivy's reach when she leaned forward for it, the man stoically folding it and putting it back in the envelope. "You're under investigation for collaboration with her in endangering the stability of the Goddess and threatening the religious power structure. You've been requested to appear at a summons next week to explain yourself. Shall I bring Charlie into this?"

Charlie was his species-law lawyer, and I huffed, arms over my chest. They'd be lucky if we even *had* a next week.

"Well?" Jenks said, landing on the table before me. "Isn't that kind of what you are doing? Collaborating?"

He was right, but it wasn't as if we had any choice. No one else could do anything about the mystics, and since it was my aura they were attracted to, I felt responsible.

"Quen, here's what I want done," Trent said, and the smaller man seemed to come to attention. "Abandon the relocation efforts at the Brimstone fields. Let them have it. I'd rather have one less endangered species than a Brimstone field anyway. Besides, with Cincinnati's and the Hollows' master vampires out for the week, demand has taken a hit. No layoffs, just shift everyone over to the secondary output." His focus blurred. "The world needs more windmills."

"Yes, Sa'han."

He wasn't writing anything down, but Quen was like one of those waiters who could remember everyone's dinner better than the girl who used a notepad and numbers.

Ivy's eyebrows were high. "You have more Brimstone fields, right?"

"What about the decree?" I said, still angry.

Trent's eyes slid to me. "A decree is nothing more than something someone is afraid to tell you to your face. Until they do, I'm ignoring it."

That made Quen even happier, and his expression twisted into a stiff mask. "If there's nothing else, Sa'han?" he said dryly.

Trent's head went back down over the open folder. "No. Thank you."

Quen slowly spun on one foot. "Ivy, Jenks. Rachel . . ."

"You're not staying?" I said as Jenks flew up to escort him to the door.

Finally Quen's bad mood cracked, and he inclined his head, smiling. "I have to take Ellasbeth to the airport."

"See?" Jenks said loudly. "Not even one day into it, and we already have one good thing happen because Trent and Rachel had sex."

"Jenks!" I shouted, but Trent barely glanced up, a smile quirking his lips. "Where are the girls?" I asked, wondering if Trent would have to leave as well.

"Jonathan." Trent closed the folder and leaned back in the chair. "He's an excellent babysitter. The girls love teasing him."

I wasn't too sure about that, but I understood the teasing part.

"Ma'am," Quen said, looking right at me as he almost clicked his heels together.

I scowled at him. "Call me that again, and I'll take care of your family planning for you."

Quen smiled, deep and full. "Rachel," he amended, then headed into the hall. "Jenks, a word?"

"What the hell is it with you people?" Jenks griped as he followed him out. "Can't you make a decision without talking to the pixy?"

"Warriors build empires around the kernel of truth that others overlook," came Quen's soft voice, and then there was nothing but his steps going fainter until the boom of the church's front door. Jenks didn't come back, and at the far end of the couch, Ivy eyed me.

Excitement settled deep in my core and spread out until it seemed as if my fingertips were tingling. Within me, the mystics rose up like leaves in the wind, excited and scared when I told them they were going home.

"So which one of you has the layout of the mortuary?" I asked, and Ivy smiled, leaning forward to push her laptop to where we all could see.

Twenty-Four

The church was quiet as Trent and I waited for Ivy and David to bring back a "borrowed" van. The pixies were out somewhere, and if I cared to listen to the mystics, I'd be able to hear photons zinging about, crashing into things to make them glow with the energy my brain understood as color. I was more interested in watching Trent do a final check on his belt pack. He looked as calm and collected in Jenks's thief black as he did in a two-thousand-dollar suit. But I already knew that. He was doing this with me, and it felt more than good; it felt right.

Bis shifted his wings from high up in the sanctuary's rafters, leaning to look out the colored squares of stained glass at a cop car zipping by, lights and sirens going. The soot he'd drawn under his eyes worried me. The kid could go almost invisible with his color shifts, but he wanted to fit in with Jenks, now sporting half-moons under his eyes to break up his pale face. I didn't want him to get hurt, but it wasn't as if I could make him stay home. Frankly, I needed his help. Bis wasn't going to let me out of his sight, saying that my aura shifted with the number of mystics behind it and that he couldn't reliably find me anymore. Which begged the question of how the mystics kept finding me. Maybe they were homing in on the soul behind the aura.

Curfew was in full swing, and the I.S. cops from Columbus were being vicious about it this side of the river with blockades and armed officers. The pervading sentiment was unless it was on fire, it could wait, and much of the burning stuff was being left to those who cared to put it out. The church had no water pressure at all. We'd either have an easy time getting to the mortuary, or one full of trials. I was betting on the latter.

The siren was fading as Trent went to the window and put one foot on the low sill to look out and tie his shoe. *Nice butt,* I couldn't help but think, and then flushed at the memory of Trent's and my earlier escapade and the feel of his skin tightening under my fingertips. My blush deepened when Trent seemed to feel my eyes on him and he turned.

Guilt pushed to the forefront and I looked away. He was being summoned before the elven courts because of me. I'd known there'd be repercussions, but I'd thought his money would shield him from the worst of it, leaving me to deal with the demons. Seeing my distress, Trent slumped. "You're not having second thoughts, are you? About us?"

My lips parted in shock. "How do you do that!"

His smile returned, and a thrill ran from the soles of my feet to my middle. "I know your tells."

"God save me from lovesick elves," Jenks moaned, his dust a cheerful silver as he went to talk to his kids. There were yammering about something, and Belle stalked into the sanctuary, fist on one hip, bow clenched in the other. Clearly there was an issue in the babysitting rules.

But Trent had moved to stand before me, a rare hint of vulnerability in the back of his eyes. "It's my fault," I said, gesturing at nothing. "The summons, I mean. If you hadn't told Ellasbeth to get out . . ."

Trent checked his watch. "I believe that was my decision, not yours."

"I could have told you to go home," I blurted, and his eyebrows rose in challenge. "I could have!" I protested, and he chuckled until I found a smile.

Trent's good humor slowly died. "And now?"

"Nothing's changed," I said, and his motions again became graceful.

"Good!" Jenks shouted as he waved his kids off and dropped down to us. "Let me know if it does so I can dust some sense into her."

Disconcerted, I dropped my eyes, then abruptly sat down as a slew of ranging mystics fell into me, making me dizzy with images of a white van and Ivy. "Ivy's on her way," I said, looking up at Trent's concern. His hand was on my shoulder, steadying me, and I thought I could feel a rising tingle of wild magic between us. "I don't know how old the image is, but she's got the van," I added. I wasn't sure what I appreciated more, that he'd have been there if I'd needed it, or that he wasn't treating me like an invalid, accepting that I'd had a moment and I was okay.

"That's probably her," he said at the unmistakable sound of an engine, and Jenks, plastered to the colored glass, gave a thumbs-up.

I stood, heart pounding. We were ready. "Okay!" I said brightly. "Jenks, Bis, Trent. This is going to be easy. We go in. Collect the mystics. We go out to the line. Done." It wasn't going to be that easy, but I could hope.

Jenks hovered between us, his kids a sullen cloud behind him. "Ah, we're coming with you." Wincing, he looked over his shoulder. "All of us."

"Seriously?" I shrugged into my black jacket and zipped it up. From outside, Ivy revved the engine, wanting us to hurry. "Who's going to watch the church?"

Jenks made a sharp wing chirp to shut his kids up. "It's not going to run away," he said. "I've seen the foundation and it doesn't have wheels. Belle will be here. But we're coming. All of us." His expression became pained. "I can't make them stay, Rache. They want to help."

I grabbed my bag from the coffee table and slung it over my shoulder. "We already have too many people." I strode for the door, but there was nothing I could do to stop them either.

"We don't take up any room," Jenks said as he paced me, his kids silently following. "And you're going to need us."

I hesitated at the door. Trent was no help, checking his watch as he deferred the decision to me. Jenks coming was a no-brainer, but a half-dozen noisy, ill-experienced pixies getting in the way might be a problem. Bis shrugged as he hung from the door frame, and pixy dust eddied when he dropped to wrap his tail across my back and under my arm in a secure hold. "I think it's a good idea," he said. "They can stick with me."

Bis taking responsibility for them—for all of them—would be a load off my mind. "Okay," I said reluctantly, and we were suddenly covered in pixy dust, Bis hunching at their ultrasonic noise. "Let's go!" I said louder, and Trent opened the door to give them somewhere to go. "Before Ivy has a cow!"

My words were confident, but I was anything but as I gave Belle a last salute and we left. Motions slow, I tugged the door closed behind me, my fingers trailing on the heavy wood as I was struck by the feeling that I might never return to open it.

Bis took off from my shoulder and the pixies dove in and out of the open windows of the van. Trent hesitated on the top step for me. "You all right?"

My feet thumped down the stairs, the shock reverberating all the way up my spine. "Jittery," I said. I was getting the worst premonition. This wasn't going to go well. Something was going to go wrong. It was more than the scent of smoke and furtive figures traveling from backyard to backyard. I'd always had the demons to fall back on, and this time, I'd be in worse trouble if they found out. They wouldn't care if the world fell apart—and while I was busy trying to explain, it would.

"It will be done in a few hours," Trent said, the sound of plastic on metal a harsh rolling as he yanked the sliding door of the van open.

I reached for a handhold . . . and faltered, rocking back to the sidewalk. The van was full of vampires. Not just vampires, but vampires with guns, and chains, and chest wraps of grenades. Trent's expression was as shocked as mine. The normal seats had been removed, replaced with two big bench seats along both sides, making it look like a SWAT van—if SWAT vans had excited vampires comparing the pros and cons of their handguns in them. Okay, on second glance, I counted only six vampires including Ivy and Nina up front, but it looked like more. *Whoa. Was that a sledgehammer?*

My attention shot to Ivy at the wheel, dressed in black with her hair up in a bun that would be hard to grab. "Ah, Ivy?" I said, ignoring the eager hands held out to drag me in. None of them were David's. "This was supposed to be a small, intimate affair."

"It just kind of happened." Ivy waved the darting pixy kids out from between us. Bis was already perched on the headrest of the front passenger seat, his big claws making dents in the vinyl. Nina looked far too eager for my liking.

"Don't be mad at Ivy," Nina said as she twisted to look at me. She was sporting a black jumpsuit that looked as if it got its start in a skydiving class—apart from the grenades sewn onto it. "She told us about the I.S. trying to control the mystics. It's not just about them killing our undead anymore. No one should have that kind of power over another. It ends here."

I backed up into Trent. Six excited vampires. My neck was tingling. "Where's David?"

A muscular vampire I remembered as being one of Piscary's bouncers pushed everyone back and told them to shut up and make a hole for us. Scott, I think. "He thought it was too crowded and is running with his pack," Scott said, the lines about his eyes telling me he was worried about his second life as well. I couldn't tell them to go home and wait.

"Get in the van, Rache!" Jenks prompted from the rearview mirror, but I balked at the muscular bodies and the quick reactions that living a life on the edge of death engendered. It might sound good on paper, but sure as pixy dust, by sunrise there'd be yelling and screaming and blood in someone's mouth.

Trent's hand touched the small of my back, and my scar tingled. "They know the risks," he said, ushering me forward when Ivy yelled at us to hurry up. "It's their masters' lives in the balance." Accepting Scott's help, Trent stepped inside. Turning, he held out his hand for me. This was a bad idea, but I reached out and let them both pull me up and in.

"Finally!" Ivy muttered, accelerating before the door was even shut.

"Slide down!" someone said, and there were more happy complaints about squishing the ammo and "who took my detonators?"

Jenks's dust was a contented gold as he sat on my shoulder. "I like these people," he said as I took the seat right behind Ivy where I could see out the front.

I looked worriedly at Nina, remembering how she'd harbored Felix without anyone knowing. Sure, he had told the Free Vampires to take a hike, but he'd also agreed to give the mystics to the I.S. in exchange for her. Grimacing, I leaned forward to Ivy, lips barely moving. "Is she clean?"

Her grip on the wheel tightened, and I backed up. "Yes," she said, eyes flicking to Nina then back to the road. "Rachel, she wants to help. To prove that she can."

I eased back, knowing the importance of that. "Then she should help," I said to make Ivy's brow ease a little, but inside, I was worried.

Someone screamed in fun as we took a corner fast to avoid a roadblock, and I was jostled into Trent. He sat me back upright, and I tried to quell a growing feeling of disaster. Everyone was having so much *fun*. Through the window, I watched the Hollows pass in the darkness. Most of the streetlights were shot out, and an eerie red sheen reminiscent of the ever-after glowed on the abandoned cars and occasional burnt-out shop front. Dark shapes darted from shadow to shadow like surface demons. It didn't help that it felt as if I'd gotten into a van of Brimstone heads on their way to a concert. "Ivy, crack the windows," I asked, but I didn't think the side windows opened any farther. *This might be an issue.*

Scott quit fiddling with his ammo and leaned across the open space between us. His face held a wide smile, and he rocked from side to side with the van's motion, his feet solidly planted on the bare floorboards. "Unless you tell us different, we'll handle the outside. Keep your escape route open. Hold anyone you might flush out."

I nodded, thinking he looked too eager, but if he was outside, he couldn't get himself killed inside. My jaw was clenched, and I blinked when one mystic talking about lights at the mortuary suddenly became six or seven yammering at me. Trent surreptitiously took my elbow to keep me from looking too spaced out. It'd gone wrong already, and we hadn't even arrived yet.

"What is it?" he breathed in my ear, but the vampires in back heard and took an interest, their eyes dilating at the shiver that passed through me.

Damn vampire pheromones, I thought, grimacing. "I'm seeing lights at the mortuary."

"They moved the run up!" Jenks shouted. "Tink's a Disney whore!"

Ivy met my eyes through the rearview mirror. "I'm more concerned about the lights behind us."

"Behind us?" Scott said, and I jumped when a sledgehammer busted the back window right out of the frame.

"Let me!" Scott demanded, but Ivy took a corner too hard. Vampires sloshed and collided, and in the mess, Scott stuck his head out the window as the guy with the hammer busted out another window. It got windy fast, and I took a grateful breath of the fresher air as four vampires hung halfway out the van and shouted at the three beater cars behind us.

"Weres!" Scott said as he came back inside, the narrow bands of blue around his irises concerning me. "We got our rabbits."

Ivy tapped the brakes, and everyone else pulled their

heads back in. Beside me, Trent was looking ill and a little amazed. I knew how he felt. Ivy was careening about as if she sweated Dramamine, but I was beginning to feel sick. "All of you shut up and look civilized!" she shouted, brown eyes almost entirely black. "We've got a roadblock I can't find a way around."

Heads dropping, they all became very busy checking their ammo. Bis had gone almost invisible apart from the pixy kids on him. Trent smelled really good beside me. Hell, everyone smelled really good. Before us, a bright spot of light turned the road into silver and gray. I could see figures with weapons in hand—big ones.

"We'll take care of this," Jenks said as Ivy began to slow, and he darted out one of the busted windows, his kids a surprisingly silent wave behind him. Bis followed, calming my thoughts somewhat as he leaped for Nina's open front window and crawled out onto the roof. There was the scrape of his nails on the metal, and then nothing.

"Shut up!" Ivy snarled like a substitute school bus driver as she slowly drove into the spot of light and halted where they told her. I.S. officers with weapons barred the road. Trent ducked his head, pulling his knit hat down lower as one of them came to the window. *Oh, really.*

"Curfew is in effect since sundown," the officer said brusquely as about five other officers surrounded us, trying to look in the windows only to find smiling vampires in the way. "Get out of the vehicle. All of you. Leave the keys in the ignition."

"We're trying to fix this," Ivy said, her hands firmly on the wheel. "You mind letting us through?"

"Get out. Now!" the officer said, and Trent looked at his feet when the man flashed a light into the back. "You'll be released at sunrise. If it was up to me, you'd be incarcerated until your trial."

"For breaking curfew?" Nina said, and the light shone fully on her.

The man's eyes widened at the grenades. Dropping back,

he made a gesture, and I shivered as a magical field went up. I sucked in my breath as a hundred mystics from who knew where flooded me, bringing a hundred different viewpoints of the roadblock. We were surrounded. The three cars that had been following us were hanging back just out of sight, engines running—waiting for the right moment.

"I didn't think those fields were legal," Trent said, and I blinked fast, trying to keep from passing out. Too many mystics; it was like looking through the world through bug eyes. Nothing made sense when you looked at it from a hundred viewpoints. No wonder the Goddess was nuts.

Scott lifted his chin, far too eager. "You stay here, missy. We'll take care of this."

"No violence!" Trent shouted, and the I.S. officer swore when the light hit him and Trent was recognized.

Mystic vision rocked me, and with a herculean effort, I managed to cycle the multiple viewpoints to one. It was getting easier to figure this out, and I gripped the edge of the seat as an engine revved and I watched almost as if it were a dream as a brown Buick with an orange hood plowed through the blockade, Weres waving their bare asses at the officers in passing.

"Get them!" the man at Ivy's door shouted, distracted, and I felt the restraining field drop.

"It's David!" Jenks shrilled as he darted in the front window. "Go! Bis has my kids!"

Three vampires dove out of the van, howling as loud as the second car of Weres as Ivy sedately put the van in drive and crossed the blockade behind it. The cop screamed at us to stop, faltering as he suddenly found himself facing confident vampires, one with a sledge. Angry, he spun to the man running the restraining charm, but he was gone, chasing after the Weres. Bis came in with the sound of sliding leather and pixy chatter, and Ivy picked up speed. Someone shot at us, but it didn't matter, and we careened around a corner and were gone. Worst-case scenario gave us thirty seconds before they'd find a car and follow; best case had vampires with hammers distracting them long enough for us to slip away.

Okay, maybe this will work, I thought as we outdistanced the mystics we'd left behind. I was getting sporadic mystic reports of laughing Weres being handcuffed and slammed against the hoods of their cars. The Weres on four paws were uncatchable, racing through the streets as they tailed us. The vampires we'd left behind were happily demolishing the roadblock.

Scott, the only vamp left beside Nina, looked positively depressed. "They'll call for backup," Nina said as she unbuckled her belt and went to sit with him. "Maybe they'll try to stop us, and then you can try your gun out."

"Maybe," he moaned, and Ivy smirked as Nina put a comforting arm over Scott's big shoulders. "You're just trying to make me feel better."

Beside me, Trent shook his head, smiling.

"Rachel?" Ivy's voice was low as she fought with her instincts. "Is that David in that last car behind us?"

I'd already heard from a mystic that it was, but I leaned to look out the broken window, my hair streaming. The truck chasing us had three people in the front, and about six wolves in the bed. As I watched, another wolf loped out of the darkness and vaulted into the truck bed, nails scraping. "Can you slow down long enough to get him in here?"

Ivy put her flashers on, and once the truck blinked its lights to acknowledge it, she abruptly pulled over. My head swung as she hit the brakes hard, and Scott's muscles bunched as he yanked the door. There was a snap as he broke the safety feature, and the door slid open even before we came to a halt. I could hear sirens. My adrenaline pulsed, making Scott's eyes flash black. This was so not good.

"Go!" David shouted as he pitched in, duster furling as Scott caught and spun him around. Three Weres on paws and with waving tails lurched in after him, and Scott slammed the door.

Nina was at the back window, head hanging out. "They're

only a couple of streets away!" she shouted, and Ivy floored it. I scrambled for a handhold, and the sound of sliding nails scraped along the back of my skull as we took a corner hard. Trent gave my shoulder a squeeze, and when I nodded that I was okay, he let go.

Hat crushed in his hand, David knelt between the two front seats, holding on as we swerved and jostled. The street lighting was marginally better, and I shivered at the wind and come-and-go shadows on the faces around me, eager for action. Smiling widely, he turned, nodding first to me, then Trent.

"Sorry I'm late. Just keep going as you are and your way should be clear."

"Should be, but isn't," Ivy said with a sigh. "Hold on. We've got another one. Damn, it's human," she added, and Scott frowned as he looked at his weapon. "This is going to be tricky. Nina, can you ease up a little?"

"Yeah, I suppose," she grumbled, kicking her grenade stash deeper under the bench.

Peeved, David slipped into the front seat, busy with his cell phone. "Sorry. This was supposed to be clear. Circle around. Give me a block or two," he asked, and without question, Ivy turned the van. There were shouts from the blockade, and a spotlight made a puddling flow as it searched, but we were down a side street and gone.

"Yes, it's me," David said into his tiny phone. "General Lee needs another rabbit at the corner of Sleepy Hollow and ah . . . Ludville."

I held on tight as we took a corner. "General Lee?"

Trent leaned to me, the scent of cinnamon rising. "Yeee-hahhh," he drawled, and I got it.

"Oh my God! Look at that!" Ivy exclaimed, and the van rocked when everyone but Trent and I flung themselves halfway out a window. Ivy slowed as a wave of brown flowed out of the darkness and to the blockade. It was the Weres clearing a path.

"You can turn around now," David said, and Ivy checked,

then double-checked both sides of the road for stragglers before turning in front of a dark storefront. I tensed as an influx of mystics warned me of something, but before I could figure it out, a blossom of orange rose up over the surrounding low buildings and trees where the roadblock was. Had been, maybe. Two seconds later, the van rocked with the sound. Nina *ooooh*ed. It was the Fourth of July, and we had the fireworks to prove it.

David muttered "thanks" into his phone and closed it. "That should do it," he said confidently. But my good mood faltered when Ivy turned the corner.

Burning chunks of car and roadblock littered the road, happy Weres with singed fur and lolling tongues pacing back and forth or licking the faces of downed humans. *Please, may no one be hurt too badly.* There were too many people. They were getting hurt.

"Damn it!" Scott complained as Ivy carefully wove her way through the burning rubble. "We haven't done anything! We can do more than look pretty, you know."

His face split in a wide grin, David turned from the front seat. "Face it. We're better organized."

"Only because the masters are sleeping," Scott grumbled, depressed, as Nina put an arm over his shoulder and tried to convince him they would see some action soon.

Which was exactly what I was afraid of. But I breathed easier as a few people began to stir, one gripping the ruff of a Were for balance as he slowly picked himself up off the pavement. Either he didn't know the Weres had caused the explosion or he thought he was a friendly dog.

Finally Ivy got through the worse of it and began to pick up speed. "What are you smiling about?" I said unhappily to Trent, and he leaned closer, grabbing my shoulder so we wouldn't bump heads as we jolted along.

"I think it's amazing that when your world collapses, you have people falling over themselves to help you, and when mine collapses, I have people fighting among themselves to get the scraps." Nodding, he looked at David, his phone to his ear as he coordinated something with Ivy. "You've done something right, Rachel, sacrificing for others the way you do."

"They're going to get hurt," I said glumly, and he lifted a shoulder as if to agree.

"Ah, guys?" Ivy said, the pace finally slowing as we found a street that wasn't blocked off. "We might have a problem."

"All right!" Scott said enthusiastically, but I didn't think Scott was going to get to bust any heads as I looked out the front window. It was the mortuary, lit up under mobile spotlights and noisy generators. FIB and I.S. cars were parked haphazardly on the street, the lawn, the lawn across the street . . . everywhere. Lines had been strung, and people dashed around looking ineffective. There were a couple of ambulances, but they weren't busy.

They had moved on them early, as Jenks had guessed. Either Edden had been lied to about the original timing, or things had changed and had required immediate action. Looking at the red clouds reflecting the light, I figured it was the latter.

"Son of a bitch!" Jenks swore, and Nina got a scared look on her face. It was over. They had them and it was over.

"Keep driving past," Trent said as he moved forward to crouch behind David. The alpha Were was again on the phone, looking for answers. "We don't know what happened yet. They might still be in there."

But I could tell they weren't. I was getting sporadic, questionable intel from the mystics, and as soon as they came in, I sent them back out for more. There'd been a fight. Lots of noise. The mystics tended to focus on the oddest things, and I was reduced to looking at the edges of their awareness to learn anything.

"I'll check it out," Jenks said as he hovered before me. His dust made me shiver, and a mystic I'd never had in me before played in it. Jenks gave me a worried look as he took in my aura. "Don't ditch me, Ivy," he added, then darted out the window, shouting for Bis.

The gargoyle sailed eagerly after him, wings billowing the cloud of dust Jenks's kids had made chasing after their dad. Scott and Nina clustered at the windows to look back at the crime scene. No one had even noticed us in the chaos.

Landon and Ayer were long gone. The air felt flat, and my skin wasn't tingling. But suddenly mystics exploded over my skin and into my mind—unfamiliar mystics pulled to me by the echo of my aura and led by an enthusiastic few. My breath slipped from me in a whimper, and I clutched the seat in vertigo as images of battle, of blood, of sudden freedom made my stomach turn. Concepts flashed past that I couldn't comprehend, but the mystics were afraid.

Death. Singular thoughts ended, echoed in me as mystics familiar with my way of thinking instructed the new ones on how to converse in this new, smaller world my mind made for them. And slowly it began to make sense where once there was only chaos.

"Is she okay?" Scott asked Trent, and I realized he was holding me upright.

"Give me a second," I breathed as, like smoke over a field, the new mystics took on the wisdom of the old and the world stopped spinning. "Better," I said, voice stronger as my eyes suddenly focused. Things shifted, and the confusion began to work for instead of against me. Images flickered through me, like watching a movie in five-second snippets, all out of order. "They're gone," I said, figuring that much out. "Landon and Ayer left before the I.S. got here. They took the captive mystics with them. A few escaped when they moved them to battery backup. They're . . . confused. Confusing."

Or at least, they had been, and with the riveting beauty of dominoes falling, the multiple images fell into place and made sense. My head came up, and every vampire's eyes went black as my fear flashed into existence. I got it. I finally understood, and it scared the crap out of me.

"They've divided them up and are distributing them across the United States." No one said anything, and I added, "It's happening! They're dispersing the captive mystics.

They're going to use them to kill all the undead. They have enough to do what they did in Cincinnati everywhere!"

"Mother pus bucket . . ." Trent whispered, shocking me as he used one of Al's favorite curses. It seemed appropriate. Ivy abruptly pulled over, and David lurched, catching himself with one hand.

"Everyone stay in the van!" Ivy shouted as she grabbed her phone. We were out of sight of the mortuary, but not that far away that I couldn't jog back in like . . . two minutes.

Immediately three Weres launched themselves out a broken window, scrambling with the sound of claws in the dark to do just that. "I've already sent someone for information," David said, and I breathed easier in the extra room.

"I told you, they're gone." I dropped my head into my hands as I imagined the chaos. Cincinnati was used to weird things happening—thanks to me—but this unrest in Chicago, New Orleans, or even San Diego was enough to give me nightmares. *Please, God. Not San Francisco.*

Ivy frowned, phone to her ear. "Yeah?" she said, angry. "And just when were you going to tell us? What happened? And don't tell me you don't know, because I just saw you."

"They're gone," David said, hand over his phone.

"I know they're gone!" I shouted. "I just saw it in 3-D in my brain! They took off in a black car, a brown Jeep, and an El Camino with a broken taillight going south! I think they're headed for the train station in Maysville. From there, they can fan out everywhere." We had to do something. If the mystics got out of Cincinnati, I'd never survive the lawsuits.

"Maysville?" David muttered. "There's nothing in Maysville."

"There's a train depot." Trent's brow was furrowed, gaze distant. "The trains don't usually stop there, but since the Cincinnati depot is under quarantine, they've adjusted the schedule." His eyes met mine. "They're taking them out of Cincinnati by train."

My gut hurt. Landon and Ayer had fought among themselves. The survivors took the mystics and left. "Where does the Maysville line go?"

Trent's lips pressed tightly and he looked at his watch. "Chicago."

Better and better.

Ivy listened to her cell phone, lips parting. "Oh." She ended the call. "Scott, will you get the door?"

The rolling sound of the door echoed, and I flinched when a bunch of mystics pulled from me with a stretchy feeling to play in the sound wave. The door slid open to show Edden standing in the dark in a bulletproof vest with an ACG breaker under it. He was tucking his own phone away, and his cross expression melted into concern upon seeing the three vampires, David, Trent, and myself. Taking his FIB hat off, he threw it into the ditch.

"Get in," Ivy said tartly, but Edden was still looking us over, eyes widening when Trent gave him a businesslike nod.

David gestured impatiently. "In or out!" he exclaimed, looking at his watch. "Rachel says they're trying to catch the Maysville train."

"Maysville?" Edden echoed as he scrambled in, then his confusion vanished. "That's right. It stops there now."

Ivy was already putting the van into drive as Scott slammed the door shut. Sitting down, the squat man's eyes lit up at Nina's arsenal; clearly he wanted to play with the grenades. Jenks's kids arrowed in as we accelerated back onto the road, but no Jenks or Bis. One pixy had a walnut, and I watched him wedge it between the roof and a visor.

I hung my head as the images of cars on the expressway suddenly began to make sense, blinking when Edden touched my knee. "Rachel, are you okay? You look like crap."

"I feel like crap." I took a deep breath and sat up. "I'm fine. Just channeling the home world a little too much."

Trent was on the phone, one finger in his ear to block out the noise. If anyone knew the train schedule, it would be

Trent. He owned most of the lines that ran through Cincinnati.

"Where am I going?" Ivy called out as we picked up speed.

"North," Trent said as he closed his phone. "They're already on the train. It will pass through Cincinnati in about fifteen minutes, and from there they hit Chicago, but I doubt that's their final destination."

"But where am I going?" she asked again, stress showing in her voice, and he got to his feet, balance shifting as he made his way up to the front. He gave David a look, and the man eased out of the front seat to take the open spot beside me.

"This is kind of unusual for you, Rachel. A group thing?" Edden said as he gave a respectful nod to Scott across from him. The vampire was clearly uneasy with the FIB captain joining our joyride, the man years older and tons more sedentary than everyone else in the van.

"Tell me about it," I grumped. Everyone wanted to help. Damn it, I felt like Frodo being chaperoned to Mordor, and like Frodo, I was beginning to wonder why I couldn't have just taken the eagles and flown out there by myself and saved everyone a lot of grief. But I suppose everyone wanted to help save the world.

"What happened?" David asked, open phone in hand. "My sources are coming up empty."

Edden brought his gaze back from Nina's weaponry. "The intel was wrong. We moved early and found the place empty."

The intel was wrong? Maybe the I.S. was lying to Edden as well and had thrown their own private party before inviting him. "That's not what I saw," I said, remembering what the mystics had shown me. "There was a fight. At least three singulars, I mean people, died."

Edden hesitated, feet spread wide to balance himself as we swayed and leaned. "Then they cleaned up after themselves, because it looks clean." His mustache bunched. "Too clean," Edden muttered, coming to the same conclusion. "Seems as if Landon and Ayer had a difference in opinion."

In a rush of wings, Jenks flew in with Bis, the pixy clearly drafting off Bis, the stronger flier. "Thanks for waiting for us, blood bag," he snarled, panting as he landed on the rear-view mirror. "We got everyone?" he asked, and a chorus of tiny, high-pitched yes's came back.

David closed his phone with a snap. Swerving, we tore through an intersection, the traffic lights black and the road empty. "It wasn't my people," David said as he tucked it away. "But I do have reports of a, and I quote, 'weird feel-ing' about sunset."

A chiming of voices in me said that was the singulars ending their incongruent thoughts, but before I could say anything, Ivy exploded with a sharp, "Are you insane?"

I jerked until I realized she was talking to Trent, still in the front seat. "And just how do you propose to get on the train?" she asked. "Those things go almost eighty miles an hour."

"Trust me." Trent leaned back, clearly miffed she was questioning him. "Get us on Rail Drive, and it will happen."

Ivy sighed and made a sharp turn.

"You know, maybe I'm not understanding what the mys-tics are trying to tell me," I said as I caught my balance in the wildly shifting van.

But Jenks was shaking his head, a blue-edged dust slip-ping from him as he hovered in the middle of the van. "No, you're right," he said. "We got the intel, Bis and me and my kids. According to the pixies across the street, a bunch of elves put three dead people in the back of the El Camino and headed south. There weren't any I.S. vehicles around at the time. Something spooked them, and they ran."

I looked sorrowfully at Trent, watching his expression become grim. Landon had cut the Free Vampires loose and taken the mystics for himself. His people were behaving badly, and there was nothing Trent could do to stop them except with muscle and magic.

"They went to the train station," Scott said, bracing himself when Ivy took a sharp turn.

"Either Landon or Ayer or both have been scooping mystics up like cotton candy on a stick ever since you got the Goddess riled up," Jenks said, a still spot of wings and dust in the careening van. "They took a dozen little boxes, and if they get to Chicago, they'll be coast to coast in a matter of days."

"Call ahead. Stop them," Scott said, and Edden nodded, surprising the young vampire.

Trent, though, shook his head. "They would know we're onto them and will disappear. We either stop them on the track where we have a chance of catching them, or nothing."

I remembered how Trent's father and mother had escaped the West Coast by hopping trains in a plague-torn United States, making it all the way to Cincinnati during the Turn. He was right. We had to catch them unawares or they'd be gone cross-country.

"If we can't head them off, we'll have only a day to find each individual cell before the vampires start to sleep," Jenks said, the van suddenly silent but for Ivy pushing the old engine into a faster pace. "Their new agenda is to shut the vampires down, coast to coast." His dust shifted to a dull orange as he looked at Trent as if he could do something. "And when that's done, there's nothing to stop them from turning their eyes on the Weres and witches."

Damn it all to the Turn and back. Between the elves' quest for superiority and the Free Vampires' holy mission, they were going to throw all of us back in the pre-Turn dark ages.

"That's not going to happen," Edden said, his thick hands opening from tight fists, and Scott looked at him as if he'd never seen a human before. "The I.S. in Chicago can catch them."

Ivy met his eyes through the rearview mirror. "I'm not trusting anything to those yahoos," she said, and Trent glumly nodded. "We have to stop that train."

"Blow it up," Scott said. "I know a guy in the Hollows—"

"We are not blowing it up," Trent interrupted, and I watched, intrigued when he stared Scott down. David met my gaze knowingly as if to say, *See?*

"There are people on it," Trent said, almost as if embarrassed.

"A hundred die to save millions," Scott protested, and David shook his head in warning.

"No." Trent sat sideways to see everyone as we raced along. "A large slice of the world's species are represented here with all our talents and ingenuity. If we can't stop a train without killing innocents, then we don't deserve the freedom we have." He hesitated. "No one gets a phone call in the morning that changes their life," he said softly. "Not if I can help it."

The van went silent, and I couldn't help but wonder how many of those calls he'd gotten himself. Two at least, from when his parents died. Another when he found out he was a father and would have to fight for his child. I was sure there was more. You can't keep your calm when all around you are losing theirs if you don't know what's truly real and what doesn't matter.

"That they're moving is a good thing," Trent said, his voice holding an unexpected confidence. "Rachel's mystic intel says the containment systems are on battery. We can procure them, move them safely to the Loveland line, and release them in an orderly, safe fashion." His gaze never went to me, but I knew his relief was enormous. "Ivy, did you bring your laptop? I need to pull up a map. If I remember right, there's a paved bike path that runs parallel to the line outside of Cincinnati. The timing might be perfect for a transfer."

Transfer? "It's under the seat," she said, but Bis had already dropped down to it, everyone watching as the gargoyle flipped it open and settled it on his crossed legs.

"How do we get across the river?" Nina asked, her mouth dropping open when Bis casually typed in Ivy's password.

"Hey!" Ivy cried out, cheeks red as she jerked her gaze from the road to him, and back again. "You! You're the one leaving crumbs on my keyboard!"

"Sorry," he said, blushing deep black as Jenks snickered. "Is this it?"

Trent slipped out of the front seat to sit where he could see the screen. David and Edden were already there, and the light from it lit the four of them in an unreal glow. "Good," Trent said, eyes pinched. "Ivy, stay the way you're going. The wheel span on this vehicle is adequate to run across the trestle. Once on the track, we can drive across the river, then get on the bike path, and—"

"At eighty miles an hour!" David protested as he dropped back, eyes wide.

"Dude," Jenks said with a chuckle. "I've got wings, and I still think that's a dumb idea."

"And pace them until we can get a team across the gap," Trent finished. "If we're lucky, we can get a call to the engine and they'll stop the train for us once we're there to take control of the situation. Edden, do you have a clean line to the FIB? I don't want a hint of this leaked to the press or the I.S. until the train is stopped and they're contained."

"I've got Rose's cell. That woman can do anything," Edden said as he peered under his glasses at his glowing cell.

It sounded good, but the reality was a little more dicey. Ivy clenched her jaw, eyes fixed to the road. Around me, everyone became quiet as they estimated their chances, comparing their strengths and reflexes to the probable fallout if they failed to even try. We were talking about jumping to a train under full steam, but everyone's culture, not to mention every vampire's second life, was in the balance.

I was getting a bad feeling. Bis and Jenks had wings. No one else did. Trent slowly closed the laptop and slid it back under the seat. "This is great!" I said sarcastically, dropping my head into my hands and swaying with the van's motion. "I like this plan! I'm excited."

"Let me get my dad," Bis said, and before I could say anything, he'd launched himself out the back broken window. I watched his dark shape vanish into the wider blackness, thinking that this much help was going to get all of us killed.

Twenty-Five

We were going just over fifty miles per hour according to the van's speedometer, but with the sliding door open and the narrowness of the paved bike path we were careening down, it felt like more. Jenks was tangled somewhere in my hair, hiding from the wind ripping through the van and out the broken windows. Forty feet away, the train raced. Watching it, I felt as if it were the industrial revolution given life, a monster of power, oblivious as it raced through the darkness in one direction and its own destruction, powered by the death of a million plants and animals a million years ago.

But it *was* going fifty, not the usual eighty. The engine had indeed been hijacked, but the engineer was backing off on the speed, probably unaware that we were here but trying to alert the next station there was trouble. Bis's dad, Etude, was ferrying us across. The adult gargoyle was about the size of a small elephant, but as light as a pony and variable as a kite. He'd helped me before when his son had been in danger, and I still felt guilty about the scars he now had on his pebbly gray skin. Scott had wanted to jump, but the only good handholds were the windows, and we were trying to stay unnoticed, hence our position at the back of the train.

It still felt too chancy for me, and I nervously tried to

explain "a dark smear on a white wall" to the mystics. They knew their kin were close, which made them hard to hold on to, but if they left me now, they'd be pulled away and lost until they could catch up.

The drive out here had gone fast, especially when Nina took the wheel at the trestle. I'd thought it a bad move, but Nina was a better driver than Ivy, if that could be believed, her squeal of delight at the first tricky part filling the van and making Scott all but rip the seats out in his effort not to jump her jugular. Edden just hung his head, muttering about grounding his son for doing the same thing fifteen years ago. The I.S. vampires manning the tracks to keep people off them had let us through just to see if we could do it. The thousand bucks Trent had dropped into their hats at both ends had helped, too, I'm sure.

My grip on the edge of the door tightened, and I looked at Trent past the strands of my hair plastered to my face from the wind. His expression was grim as Scott made a crouched landing on the roof of the last car. Etude's black wings shifted and he fell back out of sight. It would take him a moment to catch up.

Trent touched his pocket and turned to me. "Your turn."

"Me?" I stammered, pulling the hair out of my mouth as Etude landed on the roof of the van with a light thump. "Ivy can go next."

"We have only five miles of road," he said, pushing me forward as Etude looked over the edge at us and extended a clawed foot for me to sort of . . . step into. Past it, the ground raced, grass and rocks a blur. My mind was telling me his foot was safer than a harness, but I'd seen what happened when the huge gargoyle let go of the van.

"Come on, Rache!" Jenks prodded, pulling the hair behind my ear. "Scott did it."

Scott has a second life to look forward to, I thought, and the mystics in me buzzed about it, wondering how that made a difference. *It doesn't,* I told them, scared as I glanced through the front window to be sure there was no turn coming, and then . . . stepped into Etude's grip.

"You sure you know what you're doing?" I shouted up at Etude's craggy face, and Bis, his son, went spinning by, enjoying the wind.

The older gargoyle smiled. His thick grip on my waist shifted, the thick pads pressing almost painfully as he gave me a jiggle until my back rested against his leg. "Easy as cake!" he shouted, and with that being my single warning, he spread his wings. The wind snapped them open, and I gasped, my hands clenching the thick claw encircling me as we were yanked into almost a standstill.

"Ow . . ." I breathed. My lower chest hurt, but we weren't as far back as I had feared. Etude tucked me under him, his huge wings beating as he closed the gap. Ahead in the moonlight, the track ran straight into oblivion, but the bike path veered away. *Ivy. Trent,* I thought. There wasn't enough time.

"I'll get you as close as I can. Scott will catch you," Etude said, surprising me when he lowered his great head to break the wind. "Ready?"

Oh God . . . I thought, then nodded. Letting go of his gnarled foot was the hardest thing I'd ever done. Just a few feet below me, the train rocked side to side. Scott reached up to touch my feet, then my knees, and finally my waist just under Etude's claw.

"What happens when you let go?" I shouted.

"Let go?" Etude called.

"Wait!" But it was too late, and Scott's grip on me tightened as Etude's fell away. Our balance was off. I clutched at the vampire, my chest hitting his face as he went down on a knee.

"Got you," he said, voice muffled as the wind whipped over us and the train rocked.

I hadn't known you could be scared and embarrassed at the same time, and as the roof of the car hit my knees, I forced myself to let go of his shirt. "Sorry."

"Not at all," he said, grinning.

I was just in time to see Trent ripped away from the van, his exclamation muffled by wind and the sudden distance. Pulling the hair from my eyes, I looked ahead at the ribbon of gray road. Ivy stood at the door, her expression clear in the dim light, David and Edden beside her. There wasn't enough time left for her to make it, much less the two men. Etude might not be able to catch up once the van veered off. Ivy knew it as well as I.

"Catch me!" she shouted through her cupped hands, then ducked inside.

"Is she nuts?" Jenks shrilled in my ear, and Scott became three shades lighter.

The van accelerated, and Ivy reappeared at the door, looking back at us. "Ivy, no!" I yelled. "Etude can do it!"

But she was climbing onto the roof as David and Edden protested, the wind ripping her topknot to a long streamer of black. My heart pounded. Trent hadn't caught up yet, and I wedged my foot under a handhold, slowly standing up against the wind. Scott blocked a tiny slice of the wind, and I looked past him. The bike path was going to turn. She wasn't going to make it.

Lips set, Ivy inched to the front of the van, turned, and ran for the back.

"Hold on, Jenks!" I screamed, watching, then blinked as a layer of mystics seem to peel off my awareness, swirling thickly within the space of my aura as Ivy propelled herself right off the end of the van, feet still going as she leaped into space.

"Ivy!" I shouted, leaning into the wind, grasping. She was going to make it. She was going to make it! *She had to.*

"Got you!" Scott exclaimed as she fell into us. We dropped in a sliding tangle. My ankle twinged, and I gasped as my foothold caught and pain stabbed through it. The force of the wind vanished, but still it roared. My hands burned with wild magic. *Don't let go. Don't let go!* Eyes shut, I clenched her arm. We slowly slipped, and then . . . settled. Ivy was safe.

She just had to jump, I thought sourly, then thanked the mystics. I wasn't sure what they'd done, but I knew they'd been there. "Jenks, you okay?" I called out, hearing his swearing and knowing he was fine. I squinted up to find Etude blocking the wind. Bis was on his dad's shoulder, his tail wrapped around his dad's neck and literally white with fear. Trent was sandwiched facedown between Etude's massive foot and the top of the car. Etude's other foot was halfway through the outer skin of the roof, and his tail was wrapped around Scott's leg to keep him from sliding off. Ivy was in the vampire's arms. Slowly I let go of her wrist, and she looked up, thin bands of brown around her irises. Crap on toast, Nina was going to get her killed with all this risk taking. She never would've jumped otherwise. Not my careful, precise Ivy.

Shaken, I looked behind us. The road was gone. "You idiot!" I shouted as I untangled myself and sat up. "You could have been killed! Why didn't you wait for Etude!"

Ivy smiled at me over Scott's shoulder as she gave him a thankful hug. "He needs to save his strength," she said, hair streaming in the wind. "Is Jenks okay?"

"I'm fine!" he yelled, but I don't think she heard him, and I nodded.

Etude's foot lifted suddenly when Trent wiggled, still facedown on the roof of the car. Almost dancing, the big gargoyle shifted back. The man looked shaken but okay, and he grimaced as he felt his midsection carefully as he sat up. Turning to the road, his anger eased when he saw it was gone. *Thank you, Nina.*

"I don't think I'll fit in the car," Etude said, taking Bis from his shoulder and setting him on the rocking roof. "Bis, let me know if you need me." His smile widened until his black teeth showed. "My world breaker."

Bis flushed a pleased black, but I was uneasy as I looked

at them: Ivy, Bis, Trent, Scott, and Jenks tangled in my hair. If any of them died or hurt themselves, I'd never let it go. "Let's move!" I shouted, and Scott nodded. Staying low and never entirely letting go of the roof, he inched his way to the connecting bridge. It was covered to facilitate moving from car to car when necessary, and the moon glinted on the edge of steel as he cut a flap in the thick plastic and gestured us forward.

Are they here? mystics asked as they compared the real force of the wind to the memory of it of long ago. Apparently the air had thickened since they last had to plow through it with a solid body in tow.

Why don't you go find out? I directed, suggesting that they go through the calmer air within the train so they didn't risk being ripped away. A shudder raked through my soul as almost half of them streamed from me, some going through the hole Ivy was now snaking down, some through the skin of the train itself, some going through the soles of my feet. The mystics content to stay with me seemed to roll through my aura and settle in like a cat enjoys the sun. Promises to return eddied about me with the soft, binding force of a plant tendril, unexpected and worrisome.

Return to me, or their confederates still lodged in my soul? I wondered, then almost panicked when a twining of voices said it was the same thing. *You are not mine!* I shouted, trying to make my one voice louder than theirs combined. *You are going back to the Goddess! That's the entire point to this. We find the ones they stole, and you all go back!*

But they didn't seem to care, which scared the crap out of me. What if they didn't want to go back? I couldn't live my life as a mystic magnet.

"Rachel!" Trent shouted, and I blinked, looking down at his pale face and realizing that it was just Scott, Etude, and me up here. "Let's go!"

He held out a hand, and I felt his strength as I slipped mine into it. I tried to pay attention, but a growing negativity swelled in me. It was the returning mystics with news of what lay below. The captives were not in the last car, nor in the hold below it.

Worried, I carefully maneuvered myself into the tight space between the rocking cars. The returning mystics were getting uncomfortably better at sorting themselves as they arrived, binding their myriad thoughts into one in such a way that I could understand them. Sure, it was unclear at first, with multiple perspectives making it a nauseating slurry of confusion, but by the time I'd gotten myself out of the wind, enough had returned to bring it into focus. They were adapting to me on an exponential curve, and whereas yesterday I'd been struggling to keep them from destroying my friends, now I could send them on a task and have them work together to find an answer—and it was scaring the hell out of me.

My feet hit the shifting surface as the returning mystics brought back with them a wave of free mystics, escapees that had lingered close to the captive splinter. They soaked into me, pulled by their kin and attracted to my aura. In a cascading wave, their confusion at the unfamiliar thought patterns and concepts curled like smoke and vanished. Where understanding and adjustment had once taken days, now it took seconds.

I had to get them back to her, and fast.

Jenks tugged at my hair, swearing at Tink, the stars, and the moon all in one breath as he fought with the snarls. I felt him give up and cut his way free, his angry red dust spilling down my front with the strands of my hair. Ivy was between me and the first car, and Trent beside me. The car behind us was mostly empty from a quick look through the milky glass. I was getting a better image from the mystics, dropping off their intel and leaving for more, their disappointment growing at their missing kin.

Trent leaned close to me in the small space, the scent of cinnamon and wine mixing with iron and oil. "Are you okay?" he asked as we rocked, and I nodded as I held his arm for balance.

"Neither Landon or Ayer are in the last car," I said, then went over the memory again, concentrating on the faces since the mystics weren't as keen on them. "This second car doesn't look good either, but they haven't searched it as diligently."

Trent's eyes widened, and Jenks—now on Trent's shoulder—looked up from cleaning his sword. "Ah, you got that from the mystics?" Jenks asked, and I nodded, grimacing when I realized the mystics had probably done more in fifteen seconds than he could've with his first run through the train.

Realizing it, too, Trent looked over my shoulder at Ivy, something unsaid passing between them before he looked up at Scott. The vampire was still lying on the roof since there wasn't much room between the cars. "Okay. We'll assume they're forward," Trent said resolutely. "Scott, you and Etude have our back door."

"Check," he said as he pulled back, and I heard the ripping of duct tape over the wind.

A surge of adrenaline went through me. People. There were too many people. "Maybe we should disconnect the cars as we go through them."

Trent was working the door, punching in a few codes to try to get it to open. "You can't do that when the train is moving like this." Giving up, he gestured for Jenks to figure it out. "At least, you can't do it more than once," he said, smiling.

Nothing, nothing, the mystics lamented, and then a single flash of fear and hatred—and recognition.

Where? I thought, almost losing my balance as a massive amount of them went to find out. Jenks's brilliant flash of dust heralded the clicking of the lock disengaging. "First class," I said, vision wavering as the first mystics began to return. Their hatred was like quicksilver, elusive as a sunbeam. "I think they're in the first-class cab." It was a short train with only three cars.

"I'll go see," Jenks said, tugging at the door. "No offense, Rache."

"None taken."

Eyes upward, Ivy reached for the torn panel. "Scott! Hold up!"

"You're not coming?" I said to Ivy as Jenks vaulted through the crack in the door and was gone.

Already up a step, she turned. "You handle it," she said, expression grim. "I want to see what's going on in the engine. Etude can come with me. Scott has the back."

"Ivy," I protested as the wind scooped in and she levered herself out. I could find out what was going on in the engine, but as she poked her head back in, I decided she wasn't doing intel, she was busting heads. "See you when I see you," I said, reaching up, and for an instant, our fingers touched.

The luck of the Goddess goes with you, I thought, my fingertips tingling as mystics left me. They could bring me back visions if she got in trouble.

Trent cleared his throat, and I flushed. "What . . ." I muttered. "I've got enough of 'em. There's plenty left." Jenks was at the foggy window, waiting, and I reached past Trent again for the door. "You coming or not?"

"I'm coming," he said, but his smile was tinged with worry.

No one looked up as we entered. You weren't supposed to move between cars while you were under way, but the attendants did, and I ran a hand over my hair, trying to smooth it. Thief black was not attendant stripes, but a disguise charm was out. The less magic I did, the more stable the mystics were. Only when we clustered at the lock at the opposite side of the car did anyone take notice.

"The back is out of peanuts," Trent said, and the woman in the front row glared at him for his audacity. Still, no one raised a finger to stop us as Jenks tinkered with the panel until we got the green light.

We slipped into the small pass-through. First class, dead

ahead. "Leave it unlocked?" Trent asked, and I nodded. I didn't think anyone would investigate, and this way, we'd have a place to retreat.

"Well, Rache?" Jenks said as he stood on the keypad and wedged his sword behind a button just so. "What does your crystal ball say?"

I looked through the door. "There they are. Look for yourself."

It was getting harder to focus through the anger the mystics were filling me with. Overwhelmed, I leaned against the rocking train and waved Trent off. He hesitated, and at Jenks's whistle, he turned to the window. I already knew what they'd find.

Up at the front, six men were celebrating loudly and keeping the first-class attendant busy. The woman was harried, and the few other first-class passengers looked miffed, forced to listen to their noise as they sat as far back from them as they could comfortably get without being squished together in an obvious pile. I didn't see Ayer. Landon was drinking, but even through the mystics I could tell that he wasn't drunk. Little black boxes under their seats held an uncountable misery that was beginning to impinge on me. Twelve boxes, for twelve cities. They could impact eighty percent of the country's population within three days—eighty percent of the United States floundering as Cincy now was, the tenuous balance between Inderland and human crumbling as the undead starved and died.

Trent cracked the door for Jenks, returning from his own intel.

"They stink like gunpowder and wild magic," he said, wings invisible with motion though he stood on Trent's palm. "Some have been wounded but treated with first aid. I didn't see Ayer, and these guys aren't vampires." He looked at Trent. "They're all elves. Rache, we can't let them take those five people hostage."

This had been Landon's plan all along. He had used the Free Vampires, fully intending on making them the scapegoat. He'd tricked Bancroft into talking to the insane splinter to remove his voice and clear his path. He was going to use wild magic to destroy the vampire society from the inside out, eliminating an entire species to further his own. And he'd used me to take Trent's voice from the enclave, the only one who would have stood up to say no.

No wonder the demons didn't like them.

My stomach hurt, and I gave Trent's hand a squeeze. He looked ticked, a hard anger slowly fanning to life in his eyes. I thought of Ivy and Etude up at the engine. The sporadic messages from there gave me nothing, and the rocking pace of the train hadn't eased at all. Feeling overfull and slightly out of control, I looked at Trent. "You get them out. People like you."

Trent took a breath, hesitated, then pulled the shade on the window behind me. "They've got glamour glasses and Landon knows what I look like," he said, but then his brow eased. "Jenks, slick your hair back. You're the newest member of the line's elite security team."

"I am?"

The pixy rose up, and Trent rummaged in his belt pack until he found a pen and a fifty. It was probably the smallest bill he had. "You are." Trent slapped it on the rocking wall and began to write on it. "You're the line's latest endeavor to police the trains during this time of crisis, so secret even the attendants weren't told."

"I am!" Hands on his hips, Jenks hovered a few inches from the bill.

"Give this to the attendant. She can get them moving to the back, and we can get them into the next car." Tucking the pen away, Trent folded the bill up. He held it out to Jenks, then hesitated. "No swearing. Public servants don't swear."

"Damn right they don't."

Again we cracked the door, and I saw a little light go red at the attendant's station. Concerned, she tapped the panel, satisfied when it went out when the door shut behind him. I never saw Jenks make his way to the front, but I did see a glitter of dust in her work space and the woman start. She vanished behind a half-pulled curtain. Her face was white when she peeked out. Trent waved, and she ducked back.

"She's not going for it," he said, and I put a hand on his arm, stopping him.

"Wait," I said, and together we peered through the foggy plastic as the woman went from shock to fear and finally to bravery as she pulled her shoulders up and tugged her apron straight. Jenks was on her shoulder. Her hands shook as she prepared a tray of ice water, but her steps were even as she made her way to the back, pausing briefly to tell first one, then another to leave everything and make their way to the back and out of the car.

"See?" I said, and Trent leaned into me, shocking me with the scent of green and growing things among the harsh oil and diesel we rocked within. "She's got shelf loads of courage."

"Maybe," he said as he opened the door for the first woman and her preteen son. "But she's moving them out too fast."

My heart pounded, and I looked over the heads of the fleeing people to see their departure had been noted. Suddenly the pass-through was full as Trent grabbed the first and pulled her in. The woman's fear was heady, and I all but shoved her and her son through the passage. The businessman was fast behind her, but the fortysomething geek who wouldn't leave his laptop behind and was busy wrapping cords wasn't going to make it.

"Kalamack!" Landon shouted, pointing at us with a half glass of something clear and potent as he stood. "We finish this now!"

"Go! Go! Go!" I shouted, horrified when they dropped their glasses and reached under their seats.

"Too fast," Trent muttered, then ran into the car, shoving past the geeky guy to stand between him and the elves. My knees buckled as he pulled on a ley line and the mystics flashed to full alertness.

"Get. Out!" I said, breathless as I shoved the businessman to safety, then jerked when I felt a circle go up. "Trent!" I shouted, diving into the car and into the aisle as a spate of bullets popped and zinged. Mystics poured into me, and I clenched into a ball, telling them I didn't need to know what it looked like from the ceiling.

Breathless, I looked up in the sudden quiet. Damn, he had been practicing, because that was not a small circle Trent was in. The computer guy was safe with him, and I scooted out of the way when Trent dropped his circle and shoved him down the aisle.

Malcontent lay under the seats in little black boxes. I could feel the trapped mystics, angry and frustrated as they circled endlessly, never growing or becoming. Wild magic glowed from them, making me dizzy. Jenks had left the attendant, standing with Trent to dart back and forth to slash fingers and blind eyes. Trent shielded him best he could, his thrown spells raking through my soul with the ripping feel of wild magic.

Way at the front, the attendant huddled. She'd never make it through without becoming a hostage. I looked behind me as the computer guy vanished into the pass-through. They were still vulnerable. I had to break the linkage. Ivy was up at the engine with Etude, but we'd lose Scott.

"Sorry, Scott," I whispered as I crawled to the door. The cars swayed, and I stood in the pass-through, flinging an access panel up. It looked just like the movies, but there was no way I could move it without using magic.

Taking a deep breath, I grabbed a handhold and tapped the line. Ley line energy poured in, the scintillating core of wild magic now clear and obvious to me. I'd been blind before, but with the mystics reflecting and exalting in it, strength spiraled through me, lifting the mystics like a heated updraft. They swirled, adding their own force until I could hardly breathe.

"Hold it, hold it . . ." I panted, trying to focus. I couldn't think, and panic trickled through me until I found the spell

I wanted. *"Apredee!"* I shouted, then yelped when it burst from me in a pained pulse.

Every free mystic in a hundred-foot radius arrowed to me. I staggered, my grip on the handhold going slack as they hummed in the spaces inside me, looking for danger, for something to attack. I cowered, berated by the most complex mystics that it wouldn't have hurt if I hadn't tried to harness my wishes with a clunky spell, but just willed it to happen. Dizzy, I watched the fabric and steel cover begin to tear as the cars separated. The wind roared in, and I fell back to the tiny platform. A cluster of faces watched me from the retreating car. The first-class door had shut behind me. I didn't think I could open it quite yet.

There is nothing to attack! I demanded, but their combined voices wouldn't listen, and I couldn't breathe. There was danger, or I wouldn't have called. *Go away!*

The wind roared, becoming the sound of blood in my ears. The track was a mind-numbing blur, mesmerizing, and I felt my grip falter. It would be so easy to just . . . let go.

"Rachel!"

A sharp pain pinched my arm. A quick yank and my shoulder slammed into the rocking wall of the car. *Ivy!* I realized, her eyes black with fear as she stood over me between me and the numbing track. And still the mystics sang, demanding I do something wicked, something permanent.

"How's the engineer?" I slurred, and she pulled me farther from the edge.

"Hurt. Landon has control of the train. He knows we're here. Hell, everyone knows we're here. They've got a news helicopter and everything. But you did good. Everyone is safe."

An explosion shook the first-class car, red and yellow flames bursting out the windows and pulled away by the wind. Well, almost everyone was safe.

The acidic scent of sulfur shocked through me, clearing my head. *Shut up!* I screamed into my thoughts, and the mystics scattered. Damn, I should have done that ages ago.

But then a soul-ripping silence descended, broken by the wind and the rocking of the car. Scared, I looked at Ivy.

"Morgan!" Landon shouted, voice coming through the broken windows. "Get in here!"

I pushed Ivy's hands off me and yanked open the door. My God, it looked like the set of a Ring movie, everyone blond and beautiful and oozing magic. My jaw clenched, and I took three steps into the windy, demolished car. Seats were in twisted piles, the carpet burned and emergency lights glowing. The attendant was in a huddle, a weapon pointed at her. Trent was kneeling in what once was the aisle, facing me with his hands behind his head and another one of those overcompensating guns touching the back of his skull. Landon was holding it. Fear slammed into me, stopping me cold.

"What did you think you were going to accomplish with this?" he mocked, and I looked for Jenks, not seeing him and wondering if he'd been ripped away by the wind. "You seriously think you can stop me? Elves have always been stronger than demons. You're under our heel, and you don't even know it."

"Yeah?" I said, terrified at the gun at Trent's head. Mystics were screaming at me, and I shoved them to the back of my thoughts. The gun at Trent's head was the only thing that mattered.

"Drop the line or he's dead," Landon said, shoving the butt of the weapon into Trent, his head bowed and clearly dazed.

"Don't," I said, hand outstretched as I did what he said. But still the wild magic flowed. It was pure mystic energy that was making my hair float and my skin tingle. "Please. It's not a line."

"Drop it!" he screamed at me, face contorted, and I almost passed out.

"It's not a line!" I shouted, panicking. "It's the mystics! Please!"

Trent's eyes met mine, his fear for me, not himself. Oh

God, was I going to lose him just when I found out what he meant to me?

"Landon?" one of the men interrupted, a handheld scanner in his hand. "She's right. It's free-ranging mystics." He swallowed as he looked up at me, suddenly pale. "Sir?"

Landon smiled, probably unaware that he had pulled back from Trent almost half an inch. I took a breath, shoving the voices in my head down. "Splendid. You found a way to control them. That will be handy over the next couple of months. Even better. Turn around, Morgan. Kneel. Hands on head. Keep to that order or Kalamack dies."

If I let him have the mystics, the world would be thrown into chaos. If I attacked him, Trent would die. Indecision rocked me, and my head felt as if it was going to explode.

Become! the mystics in me were screaming. *Let us become!*

"Become?" I whispered, heart pounding. "I don't know how."

You don't become, one said. *We do. Just listen.*

Landon's eyes narrowed. "Morgan . . ." he threatened, shoving the pistol into Trent's skull a little more.

Listen, more said, and in desperation, I finally did.

My breath hissed in as I suddenly understood. The mystics who'd been swimming in my neural net the past two days had been slowly adapting to how I saw the world and how to work within it. What had once been confusing had cleared without me realizing. What had once taken minutes to understand had become second nature. Looking back, I could see the tracings of their gentle progression like a path through the woods. All I had to do was step out into the sun.

So I listened, and with the ease of blowing a bubble, I knew everything they saw: the frightened engineer tending to his shot partner as a man stood over them with a gun and his desperate plan to sacrifice himself to save untold millions, Ivy behind me with her hands in fists in frustration. I could see Nina, crying for Ivy as she raced ahead to where the next road crossed the tracks, hoping to stop the train even if it meant her death. I felt the stirring energy of the Weres massing in Chicago, rival gangs uniting to storm the station and overrun the train. Even the excitement in the news helicopter and Jenks holding on to Bis as he crawled to the front to find his dad. So many people willing to sacrifice— but none of it needed to happen. The mystics had evolved, become. And Trent would not die today.

"You should let them go," I said, feeling light and unreal. Humming with light. It burned my soul, charring it even as it gave me strength.

The muzzle shoved Trent forward, and my breath slipped easily from me as I saw how I could down Landon before the bullet could get to the end of the gun. I took a step forward, and Landon's expression shifted, seeing the change in me.

"That's right," I said, the fear gone. "I'm chock-full of 'em, and if you don't let their kin go, you're going to find out how a demon plays with wild magic." *Oh God. It hurt*.

Landon's confidence faltered. Behind him, his men exchanged glances.

"I know I'm curious," Trent grumbled.

I watched as if in slow motion as Landon spun his weapon around and smashed the stock of the barrel against the back of Trent's head. Ivy jerked, and I sent a burst of sound to stop her before she set them off and started a bloodbath. I'd seen in Landon's mind. He wasn't going to kill Trent. Not yet. He wanted him as the fall guy should the trickery with the Free Vampires be realized. So not happening.

I got three more paces closer as Trent fell, shaken but not unconscious. Landon's shock when he looked up and found me there was like icing. And the gun moved from Trent to me—just as I had wanted.

"Kneel," he demanded, his eyes flicking behind me to include Ivy as well.

Ivy dropped as she was told, but I couldn't do it. Wild magic spilled through me, pure and untainted from the ley lines. Burning.

And then I smiled at Jenks. He was with Bis, the little

gargoyle clinging to the outside of the rocking car as he gave me the thumbs-up. Etude was with him. Now I could do this. Now it would end.

I wasn't meant for this, and head in agony, I looked at the boxes, their contents held by flimsy, variable battery power. Landon was stupid. He didn't deserve to hold the Goddess's leash. No one did.

"You have something that belongs to me," I said, all of them oblivious to the massing mystics in me—except for Jenks and one very scared elf with a scanner.

"Down her," Landon directed to one of his men.

"Too late," I breathed, shivering as a wave of energy skated over my skin. "Oh, far too late. They're mine. I'm taking them home."

The barrel of the gun shifted from me to Trent. "Possession is nine-tenths of the law," he said confidently, gesturing to one of his men. "I said take her!"

But the man with the scanner didn't move. "Possession is exactly it . . . Landon," I said, standing before them, before them all in the center of the rocking car. The captured and splintered mystics howled for release. We were out of Cincinnati and as close to the Loveland ley line as we were going to get. I could take them home.

I took a final step forward, mystics bringing back to me the scent of Landon's sweat, the depth of his doubt.

"Stop! Or I kill him!" Landon shouted, and I reached for them.

"Rachel!" Trent exclaimed, and Landon's finger moved on the gun.

Go, I thought, watching the flare of the gunpowder in the chamber, sending enough mystics to clog the weapon and make it misfire. And they went.

Now, I thought, asking more to shift a tiny balance in the air. The poles in the batteries hiccupped. It was enough, and with a silent explosion, the splintered mystics burst from their prison. A demon could have done so with spells and curses, but with mystics swimming in my neural net, all I had to do was ask.

Trent's eyes were on me, and I saw him blink. It took forever.

And then the gun misfired, blowing Landon back.

"Rachel!" Trent shouted, scrambling forward even as Landon fell into his men and broken chairs. The attendant cried out in fear. For an instant, the air hummed with magic.

And then the freed splintered mystics fell into me.

"No!" I screamed at the flood of unconditional hatred. It wasn't simply me in pain, but my mystics, the ones who had become, as their new nature was measured and found wrong by way of fewer numbers. I fell, the bubble in my mind shifting to allow passage of those familiar to me and hold the rest back. Frustrated and angry, the splinter shifted and changed to find a way in. Again I floundered, getting one gasp of air before they swamped me anew.

Trent's arms around me tightened, burning like fire as the mystics battled, my mind the field of their conquest. The flame of becoming raced out, hot and blue at the edges, cooling to black where it passed, but there were too many splintered mystics, and for every one that became and blended, ten were overcome.

I couldn't turn them all at once. If I couldn't slow this down, I was going to go insane.

Groaning, I pulled my mystics back to me, finding a scant infinity left. Together we huddled under a protection that held only because I kept changing it. My eyes opened. Trent held me. He was mad at me, and I smiled.

"Sorry," I panted, seeing Bis and Jenks hanging from the ceiling. "I have to go. Etude will take me to the line. I'm sorry."

"Rachel!" he pleaded, but my skin became prickles of magic, and his hands sprang away.

"I have to go!" I shouted as I blew a new hole in the side of the car. "I'm sorry! I have to go!" I said again. "Keep the news crews from following me if you can!"

Knowing I'd survive, I ran for the edge, diving off into the blackness, an infinity of mystics within me, a larger infinity trailing behind like living pixy dust. I felt them peel from me, the agony in my head abating.

"Got you!" Etude cried, and I all but sobbed in relief as his grip encircled my waist again and the force of the wind shifted.

Jenks and Bis, I thought, feeling them close. Behind and below, the train raced on, mystics emptying from it in an angry wave that I could see as a silver shimmer in the dark.

"Should I jump her?" Bis said, and I jerked my head up, numb as if from an aura burn.

"Slow," I said, my words a bare whisper, and his ears swiveled to catch them. "If we go too fast, they can't keep up." I had to take them all back to her. They were hers, not mine, and if I held them too long, the sheer power of them would drive me mad. To have let them become had been a mistake.

Etude nodded, and as Jenks buried himself in my hair, I closed my eyes to block out the dizzy sensation. Behind me, I felt the train race on without the mystics. The splinter was following me, harrowing, nipping, stabbing at my heels. Ill and nauseated, I hung in Etude's grip, thinking that I should have just called the damn eagles from the beginning and done this alone.

Twenty-Six

Damp air with streamers of fog pressed me as Etude circled the gray slump of rock that was Loveland Castle. I could feel the splintered mystics trailing us in a threatening haze almost as bright as the full moon cresting over the surrounding hills, their confusion and hatred sparking like the neurons firing in my mind. The mystics who'd become were frightened, and I tried to soothe the hurt of their expected glorious reunion gone so wrong as we descended.

My eyes opened at a sudden drop, and I let go of Etude to push my hair back. The night fog puddled in the low spaces and trees poked above like islands. I could feel the earth moving—the unseen sun seeming to grow distinct as we neared sunrise. My ley line was glowing, shining with a haze I could see even without my second sight. That wasn't right. I was afraid to open my second sight to see, but a handful of mystics brought me an image, distorted from multiple viewpoints, but clear in substance. The line was ablaze with a harsh, painful glare. It was the Goddess. She was looking for her missing thoughts, and she wasn't happy.

"Are you seeing what I'm seeing?" Jenks said, still hiding in my hair. We'd taken a moment after fleeing the train to get me on Etude's back instead of in his grip, but Jenks had opted to stay where he was, tangled and close.

"Like the fires of hell leaking out?" I said, and he snickered. "Yep." Oh, she was pissed.

Etude shifted his balance as the earth seemed to rise up, and with his wings making one last pulse of motion, we were down.

The silence was deafening. Not even a cricket or frog from the nearby stream. It was as if the humming force from the line was pressing all other sounds out of existence. My mystics swarmed at my apprehension as I swung my leg over and slid to the ground. The shock reverberated up to my knees and jolted the numbness from me. Faint in the distance was Loveland's siren. The splintered mystics were coming.

"Thank you, Etude."

He was a lumpy shadow in the moonlight, the gargoyle flicking an ear to acknowledge me. "It's a small thing. I'll wait over there if you need a ride home."

Home? The memory of my front stoop with the sign over the door shadowy in the dim light rose up, and the mystics in me pooled their excitement. None of them left to go into the line, worrying me as I pulled my fog-damp hair from my shoulder so Bis could land on it. His presence joined mine with a soft thump, and turning to the glowing line, I sighed. I'd left Ivy and Trent. If I had stayed, I would've gone insane as Bancroft had.

"They'll get over it," Jenks said, seeming to know where my thoughts were as he clambered his way out of my hair and onto Bis's head, where he stood between his ears, hands on his hips and feet spread wide.

Where my thoughts were was actually a pretty good analogy, because as soon as I turned my mind to Ivy and Trent, an image surfaced. It had been there for a while, ignored as I flew to the Loveland ley line. It was of Ivy, leaning against a FIB car, arms over her chest and her lips pressed tight. Nearby, Trent was talking persuasively to another officer, the news crews waiting by the grounded copter. Landon's men were being led away, most of them limping. We'd got them, but the victory seemed hollow.

Are you sure you want to lose this? I thought, then quashed it. Sure, it was great seeing the world through a thousand eyes, but it had hurt. No wonder Bancroft had committed suicide. The Goddess could have them—have them all. It was like being connected to a line all the time. They were never quiet, and I just wanted to sleep.

"Oh, for Tink's ever-loving humping," Jenks whispered, a dull red dust seeping from him. "I think that's them. Rachel, can you see?"

I nodded, feet shifting in the knee-high grass as I tried to dampen my aura. I didn't know what I was going to do if they ignored the line glowing like a miniature sun between us and fell into me again. If the sirens rising up in our wake hadn't been enough, I would've known it was them by little pings of energy they gave off like heat lightning. Thirty seconds. I guessed thirty seconds, and we'd know if everything was for naught or not.

Bis's tail circling around my back and armpit tightened. "You want me to do anything?"

I shook my head, heart pounding as a cloud of mystics boiled over the tree line in a glow rivaling the moonlight. *You go first,* I thought at the mystics in me, and in a reluctant, swirling wave, they lifted from my soul. *All of you,* I reiterated, and disjointed images of the last few days sparked through my mind as they left.

My thoughts were finally empty, and I took a slow breath, relishing the silence. An adrenaline-based shiver shook me when the glow from the line jumped as my mystics entered it.

"Go, go, go . . ." Jenks whispered, and I found myself backing away from the line as a cloud of splintered mystics eddied to it and balked.

"Take them!" I shouted. "Damn it all to hell! Take them!"

"Rache!" Jenks shrilled. "Get down!"

I dropped, instinctively tapping the line and making a

circle. Fear rolled up as the wet earth hit me and the long grass scraped my face. Every time I touched a line, mystics overwhelmed me. But this time there was nothing but the pure clean force of the line. She had them. She had them and they were no longer mine!

Relief echoed in my new emptiness, and with Bis standing beside me, I looked up as a white flash of energy exploded from my ley line. It lit the grove, turning the leaves razor sharp and the grass into slivers of glass. Lips parted, I watched in awe as for an instant, the world hung unmoving, and then the pure light was sucked back into the line taking everything not real with it.

The sudden silence was a shock, broken by the running creek and the lowering wail of a distant emergency siren fading to nothing. Before me, the ley line was a hint of presence, invisible as it should be. The energy in my protection circle hummed. It was simple, the one dimension of sound feeling hollow. Hand shaking, I reached out to feel the strength of it until I got too close and my aura broke the charm. I shook as the flow shifted to run through me back to the line. They were gone. Everything felt normal.

Everything felt . . . dull.

"Did we do it?" Bis asked, and I slowly sat up and brushed the dampness from my palms.

"I think we did." Aching, I rose to my feet and looked at the moon, not believing it was finished. My brow eased and I almost cried. They were gone, and all I wanted to do was go home and go to bed.

"Bis, if your dad's still around, I'd like to take him up on his offer of a ride," I said as I thought of Ivy and then Trent. I didn't want to travel through the lines right now. Maybe not ever.

He smiled, his black teeth catching the moonlight. "I'll get him." He lifted off in a downward pulse of wings, and Jenks darted after him. Somehow, I thought it would have been harder than that, and I sighed, feeling empty and one-dimensional.

Pain! Betrayal! Mystic emotion slammed into me, and I spun to the line as they darted into me, burrowing deep.

"No!" I shouted, hands over my head and cowering as more arrowed out of the line. I stumbled, falling to my hands and knees as wild magic flashed through me, and my hands gripped the soil as it burned and burned and never eased. What had happened? They'd gone in. I'd felt them leave me!

"You!" thundered a familiar voice, and I looked up past my stringy hair, gaping at Ayer standing before me, sopping wet and pale—too pale to be alive anymore. A cement block was tied to his leg, and he shambled forward, oblivious to it even as it brought him to a halt.

"Ayer?" I gasped, confused and unable to think past the mystics pouring into me, all of them frightened and making my head pound. How had he gotten here? How had he gotten twice dead?

But the answer was obvious, and I pushed up until I sat back on my heels, trying to breathe around the mystics in my head. Landon had killed Ayer. He'd dumped him in the Ohio River by the looks of it, where the cold had kept his neural net somewhat functional—because everything seemed to be working. As zombies went, he was a good one, because it wasn't Ayer anymore. It was the Goddess.

"Ah, I can explain," I said as I wobbled to my feet. The mystics were pooling in familiar places, making the pinch of wild magic almost bearable. It hurt, though, solidifying my idea that the mystics would eventually kill me, even if they didn't mean to. I wasn't a being of energy and space. I was made of mass, and I felt the power squeeze from me as my muscles bunched.

The Goddess's eyes latched on to mine, chilling in intensity. "You took them," she said, Ayer's beautiful face and voice twisted in anger until they were ugly. I'd taught her that, either through my returning mystics or when she'd possessed me. Her power visibly danced over Ayer's pale skin, cresting over him like a purple wave, little sparks of energy flashing like her eyes in the moonlight.

"You left them!" I backed up, wincing at the first cut of a thousand wings on my thoughts, and my mystics rose in outrage. "I brought them back to you! All of them! I freed them and brought them home! I don't want them! Take them!"

Again she pushed Ayer forward, and he stumbled, almost falling when the block stopped him. "I can't," she said through him, and the rope dissolved. His skin, pale with death, was glowing. "You made them become. To take them back would make *me* become. I will not become. You will be ended, trickster Morgan!"

"What?" I kept moving, the long grass hissing against my legs. "No!" I didn't understand, and Ayer's expression bunched. I choked, hands rising to my neck as suddenly a wave of her mystics covered me, clogging my mouth and blinding my eyes with pinpricks of sensation. She was trying to suffocate me, and I staggered, panic rising.

My mystics rallied, rising from my skin to drive her eyes away and making the Goddess howl. In a wave of anger, she blew the grove apart. I fell, and from the corner of my sight I saw Etude spin away. Bis and Jenks were gone as well. Shaken, I knelt on the ground, my skin prickling with fire.

"You made them become!" the Goddess said, Ayer's voice echoing in my ears as the vampire stood over me, the rank smell of dead vampire and soured river water filling my nose. "You lied. You stole them from me."

"They're right there!" I shouted, just wanting her to go away, and then I screamed as another wave of mystics arrowed to me, pain bending me double as my throat suddenly clogged with feathers.

"I brought them back!" I screamed, panicking as I tried to shove the mystics out of my mind, but they slipped around my demand, falling back into me like water. "Take them! They'll adapt!"

"They. Will. Not!" she thundered through Ayer, and the vampire's skin flamed white. "They have become. Not again! I will not become again!"

But suddenly I could breathe, and I stared as the Goddess's mystics peeled from me in a visible wave, chased away by my own mystics.

No . . . The Goddess shrieked and flailed in anger, beating at nothing I could see. They hadn't been chased away. Her mystics were changing, becoming, in a visible wave.

Shaking, I got to my feet, still trying to figure this out as Ayer stumbled backward, the Goddess wailing as the gold of my mystics slurried through her purple haze. Like rivers in reverse, tendrils of light snaked through the aura of power surrounding her. As Ayer spun and slapped, the tendrils grew, became threads, became streams, became sources for more tendrils that grew into nets.

It's the becoming, I suddenly realized. It was me, the way I'd changed the mystics in order to survive them. I was seeing the concepts and ideas I'd given them snaking through the Goddess's psyche, changing her in turn, making her become something different, in essence, killing her.

"You brought them to destroy me!" the Goddess wailed, and then her anger crested to a savage ruthlessness. "There is one Goddess!" she howled, a burst of energy spilling from her with the sound of wings in the wind. "Your thoughts will be forgotten. I will make them forget. They will be forgotten and you will die!"

Shit, this was not what I wanted to happen. "I was trying to help!" I shouted, then froze when her Ayer doll suddenly collapsed.

For a heartbeat, there was silence. The haze of her power flickered, falling in on itself with a little pop. My mystics milled in confusion in the moonlit grove stinking of ozone and crushed grass. The cement block remained, but she was . . . gone?

"Jenks?" I called hesitantly, and then screamed, stiffening when the Goddess dove into my mind, ripping through me as if to tear me to shreds.

"No!" I howled, feeling my mystics hum through the

spaces in me, driving her off as she dug, burrowed, and tried to swamp me. If she succeeded, I'd be hers utterly, becoming her forever.

"Stop!" I demanded again, wrestling for control, and with a realization come too late, the Goddess recoiled in sudden terror. She'd attacked me, but wherever her thoughts touched to destroy and rend, my memories sparked, growing like an infection among her own thoughts. Just as before when she tried to break the hold the Free Vampires had on her, the more she fought, the more she lost.

And the Goddess wept as she felt herself change, become something else.

Please, stop! I cried in panic, and the mystics carried her deeper, forcing the change. *Go back! I don't want you!*

But the mystics weren't listening. They'd seen, and they couldn't go back. They liked the world of mass. Who could have guessed the limitations of three dimensions made a world richer than four?

Feathers beat on me as she tried to escape. The Goddess's terror rose thick, twining about me even as I felt her change. *I will end you!* she vowed, the smell of burning feathers choking as she was suddenly fighting for her own existence. *I will end your thoughts! I will not become again!* A great wailing rose up, pushing through my own horror. *You promised it would never happen again!* she cried like a lost child.

I was killing her.

I fled. With a singular desire, I willed myself into the line, and then I set my mind to another far away. It was a safe place, one where I went to find solace, a place where she wouldn't find me until I could figure out what to do.

Eden Park.

Twenty-Seven

Stay here, I thought, drawing the bored mystics back to me as I huddled on the bench tucked under one of the overhanging trees at the edge of the drop-off to the river. It was the best bench on the walkway in my opinion, being in the shade in the day and in the deep shadows at night, out of sight of most of the parking and all the open grass area. From here I could see a good slice of the Hollows, lit from the full moon and street fires as people gathered to defend what was dear to them. There was no power, and small but steady lights in the Hollows gave evidence of magic. Behind me, Cincinnati imploded in on itself, mostly ignored.

The tremendous wave of captured mystics flowing back to the line had missed most of the more populated areas, but even so it was only because people were glued to their TVs that the city would get through the night somewhat intact. Images of the stopped train and promises that the I.S. and FIB had caught the people responsible were a pressure bandage that would break when the Goddess finished repairing the damage I'd done and came hunting for me.

I could feel her even now, licking her wounds and forcing the mystics I'd left behind back to her way of thinking. Just as I had survived the splintered mystics by fleeing to return stronger, so would she, leaving a wave of destruction in her wake that would rival the Turn when she came to find me.

This was so not what I had wanted to happen.

The sound of a car coming up the winding drive became obvious over the background bangs and sirens. Tired, I pulled my feet up onto the bench and put my head on my knees as Trent's heavy, bullet-resistant SUV rolled up and stopped with the sound of popping gravel. A quiver went through me, and I yanked back a wave of curious mystics.

His door thumping shut shocked through me, and a few slipped my leash, returning almost immediately with an image. His head was down, and his hand was bandaged. He had all five fingers, though, and he'd found a clean set of clothes somewhere.

"Don't touch me," I said softly as a cloud of mystics ushered him forward, feeding off a faded emotion, intensifying it.

Shoes scuffing on the sidewalk, he halted five feet back. There were no lights, and he was a dark shadow under the trees. "It's just me," he said, and his voice rose and fell, making my heart ache more.

Setting my feet down, I turned to look at him with my own eyes instead of the mystics'. "You're full of wild magic. If I touch you, she might find me." Anguish rose up, biting and thick. "I tried!" I wailed suddenly, and his head dropped in understanding. "They won't go back. They adapted to me and refused to meld with her. Now she's out to kill me, and if she doesn't manage it, then she's dead herself, changed into something new, something I made."

Trent came closer, and I stiffened until he sat at the far end of the bench. The distance made me feel better, and together we looked out over the Hollows. "How did you find me?" I said, almost whispering it.

He leaned back against the bench and sighed. "Like I always do; I know where you go when you're in trouble. Bis is worried sick. Your aura has shifted again and he can't find you."

I looked at my hand as if I could see it. "I really screwed this up."

"No, not really." The hint of his usual confidence didn't make me feel any better. "Landon has been stopped and the dewar and enclave are both denying any knowledge of what he was doing—though I doubt that is true. No one on the train died, not even the conductor who was shot. Nina didn't crash the van into the train. The Weres in Cincinnati have found an unexpected, uneasy truce in their unification. Unfortunately it's against elves. On the good side, the undead are beginning to wake up. You made the news, but the headlines are positive."

Swallowing hard, I came out with what really bothered me. "I'm sorry I left you like that." Maybe if I hadn't, things would have been different.

Trent's head shifted back and forth in denial, a dark shadow under the trees. "No. Etude can only carry one, and staying wasn't an option. You did the right thing." He hesitated. "Even if it was the hardest thing I've had to endure to date."

Frustration pulled me straight, and my back hit the hard bench. "It did no good. The Goddess can absorb the splintered mystics," I said, gesturing at nothing. "What she can't handle are those reformatted for a reality-based mind." He looked at me, and I shrugged. "That would be me. I held them too long. They changed in order to communicate with me. It seems to be a better system than she has, and it began to cascade through her. I fled to keep her from being swamped, but this has happened before, according to her, and as soon as she gets angry enough, she's going to hunt me down and crush me so that the mystics I've corrupted won't cause her to change." *Won't kill her,* I thought, miserable.

My eyes grew warm, and I wiped them before I could cry. Silent, Trent propped his ankle up on his knee in thought. "If it's happened before, the demons might know something about it."

I stiffened. "I'm *not* calling Al. I have *mystics* in me! Your Goddess!" I protested, but what worried me more was that Trent and I were a couple, and Al would know that beyond a doubt. It wasn't just that we had had sex. We were making decisions together. We were shaping the world. Damn it, we were . . . were . . .

Emotion plinked through me as Trent took my hand and leaned over the space between us. "I am not ashamed of who I love."

My heart pounded, but there wasn't a whisper of wild magic in him. "I'm not either," I whispered. It was as much as I could give right now, but it was everything. "Trent . . ."

He stood, his hand slipping from mine. "It will be okay," he said, but I couldn't see his face, shadowed in the dark. "Al can lift them out of you. Newt was catching them in a jar, so there's a way to contain them. He's been in your mind before, so Al knows what's you and what isn't." Trent looked past me to the turmoil in Cincinnati. "I won't let him hurt you."

"You can't stop him," I protested, heart thudding. "There's got to be another way."

Trent shook his head. "This is the only way."

"Trent . . ."

"It will be okay," he said, and my heart just about broke when he tucked a strand of hair behind my ear. "Algaliarept, I summon you," he said softly, and I jerked back.

"This isn't safe!" I protested, feeling as if the world was backward. He was summoning Al with no circle, and I was the one complaining.

"No, it isn't." Al's voice rolled out of the darkness, and I stood, heart pounding.

Al was on the wide sidewalk. Behind him, Cincinnati tore herself apart, a suitable backdrop to his elegant crushed green velvet frock, walking stick, and top hat. "Al." I begged for understanding, but I knew the demon hadn't grasped the depth of the situation because I was still breathing.

"Help her," Trent said simply, and by the light of the moon, I saw Al's eyes narrow.

I flinched as Al strode forward, gripping my jaw to look into my eyes. The mystics rose up, and I frantically demanded *be still, be still, be still,* terrified.

"Do you realize what you have done!" Al shoved me away.

Trent lunged, catching me before I fell, and we stood before him. Al was pissed, but he still didn't realize it all.

"Help her," Trent repeated. "This wouldn't have happened if you hadn't turned your back on her."

"Do *not* blame this anathema on *me*!" Al shouted, his voice echoing back from the town houses across the park. "I said to *walk away.* There's no solution here! You should have let the world go to *hell*!"

"They've become attached to her," Trent said, because I was too scared to say it. "You've been in her mind. You know what is her and what isn't. Take out what doesn't belong."

The top of the cane cracked as Al gripped it. "And then what?" he said, taking three steps closer. "Put them in *a jar*? Don't you understand?" He dropped his head, his eyes holding hate when he looked up. "There *is* no Goddess!" he said, hammering the words at Trent. "There never was! These voices she says she hears . . ." Al drew back in disgust. "They're in her head alone. She is insane!"

"Al!" I shouted when he reached for Trent, but Trent did nothing, grim faced as Al twined his gloved hand into Trent's shirt and pulled him close.

"And you pushed her into it," Al snarled. But then his expression went empty, and he let Trent go, backing up until he could run his eyes Trent's full length. "You slept with her," he said, but it wasn't a question.

Oh God. Now it was going to get bad.

"You slept with him!" Al exclaimed, coattails furling as he spun to me. "Y-you," he stammered, unable to find the words. "I gave you everything! And you repay me with this?"

Al recoiled when I reached for him, and my heart seemed to twist. "Al, please," I begged. "I didn't mean it to happen."

Al pulled his lips from his teeth in a savage snarl. "You *let* it happen."

My blood roared in my ears, and I wavered as a small band of mystics found me, bringing a vision of the church and a broken water glass, his chrysalis among the shards. "Go away. Go away!" I shouted, waving at nothing. "Go back to her. She wants you!"

But she can only go in the space between space, one thought, and the rest agreed. *We like the mass that defines her better.*

Al and Trent were staring at me, and I suddenly realized I had screamed it out loud.

"Please," Trent begged.

Al turned, voice flat as he said, "It's too late."

"It's not—"

"It's too late!" Al wouldn't look at me. His eyes were pained, and his hands in his white gloves scrubbed his face. "If she could be helped, she would have done it herself."

Trent's expression became hard. "You mean you can't."

"That's right. I can't." Al looked at nothing, still not acknowledging I was standing right there. "The Goddess is a myth, a deified energy source. Voices in her head," he said scornfully. "*This* is what happens when you listen to the spaces too long." Now he looked at me, and the depth of his heartache struck me cold. "Your mind invents a reason," he said softly. "Mystics are a fabrication to explain a disease. This is a psychosis." Al's eyes flicked to Trent. "Your wild magic made her insane, and you will watch her die a slow, confused, worthless death. I will have no part in it."

A psychosis? He thought I was inventing this? "The mystics are real!" I protested, feeling them rise up in me. "You can see them, record them. I'm not imagining this! The things I can do. The things I see. Explain that!"

Al looked beaten as he cast his eyes on me. "Oh, the energy is real. You can collect it. Use it. The voices are not."

Trent shook in anger. "You will do nothing?"

"Don't you understand? There's nothing to take out!" Al thundered.

My heart thudded in my chest, and I was afraid when Al looked at me again, his thick hands opening and closing. I remembered their feel around my throat, and I took a step back.

"But I can help her on her way," Al intoned, and I backed up farther. "End this travesty. We do not need another Newt."

He was going to kill me.

"Al!" I exclaimed, backpedaling, but he had me by the throat.

"Go away," he snarled, flinging a hand out at Trent, and he was tossed to the pavement, face ashen in the moonlight as he pulled himself up.

The mystics rose, swarming like bees. Trent saw them. Al felt them, his expression becoming even more disgusted. They demanded action, that I strike the demon down, that I destroy him with a word. I knew I could do it, but I didn't. I made them fall about our feet like dust as I hung in Al's gentle grip around my throat.

"You could have had everything," Al said, my face mirrored in his goat-slitted red eyes. "Everything and all time. And you threw it away. If you'd left him as your familiar, we would've overlooked it, but you freed him, and we won't allow you to give them a foot on our neck again. This, Rachel Mariana Morgan, will not be tolerated."

I closed my eyes, doing nothing as his power gathered, tingling between us. I knew to the bottom of my soul that he'd do it. I'd wounded him too deeply. He knew I'd never be any closer to him than we were today, but that I had found love with those he hated was too much.

"I'm sorry," I whispered, knowing why he'd kept Ceri as a slave for a thousand years.

"It's not nearly enough," he said softly.

"Gally!" Newt screamed, and I jerked as my air cut off. "Let her go!"

I choked, eyes flashing open to see her standing beside Trent, horrified.

I clutched at Al's wrists, struggling for air, refusing to let the mystics harm him. I wouldn't strike him. I wouldn't cause his death. Black rimmed my vision, and my lungs burned.

"She looked too long!" Al said, anguish foreign in his eyes. "She drank too deep!"

Newt put a hand on his. It was right before my eyes, the only thing I could see. "Leave."

"But . . ."

"Leave," she said again, gentle in understanding. "I'll finish this. You've done enough."

Finish? I thought, gasping when his fingers eased and I got a breath of air.

"She lay down with him!" Al protested, grip loosening even more. "An elf!"

Newt's fingers dug into Al's wrist. Blood began to drip from under her thumb. "I can tell that," she said tartly. "I knew it would happen. So did you. Why do you act surprised?"

"He is an elf!" Al shouted, and suddenly I could breathe as I found myself falling to the pavement. "A mother pus bucket of an elf! And she freed him! This is exactly how they enslaved us the last time!"

Pain lanced my hip as I hit the ground. Coughing, I rolled out of the way of Al's boot, finally coming to a stop against Trent. He pulled me farther away as I gagged on the air, my hands about my bruised throat. Newt was inches from Al, looking up as if it pissed her off.

"You allowed it to happen!" Newt exclaimed, one hand waving in the air. "We all watched you do it. She's your ward. It's your fault. And I won't let you kill her for the *audacity* of being *braver* than you!" Leaning deeper into his space, she put her hands on her hips. "You are a *coward*, Al, and you don't deserve to stand at her side, much less kill her. Go find a place to hide. A deep one. You're done here. If she's strong enough to trust him, she's strong enough to test the rest of us."

Al's anger moved from me to her. Eyes squinting, he rocked back from Newt. "We're done, Rachel," he said, his words striking right to my core. "Don't call on me again. You're no longer my student."

"Al," I said, hand to my throat when it came out in a harsh croak. Mystics spun from me, wreathing him with demands he listen, that he understand. This was not what I'd wanted. But he was blind to me and he put up a hand, stopping my next words.

"My name is Gally, and if I ever see you again, I will kill you." Spinning to make his coattails furl, he snatched his walking stick from the ground. The top stone was broken off, and he left it behind as he walked away, vanishing between one step and the next. Confused, the mystics swarmed where he had been. My focus shifted deeper, finding a burning building.

"If you hurt her, you die," Trent said above me.

Oh yeah. We weren't done yet.

He tensed as Newt strode to us, her androgynous robes snapping about her bare feet. "Don't be stupid," she said, brushing him aside so she could help me stand. "You called me."

I staggered upright, feeling dizzy. He knew Newt's name? "They can't be fake," I said as the mystics returned to me. "They're real. They're so real!"

Pain arced through me, and I jerked. Eyes watering, I realized she'd slapped me.

"They're false," she said. "Let them go."

I pulled my hand from my face, warm from the rush of blood. "I tried," I protested. "I took them right to her. I made them get in the line. They came back!" Frustrated, I ran my hands over my arms as if I could brush them away. "They keep coming back . . ."

Grimacing, Newt pinched my shoulder as she pulled me a step away from Trent. "Let them go," she demanded again.

"Look at me!" she shouted when I tried to say something. "Let them go. They're constructs of your mind, a way for your limit-bound existence to process the raw energy of creation."

"Liar!" I yanked free of her. "They're real. She knows things I can't possibly guess, and she said someone promised her becoming wouldn't happen again. Why would she say that if she wasn't real?"

Newt blinked, a bemused, almost beatific expression softening her. "I didn't think she'd remember."

I blinked, silent as I took in her suddenly shy demeanor. The Goddess had said this had happened before. Newt knew it. Newt was crazy. "You?" I said, sure of it when the demon blushed. "You!" I glanced at Trent, then pulled her farther away, asking him to stay put. He looked miffed, but he gave us space. "You know they're real," I almost hissed. "Why are you trying to convince me they aren't?"

Newt glanced behind me at Trent as he picked up the broken stone from Al's cane. "Demons do not dabble in elven religion," she said stiffly. "Even if that religion holds more power in a wish than demon magic has in an action."

My jaw dropped. Oh God. I was going to go insane. Even if I survived, I was going to go crazy. I was going to become another Newt.

Seeing my fear, Newt rolled her eyes. "Oh, stop. Mystics didn't make me insane," she grumbled. "You, though, must get rid of them, or the Goddess will kill you to prevent changing again. Let me gather them up. I can return them." A smile quirked her lips. "She's terrified of me."

I knew the feeling. "But they'll come right back," I protested.

Newt shook her head, eyes down as she remembered something. "The Goddess will kill all memory of you once she sees you dead. You took her by surprise before, but she's forewarned. You won't escape again. She is a Goddess, and you, Rachel . . ."

I stifled a shiver as Newt ran a thin hand through my hair.

"You are not," she finished.

The mystics in me quailed, and I gathered them close. It was obvious that Newt wanted them out of me, that she wanted to preserve her secret that she'd also looked too deeply, that she *knew* elven magic based on a deity was more powerful than demon magic based on the will of the self. But to let the Goddess kill them? For what? So I could go on to an eternity of loveless misery as they were stuck in?

"Why?" I said, and she made a tiny sound of surprise. "If I'm to be persecuted for who I love, then why shouldn't I be insane? I might be able to stop you all then."

Newt drew back, alarmed. "A crazy demon has power," I said, and she winced. "They listen to you. They'd listen to me! With the power of the Goddess, I could best you all, and you know it. That's why you all have this problem with wild magic to begin with."

Newt ran a hand behind her neck in a gesture of unease that I'd never seen in her before. "You're simplifying things," she said as Trent inched closer until he was right behind my elbow. "Rachel, he's an elf. A freed familiar. Maybe if there was some way to bridge our two species, they'd go along with it, but there isn't."

She was talking about children. That's why Al had kept Ceri so long. He'd been trying to find a way to bridge the gap. And he had failed.

"Yeah, I get it," I said bitterly. "They made you slaves, and you tried to kill them, and they imprisoned you in the ever-after, and you both screwed up each other's genetics so no one can have any kids. But *Trent* didn't do it. I'll let you in my mind to pull them forth so everyone can believe that mystics are a psychosis and you can keep your secret, but I don't want her killing them, and I want you to fix it so the demons leave me and Trent alone!"

My heart was pounding. Trent was at my elbow, and the mystics in me went silent. They knew of love and sacrifice, but I didn't want them to die. "Change the resonance of my soul," I suddenly said, and her head snapped up. "Change it so the mystics bound to me can't find me." *No!* they wailed, and I yelled at them to shut up. "As long as they stay out of the line, they won't contaminate her with dreams of mass."

Newt's eyes narrowed, and I took a breath to finish my threat. "And if anyone ever does anything against me or Trent, I will go find my mystics and claim them because they are real and both of us know it."

Her lip curled, and emboldened, I lifted my chin, managing to stifle my jump when she smashed the butt of her staff on the cement to crack it. In the distance, that burning building fell in a stately shower of sparks. For a moment, there was darkness there, and then the flames grew brighter.

"Now will you get them out, or does the ever-after have a new insane demon to contend with?" I asked.

Her grip on her staff tightened. "You'd give up the energy of creation for . . . him? He could leave you tomorrow and you'd have nothing but hatred and bitterness to sustain you."

I remembered the feel of Trent's skin under my fingertips, the softness of his hair, the sensation of his body over, around, and in mine. I remembered how he had stood for me when I didn't have the strength myself, and the way I fought for his freedom, his life, his children. Sure, he could leave tomorrow, but that didn't rub out how I felt now. Now was all we really had.

"I've already lost Al," I said, finding that it hurt more than I would've guessed. "Giving up being able to see around corners is a small thing."

Expression sour, she turned to Trent. "And what do you sacrifice for her?" she said mockingly. "Love is dross without sacrifice. It fades with the sun."

Trent's chin lifted. "I've lost my voice among my kin," he said, and I took a breath, dismayed. "My child may be taken from me."

"Trent!"

His fingers slipped into mine. "The silence my money has bought is no more. I will be persecuted, reviled, scorned."

"As all elves should be," Newt said, clearly not happy.

"I'll probably end up in jail," he finished, and I squeezed his hand. Never. It wouldn't happen.

"Why didn't you tell me?" I said, but when I thought back to Quen's expression as he stood in my back living room, I knew I should have guessed.

"And to top it off, I lost five generations of my father's breeding program in the ever-after to surface demons," Trent finished sourly. "I have very little left."

Newt's anger vanished, replaced by a shockingly wistful sigh. "The horse," she whispered. "She's beautiful."

"She's alive?" Trent's gloom lifted. "Rachel, with that single horse, I could rebuild . . ." He hesitated as Newt cleared her throat.

Trent swallowed hard. I looked between them, seeing her desire, his need. "She is yours," he finally said, and Newt laughed and clapped like a little girl, her staff clattering to the ground.

Eyes bright, she scooped it up, taking my elbow as she drew me closer. "Let me take them," she said, words a breath on my hand as she held it to her. "They'll come to me. I'll change your soul so they'll never find you. But you must promise to never tell the others that the Goddess and I have more in common than is, ah, prudent."

My heart pounded. I was doing it again: trusting demons. But as I looked past her to Trent standing in the moonlight, one city standing to fight, the other out of control and in flames, I decided that it was worth it. All of it. Even if it should end tomorrow.

"You'll get them to back off Trent and me?" I asked, and her smile grew wicked as she nodded.

"I'll tell them you are romancing the cure for our genetic damage from him, and you will leave him as a broken ruin when you have it. They'll believe me. You're halfway to ruining him already."

Al would know, but he wouldn't say anything. My heart pounded. "Then okay. You can take them, but I don't want them killed. Any of them."

The mystics in me wailed. I reassured them, even as I felt a pang. Gone. I'd be invisible to them. They'd be like lost children in the night, but they'd be alive.

"That is acceptable," Newt said as she looked at us. Together Trent and I nodded. I felt funny, my knees weak, and standing before her thus with our hands intertwined, I felt a bond stronger than any church could bestow fall about us. "You might want to be unconscious for this," she added, and Trent cried out as her staff swung to strike me right between the eyes.

With a sharp thud of pain, the world blessedly went away.

Twenty-Eight

A lion coughed as if clearing his throat, making me shiver
in the cool morning air and sending my white dress to
bump about my legs. Lucy's hand was slightly damp and
sticky in mine as she tugged toward the ice cone stand, singing a nonsense rhyme in time with her leaping jumps that
sent a tingle of wild magic sparking between us. Newt had
cursed my soul to keep the mystics *and* the Goddess from
recognizing me, but I could still feel the trails of self they
left. The line was alive, but I couldn't be a part of it, share it.
It was a constant reminder of what I'd lost—and it hurt, especially at night. Maybe that's why Newt was crazy.

Trent and Ray were beside me, the more reserved girl
concentrating on her toddling steps. It was a rare day in July,
perfect weather to be at the zoo and early so the girls weren't
cranky yet. Jenks was doing recon somewhere, Jonathan was
behind us with the empty stroller, and Ivy and Nina were at
a nearby stand looking for a sunhat. Now that the undead
were again awake, Felix was back in Cormel's iron grip. It
should have been a relief, but Felix's mystic-induced sanity
was showing signs of collapse. The why of which was worth
thinking about.

But today was too beautiful to worry about the undead,
and I squinted up at the sky as Lucy jumped up and down,

demanding blue ice. Trent crouched, waiting for Ray to touch the colorful pictures to tell him which one she wanted. "Blue, blue, blue!" Lucy shouted, and I smiled at his patient deferment.

"Noted," he said, taking her hands and calming her. "No one gets any ice until Ray decides. It's hard to choose when you're talking. Give her a moment."

Eyelids squeezed closed, Lucy made a herculean effort to be quiet, sweet in her white dress and sun hat. It lasted for all of five seconds, until bursting, she opened her eyes wide and began to tell Ray the colors, trying to push her sister along.

Smiling, Trent stood and pulled out his wallet. Jonathan waited behind us in the shade, irking me as he watched with his nose in the air and that distasteful look on his face. "You're really good with them, you know," I said as Ray splayed her hands over all the colors and beamed up at Trent with her cute little-girl squint.

"I've had practice. CEOs around a table are worse," he said, then turned to the man tending the cart. "Can you make one with stripes of colors?" he asked, and the man nodded, but then Trent's expression shifted to a frown. "I thought I had more cash than that," he said, and handed the man a card. "Sorry, is this okay?"

Nodding, the man took it, but it was obvious he thought we were goobers. Who uses a platinum card to buy two ice cones?

Lucy clung to the cart, eyes on the cones set out of her reach as the man ran the card. Nina's laugh caught my attention, and I turned. She'd gotten Ivy to put on a big floppy hat with peacock feathers draped down the back, and when Nina begged, Ivy fell into a seductive poise, trying it out. Nina screamed in delight and reached for another so they could vogue together. Ivy flushed, but she was smiling, and I turned away before she knew I was watching. I was so happy for her.

My smile faded, and I vowed Cormel wouldn't screw it up. They owed me for saving their miserable undead lives.

They all owed me, and if they pushed, I'd remind them of that.

Turning, I scanned the open courtyard hemmed in by eateries. Jenks should be back by now. It was starting to get busy, but if we stayed away from the kids' area, we should be okay. It had been an interesting week, what with the undead waking up and their gorging serving to bring everyone back in line with an eerie suddenness. I'd tried to contact Al, only to have him crack my mirror and prove my idea wrong that he still cared and had abandoned me to protect his assets. I also didn't like that the blue butterfly chrysalis I'd found among the broken shards had gone black, the tiny movements inside making Jenks shed a worried dust.

Trent had been in the national news all week, and not in a good way. I suspected that his invite today was to help him establish a new, homey image now that Ellasbeth was being painted as the wronged woman.

I didn't mind being a part of his publicity program, and the man did need protection. People were still terrified of genetic research, and the fact that he'd come out of the closet as an elf a few months ago wasn't helping. Two years ago, I would have been right there with them, hammering on his gates and demanding access to his files before he shredded them. *Knowledge made all the difference,* I thought, then changed my mind. Trust, maybe. But research could be stolen, perverted, twisted. Maybe they were right to protest.

"I'm sorry, sir," the man said, handing the silver card back to Trent. "Do you have another card?"

Ooooh, ouch.

"Ahhh," Trent hedged, looking back at Jonathan in the shade of the pergola. In a stiff motion, Jonathan rose, stalking forward with the warmth of a zombie.

"I've got this," I said, reaching into my bag, and Trent fidgeted as I handed over a five. "Oh, for Tink's toes," I muttered as I took the ices and handed them to the girls. "You'd think I'd just hamstrung you."

"It's not that," he said as he handed Jonathan the card. "Jon, see what's going on."

The girls looked tiny as they clustered about the tall man, and Ray clamped a hand on his pant leg for balance. "Yes, Sa'han," he said, carefully disentangling Ray's fingers and transferring them to Trent's hand.

"I don't mind paying." Jonathan was headed for the ATM, and I scanned the courtyard. It suddenly felt exposed, vulnerable. *Where is Jenks?*

Trent's tight expression eased and he gave me a surprising sideways hug as he turned us back to the twin stroller parked beside the bench in the shade. "I don't mind you paying," he said softly, his words making a tingling path down my entire side since he hadn't let go. "I simply want confirmation as to why the card isn't working."

My thoughts went to the newscasters, their eyes alight and their words fast as they smelled blood in the air surrounding the Kalamack estate. I had a good idea as to why his card wasn't working. "Maybe it's just a glitch."

"Doubt it." Expression neutral, he let me go to help Lucy up onto the bench before she spilled her cone trying to do it herself. "This might end with burgers at the pool."

I lifted Ray to sit beside her sister, taking a moment to tug her dress straight over her tights. "That sounds good to me. I missed my Fourth of July picnic." I sat, straddling the bench so I could watch Jonathan and the courtyard at the same time. Trent, who had to show a more dignified bearing, sat on the other side of the girls, his back to most of the zoo and the long-range scopes of the news vans that had followed us here. They weren't allowed in without prior arrangements, and I think that was why we were here.

To be honest, I was worried—worried about him and his money. He'd never had to go without it, and the bigger the corporation, the faster it starved to death when the funds were cut off. He was a CEO of billions, but it wouldn't mean anything if his assets were frozen. He'd be okay, sure, but what about all his employees with no work, no pay for the year or two this was going to take to sort out?

Leaning over and behind the girls, he whispered, "I have insurance for this. Relax."

Startled, I drew back. "God!" I exclaimed softly. "I hate it when you do that."

He was smiling, the wind shifting his hair about his eyes, and I felt warm when he helped Lucy, now crying over an ice headache. Slowly his smile faded, damped by Jonathan at the ATM. The tall man had Trent's card in hand and was on the phone.

"Actually, this took longer than I thought it would." Concerned, he pulled his phone from a back pocket, elbows on his knees as he pushed a few buttons.

"Sorry." Ray was distressed at the red dripping down her hand, and I rewrapped the bottom with a new napkin.

"Mmmm." His brow furrowed even more. "Maybe we should head home."

Home, I thought, leaning to look at the tiny screen. He'd brought up one of his news sites, which showed a well-groomed woman sitting next to a downward-sloping graph and the words *Kalamack Industries.* Seeing me looking, he upped the volume.

" . . . as the Kalamack investigation continues to come up empty. Though employees questioned are denying Kalamack Industries conducts any genetic research outside of legal parameters, allegations of illegal genetic tinkering and trade of genetic products persist. In a related story, claims that the chain of subtropical islands owned by the Kalamack family were really a powerhouse of Brimstone fields have evaporated into the sound of wings. Investigators at the site found only open fields and thousands upon thousands of cocoons of a rare butterfly on the verge of extinction. When asked, Trent Kalamack made this statement."

The picture shifted to one of Trent, looking calm and collected in his usual suit as he stood beside a podium at his gatehouse media room. "Our intent in replanting the cane fields was twofold, not simply helping a vanishing species to recover, but advancing the local population into more well-paying jobs and fostering new opportunities. Changing the local harvest to a more sustainable product, in this case, the trade of tourism, we would achieve both goals. A cane field will employ a family, but tourism brings in dollars from around the world and employs not just farm workers to maintain the butterflies' life cycle, but also promotes far more skilled labor and the cottage industries that tourism fosters."

I looked at Trent, remembering the conversation he and Quen had in my back living room over bugs in the Brimstone field. "Well played," I murmured, realizing that he had distributed the butterflies to all his fields, effectively eating the evidence.

Trent cleared his throat nervously. "Thank you."

"Regardless, Kalamack stock continues to plummet," the newscaster continued as she reappeared, and Trent sighed. "Whether the claims are groundless or rooted in truth, it seems more and more likely that Kalamack Industries has seen the last of its golden years."

"Sorry," I said as Jenks's dust blanked out the screen. I'd heard his wings an instant before he dropped to my shoulder, and a knot of worry eased in me.

"Enks!!" Lucy shrilled, and the pixy darted out of her sticky reach. "Pixy, pixy, pixy!"

"Yeah, I'm buying up Kalamack stock as fast as Rachel's rent check clears," Jenks said as Lucy dropped her ice, her hands outstretched as she jumped. "Watch out, cookie maker, or I'm going to own you."

Clearly amused, Trent put his phone away. Jonathan was still on the phone. Apparently Trent had a lot of accounts to check. Eyes intent, Ray watched Jenks, a brown, icy cold water dripping out the end of her cone unnoticed.

But then my head came up as a familiar scent tickled my nose. "Ah, Jenks? Why do you smell like burnt amber?"

The sound of Jenks's wings hesitated, but it was Trent's suddenly bland expression that rang the alarm bells.

"I gotta check the perimeter," the pixy said, darting off, much to Lucy's dismay.

Catching her hand before she ran after him, I dug out the little packet of Handi Wipes from my bag. "Jenks!" I shouted, but he was gone. Eyes squinting, I turned to Trent. "What have you two been up to?"

Trent took the packet and pulled one out. "Mmmm. I've been helping Newt with Red," he said as he worked at getting the blue off Lucy's fingers. "I asked Jenks to watch my back."

My lips parted, and I looked into the pergola, knowing he was up there somewhere, the chicken. "And why would you think you had to keep that from me?" I asked, but I couldn't keep the frown off my face.

Lucy twisted and squirmed, and he started on the other hand when I gave him a clean wipe. "I don't," he said, wincing. "But she saw you ride Tulpa and she's embarrassed that she can't get on Red." His lips curled into a smile as he let Lucy go and the girl ran to jump in the dust Jenks was sending down. "That stupid horse is balking at everything, and Newt is oblivious to how to handle her. It's going to be a while before she can get on her." He chuckled, using the last of the wipe to clean his own hands. "It's going to be a while before she can touch her."

I wondered where Newt had the horse, then decided she had enough room. It would be the feed I'd be worried about. "So you're under investigation for drug trafficking, illegal genetic research, and whatever else they can come up with, and you decide to go to the ever-after? Without me?"

"Of course not." Trent gave me a sideways glance. "Newt and Red came to me. The animal needed to see the moon. That's half the problem if you ask me. Soon as Red associates Newt with clean grass, she'll settle down."

I rolled my eyes, shifting my leg to sit properly as Ray set her uneaten cone down and went to stand just outside the circle of sparkles sifting down. "Oh, that's much better," I said, hoping they had a hidden glen to do this in. "You're giving riding lessons to demons."

He rubbed his chin as he watched his girls. "In exchange for storage space for a few machines I don't want to lose." Eyes rising, he looked at me. "I could do this for a living. I like horses. I like demons. It's a perfect fit."

He was joking, but there was a grain of truth to it, and I threw away Ray's cone before I reached for the wipes. "I'm sorry. I don't think they're going to stop until you lose everything." Angry, I cleaned my hands, thinking I should have thought this through a little more. We could have done something different, maybe. Tried to hide it. Put off the inevitable. But as Trent took my damp hand in his to still my frustrated motions, I knew that to try to hide it would have only made it worse when the truth came out.

"Not everything, no," he said. "But I'm not the only one giving things up. I know it was hard abandoning the mystics."

My jaw clenched, and I tried to quash my gut reaction of heartache. I knew he saw it when his grip tightened. "Does it show?" I said, miserable. I'd been able to see around corners. I'd had thousands of voices telling me of whispers halfway across the city. I'd had a million defenders, ready to turn my wish to reality. It had been godlike. Even if keeping them would've made me crazy.

Trent leaned back, his hand still holding mine. "I thought so," he said softly. "You gave that up. And Al." He let go of me, his finger tilting my chin up to look at him. "I have my own guilt to chew on."

"It's not your fault."

Sighing, he watched the girls leaping at Jenks's shifting dust. "I wouldn't change anything, though I'll admit that my end of things is turning out to be more challenging than I'd anticipated. But there's a definite upside that I hadn't counted on."

"Like what?" Jenks said as he dropped from his dust

to the stroller's bar. "Is Rachel so good in bed she's worth losing a fortune?"

"Shut up, Jenks," I said, and he laughed, sounding like wind chimes.

"I don't have to do what everyone expects anymore." Smiling, Trent pulled Ray onto his lap and gentled the tiring girl to him. "I owe you. Forever, Rachel. You freed me."

Jenks made gagging sounds when I flushed. Freed him? No. He'd freed himself. "You do know freedom is why I quit the I.S., right? And see how that turned out?"

He chuckled, but my smile faltered as I glanced at my wrist and the smooth skin there. My demon mark had vanished without fanfare last week, and with it, my last tie to Al. For some stupid reason, I missed it. Trent, though, was looking at Ivy and Nina trying on hats. "Oh, I think it turned out fine." His eyes met mine over Ray's tousled hair, and I felt warm. "A little tiring, perhaps, but okay in the end."

Beaming, I leaned in, hoping for a kiss. Jenks flew up and out of the way in disgust, but before our lips met, my eyes went over his shoulder to Jonathan. The distasteful man was not at the ATM. No, he was standing between us and Ellasbeth, striding forward under the shade with two men behind her.

Ellasbeth? I thought, freezing. Trent's lips grazed mine before he realized there was a problem and drew back. Tingles raced through me, not all of them from the spark of wild magic. "Ellasbeth," I whispered, and he turned, his jaw clenching.

"And she brought friends," Jenks said snidely. "Trent, monologue or something. I have to cut the cameras or someone's gonna be in jail tonight for assault."

"Make it fast." Trent set Ray in the stroller, buckling her in before standing.

Jenks darted up and away and wild magic prickled over my skin as Trent tapped a line. Pulse hammering, I stood as well. A lion roared as I tapped a line, my chin rising as the energy flowed through me and back to the line, connecting me to everything, to all, to the universe—even if I could see only a hairsbreadth of it now.

"Stop right there!" I said, but Ellasbeth never slowed, motioning for the men and women she'd brought to circle us. Shit, there were more than two. She'd brought at least eight. People in bright shirts and shorts were scattering, running for the edges. "I said that's close enough!" I shouted as she kept coming.

Ivy and Nina tensed, but we all froze when Jonathan dropped out of the pergola, looking ugly and alien as he knocked the man behind her to the ground and crouching over him with a ball of black death in his hands. Trent grabbed my arm to keep me from moving, and I quailed when a half-heard whisper of promised death passed Jonathan's lips.

"Give me the girls, Trent!" Ellasbeth demanded, and Lucy called for her mother in delight.

Ignoring Jonathan, Ellasbeth continued forward. The second man with her moved, and with a growl that chilled my blood, Jonathan grabbed him about the neck. Suddenly the three were on the ground, scrabbling like wrestlers for an advantage as they heaved and struggled. Wild magic skated over my awareness, and Trent's grip on me tightened. There was an abrupt pop of magic, and the two men went still. Ellasbeth came to a shocked halt as Jonathan slowly got to his feet, the two men behind her unmoving.

"Holy toad shit!" Jenks exclaimed, and my pulse raced as Jonathan shook the lingering magic from him like water. His foot nudged a man back to the ground, and I breathed a sigh of relief. They were still alive. I hadn't been sure.

"Don't move," Jonathan said to Ellasbeth, and the woman's face became white. "I will bring you down."

"What the hell was that?" Jenks said as he landed on my shoulder with the fading scent of burnt amber.

"That was Jon, defending me and mine." Trent's grim expression made me wonder how often he'd seen something like this. What did he need me for?

People were at the outskirts, watching behind trash cans and low walls. Stymied, Ellasbeth nevertheless took a step forward. "Give me my girls!" she exclaimed, flicking her eyes to Jonathan and back again.

There were Weres among the watchers I realized, circling behind Ellasbeth's men. Ivy and Nina had dropped back, rightly worried about getting caught in the magical cross fire.

Trent made sure Ray was okay before he faced her. "Ellasbeth," he said, her name holding a wealth of emotions: fatigue, disappointment, relief, and anger. "Were you waiting for the news, or did you feed it to them to hurry it along so you could make your flight out?"

"Give them to me!" she demanded, making a sideways step, closer to us and away from Jonathan.

"If you have to ask, you don't deserve them," Trent said, his bitter sarcasm clear.

"You're destitute," she said, her confidence wearing thin as she stood in the sun with her straw-yellow hair and perfect dress suit. "Or you soon will be. You can't maintain custody, and if you don't give them to me now, the accusations will become worse until you are in jail or dead. Save them the humiliation of seeing their father made a public ridicule."

Trent shifted his weight, hiding me another inch behind him. "Father. Nice of you to admit that in front of all these witnesses."

Her security had noticed the Weres. One of them motioned to Ellasbeth to leave, and she frowned. "You're making this harder than it needs to be."

"Easy is tasteless and bland," he said, and her expression twisted with anger.

"I will turn you into a pauper unless you give them to me!"

At that, Trent took a step forward. Lucy was fussing, trying to get to Ellasbeth, and I distracted her with a tiny globe of light. "Wealth is not a determining factor of parental fitness," he said softly, his words reaching everyone. "Or are you calling a million parents unfit because they work for a living? Lucy is mine by right," Trent said, his voice ringing out. "And again by ancient trial that you demanded. You stole Lucy from me, Ellasbeth. Slunk away in the night with her in your belly like a thief. I took her back. She's mine."

"You slept with that demon whore!" Ellasbeth raged, face red and arms waving. "How could you do that to me!"

My jaw clenched, but I stayed where I was. This wasn't about me. It was about Trent and Ellasbeth.

"You slept with her!" she raged. "And you think anyone will still follow you? You are done, Trent. *Done!*"

Ticked, I focused on watching her security, every single one of them flanked by at least three Weres. The scent of broken heather grew stronger; Trent was pissed. "Read your history, Ellasbeth," he said bitterly. "Demon and elf pairings happened all the time. It just so happens that both parties agreed this time. Get out of my city."

She crossed her arms, then forced them down. "It's not your city anymore."

Eerie and unreal, a muted howl rose up from behind the green. It was taken up by another, and then a third, circling us in a soft binding. When it died out, another could be heard in the distance. Two more rose from different directions, probably outside the park. Ellasbeth's people began to look at one another. One man set his weapon down, turned, and walked away.

Head lifted high, Trent moved closer to me. The girls were with us. Jonathan still had the first two men cowed. Behind her, a woman and a man left, their pace fast and stilted. "Cincinnati will always be my city," Trent said. "Even if I am penniless and wash windows to feed myself and my children. Leave. Don't come back unless it's as the thief you are so I may hunt you down."

"I'm warning you, Trent," Ellasbeth said, but her threat cut off when Jonathan let the two men up, whispering in their ears until they staggered away.

"Trent . . ." she said, then louder and in shock, "Come back here!," when the shaken men ignored her and walked away. "Get back here!" she demanded, but they kept going. All her security went with them. Trent smiled, the girls silent between us. She had lost, and I could see in Trent a pained realization. He hadn't wanted it this way, but she was forcing it on him.

"Trent," she pleaded, shoulders hunched, but it was too. late. "Come with me. I can convince them it was a mistake. This doesn't have to happen. None of it."

"And be indebted to you the rest of my life? Be your puppet? No."

"For the girls' sake," she tried next, and Ray whimpered, reaching for Trent.

"Exactly," he intoned. "For the girls' sake." Jonathan inclined his head and retreated so the two of them could see each other clearly over the fifteen feet. As I watched, Trent seemed to grow not taller, but more substantial. His aura almost glowed into the visible spectrum, and I wondered if the Goddess was watching, sending her mystics to bring witness to this. *Do they see me? Do any of them know it's me?*

"As Sa'han, I am in my rights to refuse the enclave's summons, but you can tell them this." Trent took another step, and she looked even more alone. "Birthright is given. Power is earned. I still have it, and it is growing, not failing. This lost wealth will strip the dross from me and show what I am. This union between me and the demons proves my foresight and courage. The girls are *mine*. I'm still willing to allow you to see them because I have felt the pain of being apart and it was almost too much to bear, but if you try to take them again, I will come down on you with everything I have." He took a slow breath, and I saw her shiver. "Do not push it, Ellasbeth. You've not seen the depths of what I'm capable of."

Her eyes flicked to Jonathan. She swallowed hard, eyes welling as she looked at the girls, and then, head falling, she turned. Heels clicking on the cobbles, she strode away, not acknowledging the watching people.

"'Scuse me," Jenks said tartly. "I have a little dusting to do."

Ray called out after him as he left. I was shaking, uneasy, as a few Weres peeled off from the rest and followed Ellasbeth out. Slowly the crowd faded back, leaving only the zoo security with their green uniforms and two-way radios. Jonathan came forward with a dangerous grace I remembered but had never given much credit to. He could have killed them. It would have been easy, both to do and to live with afterward, and *that* was why I was Trent's security, not him.

Trent inclined his head at the last of the Weres, and the man touched his nose before fading into the dispersing crowd. I couldn't tell what pack he belonged to, but I probably owed David a favor.

"Thank you, Jonathan," I said, numb, as the tall man took Lucy and set her in the stroller. Zoo security was beginning to ring us, and it was clear we had to leave.

"I didn't do this for you," the man growled, his long fingers ugly as he snapped the buckles around the little girl. Trent cleared his throat in rebuke, and he stood. "Excuse me," he said, the scent and feel of wild magic lingering about him as he handed Trent his card back. "I'll take the girls and find some damp towels."

They were already clean, but Trent nodded, evidently needing a moment to collect himself. I watched as Jonathan pushed the girls to a nearby water fountain.

"What did he say to them?" I asked.

"I've no idea." Trent wiped the back of his neck, and the scent of cinnamon and wine grew strong. "But Jon is probably the reason I survived and my siblings didn't." He looked up, his expression grim in the dappled shade of the pergola. "Quen is good, but Jon has no restraint and acts without thinking beyond the moment. He was with me the night my siblings died. He's like having a loaded gun on the nightstand with kids in the house. Unsafe even now."

"Are you okay?" I asked, and he touched my elbow, trying to get me to walk over to the water fountain. Nina and Ivy already had, closing in around the most vulnerable members of the group. It was time to go.

"I'm sorry about this," Trent said, glancing to where Ellasbeth had stood. "I knew she was going to try something, but I honestly thought she'd be a day or two after the media broke. And at the zoo? I am truly sorry. You being here was not my intent."

I made my steps slow, reluctant to reach the sun and the lack of privacy. "I'm glad I was. Like I said, are you okay?"

Trent hesitated, a faint smile beginning as he looked from the strange, mixed-up group. Jenks had joined them, and his dust seemed to be the glue that bound them. "Tired," he admitted, but his touch had become tighter about my waist, pulling me to him.

"No doubt," I said as we rocked back into motion. "It's after noon."

"Not that tired," he said, leaning to whisper it. "Just . . . tired? Are you . . . tired?"

Oh! Getting it, I felt myself warm. "Gosh, Trent," I whispered, both pleased and flustered. "People are watching."

"Let them watch," he said, motioning for Jonathan to take the girls and go before us. Looking as if he'd rather eat slugs, the tall man maneuvered the girls onto the path and started forward. Ivy and Nina with their new hats fell into place behind them, leaving Jenks to fall back to us. His dust sparkled as we found the sun, and tugging me closer, Trent stole a quick kiss.

"Seriously?" Jenks snarked as I turned the quick kiss into something a little more lengthy, more promising. "You've both lost just about everything, and all you can think of is sifting your dust? I will never understand you lunkers."

Trent pulled away, his eyes holding a heat that set my own libido sparkling. "Lost?" he said, our pace exactly perfect as we followed behind them. "Lost what? Money? My table at Carew Tower?"

"Your voice in the enclave," I added. "Your tee time at the golf course."

Trent sighed regretfully, but he was holding me tight. "True. Money drives the world, but when everything falls apart to leave the underpinnings of our life bare to the scrutiny of critics and thieves, the only thing remaining, the only thing that can't be taken away, is the love you hold for the people you care about." He pulled me closer, and I leaned into him, feeling warm, as if I'd finally done something real and right. "I have a very sturdy house, Jenks," Trent said. "So do you."

And understanding that perfectly, Jenks flew ahead to tease the girls.

Keep reading for a sneak peek
at the final Hollows novel

THE WITCH WITH NO NAME

coming September 2014

One

Neck craned, I squinted up between the shadowed apartments. High in the sun, dragonfly-like wings threw back the glow with the transparent sheen of glittery tissue paper. The sporadic traffic at the end of the alley was enough to cover the sound of Jenks's wings, but I could hear them in my memory as the pixy hovered before a pollution-grimed window.

The moist dirt smell of damp pavement was a hint under the light but growing scent of frightened vampire coming from my elbow. I doubted Marsha was having second thoughts, but disobeying your master vampire could have lethal consequences.

Still watching Jenks, I surreptitiously edged away from Marsha's tense, middle-class office professionalism. Her heels were this year's style, but she wouldn't be able to run in them. Her hair was a luscious handful that spilled over her shoulders in an ebony wave—again, it made her an easy target in a close fight. A curvaceous figure sealed the deal that she was beautiful. But as a living vampire, it went without saying that her looks had been selected for over the last two generations, and not for Luke's benefit, the man she'd had unfortunately fell in love with. But she knew she was vulnerable. That's why Ivy, Jenks, and I were here.

My neck was getting a crick, and I dropped my gaze to the passing cars, confident that distance and recycling bins would hide us from casual sight. A tight hum jerked my attention back in time to see Jenks dart back from a winged shadow. A blue jay squawked, and the tips of five feathers spiraled down between the buildings. Flapping wildly, the sheared bird managing to get across the street before thumping to the sidewalk.

Having already dismissed the bird, Jenks cupped his hands around his face and peered through the window. His skintight, thief black tights and knit shirt helped him blend into the shadows, and the red cap was to tell rival pixies that he wasn't there poaching, a real issue this close to Edden park. So far, no one had bothered him, but birds were a constant threat.

"I shouldn't have to do this," the woman at my elbow complained, oblivious that a third of the team here to keep her alive had just had a narrow miss. "It's my apartment!"

I took a slow breath when Jenks lifted the flap to the bathroom vent and vanished inside. "You want to risk running into Luke?" I said, and she made a sound of frustration. Yes, she did, but to do so would mean her death.

A lingering sensation that something was off dogged me, despite, or perhaps because of, the ease of the run so far. Restless, I resettled my shoulder bag. I wasn't a slouch when it came to looks, but next to this woman's structured beauty, my frizzy red hair and low heel boots fell flat.

Ivy's confident steps against the hush of the side-street traffic tightened my gut. The vampire next to me stiffened at my increased pulse, and I gave her a look to pull herself together. "Stay here," I said, not liking that Jenks was still inside. "Jenks will tell you when you can come in." Hiking my shoulder bag higher, I headed for the sidewalk.

"The hell I will." Marsha stepped as if to follow.

Spinning, I shoved her shoulder to send her thumping back against the wall. Shocked, the woman stared, not a hint of anger thanks to a lifetime of conditioning. "The hell you will," I said. "Stay here until Jenks says you can move, or we turn around and walk. Right here. Right now."

Only now did her anger show, her pupils widening and the scent of angry vampire prickling my nose. Wanting to nip this show of dominance, I stretched my awareness out and tapped the nearest ley line. Energy flowed in to make the tips of my hair float as it spooled in my chi. My skin tingled, and I leaned into her space, proving I wasn't scared of her little fangs or her greater strength. "You're under a conditional death threat, sweetheart," I breathed. "Once I verify that Luke isn't in there, you can come get what you want. But if all you're looking for is a way to die that doesn't invalidate your life insurance, do it on your own time."

Sullen, Marsha dropped her eyes, the rim of blue around her pupils returning to normal.

I rocked back, thumbs in my pockets and satisfied that she'd wait. It was unusual for a vampire to listen to anyone outside their camarilla, but she *had* come to us. Nodding, I looked up and made a sharp whistle. Immediately, Jenks peeked out of the bathroom vent and gave me a thumbs up. "Park it," I muttered, and the woman shrunk against the dumpster and out of sight.

Appeased, I started for the front entrance. The run had sounded simple enough when Ivy had brought it up over grilled cheese sandwiches and tomato soup last night. Helping a woman get her things out of her apartment was a no-brainer—until she told me the separation was being forced by two rival vampire camarillas and if Luke and Marsha didn't comply someone was going to end up dead. No way was Ivy going to do this one alone.

This was doing nothing to bolster my already low opinion of the undead vampires, the masters who manipulated everyone and everything in their decade long games. Once they noticed you, the only way to avoid being a victim was to die and become a player yourself.

But not Ivy, I thought as I emerged from the alley and she angled toward me. I wouldn't let that happen to her.

Unfortunately, the harder you squirmed, the more they squeezed.

Ivy's pace hid a thread of tension I never would've noticed if I hadn't been sharing living space with her the past three years. Sleek in her black slacks and top, she strode forward with her arms free and swinging. Her long black hair was up in a hard-to-grab bun, and even from here I could see the rim of brown around her eyes was nice and steady. She jumped at the distant sound of a door closing two streets over, though. She'd noticed something was off, too.

Her shoulders eased as she fell in beside me, and we took the steps up to the front common door together. "Luke's car is still in the lot," she said as I pulled the door open and we walked into the foyer of the old apartment building as if we belonged. "By the smell of it, it's not been run for two days."

"So he's doing what he's been told and is still alive." I glanced up at the camera. Jenks had been through the common areas, and according to him, it was fake. The scuffed tile floor was dirty in the corners, and I leaned against the stairway as Ivy leafed through Marsha's mail, pulling out everything she might want before putting the rest back in.

"They won't let one of them die without killing the other," Ivy said as she made keep and toss piles. "Otherwise the dead will claim the living as his or her scion.":

Which wouldn't do at all, I thought, looking up the dimly lit stairwell. It reminded me a little of my first place. "I don't like this."

A rare smile came over Ivy, and the letter box snapped shut with a click. "You worry too much. These two aren't that important."

My eyebrows rose. Despite my comments, Marsha was gorgeous. It would be hard for a master to let that much beauty go. "Worry? I only worry about you. I don't like this run."

Ivy handed me Marsha's mail, and I tucked it in my bag. "You just don't like the undead," she said, and I pulled my splat gun out and checked the hopper.

"Golly, I can't imagine why."

Making a soft sound of agreement, Ivy started up the stairs. I knew she wasn't interested in the mail, but it had given us a chance to stand at the foot of the stairs while she breathed the air and decided if anyone was waiting for us on the way up—Jenks's assurance or not. "Relax," she said as I fell into place behind her. "They agreed to not see each other. We go in, get her stuff, get out. End of story."

"Then why did you ask me to come with you?" I said, rounding the first landing.

Not looking back, she whispered, "Because I don't trust them."

Me either. The door downstairs clicked open, and I spun. My hold on the ley line zinged through me, but it was just Jenks and Marsha. I put a finger to my lips, and she closed the door behind her to seal out the shush of cars. Even three stories up, I could see a new, healthy fear in her. Maybe Jenks had talked to her.

The pixy's wings were a soft hum as he rose straight up in less than a second. "We're clear," he said, the silver dust slipping from him making a temporary sunbeam on my shoulder.

Clear, sure, but he couldn't detect charms unless they were active. "Keep her in the hall till I say," I asked. "And let me know if anyone pulls up."

Jenks nodded, dropping down to where Marsha was trying to creep up the stairs without her heels clicking. Ivy was waiting for me at the end of the hall, and I closed the gap quickly, eyeing the new detector charms on my bracelet. It had been a pain in the ass to make them that small, but if they were on my bracelet, I could watch them and point my gun at the same time. The wooden apple detected lethal spells, and the copper clover would glow in the presence of a strong charm. The two were not always synonymous.

Ivy was starting to smell really good, a mix of vampire incense and leather. I tried to ignore it as I gripped my splat gun tighter, amulets clinking. Marsha's front door had a corkboard to leave notes at, decorated with flowers and a smiley face with fangs. I could hear the woman's heels scrape on the stairwell, and I grimaced. It was noon, a time when most day walkers would be at work and the night walkers safely underground—but there were ways around that.

The amulets were a nice steady green and I nodded, splat gun level as I crouched opposite the door's hinges. Ivy worked the key and pushed it open to stand in the opening. Jenks flew in, confident that his first look was sufficient, but I listened as Ivy tasted the air, running it through her incredibly complex brain. "Hi, honey. I'm home," she said, and I followed her in.

I had to walk right through Ivy's scent, and even with my breath held, I shivered at the touch of pheromones she was kicking out—wafting over my skin like the memory of black silk. Though still sharing our investigation firm's letterhead, she'd been pulling away from me the last six months or so. I had a good idea why, and though I was happy for her, I missed working with her on a more daily basis.

My old vampire bite tingled at the obvious aroma of amorous vampires that permeated the one bedroom, open-floor-plan apartment. *Or maybe I just missed the intoxicating mix of sexual thrill and heart-pounding adrenaline she pumped into the air when she got tense.* Frowning at my own shallowness, I looked over the small, plush, well-decorated sunlit apartment and the evidence of their love. I knew what it was like having people tell you who not to fall in love with and my thoughts pinged on Trent before spinning away.

"Stay there," I said to Marsha, now at the door. My amulets were a nice steady green, but I was only five feet into the place. "There could be person-specific spells."

Person-specific spells: a nice way of saying a bullet with your name on it—and Jenks couldn't detect them. They were a necessity when making lethal, illegal charms. Vampire politics would keep the hit quiet, but if the spell took out an innocent, they'd track down and jail the black witch who made the lethal charm.

Senses searching, I did a quick walk through the living room before checking out the small kitchen. Ivy was in the bedroom, and I slowed, eyes on the amulet. It was easier to hide stuff among the gleaming metal and new appliances, but if there was anything here, it'd show.

"Hey!" Ivy exclaimed, muffled from the walls. My head snapped up and I lurched to get in front of Marsha. Shit, I'd been right.

"Jenks!" Ivy shouted, exasperated this time. "Why didn't you tell us about the dog?"

I slid to a stop, peeved as Jenks dusted an embarrassed red. Marsha had come in, eyes alight, and I waved for her to stay where she was.

"Sor-r-r-rry!" Jenks said as the jingle of a dog collar became obvious. "It's just a dog."

No one had been here for two days? It smelled like candles, not dog crap.

"Buddy!" Marsha called out, exuberant as she pushed around me to drop to her knees, and I eyed the small, scruffy, pound-puppy that timidly walked, not trotted, into the living room. "Come here, baby! You must be starving. I thought Luke had you!"

My eyes narrowed. I'd never had a dog, but I knew they generally underwent throes of delight when their owners came back after checking the mail, much less two days. "Ah, Marsha?" I said as the dog took a hesitant step in, his tail just hanging there.

"I think we're good," Ivy said as she came out of the back room. "You want to sweep it with your charms?"

"Sure," I said slowly, something ringing false.

"Buddy?" Marsha called again, and the dog gave me a sideways look as he passed me, a mix of excitement and hesitancy I wouldn't expect from an animal.

At my wrist, an amulet flashed red.

"Shit, it's the dog!" I shouted.

Marsha looked up, her beautiful little mouth in an O of surprise. Her hands were outstretched and the dog was almost to her. I'd never get there in time.

"*Rhombus!*" I exclaimed as I pulled on the ley line, feeling it scream into me, harsh from my demand. The energy pooled and overflowed, and I shoved it out again, my word tapping into a hard-won series of mental handsprings that harnessed the energy into a molecule thin barrier. It took the easiest form—a sphere with me in the center—and the dog predictably ran into it.

But instead of the expected yip of surprise, the energy levels spiked.

It was the only warning I got, and I cowered as a bright flash of energy exploded inside my circle, coming from the dog! The loosed power reverberated to make my circle chime like a sour bell, and I froze, skin crawling as the illegal death spell flooded over me, then fell back into the dog when it didn't find its intended victim.

"Buddy!" Marsha screamed as Ivy shoved her into the wall, covering her with her body.

"Get her out of here!" I shouted, afraid to move. The spell had invoked, but it hadn't fastened on its intended victim. It was a loose cannon, and it was trapped in here with me.

"That's my dog!" the woman protested, wild with fear as Ivy manhandled her into the hallway. "Buddy! *Buddy!*"

Slowly I realized I was unhurt. Buddy, though. . . Wincing, I looked at the dog, prostrate and beginning to shake. He wasn't dead, and he wasn't a dog. It was her boyfriend, Luke.

I hate vampires, I thought, realizing what had happened. Someone had turned Luke into a doppelganger of their dog and tacked a secondary spell onto him that would kill them both when Marsha touched him. Luke was halfway gone, but until the spell found Marsha, it wouldn't invoke fully. I had a chance.

"Marsha!" I stood, carefully watching the energy flow as I broke my own circle. "Where do you keep your salt!"

"Stay put," Ivy snarled. "Tell me."

"In the cupboard beside the stove!" the woman sobbed from the hallway. "What happened! Buddy? Buddy!"

I ran to the kitchen and snapped on the faucet. "It's not your dog, it's your boyfriend."

Maybe that had been a mistake since the woman totally freaked out. "Luke!" she screamed. "Oh, God, Luke!"

"Stay in the hall!" Ivy shouted, and the sounds of a struggle grew louder.

Salt, salt . . . I thought, pulse fast as I found a mixing bowl and dropped it into the sink. "Don't let her touch him! If she touches him, they both die!"

"Luke!" the woman sobbed, and I triumphantly found the salt. I wedged a nail under the spout and ripped it right out. Hands shaking, I shook it into the mixing bowl.

"Is he going to be okay?" Jenks asked, his dust pooling on the surface to run like mercury, but I didn't know.

"Oh God. Hurry!" Marsha begged, and I gave the salt-water a quick stir, tasting it before I picked up the bowl. The woman was hovering over the dog, terrified. My heart went out to her. Vampire masters were sons of bitches. Every last one of them. "Help him!" she screamed, her perfect face twisted in terror. Ivy held her, and I moved fast, bowl of saltwater before me.

"Stay back," I warned as I stood over the little white dog and dumped it. Water splashed, and Marsha backed up, white-faced and breathless. I had no idea if the entire concentration was optimum for breaking earth charms, but there'd be enough that was to not just turn him human, but break the lethal charm as well.

Sure enough, the dog vanished behind a thick puff of brown-and-blue aura-tainted energy. "Luke!" Marsha screamed, and Jenks frowned at her. He'd seen enough spells break to know this was normal. I backed up, tense as the cloud grew to man-size. Slowly the mist broke up to show a naked, bruised and beaten man huddled on the soggy white carpet.

Luke took a sobbing gasp of air. He was going to make

it—for now, and I eased back to sit on the edge of the cushy couch, elbows on my knees and head dropped into my hands. The amulets on my bracelet clinked, and I sighed. The saltwater had ruined them. I'd tack it onto Marsha's bill, but I didn't think she had the money. Besides, she was going to be a little busy trying to survive.

"You can touch him now," I said, realizing that Marsha was still hovering over him.

Frantic, she dropped to her knees. Water squished from the carpet, and she pulled him to her. "Oh, baby!" she gushed, oblivious that he was covered in saltwater. "Did he hurt you!"

By the bruises, clearly someone—probably his own master—had, but he raised a shaky hand and brushed her cheek. "I'm okay," he rasped, a flash of ugly memory finding me at the sight of him, his black hair was plastered to his face and his eyes were not quite open. It hurt like the devil to shift with earth magic, but his toned, athletic, and beaten body covered in easily hidden scars looked as if it was used to pain.

Crying, Marsha cradled his head to herself and rocked him. I wondered how many scars were hidden behind Marsha's expensive clothes. This sucked. Vampires looked as if they had everything, but it was a lie. My eyes shifted to Ivy, seeing her inner struggle. A big fat ugly lie.

The clatter of Jenks's wings was a short warning as he landed on my shoulder. "He looked like a dog to me," he grumped.

"That's because he was one." I plucked at my wet shirt, sticking uncomfortably to me. The question wasn't how, but why. Why had two minor vampire camarillas spent this much on a double-whammy spell like this on a simple Romeo and Juliet? It was expens-s-s-ive.

Ivy was in the hall to convince the neighbors nothing was going on. It didn't take much. Clearly they were familiar with the situation. Not happy, Ivy shut the door and stomped into the kitchen to turn the faucet off.

"I'm sorry, Marsha," Luke was saying, and the crying

woman stretched for a blanket to cover him. "When they told me I couldn't see you again, I went to a witch. She said she could turn me into a dog so I could be with you. No one would know it was me."

I watched as Ivy pulled the living room blinds. Her expression was empty, hearing far past what the man was saying. Closing the last, she sat across from me in the shadow light, worried.

"I didn't care if I was a dog," Luke continued, his eyes still not open as his hand gripped her. "I knew you wouldn't leave Buddy." His eyes opened, and I stared. They were the clearest shade of blue I'd ever seen. "I love you, Marsha. I'd do anything for you. Anything!" Crying, he pulled himself into a ball in her arms. "I'm so sorry."

My God, they'd tricked him into buying the charm that would've killed them both. Ivy and I exchanged a worried look. This was bad, but we couldn't just walk away. Jenks, too, was looking ill, and he moved to the decorative bowl of pinecones on the coffee table. He'd loved and lost more than Ivy and I combined, and this wasn't sitting well with him either. But it wasn't one master vampire we'd have to outwit, but two.

Ivy was still silent, and I sourly thought of my bank account. "You think we should help them?" I said softly, and Jenks's dust shifted to a hopeful yellowish pink.

Ivy didn't look at me. The couple on the floor was silent.

"You think we should help them," I said again, this time making it a statement.

Ivy's eyes flicked up. I could see her tremendous need to give, to make right. She'd done so much wrong, and it chewed on her in the small hours. My heart ached for her skewed view of herself, and I wished she could see herself as I did. This would rub the guilt out—for a time.

"Okay, we'll help them," I said, and Marsha gasped, her tear-wet eyes suddenly full of hope where there'd only been despair. Jenks's wings hummed his approval, and I sat up, gesturing weakly. "But I don't know what we can do."

"You can't," Marsha said, voice harsh as she held Luke. "They know everything."

Unfortunately, she was right. We couldn't simply set them up in a nice house out of state and hope that they wouldn't be found and made into an even bigger example. Ivy had been trying to wiggle out from her master her entire life only to become more entangled, so much that they'd ensnared me, too. *Trent, maybe?* I thought, but he was struggling to keep his head above the political sharks as it was.

"I don't know," I said as Luke sat up, muscles beginning to work again. "Changing into a dog was a great idea." Actually, it had been a lousy idea, but unless you practiced magic, you wouldn't know how easy it was to circumvent it. My gaze went to the soggy carpet. Obviously.

"We'll run," Marsha said, tensing as if ready to walk out that exact second.

Ivy shook her head. "You won't get past the city limits."

"Marsha, sweetheart," Luke whispered. "You know that won't work."

But I'd given her hope, and the woman wouldn't let go. "We can use the tunnels!"

Ivy looked toward the shuttered windows at the sound of a horn. "They built the tunnels."

"I can't live without you. I won't!" the distressed woman cried out, and I wondered if the place had been bugged. But if it had, Jenks would have heard the electronic whine and disabled them. We had a moment to catch our breath, and then we'd have to move.

It wasn't as if we could stake their two master vampires; there were laws against that kind of thing. Unless Marsha and Luke could come up with an iron-clad blackmail, they were stuck.

"Okay," I said, feeling the need to get moving. We'd been here too long. "There might be some law or something you can tap into. Ivy's going to need access to every document your name is on. Birth certificate, property deeds, insurance, parking tickets, tax returns, everything."

Marsha nodded, that same glow of hope back in her eyes hurting me. This wasn't going to work, but we had to try something.

Ivy rose to look out a crack in the blinds. "Do either of you have a safe house?"

"None we trust anymore," Luke said, and she let the blind fall.

"I've got one," Ivy said, coming back to help Luke stand. "You should be okay for a few days. Especially if you help out a little with the other guests coming in."

Wrapped in the afghan, Luke awkwardly got to his feet, pale and shaking. "Anything. Yes. Thank you."

Jenks took to the air, humming out under the crack in the door to check the hallway. Almost immediately he darted back in with a big thumbs up.

"We can't just walk out with them," I said, and Ivy gave me a glum smile.

"They won't try anything new until sundown," Ivy said, catching Marsha's arm before the woman went into the bedroom and shook her head to leave everything. "They'll want to be present the next time."

God, help me. I hated vampires. "Okay, let's move out."

"But he needs his clothes," Marsha was saying as I collected my splat gun from the counter. Ivy was almost carrying Luke to the door, and tears began to slip again from Marsha. I totally understood. The entire place was a perfect blending of their love. It was sucky when happiness became this costly. But if they fought this hard for it, then it would last their entire lifetime. I just hoped that lifetime would be longer than a week.

The hallway was quiet, smelling of dust and old carpet. Eyes were watching through peepholes, and it made me edgy. Marsha took Luke's elbow to help him down the stairs, and Ivy dropped back to talk to me.

"Jenks, you're going with Ivy, right?" I asked, knowing she wouldn't tell me the address of her safe house, much less take me there. Jenks, though . . .

Jenks's wings hummed into invisibility, and he rose up a hand width. "Yeah."

"No," Ivy said, frowning, and he made a face at her. "You're not coming, pixy."

"Tink's a Disney whore, like you could stop me!" he shot back.

Smiling, I edged around Ivy to keep Marsha and Luke from heading out without us. "I've got my phone on," I said, pushing them back to the mailboxes until I could look at the street.

"I'll be fine. See you at home," Ivy said, ignoring Jenks and his sword pointed at her nose. "Hey, you doing anything tonight?"

"Listen to me, you broken-fanged, moss-wiped excuse of a back-drafted blood bag!" Jenks said, a silver-edged red dust slipping from him.

I looked back inside from the street, thinking this had been nice, even with the near miss. I liked working with Ivy. Always had. We did well together—even when it had gone wrong. "I'm working security for Trent," I said, lips quirking as I saw her mentally smack her forehead. "You want me to bring you back something? It's probably going to end somewhere with food."

"Sure. That's be good," she said, turning to Marsha and Luke for some last minute instruction on how to get from here to there alive. "I'll call if I need help."

I touched her arm, and her eyes met mine in farewell. Smiling, I turned away remembering something Kisten had once said: I was there when she had her morning coffee, I was there when she turned out the light. I was her friend, and to Ivy, that was everything.

"Jenks, I've got this!" I heard, and then I shut the door, my steps light as I headed for my car. Ivy would get home okay. She was right that the masters would want to be there when they brought their children in line. Besides, everyone in Cincinnati with fangs knew Ivy.

Head up, I stomped along, eyeing the few pedestrians.

Slowly my good mood tarnished. Love died in the shadows, and it shouldn't cost so much to keep it in the sun. But as Trent would say, anything gotten cheap wouldn't last, so do what you need to do to be happy and deal with the consequences. That if love was easy, everyone would find it.

I turned the corner, my head coming up at the clatter of pixy wings. "She said no, huh?" I said as Jenks landed on my shoulder, his wings tickling my neck as he settled himself.

"Tink's little pink rosebuds," he muttered. "She threatened to dump insecticide on my summer hut. Besides, she's got it okay. God! Vampires in love. The only thing worse is you mooning over Trent."

My smile widened. Maybe I'd make cookies. The man loved cookies.

He made a rude sound, his silence telling me he was unhappy. "Sorry about the dog."

I lifted a shoulder and let it fall. "You didn't know."

"I should have."

I didn't answer, thinking about my date tonight with Trent. Well, not a date exactly, but I had to get dressed up as if it was one. I still was trying to decide to put my hair up or down. *Chocolate chip was his favorite.*

"Oh, God," Jenks moaned. "You're thinking about him. I can tell. Your aura shifted."

Embarrassed, I halted at the crosswalk, waiting for the light. "It did not."

"It did," he complained, but I knew crabbed because he couldn't say he was happy for me lest he jinx it somehow. "So it's been like what, three months? Does he still curl your toes?"

"Totally," I said, and he made a rude noise at my blissful smile. "He's a total toe curler."

"Awww, this is sweeter than pixy piss," he said with a false sarcasm. "All my girls happy. I can't tell you the last time that happened."

My smile widened, and I pushed the walk button as if it might hurry it along. "I think it was when—"

The unmistakable sound of tires screaming on pavement iced through me. My breath caught, and I turned. Jenks was gone, his white-hot sparkles seeming to burn a airborne trail back the way we'd come. A woman screamed for help, and I jumped back when a black sedan roared past me, the front fender dented. Somehow I knew, like when a picture falls off the wall, or the clock stops ticking.

"Ivy" I whispered, then turned and ran.

Two

The thumps of my feet on the pavement jarred up my spine. Dodging people turning to look, I followed Jenks's fading dust. My heart seemed to stop when I turned the corner and saw Ivy crumpled in the street. Marsha and Luke were standing above her, dazed. A car stopped even as I watched, and a man got out, white-faced and his phone in hand.

"Call 911!" I shouted as I slid to the pavement beside Ivy. *Shit. Ivy.* She had to be alive. *I shouldn't have left you.*

Jenks was a frantic, darting shape as he dusted the blood from a scalp wound. She'd hit her head. Her chest moved shallowly, and her legs were twisted. I was afraid to touch her, and my hands hovered over her, reminding me of Marsha standing over Luke.

Pain charm! I thought frantically as I searched my bag. Fingers fumbling, I dropped the charm over her head. I was putting a band aid on a concussion, but she took a clean breath.

"Did you call 911?" I exclaimed as a pair of dress shoes scuffed before us.

"No hospital."

Her voice was soft, almost not there, and both Jenks and I looked at Ivy. She was pale, and pain pinched her still-closed eyes. That was good, right? She wasn't unconscious, even if her eyes were closed. *Damn it, I should have learned how to make a healing curse!* But Al was gone and it was too late.

"Ivy." I brushed her hair back, fingers trembling. They came away warm and red, and my fear redoubled. She'd hit her head bad enough that Jenks's dust wasn't stopping it. "Ivy!" I called when her eyes didn't open. More people were ringing us. "Look at me, damn it! Look at me! Can you move your fingers and toes?"

"I think so."

Her eyes opened as I took her cold hand. The pupils were fully dilated, scaring me. I wasn't sure if it was from head trauma or my fear. The circle of people around us whispered, and when a smile of satisfaction edged over her pain, panic took me. "Ivy?"

Her hand squeezed in mine, and she moved her legs, wincing as she straightened them. She could move, and I remembered how to breathe.

"Marsha and Luke are gone," Jenks whispered as he hovered by my ear.

Like I freaking cared?

She was trying to sit up, and I gingerly helped her as the heat from the stopped car bathed us. "Little fish," Ivy said, hair coming out of the bun as she held her middle. "They weren't after them. Oh, God, I think I cracked a rib."

"Don't move," I said, stiffening as a siren lifted into the air. "The ambulance is coming."

"No hospital." Her black eyes fixed on mine, and she went whiter still as she tried to take a deep breath. "No safe house. I've been marked."

Marked? Her gaze went to the pain charm about her neck, and she gripped it tight, shocking me. She never used my magic. Avoided it. "You need a hospital," I said, and she hissed in pain as she tried to turn her head.

"No."

"Ivy, you were *hit* by a *car!*" Jenks had dusted her cuts

until they were only a slow seep, but her eyes were dilated and she hadn't taken her other hand off her middle.

"Cormel," she said softly, hatred temporarily overriding her pain. "I told you Marsha and Luke weren't worth all of this. I wasn't supposed to walk out of that apartment alive. That charm was aimed at me, too. He wants me dead . . . so you . . . will figure out how to save the souls of the undead. The car was a last effort to salvage their plan before going back with failure."

My heart seemed to catch, then it raced as I looked at the surrounding faces for anyone watching too closely—their eyes holding fear. Ivy moaned as she breathed in my alarm, but I couldn't let go of it. I couldn't distance myself. The lethal charm had been aimed at all three of them. If I hadn't been there to break it, Ivy would be dead and I'd be getting a call from the second-rising morgue.

"I don't want to become a dead thing," she whispered, then clenched in pain. "Rachel?"

I closed my eyes. Ivy moaned, her pain doubling as my panic pulsed through her, bringing her alive even as she struggled to stave off death. I couldn't do this. I couldn't be her scion. But I knew I would if it came to that. Cormel had tired of waiting for his soul. If Ivy was dead, me finding out how to return the undead their souls would move way up on my to-do list.

We had to get out of here. Even the safe houses held death, and the hospitals would only make her passing smell of antiseptic. *Why had I worked so hard to save their miserable existences?* I wondered as I found my bag and looped it over my head. But it hadn't been just the undead in the balance when I'd freed the mystics last July, it had been the entire source of magic.

Jenks dropped down as I gathered my resolve. "They're everywhere, Rache," he whispered, his fear easy to read on his narrow, pinched features, and Ivy nodded. Surrounded by onlookers, we had a small space to breathe, but we couldn't stay here.

Slowly I began to think. Trent. He had a surgery suite,

one that wasn't staffed by people who could be bought. I wasn't sure where he was, but I could text him. Ivy was sitting. Maybe she could move. "Ivy," I said, blanching at the blackness in her eyes when she looked at me from around a stray strand of hair. "Can you move?"

Her boots scraped as she shifted them under her. "If I can't, I'm dead."

A few in the crowd protested, but they backed up when Jenks rose, his fast darting shape and the sharp sword in his grip making him a threat. My stomach turned when every grip I tried to help Ivy with only brought more pain. Teeth clenched, I tucked my shoulder under her arm and rose, staggering until we found our balance. Ivy's eyes closed. We hung for a moment, waiting to see if she was going to pass out. In the nearby distance, a siren rose—but it brought death, not life.

"Okay, nice and easy," I said, and Jenks kept everyone back as we started for the curb. Ivy's head was down, and she moved with in sudden, painful limps. Step, pause. Step, pause. Her weight on me was solid, and her scent was tinged with sour acid. Tears threatened, and I ignored them. I couldn't live with Ivy if she were dead. I couldn't be her scion, but I knew I'd do it, even as it would destroy me. I'd try to keep Ivy sane, knowing it was a bitter fallacy. I couldn't kill her a second time as she wanted me to. I was a bad friend.

"I'm sorry," Ivy said as we reached the curb and she took her hand from her middle long enough to use the lamppost to help her step up.

"This isn't your fault," I barked so I wouldn't cry. "We'll get you to Trent's, and you'll be fine." His compound was almost deserted since the serious inquiries into his illegal bio labs had begun, but he probably had a surgeon on call.

Seeing her standing to catch her breath, I dug in my bag for my phone. "Can you hold this?" I said, giving her my splat gun, and she held it loosely. My fingers shook as I scrolled for Trent. He was the last person I'd called, and knowing he might not take a call but would always check a text, I wrote 911 and Eden Park and hit send.

My stomach was twisting as I tucked my phone in my back pocket. It was all I could do. But we couldn't stay here. Each moment seemed to weigh more heavily on her. She was slipping. Her living vampire endurance would mean nothing if she gave up.

"You can't go to the car, Rache." Jenks hovered before us, watching us and our backs both. "They'll run you down."

Shit. He was right. Tears of frustration pricked, and Ivy leaned against the light post. Behind her, people were turning away, leaving us to die.

"Where else can I go, Jenks!" I shouted, frustrated. "No where on earth safe from them!"

He shrugged, even as his dust grew dismal, but behind him was Eden Park, and a flash of hope lit through me. Ivy sensed it, and her eyes opened, glazed with pain.

"The park." I wiggled under her again, and we staggered into motion. "Ivy, hold on."

"The park!" Jenks echoed in disbelief, and then he nodded, rising up to fly five feet over us where he could keep watch.

The park. There was a ley line in it, thin and broken, but it was there. I couldn't jump the lines without Bis. He wouldn't be awake until the sun went down, but I could shift realities if I was standing in a line. The ever-after was a poor choice, but no one could follow us there, and maybe we could walk to the church's ley line and pop back into reality.

Ivy stumbled as we found the grass, and we almost went down. Her moan sounded almost like pleasure. Old toxins were being pulled from her tissues to cope with the pain as her body struggled to stay alive. But this time it wasn't a master satisfying his blood urge that was killing her, and her breath quickened as she took in my fear and kindled her own, long suppressed desires.

"Almost there," I panted, struggling under her weight as I scanned the open grass between us and the footbridge. It was exposed, but they probably wouldn't shoot her and risk hitting me by accident. Cormel needed me alive and Ivy dead. They only had to wait.

This was partly my fault, and I felt the helpless tears trying to start as I took more of Ivy's weight. There was no way to bind a vampire's soul to their body once they died, and as we slowly limped across the green space to Twin Lakes Bridge and the broken ley line, a warm tear ran a trail down my cheek.

"Don't cry," Ivy slurred. "It's going to be okay."

I wiped my eyes between our lurching steps, my stomach roiling. "Almost there."

Jenks dropped down, worry pinching his features. "Her aura isn't looking good, Rache."

"I know!" I shouted. "I know," I said again, softer.

"It hurts," Ivy said as I took even more of her weight. "It's not supposed to hurt, is it?"

Oh God. I knew the pain amulet was outclassed, but that the damage was too much for even the vampire toxins to mutate was scary. "Almost there. Hold on," I whispered, eyes fixed on the statue of Romulus and Remus. "You can rest when we get to the line."

But I didn't think we were going to make it, especially when Jenks's dust went an angry red. "There's two blood bags on the footbridge," he snarled, his blade catching the light. "Keep going. Don't stop no matter what you hear. I'll take care of them."

"Jenks!" I cried out as he darted away. Beside me, Ivy wheezed. Her fingers rose to touch her mouth, coming away red with blood. Immediately she curled her fingers up in a ball to hide it, but a flash of fear lit through me. Internal bleeding. My gun, too, was gone, left behind somewhere on the summer-burnt grass.

"Almost there," I said again as we moved another few feet, but inside, I was despairing. There were no hospitals in the ever-after, only demons who didn't care. I didn't think we'd make it all the way to the church. If Trent didn't show, I might have just killed Ivy trying to save her.

Ivy's breath became labored, and the sudden shouting at the bridge yanked my attention up. With a sudden flurry of motion, a woman swung wildly at Jenks, falling down the embankment and into the water, harried down the entire way by the pixy. Suddenly she was screaming as Sharps, the resident bridge troll rose up, swamping her.

Without a second look, the other vampire continued for us, leaving her to sort herself out. He was vampire-child beautiful, graceful and sure of himself—and when he looked at me, I shuddered.

Jenks darted in and away, distracting him.

"Move faster, Ivy," I begged, knowing Jenks couldn't hold off a determined vampire. Eyeing the statue of Romulus and Remus, I brought up my second sight. A faint haze, ill looking and sporadic, hung at chest height. It was Al's line, half dead because of the shallow pond someone had dug out under it, but unable to die because the other half of it lay in the dry, desolate ever-after. It reminded me of the demon himself, having given up on life, but clinging to the memory of a love he had once had so tightly that now he couldn't live or die.

He would never help me. Not now. And an old guilt pulled my brow even more tight.

From the water came a gurgling scream as the woman fought to be free of Sharps. Ivy moaned and I dropped my second sight. My eyes jerked to the controlled anger and grace striding toward us despite Jenks's darting flight and bloodied blade. The vampire knew the line was there and was trying to cut us off.

Crap on toast. I wasn't going to make it. I'd have to beat him off.

Ivy hung on my shoulder as I came to a heart-pounding halt, her head down and her breathing frighteningly raspy. A lousy twenty feet were between me and the line, and the suave man smiled when he rocked to a silent stand before us. He was the expected eight feet back, his hair moving in the light breeze as he assessed my determination, feeding off my fear even as I found a firmer stance. Eight feet. He'd fought magic users before. It was just far enough that he could dodge anything I might throw at him.

Fine. He was between me and the line, but I could still pull on it, and I allowed the line's energy to funnel down to my hand and gathered it in a tight ball of frustration. He was stunning in his black suit, but it was more than his sculpted, carefully bred-for beauty. It was his attitude of complete and utter lack of fear. He was wearing sunglasses, and an old scar on his neck said he was someone's favorite. Behind him, the woman screamed at both Jenks and Sharps as she tried to get out of the water.

"Morgan," the living vampire said, his voice holding layers of emotion, and Ivy stirred, drawn awake by either the screams at the lake or the pull in his voice.

"Go to hell!" Ivy managed, and Jenks joined me. Together we faced him, my knees shaking and Jenks's wings clattering in threat.

The man's eyes flicked to Ivy, then back to me. "Give it up."

Not happening, and I found a better grip on Ivy, my bellyful of ever-after waiting for direction. "Come and get me," I mocked, trying to lure him a foot closer.

"You're not who I'm interested in. She's almost dead. All I have to do is wait."

Son of a bastard . . . This wasn't the original team sent to kill Ivy. It was probably the one sent to collect her body, and they'd be eager for the extra kudos killing her would bring them. Behind me, a car door slammed. I didn't dare look, but from the edge of my sight, three more men in suits started across the grass. Damn it, I couldn't fight off four of them and protect Ivy too, even with Jenks.

The living vampire's beautiful brown eyes went black as he breathed in my fear. "Let us finish the job, or we beat you up and we finish the job anyway. She's dying her first death before the sun goes down."

"Over my dead body." The sun was nearing the horizon, but there were hours left in its path.

"And my broken wings," Jenks added, dusting Ivy's scalp again as blood began to mat her hair.

They were almost to us. I had to do something, him being out of range or not. I thought of Trent. Had he gotten my text? Was he on his way?

"Dead?" the vampire said, recapturing my attention. "No, he wants you alive. For now."

Frustration rose. The hazy read smear of the ley line was just behind him. Twenty lousy feet. "It can't be done!" I shouted, Jenks's dust tingling against my skin. "Tell Cormel it can't be done!"

"Then you owe him for the year he's kept you both safe," the man said. "Watching you suffer Ivy's second life will do."

"I already saved him once! I'm not paying the same debt twice."

The man chuckled, motioning for the arriving thugs to circle us. I could smell them, the rising scent of vampire incense bringing Ivy's eyes open and a new tension in her face. "You prolonged his misery is all."

He gestured, and I moved, throwing a single burst of energy at the beautiful man before turning my attention inward. *Rhombus!* I shouted, relief a slap when Jenks went contrary to his instinct and dropped down, safe inside my circle.

The rushing vampires skidded to a halt, stymied. Before me, my black and gold fist-size unfocused magic slammed into the head vampire, throwing him back four feet to fall against the base of the statue of Romulus and Remus where he blinked, stunned.

Nothing could get through my barrier unless it held my aura: not bullet, not vampire, not demon—unless he was very determined and I'd left an opening. But we were trapped in it, trapped twenty feet from safety. Damn it! This was so not fair. Every other demon could shift their aura to slip into a line, but I couldn't jump on my own, couldn't jump a lousy twenty feet. The line was so close I could almost feel it humming.

Dazed, the vampire found his feet, his beauty ruined by his snarl. "She's going to die in there!" he shouted, stalking forward to halt so close the barrier hummed a warning and I could see the first lines about his eyes. "She's going to die, and then she will fall on you!"

Ivy stared up at me, clearly in pain, clearly feeling the pinch of instincts and desires she had lied to herself were under control. Tears filled her black eyes, and she reached out, her hand shaking as it found mine. "I'm sorry," she said, and anger filled me that they had brought her to this. "Please don't let me wake as the undead. I won't remember why I love you. *Promise.* Promise me you won't let me wake as an undead."

My throat closed, and as Jenks's dust sifted red between us, I dropped down, my arms going around her. She wanted me to kill her if she should die. I couldn't do it. "I promise."

"Liar." She smiled at me, hand shaking as she touched my cheek.

Panic renewed, and I felt unreal, dizzy as I looked at vampires ringing us in the late afternoon. There was no one to help me. I had to find a way.

"She won't last an hour," the beautiful man said, anticipation making his eyes black. "She will wake as the undead. You will fix her soul to her, or die at her own hands."

Ivy shook, and I let her go, resolve filling me as I stood until the shimmer of my circle hummed just over my head. "Jenks, I need you to do something," I said, and his face went white.

"I'm not leaving you, Rache."

I eyed the twenty feet and four vampires that separated us from the line. "I'm going to kick some vampire ass and get to that line. Ivy and I can wait in the ever-after."

"With the surface demons?" Jenks barked, his wings clattering harshly.

I had no choice. "Go try to wake Bis up. He can jump us to Trent's." I looked at the pixy, seeing his fear in his tight, angular face. He didn't want to leave us, was terrified we would die without him. He was probably right.

"No!" His wings clattered as he understood what I was saying. "It's hours until sunset. Don't ask me to leave you!"

I dropped down to grab Ivy's elbow to help her stand up. "I'm sorry, Ivy. You have to help me get you to the line."

"But she can hardly walk!"

"Which means she still can!" I shouted, and Ivy clutched at me, halfway to a stand and heavy in my grip. "Jenks, please," I said softly, and he hovered helpless and angry before us. "I can't jump on my own and Bis can't find me. You have to tell him where we are."

Slowly his expression shifted from anger to a frustrated understanding. "Keep her alive," he said, and I nodded, again making promises I couldn't keep.

Scared, I turned to the vampires watching suspiciously. Behind them, Cincinnati drowsed in the late afternoon sun. Al could have jumped us right to Trent's, or the hospital, or the church. But I wasn't one of them any longer. The break had been clean—even if the jagged edges of it still dug into my soul in the quiet parts of the night.

Breath held against the pain, Ivy got her weight over her feet and wavered to a rise. I felt her clench in agony as she fought to keep from coughing, her grip on me hurting. She took one breath, then another. Head up, she stared at the men ringing us. At the bridge, the woman finally got out of the water, dripping and bleeding from scratches and with a malevolent gleam in her eye. Five now.

I sucked in the line energy, feeling it hiccup and stutter. *Does Al know I'm using his line?* I wondered, feeling Al's utter abandonment of me again—jealousy, heartache, and hatred too much for him to forgive.

"Let me go, Ivy. I have to fight," I whispered, and after the briefest of hesitations, she did, her eyes closing as she un-crimped her fingers from around my arm. I could tell it had taken all her resolve, and she swallowed her saliva back, refusing to give in to her instincts—but instincts die last and hard.

"I like it when you say my name," she said as her eyes opened. "It doesn't hurt anymore."

Shit. This wasn't good. Not good at all. "I'm glad," I whispered, wishing my knees weren't shaking. "I'm going to have to kick some ass. Can you get to the statue on your own? Maybe critique me when it's over?"

"Over a beer," she said. Her hand, wasn't so tight against her middle. I didn't know a charm for this. I had nothing.

Ivy slowly lost her balance and leaned into me again, unable to stand on her own. She wasn't going to make it, no matter what happened, and I shoved my panic down deep. "Thank you, Jenks," I whispered.

His wings clattered, and he wouldn't look at me, that same black dust sifting from him to make my skin tingle. I held Ivy close, the chill of her pressing into me as her head hung down and her breathing grew shallow. She was almost passing out. Slowly I lifted my chin and found the eyes of the waiting vampire.

"You first," I said, yanking a wad of ever-after into me. My breath came in with a sharp sound. Ivy stiffened in my grip, and I wondered if she felt it as I pulled everything I could handle into me. "Jenks, grab something!" I shouted as the building energy crested, lapped the top of my abilities, and with a spasm that seemed to shake me to my core, edged into pain as I took even more. I had to take it all. All.

"Rache!" Jenks shrilled, tugging on my hair as he wound himself up in it. "What are you doing!"

I had one shot, and I wasn't going to waste it, even if it burned my synapses to a twisted mass. "*Corrumpto!*" I shouted, letting the energy explode from me.

My knees buckled. I felt airy, light and unreal. The line hummed through me, smelling of ozone and stardust. A soundless wave sped out, flattening the grass and bowling the vampires head over heels to look like crows. Ivy shuddered, her eyes opening black and deep. Together we straightened as a distant bell rang, and then another. Across the river, the basilica's bells tolled, and tears threatened when I recognized my own church bells ringing an echo to the force of my blast.

My skin was tingling, and I almost went down as Ivy's weight suddenly became my responsibility. "Ivy!" I called, bringing up my second sight and looking for the ley line. The vampires were down. We had to move. "Come on! Just a few steps!"

But then panic took me, not that the head vampire was getting up off the pavement, but that the ley line was gone! It wasn't running where it should, through the manmade ponds and beside the statue the vampire was leaning heavily against.

"Where is it!" I shouted, and Ivy sagged in my grip. Bewildered, and head humming as if it held a hive of bees, I strengthened my second sight until reality wavered under a broken landscape of dust, cracked rock, and bloated sun hazing an empty landscape and dry riverbed. The desolation of the ever-after was complete, and the gritty wind lifted through my hair even though I still stood in reality. But there was no line. *What have I done?*

Jenks hovered before me, blinking in shock. "You're in it," he said, a weird greenish dust sifting from him. "How did you move it, Rache?"

My mouth dropped open, and I spun, shocked. I moved the line? How?

"Get her!" the vampire screamed, and the present rushed back.

"Rhombus!" I shouted, staggering under Ivy's weight as my circle sprang up heady and thick since I was standing right in the middle of the line. *I'd moved it? How? I had only tapped it.* But Jenks was right. I was standing in Al's flimsy line, and it was growing stronger, no longer dampened and drained by the ponds. I'd shifted it. I had moved it to me.

The vampires slid to a halt, one of them screaming as he touched the circle and a snap of energy struck him like lightning. We were in the line. Ivy was with me. I looked past the angry vampires, knowing the line had been behind them, knowing it couldn't be moved. But it had.

And somehow, I didn't care that I'd done the impossible.

"Sorry about the beating," I said as I melded my aura around Ivy's to shift her with me to the ever-after.

"Beating?" The vampire leaned closer, not knowing what had happened. "That wasn't a beating."

I tightened my hold on the line, feeing it start to take us. "No, the one your master is going to give you." *Thank you, Jenks. I will keep her alive.*

The man's eyes became round, fear shimmering his motion for the first time, making him somehow more captivating in the contrasting shadows of fear and power. We'd bested him, and he was going to be punished.

"No!" he shouted as I shifted my aura and the world moved around us. The red of sunset became the harsh red of the ever-after sun. His howling cry of denial evolved, peeked, and became the scream of the gritty wind. The image of his crooked fingers reaching for us dissolved, and I saw it mirrored in the broken rock surrounding us. The sound of Jenks's wings was gone. We were alone and the world was broken—just like me.

My heart thumped and I shifted Ivy's weight until she hissed in pain. I squinted at the distant, red-smeared horizon, then brought my eyes closer, sending it over the remains of the Hollows already in shadow. The spires of the basilica rose over it all, the bastion carefully preserved where most everything was left to crumble. The space where my church would have been was nothing but rock and grass. My idea to walk to it crumbled. Ivy was done.

"You can rest now," I whispered. "It's going to be okay." Heart aching, I eased her down against a boulder, and she gripped my arm, refusing to let go. My eyes shot to hers, and the utter blackness in them stitched all my fears into one smothering black piece. I couldn't kill her to prevent her undead existence. If Bis didn't find us in time . . . I . . . I didn't know.

My throat was tight as I sat beside her and pulled her head to rest against me. She could move no further, and this was as good a place as any, better than some. Whatever happened, we would face it together, away from the filth she'd struggled her entire life to escape.

RETURN TO THE HOLLOWS WITH
NEW YORK TIMES BESTSELLING AUTHOR

KIM HARRISON

WHITE WITCH, BLACK CURSE
978-0-06-113802-7

Kick-ass bounty hunter and witch Rachel Morgan has crossed
forbidden lines, taken demonic hits, and still stands. But a new
predator is moving to the apex of the *Inderlander* food chain—
and now Rachel's past is coming back to haunt her . . . literally.

BLACK MAGIC SANCTION
978-0-06-113804-1

Denounced and shunned by her own kind for dealing with
demons and black magic, Rachel Morgan's best hope is life
imprisonment—her worst, a forced lobotomy and genetic
slavery. And only her enemies are strong enough to help her
win her freedom.

PALE DEMON
978-0-06-113807-2

After centuries of torment, a fearsome creature walks free,
craving innocent blood and souls—especially Rachel Morgan's,
who'll need to embrace her demonic nature to survive.